Robert Fordyce Aickman was

He was married to Edith Ray Gregorson from 1941 to 1957. In 1946 the couple, along with Tom and Angela Rolt, set up the Inland Waterways Association to preserve the canals of Britain. It was in 1951 that Aickman, in collaboration with Elizabeth Jane Howard, published his first ghost stories in a volume entitled *We Are for the Dark*. Aickman went on to publish seven more volumes of 'strange stories' as well as two novels and two volumes of autobiography. He also edited the first eight volumes of *The Fontana Book of Great Ghost Stories*. He died in February 1981.

The Wine-Dark Sea

ROBERT AICKMAN

FABER & FABER

First published in this edition in 2014
by Faber & Faber Ltd
The Bindery, 51 Hatton Garden
London ECIN 8HN

Printed and bound by CPI Group (UK) Ltd, Croydon, CRO 4YY
Typeset by Faber & Faber Ltd

A CIP record for this book is available from the British Library

ISBN 978-0-571-31172-9

Contents

Robert Aickman

An Introduction by Richard T. Kelly

Is Robert Fordyce Aickman (1914–81) the twentieth century's 'most profound writer of what we call horror stories and he, with greater accuracy, preferred to call strange stories'? Such was the view of Peter Straub, voiced in a discerning introduction to a previous edition of *The Wine-Dark Sea*. If you grant Aickman his characteristic insistence on self-classification within this genre of 'strange', then you might say he was in a league of his own (rather as Edgar Allan Poe is the lone and undisputed heavyweight in the field of 'tales of mystery and imagination'). 'Horror', though, is clearly the most compelling genre label that exists on the dark side of literary endeavour. So it might be simplest and most useful to the cause of extending Aickman's fame if we agree that, yes, he was the finest horror writer of the last hundred years.

So elegantly and comprehensively does Aickman encompass all the traditional strengths and available complexities of the supernatural story that, at times, it's hard to see how any subsequent practitioner could stand anywhere but in his shadow. True, there is perhaps a typical Aickman protagonist – usually but not always a man, and one who does not fit so well with others, temperamentally inclined to his own company. But Aickman has a considerable gift for putting us stealthily behind the eyes of said protagonist. Having established such identification, the way in which he then builds up a sense of dread is masterly. His construction of sentences and of narrative is patient and finical. He seems always to proceed from a rather grey-toned realism where detail accumulates without fuss, and the recognisable material world appears wholly four-square – until you realise that the narrative has been built as a cage, a kind of personal hell, and our protagonist is walking towards death as if in a dream.

This effect is especially pronounced – Aickman, as it were, preordains the final black flourish – in stories such as 'Never Visit Venice' (the title gives the nod) and 'The Fetch', whose confessional protagonist rightly judges himself 'a haunted man', his pursuer a grim and faceless wraith who emerges from the sea periodically to augur a death in the family. Sometimes, though, to paraphrase John Donne, the Aickman protagonist runs to death just as fast as death can meet him: as in 'The Stains', an account of a scholarly widower's falling in love with – and plunging to his undoing through – a winsome young woman who is, in fact, some kind of dryad.

On this latter score it should be said that, for all Aickman's seeming astringency, many of his stories possess a powerful erotic charge. There is, again, something dreamlike to how quickly in Aickman an attraction can proceed to a physical expression; and yet he also creates a deep unease whenever skin touches skin – as if desire (and the feminine) are forms of snare, varieties of doom. If such a tendency smacks rather of neurosis, one has to say that this is where a great deal of horror comes from; and Aickman carries off his version of it with great panache, always.

On the flipside of the coin one should also acknowledge Aickman's refined facility for writing female protagonists, and that the ambience of such tales – the world they conjure, the character's relations to people and things in that world – is highly distinctive and noteworthy within his *oeuvre*. Aickman's women are generally spared the sort of grisly fates he reserves for his men, and yet still he routinely leaves us to wonder if they are headed to heaven or hell, if not confined to some purgatory. Among his most admired stories in this line are 'The Inner Room' and 'Into the Wood', works in which the mystery deepens upon the final sentence.

And lest we forget: Aickman can be very witty, too, even in the midst of mounting horrors, and even if it's laughter in the dark. English readers in particular tend to chuckle over 'The Hospice', the story of a travelling salesman trapped in his worst nightmare of a guesthouse, where the guests are kept in ankle-fetters and the evening meal is served in mountainous indigestible heaps ('It's turkey tonight . . .'). In the aforementioned 'The Fetch', when our haunted man finally finds himself caged in his Scottish family home, watching the wraith watching him from a perch outdoors up high on a broken wall, he still has time to reflect that 'such levitations are said to be not uncommon in the remoter parts of Scotland'. This is the sound of a refined intellect, an author amusing both himself and us.

2014 is the centenary of Aickman's birth and sees him honoured at the annual World Fantasy Convention, the forum where, in 1975, his story 'Pages from a Young Girl's Journal' received the award for short fiction that year. His cult has been secure since then, and yet those who have newly discovered his rare brilliance have quite often wondered why he is not better known outside the supernatural cognoscenti.

One likely reason is that his body of work is so modestly sized: there are only forty-eight extant 'strange stories', and there was never a novel – or, to be precise, the two longer-form Aickmans that have been published – *The Late Breakfasters* in 1964 and *The Model*, posthumously, in 1987 – were fantastical (the latter especially), not to say exquisite, but had nothing overtly eerie or blood-freezing about them. Aickman simply refused to cash in on his most marketable skills as a writer (somewhat to the chagrin of the literary agents who represented him).

He was also a relatively late starter. *We Are for the Dark*, his co-publication with Elizabeth Jane Howard to which they contributed three tales apiece, appeared from Jonathan Cape in 1951; but nothing followed until 1964, with his first discrete collection, *Dark Entries*. By the turn of the 1980s he was a significant figure in the landscape, and from there his renown might have widened. It was then, however, that he developed the cancer from which he would die, on 26 February 1981, having refused chemotherapy in favour of homeopathic treatments.

Aickman's name would surely enjoy a wider currency today if any of his works had been adapted for cinema, a medium of which he was a discerning fan. And yet, to date, no such adaptation has come about. If we agree that a masterpiece is an idea expressed in its perfect creative form then it may be fair to say that the perfection Aickman achieved in the short story would not suffer to be stretched to ninety minutes or more across a movie screen. But the possibility still exists, for sure. If Aickman made a frightening world all of his own on the page, he also took on some of the great and familiar horror tropes, and treated them superbly.

To wit: the classic second piece in *Dark Entries*, 'Ringing the Changes', is a zombie story, immeasurably more ghastly and nerve-straining than *The Walking Dead*. And the aforementioned 'Pages from a Young Girl's Journal' is a vampire story, concerning a pubescent girl bored rigid by her family's Grand Tour of Italy in 1815, until she is pleasurably transformed by an encounter with a tall, dark, sharp-toothed stranger. In other words it is about the empowering effects of blood-sucking upon adolescent girls; and worth ten of the *Twilight*s of this world. On the strength of such accomplishments one can see that, while Aickman remains for the moment a cult figure, his stories retain the potential to reach many more new admirers far and wide – rather like the vampirised Jonathan Harker at the end of Werner Herzog's *Nosferatu the Vampyre* (1979), riding out on his steed to infect the world.

Had Aickman never written a word of fiction of his own he would still have a place in the annals of horror: a footnote, perhaps, to observe that he was the maternal grandson of Richard Marsh, bestselling sensational/ supernatural novelist of the late-Victorian and Edwardian eras; but an extensive entry for his endeavours as an anthologist, who helped to define a canon of supernatural fiction through his editing of the first eight volumes of the *Fontana Book of Great Ghost Stories* between 1964 and 1972.

His enduring reputation, though, would have been based on his co-founding in 1944 of the Inland Waterways Association, dedicated to the preservation and restoration of England's inland canals. Such a passionate calling might be considered perfect for an author of 'strange stories' – also for a man who was, in some profound way, out of step with or apart from his own time. By all accounts Aickman gave the IWA highly energetic leadership and built up its profile and activities with rigour and zeal. His insistent style, however, did not delight everyone: in 1951 he argued and fell out definitively with L. T. C. (Tom) Rolt, fellow conservationist and author, whose seminal book *Narrow Boat* (1944) had inspired the organisation's founding in the first place.

When we admire a writer we naturally wish to know more of what they were like as a person. Aickman's admirers have sometimes found what they have heard of him to be a shade forbidding. Culturally he was a connoisseur who had highly finessing tastes in theatre, ballet, opera and classical music. Socially he was punctilious and fastidious, unabashedly erudite, an autodidact not shy about airing his education. His political instincts were conservative, his outlook elitist. The late Elizabeth Jane Howard – first secretary of the Inland Waterways Association, with whom Aickman fell in love and for whom he carried a torch years after her ending of their brief relationship – would tell an interviewer some years later that there were at least two sides to the man: 'He could be very prickly and difficult, or he could be very charming.'

Nonetheless, those whom Aickman allowed to know him well and whom he liked and trusted in turn clearly found him to be the most marvellous company – for a night at the theatre, say, or a visit to a rural stately home, or at a catered dinner *à deux*, after which he would be inclined to read aloud from whichever strange story he was then working on. The reader will learn more in this line from the afterwords to this series of Faber reissues, which have been written by admiring friends who had just such a privileged insight into the author.

These reissues are in honour of Aickman's 2014 centenary. Along with the present volume, readers may choose from *Dark Entries*, *Cold Hand in Mine*, another posthumously published compilation entitled *The Unsettled Dust*, and (as Faber Finds) *The Late Breakfasters* and *The Model*. Whether these works are already known to you or you are about to discover them, the injunction is the same – prepare to be entranced, compelled, seduced, petrified.

RICHARD T. KELLY *is the author of the novels* Crusaders *and* The Possessions of Doctor Forrest.

The Wine-Dark Sea

Off Corfu? Off Euboea? Off Cephalonia? Grigg would never say which it was. Beyond doubt it was an island relatively offshore from an enormously larger island which was relatively inshore from the mainland. On this bigger island was a town with a harbour, mainly for fishing-boats but also for the occasional caïque, and with, nowadays, also a big parking place for motor-coaches. From the waterfront one could see the offshore island, shaped like a whale with a building on its back, or, thought Grigg, like an elephant and castle.

Grigg had not come by motor-coach, and therefore had freedom to see the sights, such as they were; to clamber over the hot, rocky hills; and to sit at his ease every evening watching the splendid sunsets. He found the food monotonous, the noise incredible, and the women disappointing (in general, they seemed only to come to identity around the age of sixty, when they rapidly transmogrified into witches and seers); but drink was cheap and the distant past ubiquitous. The language was a difficulty, of course, but Grigg could still scramble a short distance on what remained to him of the ancient variety, which, now that a test had come, was more than he had supposed.

Most of the time it was straight, beating sunshine,

I

something that had to be accommodated to by a steady act of will, like a Scandinavian winter (at least if there was any kind of serious enterprise on hand), but sometimes the air was green or blue or purple, and then the vast bay could be among the most beautiful places in the world, especially when the colour was purple. On his second or third evening, Grigg sat outside the café, an establishment patronised almost entirely by boring, noisy males, but unself-conscious and affable, none the less. He was drinking local drinks, and, despite the din, feeling himself almost to merge with the purple evening light. In the middle of the view appeared a smallish boat, with curving bow and stern, low freeboard, and a single square sail. If it had not risen from the depths, it must have sailed from behind the small offshore island. It seemed timeless in shape and handling. It added exactly the right kind of life to the sea, air, and evening.

But Grigg noticed at once that the other customers did not seem to think so. Not only did they stare at the beautiful boat, but they stared with expressions of direct hatred that an Englishman has no practice in adopting. They fell almost silent, which was a bad sign indeed. Even the white-coated waiters stopped running about and stood gazing out to sea like the customers. All that happened was that the boat put about and sailed on to the open waters. As she turned, Grigg thought that he could discern the shapes of sailors. They must have been good at their work, because the ship made off along a dead straight line in what seemed to Grigg to be very little breeze. Already she was merely a darker purple fleck in the perceptibly oncoming evening. The hubbub in the café soon worked up again. Grigg got the impression that the ship, though unpopular, was quite familiar.

Soon his waiter was removing his glass. Grigg ordered a renewal.

'What was that ship?'

He perceived that the waiter had a little English, but doubted whether it would suffice for this. It did suffice.

'She comes from the island.' The waiter stood gazing out, either at the ship or at the island.

'Can I visit the island?'

'No. There is no boat.'

'Surely I can hire one if I pay for it?'

'No. There is no boat.' And the waiter departed.

When he returned with Grigg's ensuing *ouzo*, Grigg did not resume the subject. All the same, what the waiter said had been absurd. The island could hardly have been more than a mile way and lay in the centre of the calm, sheltered bay. Grigg had not previously thought of the island as anything more than a point of emphasis in the view, an eye-catcher, as our ancestors termed it. Now he wanted to see more.

In the town was one of the state tourist offices, to which all foreign travellers are directed to go when in need. Grigg had not visited any of them before, but now was the time. He went next morning.

The pleasant young man who seemed in sole possession spoke pretty good English and received Grigg's enquiry with sophistication.

'The fishermen do not like the island,' he said, smiling. 'They give it, as you say, a wide berth.'

'Why is that?'

'It is said to be a very *old* island.'

'But surely this is a very old country?'

'Not as old as the island. Or so the fishermen say.'

'Is that a *bad* thing? Being very old?'

'Yes,' said the young man, with perceptibly less sophistication. 'A bad thing.' He sounded surprisingly firm. Grigg recollected that the tourist officials were recruited from the police.

'Then you think that no one will take me there?'

'I am sure of it,' said the young man, again smiling. 'No one.'

'Then I shall have to swim,' said Grigg. He spoke lightly, and he would have hated to have to do it. But the young man, who could not be sure of this, tried another tack.

'There's nothing to see on the island,' he said a shade anxiously. 'Nothing at all, I assure you. Let me give you our leaflet of tourist sights. All very nice.'

'Thank you,' said Grigg. 'I've got one already.'

The young man put the leaflet away, more obviously disappointed than an Englishman would have permitted of himself.

'Then you've been to the island yourself?' asked Grigg.

'No,' said the young man. 'As I told you, there is nothing to see.'

'Last night I saw a ship sail from the island. Either

4

someone must live there or there must be some reason for going there.'

'I do not know about that,' said the young man, slightly sulky but still trying. 'I cannot imagine that anyone lives there or wants to go there.' Grigg could not suppose that this was to be interpreted quite literally.

'Why shouldn't they?'

'The Turks. The Turks made the island unlucky.'

Long before, Grigg had realised that throughout Hellas everything bad that cannot be attributed to the evil eye or other supernatural influence is blamed upon the Turks; even though the stranger is apt on occasion to suspect, however unworthily, that the Turks provided the last settled and secure government the region has known. And he had furthermore realised that it is a subject upon which argument is not merely useless but impossible. The Turks and their special graces have been expunged from Hellenic history; their mosques demolished or converted into cinemas.

'I see,' said Grigg. 'Thank you for your advice. But I must make it clear that I do not undertake to follow it.'

The young man smiled him out, confident that the local brick wall would fully withstand the pounding of Grigg's unbalanced and middle-aged head.

And so it seemed. Contrary to legend, Grigg, as the day wore on, discovered that few of the fishermen seemed interested in his money: to be more precise, none of them, or none that he approached, and he had approached many. It did not seem to be that they objected to going

5

to the island, because in most cases he had not reached the point of even mentioning the island: they simply did not want to take him anywhere, even for what Grigg regarded as a considerable sum. They appeared to be very much preoccupied with their ordinary work. They would spend one entire day stretching their saffron-coloured nets to dry on the stones of the quay. Naturally the language barrier did not help, but Grigg got the impression that, in the view of the fishermen, as of various others he had met, tourists should adhere to their proper groove and not demand to wander among the real toilers, the genuine and living ancestors. Tourists were not to be comprehended among those strangers for whom, notoriously, the word is the same as for guests.

None of the separate, discouraging negotiations had taken long, and by the evening of that same day Grigg had combed the port and now found time on his hands. Thinking about it all, over an early drink, he wondered if word could have gone round as to the real destination of his proposed excursion. He also wondered if the island could be an enclave of the military, who were often to be found embattled in the most renowned and unexpected corners of the land. It seemed unlikely: the young man would have been proud to tell him so at once, as a young cowherd had told him at the ancient castro above Thessalonika. Besides, the ship he had seen could hardly have served for war since the Pericleans. It struck him to wonder whether the ship had returned during the night. He felt sure that it belonged to the island and not elsewhere. He even thought of buying a pair of field-glasses, but desisted because they would have to be carried all the way home.

Over his next *ouzo*, Grigg went on to consider why it mattered to him about reaching the island, especially when so much difficulty seemed to be involved. He decided that, in the first place, it had been the beautiful ship. In the second place, it had been the hostility to her of the people in the café. Grigg was one whose feelings were usually contrary to any that might be expressed in mass emotion; and he was confirmed in this when the popular feeling was so morally narrow and so uniform as, commonly, among the Hellenes. In the third place, it was undoubtedly the mysterious business about the island being bad because very old. A perceptive traveller in Hellas comes to think of the Parthenon as quite modern; to become more and more absorbed by what came earlier. Soon, if truly perceptive, he is searching seriously for centaurs.

All the same, Grigg quite surprised himself by what he actually did. Walking along the hard road in the heat of the next mid-afternoon, with almost no one else so foolish as to be about at all, apart from the usual discontented coach trip, he observed a small boat with an outboard motor. She was attached, bow on, to a ring. He could borrow her, visit the island, be back almost within an hour, and pay then, if anyone relevant had appeared. He was sure that it was now or never. He was able to untie the painter almost at his leisure, while the coach-party stared at him, welcoming the familiar activity and the familiar-looking man who was doing it.

The engine started popping at the first pull. A miracle, thought Grigg, who had experience of outboards: fate is with me. In a matter of hardly more than seconds in all, his hand was on the helm and he was off.

To anyone that loves the seas of Britain or the great sands of Belgium and Holland, there is something faintly repulsive about the tideless Mediterranean and Aegean, which on a calm day tend to be at once stagnant and a little uncanny. Dense weed often clogs the shallows, uncleaned by ebb and flow; and one speculates upon fathom five and millennia many of unshifting spoil. While he was still near the shore, Grigg's enjoyment was mitigated also by the smell, much more noticeable than from the land; but soon the pleasure of being afloat at all worked on him, and within minutes there was nothing in his heart but the sun, the breeze, the parting of the water at the prow of the boat, and the island ahead. After a spell, he did half look over his shoulder for a possible gesticulating figure on the quay. There was no one. Even the coach-party was re-embarked and poised to go elsewhere. And soon the lights that sparkled on the miniature waves were like downland flowers in spring.

Upon a closer view, the building on the island's back proved to be merely the central section, or keep, of saffron-coloured fortifications that included the whole area. In view of what the man at the tourist office had said, they had presumably been erected by the Turks, but one never quite knew whether there had not been contributions from the Venetians, or the Normans, or the Bul-

8

gars, or the Cyclops, or, at different times, from them all. Some of the present structures seemed far gone in decay, but all of them were covered with clusters and swags of large, brightly coloured flowers, so that the total effect was quite dazzling, especially when seen across a few hundred yards of radiant blue sea. Grigg perceived that the island was simply a rock; a dark brown, or reddish-brown rock, which stood out everywhere quite distinctly from the lighter hue of the stonework.

Then he saw that the sunlight was glinting on glass in at least some of the windows, small and deepset though they were. To his right, moreover, an ornamental balustrade, hardly a part of the fortress, descended the sloping back of the island until it ended almost at sea-level. Grigg thought that the rock might continue to slope in the same gentle degree under the water, so that it would be as well to go cautiously and to keep well out; but it seemed, none the less, the likeliest end of the island for a landing. He rounded the island in this way without incident, and saw that on the far side there was a square stone harbour, though void alike of craft and citizens. He cut off his noisy engine and drifted in. He marvelled more than ever at the number, the size, and the gorgeousness of the flowers. Already, still out at sea, he could even smell them: not the smell of one particular species, but a massed perfume, heavy and almost melodious, drifting across the limpid water to meet and enfold him. He sailed silently in like a coasting bird, and settled perfectly at the harbour steps, as one commonly does when not a soul is looking. Grigg sprang ashore, climbed the steps, which were made of marble, and made fast to one of the rings in the stone-work at the top. He observed that here the ocean-verge was uncluttered with weed, so that he could look down-wards many yards through the water and the shoals of fish to the sunny sand below.

Having but borrowed the boat, he meant, of course, to remain for only a matter of minutes; merely to make up his mind as to whether there was anything on the island to justify the difficulty of a renewed effort for a more conventional visit. At once, however, he realised how glad he was to be alone, how greatly a professional boatman would have spoiled his pleasure.

On this side of the long sloping balustrade were wide steps; a marble staircase leading from port to citadel. They were immaculate: even, level, and almost polished in their smoothness. Grigg ascended. On his right was the bare brown rock. He noticed that it was strikingly rough and gnarled, with hardly anywhere a flat area as big as a lace handkerchief. He put his hand on this rough rock. It was so hot that it almost burnt him. Still, soil had come from somewhere: as well as the wonderful flowers, there were fruit trees ahead and heavy creepers. Curiously coloured lizards lay about the steps watching him. He could not quite name the colour. Azure, per-haps; or cerulean. When he reached the citadel, there were nectarines hanging from the branches spread out against the yellow walls. They seemed much ahead of their time, Grigg thought, but supposed that so far south the seasons were different. He was feeling more and more a trespasser. The island was quite plainly inhabited and cared for. There was nothing about it which accorded with the impression given at the tourist office.

The citadel had wooden gates, but they were open. Grigg hesitated. There was nothing to be heard but the soft sea and the bees. He listened, and entered the citadel.

The structure ranged round three sides of a stone-paved courtyard. The fourth side, which faced away from the bigger island, had either fallen or been bombarded into ruin, and then perhaps been demolished, so that now there was nothing left but high, rough edges of yellow masonry framing the view of the open sea, vast, featureless, and the colour of the sky. Again there were flowers everywhere, with a big flowering tree near the centre of the court. The glazed windows stood open, and so did several doors. Grigg did not care to enter: the place was clearly lived in, and he had no justification for being there.

Still he did not feel as yet like returning.

On the far side of the courtyard was another open gateway. Grigg passed cautiously through it. There seemed nothing to worry about. As usual, no one was to be seen. There were not even the farm animals he had half expected. There was nothing but a tangle of collapsed defence structures from past centuries, starting with an irregular wall which ringed this entire end of the island at little above sea-level. Between the many ruined buildings was dense, sharp grass, reaching above Grigg's knees, and unpleasantly suggestive also of snakes. None the less, he ploughed on, convinced by now that this was his only chance, as he would never be able to find a reason for coming back.

A considerable garrison must have been installed at one time, or at least contemplated. The place was still like a maze, and also gave the impression, even now, of having been abandoned quite suddenly, doubtless when the Turks departed. There were still long guns, mounted and pointed out to sea, though drawn back. There were straggling, dangerous stacks of stone, and other obviously ancient heaps that might once have been heaps of anything. Grigg was far too hot and increasingly lacerated, but he determined to scramble on, as there was a circular tower at the end of the island, which, if climbable, might offer a more revealing panorama. Anyway, who that had imagination, could reach the island in the way Grigg had reached it, and not at least try to climb that tower?

When at long last attained, the tower seemed to be in almost perfect order. Grigg dragged open the parched door, and wound his way up and up through the spiders and other crepusculae. The circular stone stair emerged through a now uncovered hole in the stone roof, so that the top steps were shapeless and treacherous beneath deep, lumpy silt which had drifted in from the atmosphere.

And then there was a revelation indeed. As Grigg emerged and looked out over the low battlements, he saw on the instant that another boat had entered the small harbour, almost a ship; in fact, without doubt, *the* ship. She was painted green, and her single blue sail had already been struck. Grigg perceived that now he could hardly depart from the island without explanations.

He descended the tower, not having studied the other features of the prospect as carefully as he otherwise would have done. As he stumbled back through the débris and thick, dry vegetation, he grazed and sliced himself even more than on the outward scramble. He felt very undignified as he re-entered the citadel, especially as he was hotter than ever.

Standing in the courtyard were three women. They all appeared to be aged between thirty and forty, and they all wore identical greeny-brown dresses, plainly intended for service.

'Good afternoon,' said one of the women. 'Do you wish to stay with us?' She had a foreign accent, but it struck Grigg at once as not being Greek.

'Can one stay?' It was a foolish rejoinder, but instinctual.

'We do not run an hotel, but we sometimes have guests. It is as you wish.'

'I am staying in the town. I couldn't find out anything about the island, so I borrowed a boat to see for myself.'

'How did you do that?' asked one of the other women, in what seemed to Grigg to be the same foreign accent. She had dark hair, where the other two were fair, and a darker voice than the first speaker.

'Do what?'

'Borrow a boat. They would never lend you a boat to come here.'

'No,' said Grigg, certain that he was blushing under the singularly direct gaze of his interrogator's black eyes. 'It was difficult.' After pausing for a second, he took a small plunge. 'Why should that be?'

'The Greeks are stupid,' said the first woman. 'Violent and vengeful, of course, too; quite incapable of government; but, above all, stupid. They can't even grow a tree. They can only cut them down.' She placed her hand on the bole of the beautiful flowering tree which grew in the courtyard. It was a rather fine movement, Grigg thought, much more like the Greeks of myth than any of the Greeks he could remember actually to have seen.

'They certainly seem to have a particular feeling about this island.'

No further explanation was forthcoming. There was merely another slight pause. Then the first woman spoke.

'Do *you* have any particular feeling about this island?'

'I think it is the most beautiful place I have ever visited,' replied Grigg, hardly knowing whether or not he exaggerated.

'Then stay with us.'

'I have to take back the boat. As I said, I have only borrowed it.'

The third woman spoke for the first time. 'I shouldn't take back the boat.' She spoke with the same accent as the others, and her tone was one of pleasant warning.

'What do you mean?' asked Grigg.

'You'll be torn to pieces if you do.'

'Oh, surely not,' said Grigg, laughing uneasily.

'Didn't you steal the boat?' The woman was smiling quite amicably. 'Or at least borrow it without asking?'

'As a matter of fact, yes.'

'And haven't you borrowed it so as to come here?'

'Yes.'

'They'll tear you to pieces.' She spoke as if it were the most foregone of conclusions; but, seeing that Grigg still doubted, she added in friendly seriousness, 'Believe it. It's true. If you leave us, you can't go back. You'll have to go somewhere else. A long way off.'

Inevitably, Grigg was impressed. 'But tell me,' he said, 'why shouldn't I – or anyone else – come here?'

The woman with the black eyes looked hard at Grigg. 'They believe we're sorcerers – sorcer*esses*,' she corrected herself, tripping over the language.

Grigg was familiar with such talk among southern peasants. 'And are you?' he asked lightly.

'Yes,' said the dark woman. 'We are.'

'Yes,' confirmed the first woman. 'We are all sorceresses.' There was about about the statement neither facetiousness nor challenge.

'I see,' said Grigg gravely; and looked away from them out to the open ocean, empty as before.

'People who come here usually know that already,' said the first woman; again in some simple explanation.

Grigg turned back to them and stared for a moment. They really were, he realised, most striking to see, all three of them: with beautifully shaped, muscular, brown limbs; strong necks and markedly sculptural features;

15

and a casual grandeur of posture, which was perhaps the most impressive thing of all. And their practical, almost primitive, garments suited them wonderfully. The two fair women wore yellow shoes, but the dark woman was bare-footed, with strong, open toes. Grigg was struck by a thought.

'Yesterday I saw your ship,' he said. 'In a way, it was why I came. Do you sail her yourself?'

'Yes,' said the first woman. 'We have sometimes to buy things, and they will sell us nothing here. We built the boat on a beach in Albania, where no one lives. We took wood from the forests behind, which belong to no one.'

'I believe that now they belong to the People's Republic,' Grigg said, smiling.

'That is the same thing,' said the woman.

'I suspect that you are right about my little boat,' said Grigg. 'They tell you to act more regularly on impulse, but I often act on impulse, and almost always find that it was a mistake, sometimes a surprisingly bad one.'

'Coming here was not necessarily a mistake,' said the first woman. 'It depends.'

'I wasn't thinking about that part of it,' said Grigg, convicted of rudeness. 'I like it here. I was thinking of what will happen when I go back – whenever I go back.'

'One of us will guide you to somewhere you'll be safe. Now, if you wish.'

'Thank you,' said Grigg. 'But I only borrowed the boat and must really return it.'

'Take it back during the night,' said the third woman,

with unexpected practicality.

And thus it was that Grigg decided to stay; at least until it was dark.

There was work to be done: first, the unloading of the ship. Grigg naturally offered to help, but the women seemed very cool about it.

'The tasks are disposed for the three of us,' said the woman who had spoken first, 'and you would find it very hot.'

Grigg could not deny this last statement, as he was already perspiring freely, though standing still. None the less, he could hardly leave it at that.

'As you are permitting me to intrude upon you,' he said, 'please permit me to help.'

'You are not an intruder,' said the woman, 'but you are a stranger, and the tasks are for me and my sisters.'

She made Grigg feel so completely unqualified that he could think of nothing to say. 'The house is open to you,' continued the woman. 'Go wherever you like. The heat is not good unless you are accustomed to it.' The three women then went out through the harbour gateway and down the long flight of marble steps to the ship. Grigg looked after them as they descended, but none of them looked back.

Grigg entered through one of the doors and began to prowl about. There were many rooms, some big, some small, but all well proportioned. All were painted in different colours, all perfectly clean, all open to the world, and all empty. The whole place was beautifully tended, but it was hard to see for what, at least by accepted standards.

Grigg ascended to the floor above. The marble staircase led to a landing from which was reached a larger and higher room than any of the others. It had doubtless been the main hall of the citadel. Three tall windows opened on to small decorative balconies overlooking the courtyard. On a part of the floor against the wall opposite these windows were rectangular cushions packed together like mah-jong pieces, to make an area of softness. There were smaller windows high in the wall above them. There was nothing else in the room but a big circular bowl of flowers. It stood on the floor towards one corner, and had been hewn from pink marble. Grigg thought that the combined effect of the cushions, the flowers, and the proportions of the room was one of extreme luxury. The idea came to him, not for the first time, that most of the things which people buy in the belief that they are luxuries are really poor substitutes for luxury.

The other rooms on that floor of the citadel were as the rooms below, spotless, sunny, but empty. On the second floor there were several rooms furnished as the hall; with in one place a mass of deep cushions, in another a mass of flowers, and nothing else. Sometimes the flowers were in big iron bowls mounted on tripods; sometimes in reservoirs forming a part (but the dominant part) of a statuary group. On the first and second floors, the rooms led into one another, and most of them had windows, overlooking the larger island from which Grigg had come, the other overlooking the open sea. It was true that there were doors, in coloured wood; but all, without exception, stood open. There was nothing so very unusual about the building, agreeable though it was, and nothing in the least mysterious in themselves about its appurtenances, but before Grigg had completed his tour and emerged on to the flat roof, he had begun to feel quite depressed by the recollection of how he and his neighbours dwelt, almost immersed beneath mass-produced superfluities, impotent even as distractions.

On the roof was a single stone figure of a recumbent man, more than life-size. It reposed at one end of the roof with its back to the harbour, and it was from the other end of the roof that Grigg first saw it, so that he had a longish walk across the bare expanse before he came up to it, like a visitor to Mussolini in the great days.

The figure was, inevitably, of the kind vaguely to be termed classical; but Grigg doubted whether, in any proper sense, it was classical at all. It was not so much that it was in perfect order, as if it had been carved that same year, and glossy of surface, both of which things are rare with ancient sculpture, but rather the sentiment with which the figure was imbued, and which it projected as an aura, the compulsive implication of the artist's work, if indeed there had ever been an artist.

It was a male of advanced years, or alternatively, perhaps, ageless, who reclined with his head on his right hand which rose from the elbow on the ground, a position which Grigg had always found to be especially un-comfortable. The hair straggled unkempt over the low cranium. The big eyes protruded above the snub nose, and from the thick lips the tongue protruded slightly also. There was a lumpy chin, unconcealed by a beard. The rest of the body was hirsute, long-armed, and mus-cular; hands, feet, and phallus being enormous. The man appeared to be lying on the bare and wrinkled earth; or possibly, it struck Grigg, on rocks. The folds in the stone ground of the statue (it seemed to be some other stone than the usual marble) were very similar to the folds in the rock which he had noticed as he walked up from the harbour. There was something compressed and drawn together about the man's entire attitude, almost like a foetus in the womb, or an immensely strong spring, compressed against the moment of use. Grigg thought that the man did not so much stare at him, though staring he certainly was, as right through him and beyond him, probably far beyond. As Grigg gazed back, a small spurt of dirty water bubbled from the man's open mouth. It dribbled from his tongue and discoloured the forearm supporting his head. There must have been a pump to supply the fountain, and Grigg was not surprised, considering the obvious mech-anical problems, that it did not work very well.

Grigg advanced to the balustrade surrounding the citadel roof and looked over the harbour. The women were still at work unloading the ship. One of them, the smaller of the two with fair hair, who had been the last to speak when Grigg appeared, was carrying up the wide steps a large green cask, mounted on her right shoulder.

Grigg felt very uncertain what to do. He could hardly just stand about while the women were working so industriously, but he felt that the rejection of his services had been singularly final, and he also felt that if he succeeded in insisting, then he would almost certainly make a fool of himself in the great heat and with a routine of which he was ignorant. He had nothing even to read, nor had he seen anything to read on the entire island. He decided, pusillanimously, to stay where he was, until things below perhaps quieted down.

He sank upon the stones of the roof at a place where the balustrade gave a little shade. He had in mind to stretch out for a siesta, but the stones were so hard and so level that he found himself propping his head on his hand, like the stone man he had just been looking at. He gazed out to sea between the columns of the balustrade, but the attitude soon proved every bit as uncomfortable as he had always thought, and he began instead to sprawl upon his back, pushed as close against the balustrade as he could manage, in the need for as much shade as possible. He reflected that again he was imitating the stone man, so drawn in on himself.

It was, in any case, quite useless, and, like most useless things, useless almost immediately. Not only was the sun unbearable, but the stored heat of the stone was even more unbearable and worse even than its hardness, though stone is harder in the Hellenes than anywhere else. After only a few minutes, Grigg felt as stiff and parched as an old tobacco leaf; so much so that he had difficulty in rising to his feet, and was glad that his middle-aged muddling, the dropsy of a welfare society, was not under observation.

He descended to the floor below and sank himself on the cushioned area in one of the luxurious rooms; he neither knew nor cared which. Through the open windows had flown in some very tiny, curiously coloured birds. Grigg could not quite name the colour: some kind of bright blue, aquamarine perhaps. The birds fluttered immoderately, like moths; and, from their throats or wings or both, came a faint, high, silvery, unceasing chant, as of honey heard dripping from the very summit of Hymettus. Grigg normally liked a bird in the room no more than other men like it; but all he did about the birds now was fall dead asleep.

At some time during his sleep, he had a nightmare. He dreamed that lizards, not small blue ones, but quite large black ones, possibly eighteen inches long, were biting off his own flesh. Already they had devoured most of the flesh on his feet and legs, so that he could see the bare, red bones extending upwards to the knees. It was difficult to look, however. There was something in common between his attitude, lying uncomfortably on his back, and the attitude he had been forced into on the roof. He did not seem to be tied down in any way, or even drugged, but he was too stiff to move very much, none the less. Gnawing away even now were eight or ten lizards, with long angular legs, big clawed feet, and oversized necks, heads, and eyes; and there were many other similar lizards, standing silently

22

in the background, a terrifying number, in fact. Perhaps they are waiting their turn, Grigg thought; and then remembered that it was something which animals are seldom observed to do. One curious thing was that the gnawing did not exactly hurt: it was quite perceptible, but Grigg felt it as a nervous *frisson* charging his whole body, half painful but half pleasurable, like a mild current of electricity from a machine on the pier. Grigg could not decide whether or not he was wearing clothes. When he looked, he could see his bare legs (very bare in fact); while, at the same time, he *felt* as if he were fully dressed. But, then again, the lizards had already pecked at other patches of his body. He trembled to think what it would be like when they reached his head.

But before they did, Grigg was awake, or, rather, awakened.

The scene seemed hardly less strange, because there were several things to be taken in at once.

In the first place, the whole room was filled with a dim and dusky red light, which Grigg soon realised was probably just the last of the sunset, suggesting that he had slept a long time.

In the second place, the room seemed to be what he could only regard as moving about. There was a steady pitching, up, down, up; and with it was incorporated a sick-making diagonal tilt. It was by no means a single lurch, but a persistent, though far from regular, heaving and plunging.

'An earthquake,' cried Grigg very loudly to the

twilight; now much more fully awake.

He tried to leap up, but then realised a third thing: in some way he was being restrained.

He awoke completely. There was a weight on his chest, and bonds round his arms. He perceived that it was a human being who was imprisoning him, holding him down.

It was one of the three women. She lifted her head, though without releasing him, and he perceived that it was the woman he had last seen carrying the green cask on her shoulder up the steps.

'It will end,' she said. 'Lie still and it will be over.'

'It *is* an earthquake?' enquired Grigg in a whisper.

'Yes,' she said. 'An earthquake.' Her tonelessness was probably deliberate and intended to reassure. She tightened her hold on him, and as she moved her head, he felt her hair against his face in the near darkness.

'What's your name?' asked Grigg in the same whisper.

'My name is Tal.'

'You are beautiful.'

'You are strong.'

Grigg had not, before she spoke, felt at all strong.

'I could hardly hold you.' She spoke as if she had saved him from some great peril.

'I was dreaming. I still am dreaming.'

'Then I am part of the dream.'

'The whole island is a dream but it is a very lovely island.'

'It is an island of love.'

Suddenly he realised that she was naked.

The last of the sunset, setting fire to his body, kindled it into a blaze. The two of them rolled on to the warm floor.

'It is my first earthquake,' he said. 'I always thought earthquakes were bad.'

And in a few flushed minutes before it was absolutely and finally dark, in that region where darkness comes quickly, he had possessed her, with uttermost rapture, a rapture not previously imaginable.

He heard her voice through the darkness speaking, he divined, from the doorway. She sounded as cool as the night was still warm.

'There is a meal.'

'I am hungry for it.'

The earthquake had ended. It was as if they two had ended it.

'Can you find your way down without a light?'

'I'm sure I can.' After all, she had given him the eyes of a cat, of a muscular, blonde cat.

'We eat in the courtyard.'

'I could devour an ox,' commented Grigg happily, and abandoning all restraint.

'We eat fruit,' she said, and he could hear her leaving him through the darkness.

'Tal!' he cried after her, but softly. He wanted to kiss her, to ravish her again, but she did not return.

*

There she was, however, eating nectarines with the others, as soon as he had groped his way down. There were grapes, nuts, and oranges, not in dishes but strewn with the nectarines about the stones of the court. Grigg thought it was just as if all the fruit had been scattered from a cornucopia. There were also a whole chest of figs and heavy lumps of small dates in a big brown canvas bag. The three women had brought out cushions and were eating in what is supposed to have been the Roman style. There were cushions for Grigg too, and soon he was peeling an orange. The sky was now full of stars.

'I am Lek,' said the other fair woman.

'I am Vin,' said the dark woman. She was still bare-footed, Grigg noticed.

As Tal said nothing, Grigg wondered how much was known.

'I am Grigg.'

'Be welcome, Grigg,' said Lek, the woman who had spoken to him first, that afternoon in this same court-yard; 'be assured of all our loves.'

'Thank you,' replied Grigg. 'I am happy.'

Vin threw him a nut; or rather, if he had not been able to see her warm smile in the now clear starlight, he might have supposed that she had thrown a nut at him, so hard did it hit. What was more, he noticed that there were no nutcrackers and no substitute for them. The women split the nuts open by biting them, which was entirely beyond him to do. It was quite a serious matter, because he really could not subsist entirely on fruit. He had, after all, eaten nothing since

breakfast. However, he looked with surreptitious meaning at Tal, and felt compensated but less than reassured.
Moreover, the night, instead of growing cooler, seemed
to be growing steadily warmer.

'Don't earthquakes usually do damage?' he asked.

'Elsewhere they do,' replied Lek, splintering a nut.
'Not here.'

'Our earthquakes are not like other people's earthquakes,' said Vin. She did not say it banteringly, but
rather as if to discourage further questions. She too, was
carefully picking scraps of nut from splinters of shell.

'I see,' said Grigg. 'Or rather, I don't see at all.'

'We do not claim to be like other people in any way,'
explained Lek. 'As I told you, we are sorceresses.'

'I remember,' said Grigg. 'What exactly does that
mean?'

'It is not to be described,' said Lek.

'I feared as much,' said Grigg, glancing again at Tal,
who so far had not spoken at all.

'You misunderstand,' said Lek. 'I mean that the
description would be without meaning. The thing can
only be felt, experienced. It is not a matter of conjuring,
of turning lead into gold, or wine into blood. We can
do all those things as well, but they are bad and to be
avoided, or left behind.'

'I think I have heard something of the kind,' said
Grigg. 'I am sorry to be inquisitive. All the same, it
might have been nice if you could have prevented that
earthquake.'

'There was no reason to prevent it.'

27

'Sorry,' said Grigg, tired of the mystification. 'It is none of my business, anyway.'

'That depends,' said Lek.

'Upon whether you decide to stay or go,' said Vin. As she spoke, she took off her plain, greeny-brown dress. She did it casually, as a woman might remove a scarf when she finds it too hot. Vin was wearing no other garment, and now lay naked on the cushions, her back against the low wall, behind which stretched the sea.

'On this island,' continued Lek, 'we live as all people once lived. But long ago they thought better of it and started looking for something else. They have been looking, instead of living, ever since.'

'What have they been looking for?'

'They call it achievement. They call it knowledge. They call it mastery. They even call it happiness. You called it happiness just now, when Vin threw a nut at you, but we are prepared to treat that as a slip of the tongue by a newcomer. And do you know who started it all?'

'I would rather you told me.'

'The Greeks started it. It was their stupidity. Have you not seen how stupid the Greeks are?'

'As a matter of fact, I have. It is not at all what one is led to expect. I have been continuously surprised by it.'

'Nothing to be surprised at. It is the same quality that made the Greeks separate man from nature in the first place, or rather from life.'

'You mean the ancient Greeks?' asked Grigg, staring at her.

'The same Greeks. All Greeks are the same. All stupid. All lopsided. All poisoned with masculinity.'

'Yes,' said Grigg, smiling. 'As a matter of fact, I have noticed something like that. It is not a country for women.' His eyes drifted to Vin's naked body, gleaming in the starlight.

'Once it was. We ruled once, but they drove us out,' said Lek, more sadly than fiercely. 'We fought, and later they wrote silly plays about the fight, but they defeated us, though not by the superior strength on which they pride themselves so much.'

'How, then?'

'By changing our world into a place where it was impossible for us to live. It was impossible for them to live in such a world also, but that they were too stupid to know. They defeated us in the same way that they have defeated everything else that is living,'

'Tell me,' said Grigg. 'What makes you think that I am any different? After all, I am a man, even though not a Greek. Why on earth should I be any kind of an exception?'

'There is no earth here,' said Lek. 'Haven't you noticed?'

'Nothing but rock,' cried Grigg. 'But there are more flowers than anywhere? And these wonderful nectarines?'

'They live on rock,' said Tal, speaking for the first time.

'You are different,' said Lek, 'simply because you have both set out and arrived. Few try and fewer succeed.'

'What happens to them?'

'They have set-backs of various kinds.'

'I didn't find it in the least difficult,' said Grigg.

'Those meant to succeed at a thing never do find the thing difficult.'

'Meant? Meant by whom?'

'By the life of which they are a part, whether they know it or not.'

'It is very mystical,' said Grigg. 'Where is this life to be found?'

'Here,' said Lek, simply. 'And it is not mystical at all. That is a word invented by those who have lost life or destroyed it. A word like *tragedy*. The stupid Greeks even called the plays they wrote about their fight with the women *tragedies*.'

'If I stay,' began Grigg, and then stopped. 'If I stay,' he began again, 'how do I make payment? I do not necessarily mean in money. All the same, how?'

'Here there are no bargains and no debts. You do not pay at all. You submit to the two gods. Their rule is light, but people are so unaccustomed to it that they sometimes find it includes surprises.'

'I have seen one of the gods. Where is the other?'

'The other god is female and therefore hidden.'

Grigg noticed that a considerable tremor, very visible in the case of Vin, passed through all three of their bodies.

'I still do not understand,' he said, 'why there is no one else. We are not all that far away. And the voyage is really quite easy. I should have thought that people would be coming all the time.'

'It might be better,' said Lek, 'to rejoice that you are the one chosen. But if you wish to go, go now, and one of us will guide you.'

Grigg didn't go. It wasn't Lek's riddling talk that prevented him, but much simpler things: Tal; the charm and strangeness of the empty rooms; not least the conviction that the women were right when they said he could not return to his starting-point, and uncertainty as to where else he could practicably make for. He told them that he would stay for the night. A plan would be easier to evolve in the sunshine.

'You don't mind if I grow a beard?' he said. 'I've brought nothing with me.'

They were very nice about his having brought nothing with him.

'Enchanted islands are hard to understand,' he said. 'I've always thought that. It worried me even as a child. The trouble is that you can never be sure where the enchantment begins and where it ends.'

'You learn by experience,' said Tal.

'Do you – do we – really live entirely on fruit?'

'No,' said Lek. 'There is wine.'

Vin rose and walked out through the gateway that led down to the harbour. She moved like a nymph, and her silhouette against the night sky through the arch was that of a girl-athlete on a vase.

Wine was not the sustenance that Grigg, fond though he was of it, felt he most needed at the moment, but he said nothing. They were all silent while waiting for Vin to return. The tideless waves flapped against the surrounding rock. The stars flickered.

Vin returned with a little porcelain bowl, not spilling a drop of the contents as she stepped bare-footed over the uneven stones. The bowl was set among them, small cups appeared, and they all drank. There was little wine left when all the cups had been filled. The wine was red. Grigg thought it was also extremely sweet and heavy, almost treacly in texture; he was glad that he did not have to drink more of it. They followed the wine by drinking water from a pitcher.

'Where do you find water?' asked Grigg.

'From springs in the rock,' answered Lek.

'More than one spring?'

'There is a spring of health, a spring of wisdom, a spring of beauty, a spring of logic, and a spring of longevity.'

'And the water we are drinking?'

'It is from the spring of salutation. Alas, we do not drink from it as often as we should like.'

Here Tal departed and came back with the green cask which Grigg had earlier seen her carrying. It contained a different wine, and, to Grigg, a more accustomed.

Tal had also brought a lantern. They settled to ancient games with coloured stones, and lines drawn with charcoal on the rocky floor. These games again were new to Grigg: not only their rules and skills, but, more, the spirit in which they were played. The object appeared to be not so much individual triumph as an intensification of fellow-feeling; of love, to use Lek's word of welcome to him. Most surprising of all to Grigg was the discovery that he no longer felt underfed, although he had eaten neither meat nor grain. He felt agog (it was the only word) with life, air, warmth, and starlight. Time itself had become barbless and placid.

'Sleep where you will,' said Lek. 'There are many rooms.' Vin picked up her dress and they all entered the citadel.

'Good night,' they said.

'He tried to catch Tal's eye, but failed.

They were gone.

Grigg did not feel like sleep. He decided to walk down to the harbour.

The lizards were still sprawling and squirming on the steps, which Grigg thought odd for such creatures, and unpleasingly reminiscent of his dream. The scent of the massed flowers was heavier than ever. He went slowly down through the stars and the blossoms, and climbed aboard his boat, now lying alongside the much bigger sailing-ship; looked at the engine, which appeared to be untouched (though he could think of no real reason why it should be otherwise); and sat on the stern seat thinking.

He decided that though the way of life on the island seemed to him in almost every way perfect, he was far from sure that he himself was so innately the designated participant in it as to justify his apparently privileged journey and landfall. He was far from pleased by this realisation. On the contrary, he felt that he had been corrupted by the very different life to which he had been so long accustomed, and much though he normally disliked it. He doubted whether by now he was capable of redemption from that commonplace existence, even by enchantment. The three women had virtually agreed that enchantment has its limitations. Grigg felt very much like starting the outboard forthwith, and making off to face the difficult music.

'Be brave.'

Grigg looked up. It was Vin who had spoken. She had resumed her dress and was leaning over the gunwale of the ship above him.

'But what does courage consist in? Which is the brave thing to do?'

'Come up here,' said Vin, 'and we'll try to find out.'

Grigg climbed the narrow harbour steps, walked round the end of the little basin, and stepped over the side of the curved ship. Vin had now turned and stood with her back against the opposite side, watching him. Grigg was quite astonished by how beautiful she looked, though he could hardly see her face through the darkness. It mattered little: Vin, standing there alone, was superb. She seemed to him the living epitome of the elegant ship.

'We don't really exist, you know,' said Vin. 'So, in the first place, you need not be scared of us. We're only ghosts. Nothing to be frightened of.'

He sat on a coil of rope in front of her, but a little to the side, the harbour-mouth side.

'Do you chuck about ropes like this?'

'Of course. We're strong.'

'Do you eat absolutely nothing but fruit?'

'And drink the wine I brought you to drink.'

'I thought it was no ordinary wine.'

'It makes you no ordinary person.'

'I don't feel very different.'

'People don't feel very different even after they have died. The Greek Church says that forty days pass before people feel any different.'

'Is that true?'

'Quite true. Not even the Greeks are wrong all the time. And the dead still feel the same even *after* forty days unless the proper masses are said. You can't go to Heaven without the masses, you know.'

'Or, presumably, to Hell?'

'As you say, Grigg.'

Grigg was struck by a thought.

'Is that in some way why you're here now?'

Vin laughed, gurgling like her own thick, sweet, red wine. 'No, Grigg. We're not dead. Feel.'

She held out her left hand. Grigg took it. It was curiously firm and soft at the same time, strong but delicate. Grigg found himself most reluctant to relinquish it.

'You're alive,' said Grigg.

Vin said nothing.

'Tell me,' said Grigg, 'what there is in the wine?'

'Rock,' said Vin softly.

Grigg was absurdly reminded of those claims in wine-merchants' catalogues that in this or that brand can be tasted the very soil in which it was grown.

'Don't laugh,' said Vin, quite sharply. 'The rock

35

doesn't like it.'

Grigg had no idea what she meant, but he stopped laughing at once. The mystery made her words all the more impressive, as sometimes when an adult admonishes a child.

'Where did you all come from?' asked Grigg. 'To judge by what you say, you can't be Greek. And you don't sound Greek. You speak English beautifully, which means you can't be English. What are you?'

'Lek comes from one place. Tal from another. I from a third. Where I come from the people wear no shoes.'

'Lek spoke of you as sisters.'

'We are sisters. We work and fight side by side, which makes us sisters.'

'Are there no more of you?'

'Men have broken through from time to time, like you. The rock is surrounded, you know. But none of the men have stayed. They have killed themselves or sailed away.'

'Have none of them sailed back? After all, it's not far.'

'Not one. They have always had something to make it impossible. Like your stolen boat.'

'I suppose that's inevitable. One couldn't think of finding a place like this and still being able to go back.' He thought about it, then added, 'Or forward either, I daresay.'

'Grigg,' said Vin, 'burn your boat. I will make fire for you.'

The shock of her words made him rise to his feet, charged with the instinct of flight.

On the instant her arms were round him, holding him very tightly. 'Burn it, burn it,' she was crying passionately. 'Will you never understand? You might have done it hours ago.'

Without thinking of what he was doing, he found that his arms were round her too, and they were kissing.

'Watch me make fire,' she shouted. In the instant they had become lovers, true lovers, sentiment as well as passion, tender as well as proud.

She darted across the ship, leapt the gunwale, and ran round the little quay, all the while dragging Grigg by the hand. She seemed to part the thin painter with a single pull and drew the boat out of the basin. Despite the absence of tide or wind, the boat drifted straight out into the darkness of the open sea.

'Day and night, the sea runs away from the rock,' cried Vin.

They stood together, their arms tightly round one another's waists, watching the boat disappear.

Grigg could not sense that she did anything more, but suddenly, far out, there was a beautiful rosy glow, like the sunset, it was contained and oval, and in the middle of it could be seen the transfigured outline of the boat, gleaming whitely, like the Holy Grail, too bright to stare at for more than a moment. Outside the fiery oval, the whole air was turning a faint, deep pink.

'My God,' cried Grigg, 'the petrol in the outboard. It will explode.'

'On to the ship,' said Vin, and hauled him back round the basin and aboard.

They hid, clinging together, in a small hold made simply by thick planks stretched at gunwale-level across the bow. The flush in the night sky was intensifying all the time. Then there was a loud concussion; the sky turned almost scarlet; and, not more than a few minutes later, he possessed Vin as if she had been hardly more than a little girl.

Hand in hand, they ascended the wide steps to the citadel. At the gateway, they looked back. The burning boat had still not sunk, because it could just be seen, a faint horizontal cinder, drifting into the blackness. The pink in the air was once more faint, and apparently turning to silver.

'The moon,' said Vin. 'The moon is drawing near and shining through the water.'

'The flowers go to meet the moon even more eagerly than the sun. You can hear them. Listen, Vin.'

They stood in silence.

'Sleep with me, Vin.'

'We sleep apart.'

It was as Tal had said 'We eat fruit'. And it proved to be equally true.

He stole through the empty rooms, seeing no one. Now very tired, he lowered himself on to a pile of cushions, but not the pile on which he had lain with Tal, and not in the same room.

None the less, he could not easily sleep. It came to him with a nervous shock, as happens after long absorption, to recall that, only that same morning, the island, the rock, as the women always named it, had been no more than an obsessive premonition, he no other than an ordinary mortal, eternally going through the motions. He felt now that in the very moment he had first sighted the rock, he had begun to change. And there was almost certainly no going back; not just in symbol or allegory, but in hard, practical terms, as the world deems them.

Grigg lay listening to the lapping, trickling waves; smelling the night flowers. Was it never cooler or colder than this? Never?

Grigg would not have believed it possible, as he reflected on his third morning, that he could live so happily without occupation. There were a few jobs to be done, but so far the women had done all of them, and Grigg had felt no real compunction, as the jobs had seemed to be as complete a part of their lives as breathing – and as automatic and secondary. There had been almost nothing else: no reading, no struggling with the environment, no planning. Grigg had always truly believed that he, like others, would be lost without tasks; that pleasures pall; and that ease exhausts. Now he was amazed not only by the change in his philosophy, but by the speed with which it had come about. Obviously, one had to say, it was far, far too soon to be sure; but Grigg felt that obviousness of that kind was, as far as he was concerned, already a thing of the past. Indeed, nothing, probably nothing at all, was obvious any more. Perhaps it was that Tal and Vin had purged him of the obvious within little more than his first twelve hours on the island.

Not that anything of that kind had so far happened again. Vin had withdrawn into an attitude of loving casualness, as Tal had done: the attitude which characterised all three of the women, and which Grigg found especially charming, so that he had not even made any serious attempt to intensify things with either of them.

Later that day, the three women had been singing. Now there was a pause, while they all lay listening to the waves and flowers singing for them.

'I am content,' said Grigg. 'But what do I do all day?'

Vin replied. 'The Greek Church says that work was the fruit of sin. Here the fruit is more wholesome.'

And, indeed, for a moment Grigg almost felt that he knew what the Garden of Eden had really been like: not the boring, moral attenuation of it; but the physical splendour, with flowers perfumed like these, with tiny, aquamarine birds, singing like honey, with indifference as to whether one was clothed or naked, with beauty to make it indifferent.

'The Greek Church,' said Lek, 'had once a prophet. "Take no thought for the morrow," he said; and spoke of lilies.'

'But not of lilies only,' said Grigg. 'Far from it, alas.'

'You must not expect a Greek prophet to be always wise. The Greeks used to decorate their houses with flowers, and sing songs. Now they buy tinsel from shops and listen to radios. The Greek radios are the noisiest in the world. It is not surprising that Greek prophets often

40

make mistakes.'

'You can't prophesy,' said Tal, 'when there's such a noise that no one can hear you.'

'But the radio is new,' objected Grigg.

Lek would have none of it. 'The radio has been with us since the dawn of time,' she said.

'I believe that men thought of it when they took over the world,' said Tal.

'I prefer listening to you,' said Grigg. 'Sing me the song the sirens sang.'

So they did.

On one occasion, two rather unpleasant things happened on the same day.

The first was that Grigg, roaming about the citadel, as he was so often told he was perfectly free to do, came upon a shut door. It was in the basement, or cellar, where he had previously hesitated to go: a sequence of low rooms, as it proved, sunk into the rock, which, quite unmodified, formed the irregular floor. The rooms were ill-lighted by small windows high in the walls. Grigg had tried the door, which was deep in the furthest rocky wall, and opened it, before he realised that it was the first door he had had to open at all; the others, as far as he could remember, having stood wide before him, at least when originally met with. He thought of Alfred de Musset's proverb: A door is either open or shut.

Inside, it was totally black; as thick, Grigg found himself thinking, as that wine. He hesitated to take even one step inside, but craned in, listening, and drawing the door close behind him. A long way below, as it seemed, was a noise: Grigg wondered if it could come from the bottom of a deep pit. At first he thought it sounded like the ebb and flow of the waves, and supposed there might be a rift in the rock; but then, in a curious way, it sounded more like a gigantic process of ingestion, as if, perhaps, a press were reducing a miscellany of organic matter to, as people say, pulp. The sound rose and fell, though something less than rhythmically, but never quite ceased; and every now and then a smell rose from the pit, if pit there was, a smell akin to the noise, in that it might have been of long-rotted tideless seaweed or, alternatively, of vaguer and terrestrial decomposition. The smell, though unpleasant, came only in strong whiffs, and Grigg wondered why it was apparently uncontinuous. Could something below be opening and shutting, appearing and withdrawing? Noise, smell, and darkness were plainly related to the formations of the rock, but Grigg found the place disturbing, as a child often finds a room he has entered without clear authority.

None the less, it was fascinating, and Grigg could not quite go, either: still like the transfixed child. He felt less than ever inclined to proceed further, but remained half-in, half-out, trying to peer through the blackness, but dreading at the same time. And, in the end, something terrible happened, or something which Grigg found terrible: it was as if the pit spoke. There was a sudden growling roar; a noise entirely different from what had gone before; and Grigg was sure that there were clear words. He could not understand them, and they did not sound like Greek, but words he knew they were, and addressed to him. The personal note was unmistakable, it was as if the pit and the darkness, the noise and the smell, had been watching him, and were now warning him off, and leaving no possibility of mistake.

Grigg reeled back and slammed the door. Stumbling over the rocky floor, he hastened into the sunlight. Even before he had reached the courtyard, he had begun to realise that he had merely been the victim of an aural hallucination – an hallucination of a quite common type, indeed; almost the sort of thing staged for tourists visiting Mediterranean grottoes. When he found himself alone in the courtyard, he realised that he had nearly made a serious fool of himself. Even though the first terror had by then ebbed, there was no knowing what idiotic thing he might have said if there had been anyone to listen.

He climbed over the courtyard wall and stretched out on the rock finally to recover his wits.

That same evening, he heard the women shouting and laughing, out beyond the gateway to the harbour. He went to look. The sky was almost emerald green and they moved in magnificent silhouette against it. The three of them stood above the water's edge and below the harbour causeway, on the side of the island away from the basin. Grigg found the beauty of their movement incomparable. He stood watching them for some time, as if they presented a merely formal spectacle, of maenads on a vase, or ballet dancers, before he clearly realised that they were not merely throwing stones, but very much aiming at a target. He walked down the causeway, and stood behind them, looking over their heads.

Floating in the emerald sea beneath the emerald sky was a body; though it was unlikely to be afloat much longer, as the women knew how to throw, and every stone hit true and hard. Grigg could see the body quite well: it had belonged to a fat, elderly, clean-shaven man with a big, bald head, and was dressed in a dark, conventional suit, of which the open jacket spread out in the water, like a pair of fins. All round the body the sea was red, like the death of a whale. Grigg shuddered as he thought of the whale.

The skilled throwing went on for another minute or two, a marvel of ancient beauty, and then, suddenly, the body collapsed and sank. Grigg could hear the water pouring in, as into a pierced gourd. The women, apparently still unaware of him, stood in lovely silent attitudes and watched it go. When they saw nothing left but the fading patch of carmine, they turned, saw Grigg, and advanced laughing and gesticulating, their hair dishevelled and their faces flushed with excitement.

'Who was he?' asked Grigg.

'A tourist. They fall out of boats.'

'They fall off pier-heads.'

'They fall from Heaven.'

Grigg felt as once he had done when he found himself encompassed by English and American enthusiasts for the bull-fight. But now, at least, the central object had been dead to start with. Or so he could but suppose.

*

But this was not the only time when Grigg saw blood in the sea.

After he had been, as he thought, about three weeks on the island, or perhaps as much as a month, there was a great storm. There had been little forewarning, or little that Grigg had been able to sense; and the women had said nothing. The first lightning leapt at him in his room, taking him completely by surprise as he lay there musing in the warm darkness, some time after midnight. It was curious pink lightning, condensing, as it seemed, the entire firmament into a single second; and the thunder which followed might well have torn apart the total citadel ... except that, to Grigg's astonishment, there was no thunder, nothing of the kind beyond a faint rumble, more as if the Olympians had been overheard conversing than as if there had been an electrical discharge. On the instant, there followed another flash and brief rumble of distant talk; and then another. Grigg now listened for rain, of which there had been none that he was aware of since his arrival; but though, according to the laws of nature, it must have been raining somewhere, all there seemed to be here was a rising wind. Lightning was flickering from cherry-blossom almost to scarlet; but Grigg hardly noticed it as the wind rose and rose, like a cataract of water charging through the widening burst in a dam and sweeping down a valley, presenting to Grigg a similar picture of instant danger and catastrophe. He caught up the garment the women had

45

woven for him and hastened round the big dark room shutting windows, like a suburban housewife. Those in one of the walls were too high for him to reach, but at least there was as yet no question of water pouring in.

'There have always been storms like this.'

It was Lek's voice. Grigg could just perceive her shape standing by the door. 'There is nothing to be afraid of. The citadel is built to remain standing.' A flash of rosy lightning filled the room, so that, for a second, Grigg saw her with unnatural clarity, as if she had been an angel. 'Come and look.'

Lek clasped his hand and led him out. They ascended the pitch-black, stone stair. 'Do not falter,' said Lek. 'Trust me.' Grigg, feeling no doubt at all, went up the hard, dark steps without even stubbing a toe. They came out on the roof.

The sky was washed all over with the curious pink of the lightning. Grigg had never seen anything like it before, and had never known so strange a wind, roaring, but warm, and even scented. Faintly massed against the rosy dimness at the other end of the flat roof was the recumbent shape of the male god. Lek stood looking at the god, herself a lovely, living statue. Grigg was filled with awe and revelation.

'Tal is earth,' he said, somehow speaking above the roar of the wind.

As far as he could see, Lek moved not an eyelid.

'Vin is fire.'

He thought she faintly smiled.

'And you are air.'

A smile it was. There could be no doubt about it. And her eyes were far-distant vastnesses. The wind hummed and sang. Grigg kissed Lek, lightly as a leaf.

'Come nearer to the god,' said Lek, drawing him onward through the hurricane. 'It is for him. Everything is for him.'

And for the prostrate Grigg, as the warm wind blew and blew, the heavens opened.

This time, just as much as he had finally forgotten to ask questions, so, at the end, he made no foolish demands.

On another night, conceivably a week later, Grigg was awakened by what must have been an unusual sound. He sat up and listened. There was nothing at all loud to be heard, but there was an unmistakable clinking and clanking in the island night, systematic, purposive, human. It occurred to Grigg immediately that there was an intruder – one intruder at least.

He put on his garment and descended, without disturbing the women, presumably on the floor below.

He stood in the courtyard avoiding the gaze of the stars in order the better to judge where the noise was coming from.

He padded across the courtyard stones to the gateway leading to the tower he had climbed when first he came.

On the top of the tower, visible above the roofs of the intervening ruins, he could just make out a figure; blacker than the night, and palpably at some manner of work.

Grigg hesitated for a considerable number of moments. Should he try to investigate on his own, or should he first rouse the women? He probably decided on the former because he still felt short of experience and knowledge that were not mediated by what the women themselves called sorcery. He half-welcomed a moment to investigate on his own.

He started to scramble, as quietly as was possible, through the rough foundations and tough thickets. Possibly he could not be quiet *enough* under such adverse conditions, because when at length he reached the tower, the black figure was gone, and a small black motor-boat was chugging across the black sea. The top of the tower had been screened from his view by the old fortress walls for much of the time he had been scrambling through the miniature Turkish jungle. The boat was the first he had seen so near the island. He watched it until, lightless, void of all detail, it merged into the black night.

He had little doubt that it meant trouble, and he made a considerable search, even climbing the spidery tower, only when halfway up reflecting that someone might still be there, someone who had remained when the boat had left. His heart missed a beat, compelling him to pause in the tight, dusty darkness, but he continued upwards. There was no one, nothing but the stars drawn nearer, and there was no sign of intrusion, change, or recent damage; either about the tower or about the entire extremity of the island: nothing, at least, that Grigg could find or see as he plunged about, slashing and abrading himself, in the darkness beneath the uninvolved stars. He could not even make out how the interloper could possibly have managed to moor a boat and mount the sharp rock.

Grigg sought and thought so conscientiously that the first light of dawn was upon him as he clambered back to the citadel. Ineffable, he thought, was the only word for such beauty: faint grey, faint blue, faint pink, faint green; and the entire atmosphere translucent right through to the centre of the empyrean, and on to the next centre, as if, while it lasted, distance was abrogated, and the solitary individual could casually touch the impersonal core of the universe.

Back in the courtyard, he stood with his hands on the familiar wall, gazing across the tranquilly colourless, early-morning sea.

Re-ascending the citadel staircase, he tiptoed into the big hall where the women slept. The three of them lay there, touching; in dark red robes (Grigg could think of no other noun); their faces pale and their lips full, with sleep; their relaxed bodies as undefined as the good, the true, and the beautiful. Grigg stood away from the wall, motionlessly gazing, filled with the apprehension of tragedy. He stood for a long time, then dragged at his numb limbs, and went on up. There was a scorpion-like creature on his coloured cushions, which, as it refused to be driven out, he had to kill before settling down to his resumed slumbers.

And the next morning, there, once more, was the redness in the sea; and this time, the sea was blood-red, not in a large, repulsive, but all too explicable patch, but red as far as Grigg, gazing appalled from his high window, could see; as if all the way across to the larger, mainland island. It was fearful, nightmarish, infernal. Macbeth's dream had materialised: the green *was* one red.

Moreover, there was a second sound that was new to the island.

Grigg went down, his feet heavy.

On the floor below, the women were lamenting. In their greeny-brown dresses, they clung together, shadowy and large-eyed, wailing and babbling in some tongue of which Grigg knew nothing, doubtless their own. Even in their mortification and misery, they were as beautiful as in their previous joy.

'What has happened?'

The women stopped wailing when they saw him, and Lek spoke.

'The rock is dead.'

Not at all understanding, Grigg could not but blurt out, 'There was a man here last night. One man at least. I saw him.'

'You *saw* him,' said Vin. 'And you did not kill him?'

'Or let *us* kill him,' said Tal.

There was a difficult pause. Grigg gazed into their tear-stained faces.

'I saw him on top of the tower. I could not get to him in time across the ruins in the darkness. When I reached the tower, he was gone. I saw and heard his boat quite a long way off.'

'Why did you not tell us?' asked Lek. 'Why did you

not trust us?'

To such a question conventional answers abound, but Grigg could not bring one of them to his lips. Guilt in him was reinforced by fear. He felt that he might be made to suffer, and he felt that he deserved the suffering.

'What does it mean,' he asked, 'when you say the rock is dead?'

A tremor passed through them and Vin began once more to weep.

'The rock was a living rock,' said Lek softly. 'The rock gave us wine and water. The rock was the other god, the female god, so, while the rock was alive, you could not be told. Now they have killed the rock with a machine, so that it does not matter what is said.' As Lek spoke, Tal burst into tears and moans.

'Is there nothing I can do?'

'There is nothing that anyone in the world can do.

'This was the last living rock, and now the last living rock is dead. There is nothing but to mourn, to forgive, and to go.'

'I do not expect to be forgiven,' said Grigg. 'I deserve to die.' The words came out quite naturally; which was something he would never before have thought possible.

Lek stepped forward, took his hands, and kissed them. Then Vin and Tal did the same, leaving their tears on his mouth.

'Let me at least mourn with you.'

Lek smiled sadly, and indeed he found that the power

to mourn, the power to mourn anything, was not in him.

They walked in line down the causeway, among the flowers, the birds, and the lizards; with Grigg bringing up the rear. The green and grey of the sea had absorbed nearly all the red, though there was still a faint, shimmering glow beneath the surface, melting away as Grigg watched. They took nothing.

The women spread the big, blue sail, and expertly steered the ship out of the basin into the hot morning. Grigg stood at the stern, looking back along the spreading plume of her wake.

Then Lek was standing beside him.

'How long can you swim?'

Grigg looked into her eyes.

'Possibly for half an hour,' he said. 'At least, in smooth, warm water.'

So when they neared a spit of land, he went overside in the summer clothes he had worn when he had originally cast off in his borrowed motor-boat. It was his initiation into the last of the four elements. He went without touching any of the women, and in the event, he was immersed for not much more than ten minutes before fetching up, dripping and bearded, on a pebbly strand. Even so, it was enough for the ship to have sailed almost to the horizon, so skilfully was she navigated.

The Trains

On the moors, as early as this, the air no longer clung about her, impeding her movements, absorbing her energies. Now a warm breeze seemed to lift her up and bear her on: the absorption process was reversed; her bloodstream drew impulsion from the zephyrs. Her thoughts raced from her in all directions, unproductive but joyful. She remembered the railway posters. Was this ozone?

Not that she had at all disliked the big industrial city they had just left; unlike Mimi, who had loathed it. Mimi had wanted their walking tour to be each day from one Youth Hostel to another; but that was the one proposal Margaret had successfully resisted. Their itinerary lay in the Pennines, and Margaret had urged the case for sleeping in farmhouses and, on occasion, in conventional hotels. Mimi had suggested that the former were undependable and the latter both dreary and expensive; but suddenly her advocacy of Youth Hostels had filled her with shame, and she had capitulated. 'But hotels look down on hikers,' she had added. Margaret had not until then regarded them as hikers.

Apart from the controversy about the city, all had so far gone fairly well, particularly with the weather, as their progress entered its second week. The city Margaret had found new, interesting, unexpectedly beautiful and romantic: its well-proportioned stone mills and uncountable volcanic chimneys appeared perfectly to consort with the high free mountains always in the background. To Mimi the place was all that she went on holiday to avoid. If you had to have towns, she would choose the blurred amalgam of the Midlands and South, where town does not contrast with country but merges into it, neither town nor country being at any time so distinct as in the North. To Margaret this, to her, new way of life (of which she saw only the very topmost surface), seemed considerably less dreadful than she had expected. Mimi, to whom also it was new, saw it as the existence from which very probably her great-grandfather had fought and climbed, a degradation she was appalled to find still in existence and able to devour her. If there had to be industry, let the facts be swaddled in suburbs. The Free Trade Hotel (RAC and AA) had found single rooms for them; and Mimi had missed someone to talk to in bed.

They had descended to the town quite suddenly from the wildest moors, as one does in the North. Now equally suddenly it was as if there were no towns, but only small, long-toothed Neanderthals crouched behind rocks waiting to tear the two of them to pieces. Air roared past in incalculable bulk under the lucent sky, deeply blue but traversed by well-spaced masses of sharply edged white cloud, like the floats in a Mediterranean pageant. The misty, smoky, reeking air of the city had enchanted Margaret with its perpetually changing atmospheric effects, a meteorological drama unavailable in any other environment; but up here the air was certainly like itself. The path was hard to find across the heather, the only landmarks being contours and neither of them expert with a map; but they advanced in happy silence, all barriers between them blown down, even Margaret's heavy rucksack far from her mind. (Mimi took her own even heavier rucksack for granted at all times.)

'Surely that's a train?' said Margaret, when they had walked for two or three hours.

'Oh God,' said Mimi, the escapist.

'The point is it'll give us our bearing.' The vague rumbling was now lost in the noisy wind. 'Let's look.'

Mimi unstrapped the back pocket on Margaret's rucksack and took out the map. They stood holding it between them. Their orientation being governed by the wind, and beyond their power to correct mentally, they then laid the map on the ground, the top more or less to the north, and a grey stone on each corner.

'There's the line,' said Margaret, following it across the map with her finger. 'We must be somewhere about here.'

'How do you know we're not above the tunnel?' enquired Mimi. 'It's about four miles long.'

'I don't think we're high enough. 'The tunnel's further on.'

'Couldn't we strike this road?'

'Which way do you suggest?'

'Over the brow of the next hill, if you were right about that being a train. The road goes quite near the railway and the sound came from over there.' Mimi pointed, the web of her rucksack, as she lay twisted on the ground, dragging uncomfortably in the shoulder strap of her shirt.

'I wish we had a canvas map. The wind's tearing this one to pieces.'

Mimi replied amiably. 'It's a bore, isn't it?' It was she who had been responsible for the map.

'I'm almost sure you're right,' said Margaret, with all the confidence of the lost.

'Let's go,' said Mimi. With difficulty they folded up the map, and Mimi returned it to Margaret's rucksack. The four grey stones continued to mark the corners of a now mysterious rectangle.

As it chanced, Mimi was right. When they had descended to the valley before them, and toiled to the next ridge, a double line of railway and a stone-walled road climbed the valley beyond. While they watched, a train began slowly to chug upwards from far to the left.

'The other one must have been going downhill,' said Mimi.

They began the descent to the road. It was some time since there had been even a sheep path. The distance to the road was negligible as the crow flies, but it took them thirty-five minutes by Mimi's wrist-watch, and the crawling train passed before them almost as soon as they started.

'I wish we were crows,' Mimi exclaimed.

Margaret said, 'Yes,' and smiled.

They noticed no traffic on the road, which, when

reached, proved to be surfaced with hard, irregular granite chips, somewhat in need of re-laying and the attentions of a steamroller.

'Pretty grim,' said Mimi after a quarter of an hour. 'But I'm through with that heather.' Both sides of the valley were packed with it.

'Hadn't we better try to find out exactly where we are?' suggested Margaret.

'Does it really matter?'

'There's lunch.'

'That doesn't depend on where we are. So long as we're in the country it's all one, don't you think?'

'I think we'd better make sure.'

'OK.'

Mimi again got out the map. As they were anchoring it by the roadside, a train roared into being and swept down the gradient.

'What are you doing?' asked Margaret, struggling with a rather unsuitable stone.

'Waving, of course.'

'Did anyone wave back?'

'Haven't you ever waved to the driver?'

'No. I don't think I have. I didn't know it was the driver you waved to. I thought it was the passengers.' The map now seemed secure.

'Them too sometimes. But drivers always wave to girls.'

'Only to girls?'

'Only to girls.' Mimi couldn't remember when she hadn't known that. 'Where are we?' They stared at the

57

map, trying to drag out its mystery. Even now that they were on the road, with the railway plain before them crossing contour after contour, the problem seemed little simpler.

'I wish there was an instrument which said how high we were,' remarked Mimi.

'Something else to carry.'

Soon they were reduced to staring about them.

'Isn't that a house?' Mimi was again pointing the initiative.

'If it is, I think it must be "Inn".' Margaret indicated it. 'There's no other building on the map this side of the railway tunnel, unless we're much lower down the valley than we think.'

'Maps don't show every small building.'

'They seem to in country districts. I've been noticing. Each farm has a little dot. Even the cottage by the reservoir yesterday had its dot.'

'Oh well, if it's a pub, we can eat in the bar. OK by me.'

Again they left behind them four grey stones at the corners of nothing.

'Incidentally, the map only shows one house between the other end of the tunnel and Pudsley. A good eight miles, I should say.'

'Let's hope it's one of your farms. I won't face a night in Pudsley. We're supposed to be on holiday. Remember?'

'I expect they'll put us up.'

The building ahead of them proved long deserted. Or

possibly not so long; it is difficult to tell with simple stone buildings in a wet climate. The windows were planked up; slates from the roof littered the weedy garden; the front door had been stove in.

'Trust the Army,' said Mimi. 'Hope tonight's quarters are more weatherproof. We'd better eat. It's a quarter past two.'

'I don't think it's the Army. More like the agricultural depression.' Margaret had learnt on her father's estate the significance of deserted farmhouses and neglected holdings.

'Look! There's the tunnel.'

Margaret advanced a few steps up the road to join her. From the black portal the tunnel bored straight into the rock, with the road winding steeply above it.

'There's another building,' said Margaret, following the discouraging ascent with her eyes. 'What's more, I can see a sign outside it. I believe the map's wrong. Come on.'

'Oh well,' said Mimi.

Just as they were over the tunnel entrance another train sped downwards. They looked from above at the blind black roofs of the coaches, like the caterpillar at the fair with the cover down.

It was hard to say whether the map was wrong or not. The house above the tunnel, though apparently not shown, was certainly not an inn. It was almost the exact opposite: an unlicensed Guest House.

'Good for a cup of tea,' said Mimi. 'But we'd better eat outside.'

A little further up the road was a small hillock. They ascended it, cast off their heavy rucksacks, loosened their belts a hole or two, and began to eat corned beef sandwiches. The Guest House lay below them, occupied to all appearances, but with no one visible.

'Not much traffic,' said Margaret, dangling a squashed tomato.

'They all go by train.'

The distant crowing of an engine whistle seemed to confirm her words.

The sharp-edged clouds, now slightly larger, were still being pushed across the sky; but by now the breeze seemed to have dropped and it was exceedingly hot. The two women were covered with sweat, and Mimi undid another button of her shirt.

'Aren't you glad I made you wear shorts?'

Margaret had to admit to herself she was glad. There had been some dissension between the two of them upon this point; Margaret, who had never worn shorts in her life before, feeling intensely embarrassed by Mimi's proposal, and Mimi unexpectedly announcing that she wouldn't come at all unless Margaret 'dressed like everybody else'. Margaret now realised that for once 'everybody' was right. The freedom was delightful; and without it the weight of the rucksack would have been unendurable. Moreover, her entire present outfit had cost less than a guinea; and it mattered little what happened to it. That, she perceived, was the real freedom. Still, she was pleased that none of her family could see her.

'Very glad indeed,' she replied. 'I really am.'

Mimi smiled warmly, too nice to triumph, although the matter was one about which Margaret's original attitude had roused strong feelings in her.

'Not the ideal food for this heat,' said Margaret. 'We'll come out in spots.'

'Lucky to get corned beef. Another girl and I hiked from end to end of the Pilgrim's Way on plain bread and marge. It was Bank Holiday and we'd forgotten to lay anything in.' Then, springing to her feet with her mouth full, she picked up her rucksack. 'Let's try for a drink.' She was off down the road before Margaret could rise or even speak. She was given to acting on such sudden small impulses, Margaret had noticed.

By the time Margaret had finished her final sandwich, Mimi had rung the Guest House bell and had been inside for some time. Before following, Margaret wiped the sweat from her face on to one of the large handkerchiefs Mimi had prudently enjoined; then from one of the breast pockets of her shirt produced a comb and mirror, rearranged her hair so far as was allowed by sweat and the small tight bun into which, with a view to efficiency on this holiday, she had woven it, and returned the articles to her shirt pocket, buttoning down the flap, but avoiding contact as far as possible with her sticky body. She approached the front door slowly, endeavouring to beget no further heat.

The bell, though provided with a modern pseudo-Italian pull, was of the authentic country-house pattern, operated by a wire. The door was almost immediately opened by a plain woman in a Marks and Spencer overall.

'Yes?'

'Could I possibly have something to drink? My friend's inside already.'

'Come in. Tea or coffee? We're out of minerals.'

'Could I have some coffee?'

'Coffee.' The word was repeated in a short blank tone. One would have supposed she had to deal with sixty orders an hour. She disappeared.

'Well, shut the door and keep the heat out.'

The speaker, a middle-aged man wearing dirty tennis shoes, was seated the other side of a round wooden table from Mimi, who was stirring a cup of tea. There was no one else in the room, which was congested with depressing café furniture, and decorated with cigarette advertisements hanging askew on the walls.

'You know what they say in New York?' He had the accent of a north-country businessman. His eyes never left Mimi's large breasts distending her damp khaki shirt. 'I used to live in New York. Ten years altogether.'

Mimi said nothing. It was her habit to let the men do the talking. Margaret sat down beside her, laying her rucksack on the floor.

'Hullo.' His tone was cheekier than his intention.

'Hullo,' said Margaret neutrally.

'Are you two friends?'

'Yes.'

His gaze returned to the buxomer, nakeder Mimi.

'I was just telling your friend. You know what they say in New York?'

'No,' said Margaret. 'I don't think so. What do they say?'

'It isn't the heat. It's the humidity.'

He seemed still to be addressing Margaret, while staring at Mimi. Giving them a moment to follow what he evidently regarded as a difficult and penetrating observation, he continued, 'The damp, you know. The moisture in the atmosphere. The atmosphere's picking up moisture all the time. Sucking it out of the earth.' He licked his lower lip. 'This is nothing. Nothing to New York. I lived there for ten years. Beggars can't be choosers, you know.'

A door opened from behind and the taciturn woman brought Margaret's coffee. The cup was discoloured round the edge, and the saucer, for some reason, bore a crimson smear.

'One shilling.'

Startled, Margaret produced a half-crown from a pocket of her shorts. The woman went away.

'Nice place this,' said the man. 'You've got to pay for that these times.'

Margaret lifted up her cup. The coffee was made from essence and stank.

'What did I say? How's that for a cup of coffee? I'd have one myself, if I hadn't had three already.'

'Are you staying here?'

'I live here.'

The woman returned with one and sixpence, then

departed once more.

'There's no need for a gratuity.'

'I see,' said Margaret. 'Is she the proprietress?'

'It's her own place.'

'She seems silent.' Immediately Margaret rather regretted this general conversational initiative.

'She's reason to be. It's no gold mine, you know. I'm the only regular. Pretty well the only customer by and large.'

'Why's that? It's a lovely country, and there's not much competition from what we've seen.'

'There's none. Believe me. And it's not a nice country. Believe me again.'

'What's wrong with it?' This was Mimi, who had not spoken since Margaret had entered.

'Why nothing really, sister, nothing really. Not for a little girl like you.' Margaret noticed that he was one of the many men who classify women into those you talk to and those with whom words merely impede the way. 'I was just kidding. I wouldn't be here else. Now would I? Not living here.'

'What's wrong with the place?'

Margaret was surprised by Mimi's tone. She recollected that she had no knowledge of what had passed between the two of them while she had been combing her hair on the little hill.

'You know what the locals say?'

'We haven't seen any locals,' said Margaret.

'Just so. That's what I say. They don't come up here. This is the Quiet Valley.'

'Oh really,' cried Margaret, not fully mistress of her motives all the same. 'You got that name out of some Western.'

But he only replied with unusual brevity, 'They call it the Quiet Valley.'

'Not a good place to start in business!' said Margaret.

'Couldn't be worse. But she just didn't know. She sank all she had in this place. She was a stranger here, like you.'

'What's wrong with the valley?' persisted Mimi, her manner, to Margaret's mind, a little too tense.

'Nothing so long as you stay, sister. Just nothing at all.'

'Is there really a story?' asked Margaret. Almost convinced that the whole thing was a rather dull joke, she was illogically driven to enquire by Mimi's odd demeanour.

'No *story* that I've heard of. It's just the Quiet Valley and the locals don't come here.'

'What about you? If it's so quiet why don't you move?'

'I like quiet. I'm not one to pick and choose. I was just telling you why there's a trade recession.'

'It's perfectly true,' said Margaret, 'that there seems very little traffic.' She noticed Mimi refasten the shirt button she had undone to cool herself. The man averted his eyes.

'They all take the railroad. They scuttle through shut up like steers in a wagon.'

Mimi said nothing, but her expression had changed.

'There seem to be plenty of trains for them,' said Margaret, smiling.

'It's the main line.'

'One of the drivers waved to us. If what you say is true, I suppose he was glad to see us.'

For the first time the man concentrated his unpleasing stare on Margaret.

'Now as to that—' His glance fell to the table and remained there a moment. 'I was just wondering where you two reckon on spending the night.'

'We usually find a farmhouse,' said Margaret shortly.

'It's wild on the other side, you know. Wilder than here. There's only one house between the tunnel and near Pudsley.'

'So we noticed on the map. Would they give us a bed? I suppose it's a farm?'

'It's Miss Roper's place. I've never met her myself. I don't go down the other side. But I dare say she'd help you. What you said just now—' Suddenly he laughed. 'You know how engine drivers wave at girls, like you said?'

'Yes,' said Margaret. To her apprehension it seemed that an obscene joke was coming.

'Well, every time a train passes Miss Roper's house, someone leans out of the bedroom window and waves to it. It's gone on for years. Every train, mark you. The house stands back from the line and the drivers couldn't see exactly who it was, but it was someone in white and they all thought it was a girl. So they waved back. Every train. But the joke is it's not a girl at all. It can't be. It's gone on too long. She can't have been a girl for the last twenty years or so. It's probably old Miss Roper herself. The drivers keep changing round so they don't catch on. They all think it's some girl, you see. So they all wave back. Every train.' He was laughing as if it were the funniest of improprieties.

'If the drivers don't know, how do you?' asked Mimi.

'It's what the locals say. Never set eyes on Miss Roper myself. Probably a bit of line-shooting.' He became suddenly very serious and redolent of quiet helpfulness. 'There's a Ladies' Room upstairs if either of you would like it.'

'Thank you,' said Margaret. 'I think we must be getting on.' The back of her rucksack was soaked and clammy.

'Have a cigarette before you go?' He was extending a packet of some unknown brand. His hand shook like the hand of a drug addict.

'Thanks,' said Mimi, very offhand. 'Got a match?' He could hardly strike it, let alone light the cigarette. Looking at him Margaret was glad she did not smoke.

'I smoke like a camp fire,' he said unnecessarily. 'You have to in my life.' Then, when they had opened the door, he added, 'Watch the weather.'

'We will,' said Margaret conventionally, though the heat had again smothered them. And once more they were toiling upwards beneath their heavy packs.

They said nothing at all for several minutes. Then Mimi said, 'Blasted fool.'

'Men are usually rather horrible,' replied Margaret.

'You get used to *that*,' said Mimi.

'I wonder if this really is called the Quiet Valley?'

'I don't care what it's called. It's a bad valley all right.'

Margaret looked at her. Mimi was staring defiantly ahead as she strode forward. 'You mean because there are no people?'

'I mean because I know it's bad. You can't explain it.'

Margaret was inexpert with intuitions, bred out of them perhaps. The baking, endless road was certainly becoming to her unpleasant in the extreme. Moreover, the foul coffee had given her indigestion, and the looseness of her belt made it impossible to loosen it further.

'If you hadn't heard that train, we'd never have been here.'

'If I hadn't heard it, we'd quite simply have been lost. The path on the map just gave out. That's apt to happen when you merely choose paths instead of making for definite places.'

In her vexation Margaret raked over another underlying dissimilarity in their approaches to life, one already several times exposed. Then reflecting that Mimi had been perfectly willing to wend from point to point provided that the points were Youth Hostels, Margaret added, 'Sorry Mimi. It's the heat.'

A certain persistent fundamental disharmony between them led Mimi to reply none too amicably, 'What exactly do you suggest we *are* going to do?'

Had Margaret been Mimi there would have been a row: but, being Margaret, she said, 'I think perhaps we'd better take another look at the map.'

This time she unslung her rucksack and got out the map herself. Mimi stood sulkily sweating and doing nothing either to help or to remove the sweat. Looking at her, Margaret suddenly said, 'I wonder what's become of the breeze we had this morning?' Then, Mimi still saying nothing, she sat down and looked at the map. 'We could go over into the next valley. There are several quite large villages.'

'Up there?' Mimi indicated the rocky slope rising steeply above them.

'The tunnel runs through where the mountains are highest. If we go on a bit, we'll reach the other end and it may be less of a climb. What do you say?'

Mimi took a loose cigarette from a pocket of her shirt. 'Not much else to do, is there?' Her attitude was exceedingly irritating. Margaret perceived the unwisdom of strong Indian tea in the middle of the day. 'I hope we make it,' added Mimi with empty cynicism. As she struck a match, in the very instant a gust of wind not only blew it out but wrenched the map from Margaret's hands. It was as if the striking of the match had conjured up the means to its immediate extinction.

Margaret, recovering, closed the map; and they looked behind them. 'Oh hell,' said Margaret. 'I dislike the weather in the Quiet Valley.' A solid bank of the dark grey cloud had formed in their rear and was perceptibly closing down upon them like a huge hood.

'I hope we make it,' repeated Mimi, her cynicism now less empty. They left their third set of grey stones demarcating emptiness.

Before long they were over the ridge at the top of the valley. The prospect ahead entirely confirmed the sentiments of the man at the Guest House. The scene could hardly have been bleaker or less inviting. But as it was much cooler, and the way for the first time in several hours comfortably downhill, they marched forward with once-more tightened belts, keeping strictly in step, blown forward by a rising wind. The recurring tension between them was now dissipated by efficient exertion under physically pleasant conditions; by the renewed sense of objective. They conversed steadily and amiably, the distraction winging their feet. Margaret felt the contrast between the optimism apparently implicit in the weather when they had set out, and the doom implicit in it now; but she felt it not unagreeably, drew from it a pleasing sense of tragedy and fitness. That was how she felt until well after it had actually begun to rain.

The first slow drops flung on the back of her knees and neck by the following wind were sweetly sensuous. She could have thrown herself upon the grass and let the rain slowly engulf her entire skin until there was no dry inch. Then she said, 'We mustn't get rheumatic fever in these sweaty clothes.'

Mimi had stopped and unslung her rucksack. Mimi's rucksack was the heavier because its contents included a robust stormproof raincoat; Margaret's the less heavy because she possessed only a light town mackintosh. Mimi encased herself, adjusted her rucksack beneath the shoulder straps of the raincoat, tied a sou'wester tightly beneath her chin, and strode forward, strapped and buttoned up to the ears, as if cyclones were all in a day's work. After a quarter of an hour, Margaret felt rain beginning to trickle down her body from the loose neck of her mackintosh, to infiltrate through the fabric in expanding blots, and to be finding its way most disagreeably into the interior of the attached hood. After half an hour she was saturated.

By that time they had reached the far end of the tunnel and stood looking down into a deep, narrow cutting which descended the valley as far as the gusts of rain permitted them to see. Being blasted through rock, the cutting had unscalably steep sides.

'That's that,' said Margaret a little shakily. 'We'll have to stick to the Quiet Valley.'

'It looks all right the other side,' said Mimi, 'if only we could get over.' Despite her warm garb, she too seemed wan and shivery. On their side of the railway, and beyond the road that had brought them, was a sea of soaking knee-high heather; but across the cutting the ground rose in a fairly gentle slope, merely tufted with vegetation.

'There's no sign of a bridge.'

'I could use a cup of tea. Do you know it's twenty-five past six?'

As they stood uncertain, the sound of an ascending train reached them against the wind, which, blowing strongly from the opposite direction, kept the smoke within the walls of the cutting. So high was the adverse gale that it was only a minute between their first hearing the slowly climbing train and its coming level with them. Steam roared from the exhaust. The fireman was stoking demoniacally. As the engine passed to windward of the two women far above, and the noise from the exhaust crashed upon their senses, the driver suddenly looked up and waved with an apparent gaiety inappropriate to the horrible weather. Then he reached for the whistle lever and, as the train entered the tunnel, for forty seconds doubled the already unbearable uproar. It was a long tunnel.

The train was not of a kind Margaret was used to (she knew little of railways); it was composed neither of passenger coaches nor of small clattering trucks, but of long windowless vans, giving no hint of their contents. A nimbus of warm oily air enveloped her, almost immediately to be blown away, leaving her again shivering.

Mimi had not waved back.

They resumed their way. Margaret's rucksack, though it weighed like the old man of the sea, kept a large stretch of her back almost dry.

'Do the drivers always wave first?' asked Margaret for something to say.

'Of course. If you were to wave first, they probably wouldn't notice you. There's something wrong with girls who wave first anyway.'

'I wonder what's wrong with Miss Roper?'

'We'll be seeing.'

'I suppose so. She doesn't sound much of a night's prospect.'

'How far's Pudsley?'

'Eight miles.'

'Very well then.'

Previously it had been Mimi who had seemed so strongly to dislike the valley. It was odd that, as it appeared, she should envisage so calmly the slightly sinister Miss Roper. Odd but practical. Margaret divined that her own consistency of thought and feeling might not tend the more to well-being than Mimi's weathercock moods.

'Where exactly does Miss Roper hang out, do you suppose?' enquired Mimi. 'That's the first point.'

The only visible work of man, other than the rough road, was the long gash that marked the railway cutting to their left.

'The map hasn't proved too accurate,' said Margaret.

'Hadn't we better look all the same? I'm really thinking of you, dear. You must be like a wet rag. Of you and a cup of tea.'

The wind was very much more than it had so far at any time been, but they could find no anchoring stones. Walls had long since ceased to line the road, and there appeared to be no stones larger than pebbles. While they were poking under clumps of heather, a train descended, whistling continuously.

In the end they had to give up. The paper map, on being partly opened, immediately rent across. The downpour would have converted it into discoloured pulp in a few moments. They were both so tired and hungry, and Margaret, by general temperament the more determined, so wet, that they had no heart in the struggle. Mimi stuffed the already sodden lump back into Margaret's rucksack.

'We'd better get on with it, even if we have to traipse all the way to Pudsley,' she said, re-tying a shoelace and then tightening her raincoat collar strap. 'Else we'll have you in hospital.' She marched forward intrepid.

But in the end, the road, which had long been deteriorating unnoticed, ended in a gate, beyond which was simply a rough field. They had reached a level low enough for primitive cultivation once to have been possible. Soaked and wretched though she was, Margaret looked back to the ridge, and saw that the distance to it was very much less than she had supposed. They leaned on the gate and stared ahead. Stone walls had reappeared, cutting up the land into monotonously similar untended plots. There were still no trees. The railway had now left the cutting and could presumably be crossed; but the women did not make the attempt, as visible before them through the flying deluge was a black house. It stood about six fields away: no joke to reach.

'Why's it so black?' asked Margaret.

'Pudsley. Those chimneys you're so fond of.'

'The prevailing wind's in the other direction. It's behind us.'

'Wish I had my climbing boots,' said Mimi, as they waded into the long grass. 'Or Wellingtons.' The grass soaked the double hem of Margaret's mackintosh, which she found a new torture. Two trains passed each other, grinding up and charging down. Both appeared to be normal passenger trains, long and packed. Every single window was closed. This produced an odd effect, as of objects in a bottle; until one realised that it was, of course, a consequence of the weather.

By the time they had stumbled across the soaking fields, and surmounted the high craggy walls between, it was almost completely dark. The house was a square, gaol-like stone box, three storeys high, built about 1860, and standing among large but unluxuriant cypresses, the first trees below the valley ridge. The blackness of the building was no effect of the light, but the consequence of inlaid soot.

'It's right on top of the railway,' cried Mimi. Struggling through the murk, they had not noticed that.

There was a huge front door, grim with grime.

'What a hope!' said Mimi, as she hauled on the bell handle.

'It's a curious bell,' said Margaret, examining the mechanism and valiant to the soaking, shivering end. 'It's like the handles you see in signal boxes.'

The door was opened by a figure illumined only by an oil lamp standing on a wall bracket behind.

'What is it?' The not uneducated voice had a curious throat undertone.

'My friend and I are on a walking tour,' said Margaret, who, as the initiator of the farmhouses project, always took charge on these occasions. 'We got badly lost on the moors. We hoped to reach Pudsley,' she continued, seeing that this was no farmhouse, open to a direct self-invitation. 'But what with getting lost and the rain, we're in rather a mess. Particularly me. I wonder if you could possibly help us? I know it's outrageous, but we *are* in distress.'

'Of course,' said another voice from the background. 'Come in and get warm. Come in quickly and Beech will shut the door.' This slight inverted echo of the words of the man at the Guest House stirred unpleasing associations in Margaret's brain.

The weak light disclosed Beech to be a tall muscular figure in a servant's black suit. The face, beneath a mass of black hair, cut like a musician's, seemed smooth and pale. The second speaker was a handsome well-built man, possibly in the late forties, and also wearing a black suit and tie, which suggested mourning. He regarded the odd figures of the two women without any suggestion of the unusual, as they lowered their dripping rucksacks to the tiled floor, unfastened their outer clothes running with water, and stood before him, two dim khaki figures, in shirts and shorts. Margaret felt not only ghastly wet but as if she were naked.

'Let me introduce myself,' said the master of the house. 'I am Wendley Roper. I shall expect you both to dine with me and stay the night. Tomorrow will put an entirely different face on things.' A slight lordliness of manner, by no means unattractive to Margaret, suggested that he mingled little with modern men.

Margaret introduced Mimi and herself; then said, 'We heard higher up the valley that a Miss Roper lived here.'

'My aunt. She died very recently. You see.' He indicated his clothes.

'I am so sorry,' said Margaret conventionally.

'It was deeply distressing. I refer to the manner of her death.' He offered the shivering women no details, but continued, 'Now Beech will take you to your room. The Rafters Room, Beech. I fear I have no other available, as the whole first floor and much else is taken up by my grandfather's collection. I trust you will have no objection to occupying the same room? It is a primitive one, I regret to say. There is only one bed at present, but I shall have another moved up.'

They assured him they had no objection.

'What about clothes? My aunt's would scarcely serve.' Then, unexpectedly, he added, 'And Beech is too big and tall for either of you.'

'It's quite all right,' said Margaret. 'Our rucksacks are watertight and we've both got a change.'

'Good,' said Wendley Roper seriously. 'Beech will conduct you, and dinner will be served when you've changed. There'll be some hot water sent up.'

'You are being most extraordinarily kind to us,' said Margaret.

'We should take the chances life brings us,' said Wendley Roper.

Beech lit a second oil lamp which had been standing on a large tallboy, and, with the women carrying their rucksacks, imperfectly illuminated the way upstairs. On the first-floor landing there were several large doors, such as admit to the bedrooms of a railway hotel, but no furniture was to be seen anywhere, nor were the staircase or either landing carpeted. At the top of the house

Beech admitted them to a room the door of which required unlocking. He did not stand aside to let them enter first, but went straight in and drew heavy curtains before the windows, having set down the light on the floor. The women joined him. This time there was a heavy brown carpet, but the primitiveness of the room was indisputable. Beyond the carpet and matching curtains, the furnishings consisted solely of a bedstead. It was a naked iron bedstead, crude and ugly.

'I'll bring you hot water, as Mr Roper said. Then a basin and towels and some chairs and so forth.'

'Thank you,' said Margaret. Beech retired, closing the door.

'Wonder if the door locks?' Mimi crossed the room. 'Not it. The key's on Beech's chain. I don't fancy Beech.'

'Can't be helped.' Margaret had already discarded her clothes, and was drying her body on a small towel removed from her rucksack.

'I'm not wet through, like you, but God it's cold for the time of year.' Mimi's alternative outfit consisted of a dark grey polo-necked sweater and a pair of lighter flannel trousers. Soon she had donned it, first putting on a brassière and knickers to mark renewed contact with society. 'Bit of a pigsty, isn't it?' she continued. 'But I suppose we must give thanks.'

'I rather liked our host. At least he didn't shilly-shally about taking us in.' Margaret was towelling systematically.

'Got a nice voice too.' Mimi decided that she would be warmer with her sweater inside her trousers, and made the alteration. 'Unlike Beech. Beech talks like plum jam. Where, by the way, are the rafters?'

The room, which was much longer than it was wide, and contained windows only in each end wall, a great distance apart, was ceiled with orthodox, though cracked and dirty, plaster.

'I expect they're just above us.'

'Up there?' Mimi indicated a trap-door in a corner of the ceiling.

Margaret had not previously noticed it. But before she could speak, the room was filled with a sudden rumbling crescendo, which made the massive floorboards vibrate and the light bed leap up and down upon them. Even the big black stones of the walls seemed slightly to jostle.

'The trains!'

Dashing to a window, Mimi dragged back the curtains, and lifting the sash, waved, her mood suddenly one of excitement, as the uproar swept down towards Pudsley.

Then she cried, 'Margaret! The window's barred.'

But Margaret's attention was elsewhere. During the din the door had opened, and Beech, a large old-fashioned can steaming in one hand, a large old-fashioned wash-basin dangling from the other, was in the room, and she absurdly naked.

'I beg your pardon,' he was saying. 'I don't think you heard me knock.'

'Get out,' said Mimi, flaming, her soul fired by an immemorial tabu.

'It's perfectly all right,' intervened Margaret, grasping the small wet towel.

'I'll fetch you some towels.'

He was gone again. He seemed totally undisturbed.

'He couldn't help it,' said Margaret. 'It was the train.'

Mimi lowered the window and re-drew the thick curtains. 'I've an idea,' she said.

'Oh! What? About Beech?'

'I'll tell you later. I'm going to wait at the door.'

Soon Beech returned with two large and welcome bath towels and a huge, improbable new cake of expensive scented soap. Margaret had filled the rose-encircled basin with glorious hot water; but before washing, Mimi stood by the door to receive two simple wooden bedroom chairs, a large wooden towel-horse and a capacious chamber-pot, before Beech descended to assist with dinner. 'I'll set you up another bed and bring along some bedding later,' he said, as his tall shape descended the tenebrous stair, now lit at intervals by oil lamps flickering on brackets.

Mimi rolled up the sleeves of her sweater and immersed her rather fat arms to the elbows. Margaret was drawing on a girdle. Her spare clothes consisted in another shirt, similar to the one the rain had soaked, but stiff and unworn, a cream-coloured linen skirt of fashionable length, and a tie which matched the skirt. She also had two pairs of expensive stockings, and a spare pair of shoes of lighter weight than Mimi's. Soon she was dressed, had knotted her tie, and was easing the stockings up what she felt must be starkly weather-roughed legs. She felt wonderfully dry, warm, and well. Her underclothes felt delightful. She felt that, after all, things might have turned out worse.

While Margaret was dressing, Mimi had been scrubbing her hands and forearms, then submitting her short hair to a vigorous, protracted grooming with a small bristly hairbrush. She was too busy to speak. She concentrated upon her simple toilet with an absorption Margaret would not have brought to dressing for her first dinner in evening clothes with a man.

With one stocking attached to its suspender, the other blurring her ankle, Margaret leaned back comfortably and asked, 'What was your idea?'

Mimi returned brush and comb to her rucksack. 'I think it's obvious. Old Ma Roper was mad.'

Margaret's warm world waned a little. 'You mean the window bars? This might have been a nursery.'

'Not only. You remember what he said? "The manner of her death was deeply distressing." And that's not all.'

'What else?'

'Don't you remember? Her waving to the trains?'

'I don't think that means she was mad. She might merely have been lonely.'

'Long time to be lonely. Let's go down if you're ready.'

Beech was waiting for them in the gloomy hall. 'This way, please.'

He opened a huge door and they entered the dining room.

Very large plates, dishes, and cutlery covered the far

end of a heavy-looking wooden table, at the head of which sat their host, with a place laid on either side of him. The room was lit by two sizzling oil lamps, vast and of antiquated pattern, which hung from heavy circular plaster mouldings in the discoloured ceiling. The marble and iron fireplace was in massive keeping with the almost immovable waiting-room chairs. On the dark-green lincrusta of the walls engravings hung behind glass so dirty that in the weak green light it was difficult to make out the subjects. A plain round clock clicked like a revolving turnstile from above the fireplace. As the women appeared, it jerked from 2:26 to 2:27. By habit Mimi looked at her watch. The time was just after eight o'clock.

'Immediately you entered the house, the rain stopped,' said Wendley Roper by way of greeting.

'Then we'd better be on our way after dinner,' said Mimi.

'Most certainly not. I meant only that if you'd arrived a few minutes later, I might have lost the pleasure of your company. Will you sit here?' He was drawing back the heavy chair for Mimi to sit on his right. Beech performed the like office for Margaret. 'I should have been utterly disconsolate. You both look remarkably attractive.'

Beech disappeared and returned with a tureen so capacious that neither of the women would have cared to lift it. Roper ladled out soup into the huge plates. As he did so, a train roared past outside.

'I suppose the railway came after the house had been

here some time?' asked Margaret, feeling that some reference to the matter seemed called for.

'By no means,' answered Roper. 'The man who built the railway built the house. He was my grandfather, Joseph Roper, generally known as Wide Joe. Wide Joe liked trains.'

'There's not much else for company,' remarked Mimi, engulfing the hot soup.

'This was one of the last main line railways to be built,' continued Roper. 'Everyone said it was impossible, but they were keen all the same, partly because land in this valley was very cheap, as it still is. But my grandfather was an engineering genius, and in the end he did it. The engravings in this room show the different stages of the work.'

'I suppose he regarded it as his masterpiece and wanted to live next to it when he retired?' politely enquired Margaret.

'Not when he retired. As a matter of fact, he never did retire. He built this house right at the beginning of the work and lived here until the end. The railway took twenty years to build.'

'I don't know much about railway building, but that's surely a very long time?'

'There were difficulties. Difficulties of a kind my grandfather had never expected. The cost of them ruined the company, which had to amalgamate in consequence. They nearly drove my grandfather mad.' Margaret could not stop herself from glancing at Mimi. 'Everything conspired together against him. Things happened which he had not looked for.'

Beech reappeared and, removing the soup, substituted a pile of sausages contained in a rampart of mashed potato. As he manoeuvred the hot and heavy dish, Margaret noticed a large, dull coal-black ring on the third finger of his left hand.

'Primitive fare,' apologised Roper. 'All you can get nowadays.'

None the less, the two women found it unbelievably welcome.

'I do see now what you might call railway influences about the house,' said Margaret.

'My grandfather lived in the days when a railway engineer was responsible for every detail of design. Not only of the tunnels and bridges, but the locomotives and carriages, the stations and signals, even the posters and tickets. He had sole responsibility for everything. An educated man could never have stood the strain. Wide Joe educated himself.'

At intervals through dinner, passing trains rattled the heavy table and heavy objects upon it.

'Now tell me about yourselves,' said Wendley Roper, as if he had just concluded the narrative of his own life. 'But first have another sausage each. There's only stewed fruit ahead.' They accepted.

'We're civil servants,' said Mimi. 'That's what brought us together. I come from London, and Margaret comes from Devonshire. My father is a hairdresser and Margaret's father is a Lord. Now you know all about us.'

'An entirely bankrupt Lord, I regret to say,' added Margaret quietly.

'I gather more Lords are bankrupt in these times,' said Roper sympathetically.

'And many hairdressers,' said Mimi.

'Everyone but civil servants, in fact?' said Roper.

'That's why we're civil servants,' replied Mimi, eviscerating her last sausage from its inedible skin. 'Though you don't seem altogether bankrupt,' she added. Food was increasing her vitality.

He made no reply. Beech had entered with a big glass bowl, deeply but unbeautifully cut, filled with stewed damsons.

'The local fruit,' said Roper despondently.

But they even ate stewed damsons.

'I am absolutely delighted to have you here,' he remarked when he had served them. 'I see almost no one. Least of all attractive women.'

His tones were so direct and sincere that Margaret immediately felt pleased. Having, until this year she took a job, lived all her life against a background of desperate and, as she thought, undeserved money troubles, and in a remote country district, she had had little to do with men. Even such a simple compliment from a good-looking and well-spoken man still meant disproportionately much to her. She observed that Mimi seemed to notice nothing whatever.

'I don't know what would have become of us without you,' said Margaret.

'Food for the crows,' said Mimi.

Suddenly the conversation loosened up, becoming comparatively cordial, intimate, and general. Roper disclosed himself as intelligent, well-informed, and a good listener to those less intelligent and well-informed, at least when they were young women. Mimi's conversation became much steadier and more pointed than usual. Margaret found herself saying less and less, while enjoying herself more.

'Beech will bring us coffee in the drawing room,' said Roper, 'if drawing room's the right expression.'

They moved across the hall to another bleak apartment, this time walled with official-looking books, long series of volumes bound in dark-blue cloth or in stout, rough-edged paper. Again there were two complicated but not very efficient lamps hissing and spurting from the coffered ceiling. The furniture consisted in old-fashioned leather-covered armchairs and sofas; and, before the window at the end of the room, a huge desk, bearing high heaps of varied documents, disused and dusty. About the room in glass cases were scale models of long-extinct locomotives and bygone devices for ensuring safety on the railways. Above the red marble mantel was a vast print of a railway accident, freely coloured by hand.

'You do keep things as the old man left them,' said Mimi.

'It is a house of the dead,' said Roper. 'My aunt, you know. She would never have anything touched.'

Beech brought coffee: not very good and served in over-large cups; but pleasantly warm. Margaret still found the house cold. She hoped she was not ill after the soaking and strain of the day. She continued, however, to listen to Mimi and Roper chatting together in surprising sympathy; every now and then made an observation of her own; and, thinking things over, wondered that on the whole they had turned out so well. It was Margaret who poured out the coffee.

What were Mimi and Roper talking about? He was asking her in great detail about their dull office routine; she was enquiring with improbable enthusiasm into early railway history. Neither could have had much genuine interest in either subject. It was all very unreal, but comfortable and pleasing. Roper, many aspects of whose position seemed to Margaret to invite curiosity, said nothing of himself. Every now and then a train passed.

'A pension at sixty doesn't make up for being a number all your life. A cipher. You want to get off the rails every now and then.'

'You only get on to a branch line, a dead end,' said Roper with what seemed real despondency. 'It's difficult to leave the rails altogether and still keep going at all.'

'Have you ever tried? What *do* you do?' It was seldom so long before Mimi asked that. She despised inaction in men.

'I used to work in the railway company's office. All the Ropers were in the railway business, as you will have gathered. I was the only one to get out of it in time.'

'In time for what?'

'In time for anything. My father was the company's

Chief Commercial Manager. Trying to meet the slump killed him. Things aren't what they used to be with railways, you know. My grandfather was run over just outside that window.' He pointed across the dusty desk at the end of the room.

'What a perfectly appalling thing!' said Margaret. 'How did it happen?'

'He never had any luck after he took on this job. You know how two perfectly harmless substances when blended can make something deadly? Building the railway through this valley was just like that for my grandfather. A lot of things happened . . . One thing the valley goes in for is sudden storms. On a certain night when one of these storms got up, my grandfather thought he heard a tree fall. You noticed the trees round the house? The original idea was that they'd provide shelter. My grandfather thought this tree might have fallen across the line. He was so concerned that he forgot the time-table, though normally he carried every train movement in his head. You can guess what happened. The noise of the approaching train was drowned by the wind. Or so they decided at the inquest.'

When a comparative stranger tells such a story, it is always difficult to know what to say, and there is a tendency to fill the gap with some unimportant question. 'And was the tree across the line?' asked Margaret.

'Not it. No tree had fallen. The old man had got it wrong.'

'Then surely they were rather lax at the inquest?'

'Wide Joe had always been expected to meet a bad

end, and the jury were all local men. He was pretty generally disliked. He made his daughter break off her engagement with a railwayman at Pudsley depot. Marrying into the lower deck, and all that. But it turned out he was a bit wrong. The man got into Parliament and ended by doing rather better for himself than my grandfather had done by sticking to the railway. By then, of course, it was too late. And my grandfather was dead in any case.'

'That was your aunt?' enquired Mimi.

'Being my father's sister, yes,' said Roper. 'Now let us change the subject. Tell me about the gay world of London.'

'We never come across it,' said Mimi. It's just one damn thing after another for us girls.'

The moment seemed opportune for Margaret to get her pullover, as she still felt cold. She departed upstairs. In some ways she would have been glad to go to bed, after the exhausting day; but she felt also an unexplained reluctance, less than half-conscious, to leave Mimi and Roper chatting so intimately alone together. Then, ascending the dim staircase with its enormous ugly polished banisters in dark wood, she received a shock which drove sleep temporarily from her.

The incident was small and perfectly reasonable; it was doubtless the dead crepuscularity of the house which made it seem frightening to Margaret. When she reached the first-floor landing she saw a figure which seemed hastily to be drawing back from her and then to retreat through one of the big panelled doors. The impression of furtiveness might well have resulted solely from the exceedingly poor lighting. But as to the opening and shutting of the door, Margaret's ears left her in no doubt. And upon another point their evidence confirmed the much less dependable testimony of her eyes: the withdrawing feet tapped; the half-visible figure was undoubtedly a woman's. She appeared to be wearing a dark coat and skirt, which left her lighter legs more clearly discernible.

Stamping on absurd fears, quite beyond definition, Margaret ascended the second flight and entered the bedroom. After all, it was quite probable that Beech did not do all the work of the house: most likely that Roper's staff should consist of a married couple. Margaret sat upon one of the hard chairs Beech had brought, and faced her fear more specifically. It took shape before the eyes of her mind: a faceless waxwork labelled 'Miss Roper', mad, dead, horribly returned. The costume of the figure Margaret had seen was not that of the tragic Victorian in Wendley Roper's narrative: but then Miss Roper had died only recently, and might have kept up with the times in this respect, as more and more old ladies do. That would be less likely, however, if she had really been mad, as Mimi had suggested, and as the tale of the broken engagement would certainly require had it been told by one of the period's many novelists.

The room Margaret was in had seen it all. Suddenly, as this fact returned to memory, the grimy dingy papered walls seemed simultaneously to jerk towards her, the whole rather long and narrow attic to contract upon her threateningly. Though enormously larger, the room suddenly struck Margaret as having the proportions of a railway compartment, a resemblance much increased by the odd arrangement of the windows, one at each end. Old-fashioned railway carriage windows were commonly barred, Margaret was just old enough to have noticed. This recollection brought rather more comfort than was strictly reasonable. Relaxing a little, Margaret found that she had been seated motionless. Her muscles were stiff and she could hear her heart and pulses, whether or not proceeding at the normal rate it was hard to say. Some time must have passed while she had sat in what amounted to a trance of fear. But their only watch was on Mimi's wrist, her own having been stolen while she washed in the Ladies' Lavatory of an expensive restaurant to which her father had taken her for her birthday. Above all, she was colder than ever. She extracted the pullover from her rucksack and put it on. It was V-necked and long-sleeved. The warmth of its elegant, closely woven black wool was cheering. Before once more descending, Margaret adjusted the lamp which had been left in the bedroom. Then she recalled Roper's remark that the whole first floor of the house was occupied by his grandfather's collection; which for some reason did not make the actions of the woman she had seen seem more reassuring. But a minute later she crossed the first-floor landing firmly, though certainly without making any investigation; and reached the door of the preposterous 'drawing room' without (she was quite surprised to realise) any particular incident.

Immediately she entered, however, it was obvious that the atmosphere in the room had very much altered since she had left. Her fears were cut off like the change of scene in a film, to be replaced by a confused emotion as strong and undefined as the very different sensations which had accompanied the short period between her glimpsing the woman on the stairs and reaching the chair in her bedroom. Not only were Mimi and Roper now seated together on the vast leather-covered sofa before the empty fireplace, but Margaret even felt that they had vulgarly drawn further away from each other upon hearing her return.

'Hullo,' said Mimi cheekily. 'You've been a long time.'

For a moment Margaret felt like giving the situation a twist in her direction (as she felt it would be), by relating some of the reason for her long absence; but, in view of the mystery about Miss Roper, managed to abstain. Could it be that Miss Roper was not dead at all? she suddenly wondered.

'Mind your own business,' she replied in Mimi's own key.

'I hope you found your way,' said Roper politely.

'Perfectly, thank you.'

There was a short silence.

'I fear Beech has gone to bed, or I'd offer you both some further refreshments. I have no other servant.'

After the initial drag of blood from her stomach, Margaret took a really hard pull on her resolution.

'Do you live alone here with Beech?'

'Quite alone. That's why it's so pleasant to have you

two with me. I've been telling Mimi that normally I have only my books.' It was the first time Margaret had heard him use the Christian name.

'He leads the life of a recluse,' said Mimi. 'Research, you know. Dog's life, if you ask me. Worse than ours.'

'What do you research into?' asked Margaret.

'Can't you guess, dear?' Mimi had become very much at her ease.

'Railways, I'm afraid. Railway history.' Roper was smiling a scholar's smile, tired and deprecating, but at the same time uniquely arrogant. 'If you're a Roper you can't get it quite out of the blood. I've been showing Mimi this.' He held out a book with a dark-green jacket.

'*Early Fishplates*,' read Margaret, 'by Howard Bullhead.' The print appeared closely packed and extremely technical. The book was decorated with occasional arid little diagrams.

'What has this to do with railways?'

'Fishplates,' cried Mimi, 'are what hold the rails down.'

'Well, not quite that,' said Roper, 'but something like it.'

'Who's Mr Bullhead?'

'Bullhead is a rather technical railway joke. I'm the real author. I prefer to use a pseudonym.'

'The whole book's one long mad thrill,' said Mimi. 'Wendley's going to sell the film rights.'

'I can't get it altogether out of my blood,' said Roper again. 'The family motto might be the same as Bismarck's: Blood and Iron.'

93

'Do you *want* to get it out?' asked Margaret. 'I'm sure it's a fascinating book.'

But Mimi had leapt to her feet. 'What about a cup of tea? What do you say *I* make it?'

Roper hesitated for a moment. Margaret thought that disinclination to accede conflicted with desire to please Mimi.

'I'll help.' Normally tea at night was so little Margaret's habit that Mimi stared at her.

'That would be very nice indeed,' said Roper at last. Desire to please Mimi had doubtless prevailed, though indeed it was hard to see what else he could say. 'I'll show you the kitchen. It's really very nice of you.' He hesitated another moment. Then they both followed him from the room.

Before the kettle had boiled in the square cold kitchen, Margaret's mind was in another conflict. Roper no longer seemed altogether so cultivated and charming as towards the end of dinner; there were now recurrent glimpses in him of showiness and even silliness. The maddening thing was, however, that Margaret could no longer be unaware that she found him attractive. Some impulse, of which her experience was small and her opinion adverse, was loose in her brain, like the spot of light in a column of mercury. Upon other matters her mind was perfectly clear; so that she felt like two people, one thinking, one willing. Possibly even there was a third person, who was feeling; who was feeling very tired indeed.

Mimi, sometimes so quick to tire, seemed utterly

unflagging. She darted about the strange domesticities, turning taps, assembling crocks, prattling about the gas cooker: 'Your gas doesn't smell. I call that service.'

'The smell is *added* to coal gas as a safety precaution,' said Roper.

'Why don't they choose a nice smell, then?'

'What would you suggest?'

'I don't mean Chanel, but new-mown hay or lovely roses.'

'The Gas Board don't want all their customers in love with easeful death.'

'What's your favourite method of committing suicide?'

Though this was one of Mimi's most customary topics, Margaret wished that she had chosen another. But Roper merely replied, 'Old age, I think.' He seemed fascinated by her. Neither he nor Margaret was doing anything to help with the preparations. In the end Mimi began positively to sing and the empty interchange of remarks came to an end.

As Mimi was filling the teapot, Roper unexpectedly departed.

'Do you like him?' asked Margaret.

'He's all right. Wonder if there's anything to eat with it.' Mimi began to peer into vast clanging bread bins.

'Have you found out anything more about him?'

'Not a thing.'

'Don't you think it's all rather queer?'

'Takes all sorts to make a world, dear.'

'It seems to take an odd sort to make a railway. You

yourself suggested—' But Roper returned.

'I thought we might end this delightful evening in my den; my study, you know. It's much warmer and cosier. I don't usually show it to visitors. I like to keep somewhere quite private. For work, you know. But you are no ordinary visitors. I've just looked in and there's even a fire burning.' This last slightly odd remark was not to Margaret made less odd by the way it was spoken; as if the speaker had prepared in advance a triviality too slight to sustain preparation convincingly. 'Do come along. Let me carry the tray.'

'I've been looking for something to eat,' said Mimi. 'Do you think Beech has laid by any buns or anything?'

'There's some cake in my den,' said Roper, like the hero of a good book for boys.

This time the door was open and the room flooding the hall with cheerful light.

It was entirely different from any other room they had entered in that house: and not in the least like a den, or even like a study. The lamps were modern, efficient, adequate, and decorative. The furniture was soft and comfortable. The railway blight (as Margaret regarded it) seemed totally absent. As Roper had said, there was an excellent fire in a modern grate surrounded by unexciting but not disagreeable Dutch tiles. This seemed the true drawing room of the house.

'What a lovely lounge!' cried Mimi. 'Looks like a woman in the house at last. Why couldn't we come in here before?' Her rapidly increasing command of the situation seemed to Margaret almost strident.

'I thought the occasion called for more formality.'

'Dog in the manger, if you ask me.' Mimi fell upon a sofa, extending her trousered legs. 'Pour out, Margaret, will you?'

Margaret, conscious that whereas Mimi ought to be appearing in a bad light, yet in fact it was she, Margaret, who, however unjustly, was doing so, repeated with the tea the office she had already performed with the coffee. Roper, who had placed the tray on a small table next to an armchair in which Margaret proceeded to seat herself beside the fire, carried one of the big full cups to Mimi. He poured her milk with protective intimacy and seemed to find one of her obvious jokes about the quantity of sugar she required intoxicatingly funny. He moved rather well, Margaret thought. Mimi, moreover, had been right about his voice. His remarks, however, though almost never about himself, seemed mostly, in the light of that fact, remarkably self-centred. It would be dreadful to have to listen to them all one's life.

Suddenly he was bearing cake. Neither of the women saw where it came from but, when it appeared, both found they still had appetites. It tasted of vanilla and was choked with candied peel.

In the kitchen Margaret had noticed that despite the late hour the traffic on the railway had seemed to be positively increasing; but in the present small room the noise was much muffled, the line being on the other side of the house. None the less, frequent trains were still to be heard.

'Why are there so many trains? It must be nearly midnight.'

'Long past, dear,' interjected Mimi, the time-keeper. The fact seemed to give her a particular happiness.

'I see you're not used to living by a railway,' said Roper. 'Many classes of traffic are kept off the tracks during ordinary travelling hours. What you hear going by now are the loads you don't see when the stations are open. A railway is like an iceberg, you know: very little of its working is visible to the casual onlooker.'

'Not visible, perhaps. But certainly audible.'

'The noise does not disturb you?'

'No, of course not. But does it really go on day and night?'

'Certainly. Day and night. At least on important main lines, such as this is.'

'I suppose you've long ceased to notice it?'

'I notice when it's not there. If a single train is missing from its time, I become quite upset. Even if it happens when I'm asleep.'

'But surely only the passenger trains have time-tables?'

'My dear Margaret, every single train is in a time-table. Every local goods, every light engine movement. Only not, of course, in the time-table you buy for six-pence at the Enquiry Office. Only a small fraction of all the train movements are in that. Even the man behind the counter knows virtually nothing of the rest.'

'Only Wendley knows the whole works,' said Mimi from the sofa.

The others were sitting one at each side of the fire in front of which she lay and had been talking along the length of her body. Margaret had realised that this was the first time Roper had used her Christian name. It seemed hours ago that he had called Mimi by hers. Suddenly, looking at Mimi sprawling in her trousers and tight high-necked sweater, Margaret saw the point, clearer than in any book: Mimi was physically attractive; she herself in all probability was not. And nothing else in all life, in all the world, really counted. Nothing, nothing. Being cleverer; on the whole (as she thought) kinder; being more refined; the daughter of a Lord: such things were the dust beneath Mimi's chariot wheels, items in the list of life's innumerable unwantable impedimenta. Margaret stuck out her legs unbecomingly.

'Can I have another cup of tea?' said Mimi. Her small round head was certainly engaging.

'There you are,' said Margaret. 'Now will you both forgive me if I go to bed? I think I could do with some sleep after my soaking.'

'I'm a beast,' cried Mimi, warmly sympathetic. 'Is there anything I can do? What about a hot water bottle, Wendley? Margaret is always as helpless as a butterfly. I have to look after her.' She was certainly rather sweet too.

'Not a hot water bottle, please,' replied Margaret. 'They're not in season yet. I'll be all right, Mimi. See you later. Good night.'

Between sympathy and the desire to get her out of

the room, Margaret thought on her way upstairs, Mimi had absolutely no conflict whatever; she merely took her emotions in turn, getting the most out of all of them, and no doubt giving the most also.

This time there was no vague figure which crept back from the stairs: or possibly it was that Margaret's thoughts attended a different will-o'-the-wisp. Immediately she entered the bedroom, she noticed that the promised second bed had arrived, as lean and frugal as the first. In the long room the two beds had been set far apart. Margaret was unable to be sure whether the second bed had or had not been there when she had last entered the room.

Her mind still darting and plunging about the scene downstairs, she selected the bed which stood furthest from the door. At that moment Mimi seemed to her in no particular need of consideration. Margaret dashed off her clothes in the clammy atmosphere, dropping the garments with unwonted carelessness upon one of the two dark, thin-legged chairs; then, as a train pounded past, rattling the small barred windows at each end of the room and causing the curtains to shake apart, letting in the infernal glare outside, she climbed into her pyjamas and into the small, tight bed. She now realised for the first time that there were no sheets, but only clinging blankets. To put out the single oil lamp was more than her courage or the cold permitted. She buttoned her jacket to the top and wished it had long sleeves. It had been only an absurd dignity, a preposterous aggression, which had led her to reject a hot water bottle.

She was quite unable to sleep. Her mind had set up a devil's dance which would not subside for hours at the best. The bed was the first really uncomfortable one in which Margaret had ever slept: it was so narrow that blankets of normal size could be and were tucked in so far that they overlapped beneath the occupant, interlocking to bind her in; so narrow also that the cheap hard springs of the wire framework gave not at all beneath the would-be sleeper's weight; and the mattress was inadequate to blur a diamond pattern of hard metallic ridges. Although she liked by day to wear garments fitting closely at the throat, Margaret found that the same sensation in bed, however much necessitated by the temperature, amounted to suffocation. Nor had she ever been able, since first she could remember, to sleep with a light in the room. Above all, there were the trains: not so much the periodical thunder rollings, she found, as the apparently lengthening intervals of waiting for them. Downstairs the trains had seemed to become more and more frequent; here they seemed to become slowly sparser. It was probably, Margaret reflected, a consequence of the slowness with which time is said to pass for those seeking sleep. Or perhaps Wendley Roper would have an answer in terms of graphicstatics or inner family knowledge. The ultimate effect was as if the train service were something subjective in Margaret's head, like the large defined shapes which obstruct the vision of the sufferer from migraine. 'No sleep like this,' said Margaret to herself, articulating with a clarity which made the words seem spoken by another.

She forced herself from the rigid blankets, felt-like though far from warm, opened the neck of her pyjama jacket, and extinguished the light, which died on the lightest breath. What on earth was Mimi doing? she wondered with schoolgirl irritation.

Immediately she had groped into the pitch-dark bed, a train which seemed of an entirely new construction went past. This time there was no blasting of steam and thundering or grinding of wheels: only a single sustained rather high-pitched rattling; metallic, inhuman, hollow. The new train appeared to be descending the bank, but Margaret for the first time could not be sure. The sound frightened Margaret badly. 'It's a hospital train,' her mother had said to her long ago on an occasion of which Margaret had forgotten all details except that they were horrible. 'It's full of wounded soldiers.'

In a paroxysm of terror, as this agony of her childhood blasted through her adult life, Margaret must have passed into sleep, or at least unconsciousness. For the next event could only have been a dream of hallucination. The room seemed to be filling with colourless light. Though even now this light was extremely dim, the process of its first appearance and increase seemed to have been going on for a very long time. As she realised this, another part of Margaret's mind remembered that it could none the less have been only a matter of minutes. She struggled to make consistent the consciousness of the nearly endless with the consciousness of the precisely brief. The light seemed, moreover, the exact visual counterpart of the noise she had heard made by the new train. Then Margaret became aware of something very horrible indeed: it began with the up-turned dead face of an old woman, colourless with the exact colourlessness of the colourless light; and it ended with the old woman's crumpled shape occultly made visible hanging above the trap-door in the corner of Margaret's compartment-shaped room. Up in the attic old Miss Roper had hanged herself, her grey hair so twisted and meshed as itself to suggest the suffocating agent.

Margaret's hands went in terror to her own bare throat. Then the door of the room opened, and someone stood inside it bearing a light.

'I don't think you heard me knock.'

As when she and Mimi had arrived she had noticed in Roper's first words the echo of the man at the Guest House, so now was another echo – of Beech's cool apology for that bedroom contretemps which had so fired Mimi's wrath. To Margaret it was as if a nightmare had reached that not uncommon point at which the sufferer, though not yet awake, not yet out of the dream, yet becomes aware that a dream it is. Then all was deep nightmare once more, as Margaret recalled the shadow woman on the stairs, and perceived that the same wo-man was now in the room with her.

Margaret broke down. Still clutching her throat, she cried repeatedly in a shrill but not loud voice. 'Go away. Go away. Go away. Go away.' It was again like her child-hood.

The strange woman approached and, setting down

the lamp, began to shake her by the shoulders. At once Margaret seemed to know that, whoever else she was, she was not the dead Miss Roper; and that was all which seemed to matter. She stopped wauling like a terror-struck child: then saw that the hand still on one of her shoulders wore a dull coal-black ring; and, looking up, that the face above her and the thick black hair were Beech's, as had been that indifferently apologetic voice. Nightmare stormed forward yet again; but this time only for an adult speck of time. For Margaret seemed now to have no doubt whatever that Beech was indeed a woman.

'Where's your friend?'

'I left her downstairs. I came up to bed early.'

'Early?'

'What's the time? I have no watch.'

'It's half past three.'

The equivocal situation returned to life in Margaret's mind in every detail, as when stage lights are turned on simultaneously.

'What business is it of yours? Who are you?'

'Who do you think I am?'

'I thought you were the manservant.'

'I looked after old Miss Roper. Until she died.'

'Did that mean you had to dress like a man?' The woman now appeared to be wearing a dark grey coat and skirt and a white blouse.

'Wendley could hardly live alone in the house with a woman he wasn't married to. Someone he had no intention of marrying.'

'Why haven't you left, then?'

'After what happened to Miss Roper?'

'What did you do to Miss Roper?' Margaret spoke very low but quite steadily. All feeling was dead in her, save, far below the surface, a flickering jealousy of Mimi, a death-wish sympathy with the murdering stranger beside her. So that Margaret was able to add, steadily as before, 'Miss Roper was mad, wasn't she?'

'Certainly not. Why do you say that?'

'Her father preventing her marrying. The bars on the windows.'

'You can be crossed in love without going mad, you know. And madhouse windows are not the only ones with bars.' The large white hand with the black ring on the engagement finger had continued all this time to rest on Margaret's shoulder. Now with a sharp movement it was withdrawn.

'So this was simply a prison? Why? What had Miss Roper done?'

'Something to do with the railway. Some secret she had from the old man and wouldn't tell Wendley. I never asked for details. I was in love. You know what that means as well as I do.'

'What sort of secret? And why did it have to be a secret?'

'I don't know what sort of secret. I don't care now. She wanted to keep it secret from Wendley because she knew what he would do with it. She spent all her time trying to tell other people.'

'That's why . . .' Margaret was about to say 'that's why

she waved', then stopped herself. '*What* would Wendley have done with it?'

'Your friend should have some idea of that by this time.' This unexpected remark was delivered in a tone of deepest venom.

'What do you mean? Where is Mimi?' Then a sudden hysteria swept over her. 'I'm going to find Mimi.' She struggled out of the crib-like bed, bruising herself badly on the ironwork. The trains seemed to have long ceased and everything was horribly quiet in the Quiet Valley.

The woman, approaching the cheap little bedroom chair on which Margaret's clothes lay tumbled where she had dropped them, picked up Margaret's tie, and held it between her two hands twelve inches or so apart.

In the negligible light of one oil lamp there began a slow chase down the long narrow room.

'You're not on his side really,' cried Margaret, everything gone. 'You know what's happening downstairs.'

The woman made no answer, but slightly decreased the distance between her hands. Margaret perceived how foolish had been her error in deliberately selecting the bed furthest from the door. None the less, a certain amount of evasion, as in a childhood game of 'Touch', was possible before she found herself being forced near the end wall, being corralled almost beneath the trapdoor in the ceiling above. If only she could have reached the other door, the door of the room! Much would then have been possible.

As they arrived at the corner beneath the trap,

Margaret's heel struck Mimi's open rucksack, dropped there by its casual owner, hitherto forgotten or unnoticed by Margaret, and concealed by the dim light. Margaret stooped.

Three seconds later her adversary was lying back downwards on the floor, bleeding darkly and excessively in the gloom, Mimi's robust camping knife through her rather thick white throat. 'Comes from Sweden, dear,' Mimi had said. 'Not allowed to sell them here.'

It did not take Margaret long, plunging into the pockets in the dead woman's jacket, to find Beech's bunch of keys. This was fortunate, as the scream of the murdered woman, breaking into the course of events below, was followed by running footsteps on the murky stairs. The agile Mimi burst into the room crying, 'Lock it. For God's sake lock it'; and Margaret had raced the length of the Rafters Room and locked it before Wendley Roper, heavy and unused to exercise, had arrived at the landing outside. The large key turned in the expensive, efficient lock with a grinding snap he could not have mistaken. The railway hotel door was enormously thick, a beautiful piece of joinery. Margaret waited, her body drooping forward, for Roper to begin his onslaught. But it was a job for an axe, and nothing whatever happened; neither blows on the door, nor a voice, nor even retreating footsteps.

Mimi, ignorant that the room had a third occupant, was seated on the side of her bed with her hands distending her trousers' pockets. She was panting slightly, but her hair was habitually cut too short ever to show much disorder. Margaret had previously thought her manner strident; it was now beyond bearing. She began to blow out a stream of curses, particularly horrible in the presence of the dead woman.

'Mimi, my dear,' said Margaret gently. 'What are we going to do?' Still in her pyjamas, she was shivering spasmodically.

Mimi, keeping her hands in her pockets, looked round at her. 'Catch the first departure for Hell, I should say.'

Though she was not weeping, there was something unbearably desolate about her. Margaret wanted to comfort her: Mimi's experiences had been unimaginably worse even than her own. She put her cold arms round Mimi's stiff hard body; then tried to drag Mimi's hands from her pockets in order to take them in her own. Mimi, though offering no help, did not strongly resist. As Margaret dragged at her wrists, one of her own hands round each, a queer little trickle fell to the floor on each side of her. Mimi's pockets were tightly stuffed with railway tickets.

Dropping Mimi's wrists, Margaret picked up one of the tickets and read it by the light of the strange woman's lamp: 'Diamond Jubilee Special. Pudsley to Hassell-wicket. Third Class. Excursion 2s. 11d. God Save Our Queen.' Mimi's fists were clenched round variegated little bundles of pasteboard rectangles.

It was impossible to tell her about the dead woman.

'I'm going to dress. Then we'll get out.' Margaret began to drag on the clothes she had worn for dinner.

She buttoned the collar of her shirt, warm and welcome about her neck. She looked for her tie, and could just see it in one hand of the dead woman as she lay compact on the floor at the end of the room behind Mimi's back.

'I'll pack our rucksacks.' Fully dressed, Margaret felt more valiant and less vulnerable. She groped at the feet of the corpse for Mimi's rucksack and assembled the scattered contents. But, though feeling the omission to be folly, she did not go back for Mimi's knife. In the end, she had packed both rucksacks and was carefully fastening the straps. Mimi had apparently emptied her pockets of tickets, leaving four small heaps on the dark carpet, one from each fist, one from each pocket; and was now sitting silent and apparently relaxed, but making no effort to help Margaret.

'Are you ready? We must plan.'

Mimi gazed up at her. Then she said quietly, 'There's nowhere for us to go now.' With the slightest of gestures she appeared to indicate the four heaps of tickets.

No argument that Margaret used would induce Mimi to make the least effort. She just sat on the bed saying that they were prisoners and there was nothing they could do.

Feeling that Mimi's reason might have been affected, though of this there was no sign, Margaret began to contemplate the dreadful extremity of trying to escape alone. But apart from the additional perils to body and spirit (there was no knowing that Roper was not standing outside the door), she felt that it would be impossible for her to leave Mimi alone to what might befall.

She set down her rucksack on the floor beside Mimi's. When filled, she always found it heavy to hold for long.

'Very well. We'll wait till it's light. It should be quite soon.'

Mimi said nothing. Looking at her, Margaret saw that for the first time she was weeping. Margaret once more put her arms round her now soft body, and the two women tenderly kissed. They came from very different environments and it was the first time they had ever done so.

The desperate idea entered Margaret's mind that help might be obtained. Surely there must be visitors to the house of some kind sometimes; and neither she nor Mimi was a powerless old woman. Margaret's eyes unintendingly went to the knife in the victim's throat.

For a long time the two women sat close together saying little.

Margaret had not for hours given a thought to the railway outside. Since that strange and dream-like new train, nothing had passed. Then, from the very far distance, came the airy ghost of an engine whistle: utterly impersonal at that hour and place, but, to Margaret, filled with promise.

She rose and drew back the curtains from one of the queer barred windows.

'Look! It's dawn.'

A girdle of light was slowly edging over the horizon, offering a fine day to come, unusual in such mountainous country. Margaret, aflame for action, looked quickly about the room. She herself was wearing colours unlikely to stand out in the yet faint light. Mimi's grey was hardly more helpful. There was only one thing to be done. Leaping across the room, Margaret ripped a large piece of material from the dead woman's white blouse patched with blood. Then as in the growing radiance Mimi turned and for the first time saw the body, Margaret, throwing up the narrow window, waved confidently to the workmen's train which was approaching.

Your Tiny Hand Is Frozen

It was on the third night that the trouble with the telephone started. Edmund St Jude had been a light sleeper for years; but the previous day had been occupied with steady and unwonted domestic tasks, and when the telephone began to ring he was slumbering heavily and dreaming vividly. For some time, indeed, it was in this dream that the bell rang: then he found that he was sitting crouched in bed, shuddering a little, and totally uncertain how far the dream had ended. Moonlight drifted in through the glass mansard of the studio north light, but the telephone, being on a low table immediately beneath the sill, was in darkness. In the absence of other sounds to muffle or compete, the peals of the bell were thrown back and forth from wall to wall, icy and imperative.

Clutching his personality, jeopardised by the dream, about him, Edmund resolved not to answer. At that hour it could only be a wrong number . . . or a friend of Teddie's, he suddenly thought. The bell continued to ring. What time was it? His beautiful hunter, symbol of his former life, lay on a chair by the bed. It was twenty-five minutes past five. That the caller could be for Teddie seemed improbable. The bell continued to ring.

In the end, Edmund, who was an amiable man, always yielded to importunity. He crawled out into the autumnal November moonlight and lifted the instrument from its black bed. His aunt, with whom he had previously resided for a number of years, had contrived to retain an instrument of the earlier candlestick pattern; to which Edmund's reflexes were accordingly accustomed, especially in the middle of the night. He fumbled slightly, almost dropping this newer contraption. Now the silence was as disconcerting as the former noise.

'Hullo.'

There was no answering sound of any kind.

'Hullo.'

After a silence of seconds, there was a loud sharp click. It was as if the caller had counted one, two, three, and then, as if by premeditation, rung off.

'*Hullo*,' said Edmund futilely. But nothing happened. It was not an hour for the operator forthwith to ask what number he wanted.

Edmund replaced the telephone and sped back to bed. He slept again, but now lightly and brokenly, as he usually did.

The episode amounted to little, and Edmund, had he been permitted, would probably soon have forgotten it, especially among the many other nuisances of which his new life seemed largely composed. But during the next few weeks the incident was repeated again and again. Almost always it happened if not during the hours of daylight, which now were daily shrinking, then at least during the hours when Edmund was up and about; although there were further night alarms on at least two occasions.

One of these night calls was especially curious. The telephone rang almost immediately after Edmund had got into bed. Suspecting, with a sinking of his already low spirits, that it was one of the unaccountable calls, but knowing that for him there was no escape in letting the bell go on ringing (two minutes and fifty seconds had proved his maximum period of endurance to date, counted out upon the second-hand of his hunter), he at once switched on the weak bedside light, rose, and answered.

'Hullo.'

There was the usual silence.

'Hullo.'

Not for the first time, he was permitted to speak thrice.

'Hullo.'

There came the click; and then a sound which was new. Edmund heard it before he put back the telephone, but that it came after and not before the dismissive click he was sure. It was a sound which could be nothing but a light short laugh. It seemed to mock his certainly derisory plight. It upset him very much. But no such quirk, additional to the mischief of the calls themselves, occurred again.

There appeared no method or regularity about the calls. Several days would pass without one; then there would be three in twenty-four hours. The apparent chanciness of the calls played its part in for long dissuading Edmund, who always delayed such approaches, from communicating with the Exchange. He was also deterred by the extreme rarity of his other calls, received or initiated. He felt that this put him in a weak position to complain, and would make his complaint seem ridiculous. The whole telephone installation was only a survival from Teddie's occupancy, and it was one of several with which he would have dispensed.

Another was a habit which seemed common to many of Teddie's friends of calling without previous announcement. The callers consisted of rather commonplace young women, obviously in great need of a good gossip, and of well-set-up young men with the wrong kind of haircut and few overt stigmata of imagination. Edmund, who could afford few friends of his own, had known few of Teddie's. He was now much surprised by the implications with regard to Teddie's nature and character which these stray visitors conveyed. As he was engaged to marry Teddie, he was also somewhat concerned.

On one occasion, when Edmund was standing at the studio door trying to ward off a large youth who said his name was Toby, the telephone rang. It proved to be one of the mysterious calls, but by the time Edmund had heard the usual click and had replaced the instrument, he perceived that his visitor had followed him into the studio.

'Nothing wrong, I hope?'

With each successive call, Edmund was becoming fractionally more irritated, and also perturbed; so that the young man's question was as unwelcome as his presence.

'Nothing,' said Edmund stonily. Then he thought. He was beginning to need a confidant. 'Nothing *wrong*,' he continued. 'But perhaps something unusual. The telephone rings. I answer it. And then the person at the other end rings off. That's all. But it happens again and again.'

'Nothing unusual about that,' said Toby, failing to grasp the essence of the matter. 'We all get it.' His manner was insensitive and insufferable. 'Now tell me, St Jude.' He was also over-familiar. 'How long has Teddie had TB? I never knew she had it at all.'

'No one knew,' replied Edmund. 'But I'm sorry. I was working. I must get on, you know. I'll tell Teddie you called.'

'OK.' Toby had evidently given Edmund up. He shrugged his bulging shoulders and departed without further comment. Edmund had to shut the door behind him.

Annoyance with Toby seemed to imbue Edmund with the small increment of aggression required for him to complain to the Exchange.

'It must have happened more than thirty times now,' he concluded. 'I mean since I arrived here, about three weeks ago.'

'Are you the subscriber?' asked the Exchange.

'No, Miss Taylor-Smith's the subscriber. But I'm her subtenant.'

'Have we been notified?'

'I don't think so. The arrangement's only temporary.'

'Please send us full particulars or we may have to

discontinue the service.'

'I'll write to you. But these calls—'

'I'm sorry, but if you don't tell us when there's a new subscriber—'

'That's nothing to do with it.'

'If you'll complete a new Application Form, we'll go into the matter further.'

The odd thing was that after that the calls ceased. Edmund never wrote to the Exchange. His inclination was to ask for the telephone to be removed from the studio as soon as possible, but he reflected that this might be unfair to Teddie, as it was understood that telephones were by most people both sought after and hard to obtain, and Teddie probably needed one in order that she might communicate with the parents of her sitters. So Edmund did nothing. None the less the call which came when Toby was there was the last unexplained call Edmund received for a long time.

It was when Christmas approached that the climate of unsuccess in which Edmund nowadays passed too much of his life became annually most intolerable. Every year since the sale of the family's ancient manors and estates had so nearly extinguished his income, he had participated in his aunt's sober Christmas celebrations, if only because she so clearly counted upon him to do so. Now, however, he seemed to have a measure of choice. It was unfortunate that the family débâcle and his past feeling of obligation to his aunt had combined to terminate the previous modest influx of Christmas invitations; but at least he once more had premises where, to the extent his means permitted, he himself could offer hospitality.

Not that the position was unequivocal. He was, after all, only a superior caretaker, with love the consideration in place of cash; and the atmosphere of the studio remained Teddie's entirely. He looked carefully round, before making a list of friends who might join him for Christmas Dinner, bringing, if possible, some festive contributions of their own. Lacking the presence of Teddie to indicate that they were but stock-in-trade (the expression was hers), the pictures of children which covered all the walls made a scheme of decoration that was oppressively insipid. Conspicuously embarrassing were the two biggest works: one a much enlarged reproduction of Reynolds's *The Age of Innocence*, specially photoprinted with the maximum fidelity accessible to science, and intended both as lure to parents and as reassurance that Teddie's muse had strict principles; the other Teddie's own *Children of Mr and Mrs Preston Brook*. This work had been shown, upon Mr Brook's instructions, at a number of exhibitions; after which Mr Brook, a successful manufacturer of vegetable sundries, had so far failed to take possession of his property. The picture hung above the electric heater, and still bore a nameplate, with 'Edwina Taylor-Smith MSPC' in prominent capitals. Edmund could still hear Teddie saying, 'Edwina. It's a noise like a slowly squeaking wheel.'

Twenty-five minutes later Edmund had made little progress with his list. Most of his acquaintances were too rich, too distant, or too obviously provided already with better fare than his. Almost all were married; commonly to spouses who were either unknown or unsuitable. With many he had lost all touch. There were three or four men who were possible, being generally situated much as he was; but Edmund was shocked and disheartened by the specific demonstration that women, other than Teddie, had almost disappeared from his life. None the less a start had to be made if he was not to spend Christmas in solitude. Edmund lifted the telephone and dialled the number of his friend Tadpole, who had been at Oriel with him.

He could hear the bell begin to ring immediately. It continued ringing. Reluctant to acknowledge the evaporation of his first essay, he allowed it to ring long after the time had expired when his friend, who lived in chambers, could be expected to answer. He began to think of the exigent ringing which had marked the unexplained calls he himself had been receiving until about a month before; when the noise stopped and a voice spoke. By then the rhythmic thrumming of the bell in his ear had slightly hypnotised Edmund, and the voice made him start. Still, it seemed to him an unknown voice. And it said something quite unintelligible to him.

'I beg your pardon?'

Again the voice said something unintelligible, but this time longer. Edmund could hear only a rather high-pitched gabbling.

'I wanted to speak to Mr Pusey. Is he in?'

The reply seemed to be two short, sharp sentences, but Edmund could not distinguish a single word. It occurred to him even that the sounds might not be vocal, but might come from the telephone system itself.

'I'd better ring off and try again,' said Edmund, unsure that he was not merely speaking to himself.

There was a much softer gabbling, which diminished into silence.

Edmund rang off.

After a minute or two, he tried again. This time the bell simply rang, and went on ringing. Palpably though depressingly, Tadpole was out.

Edmund made three more calls. One of his friends was spending Christmas in Paris; one would have to let him know later (Edmund was certain that he was hoping for something better to offer itself); and one, like Tadpole, did not reply. Edmund decided to write off to the remaining names on his list. If only he could write, 'Evelyn Laye will be there, so we'll be sure of some good talk!'

During the following seven days, Edmund used the telephone more than was his wont. He began to ring up everyone he had met, however casually, during the previous year. Probably because his contact with them had been so casual, none of them seemed to want to spend Christmas with him. In the course of one of these, usually brief, calls, the somewhat uneasy conversation was at one point intruded upon by a repetition in the background of the indistinct gabbling talk.

'Can you hear that sound?' asked Edmund, interrupting his acquaintance's meagre trickle of explanation.

'What sound, old boy?'

'Like someone talking gibberish.'

'Some woman on a cross-line, I expect.'

'You think it's a woman?'

'How do I know, old boy? But look here, as I was saying, Nell and I – but of course, you've not met Nell – we always go to stay with her people up in Galloway—'

By the end of the week, his friend who had wavered decided against him. Something better had duly appeared. Of those Edmund had written to, one had replied pleading a previous commitment by return of post. The others had not replied at all. Upon Edmund descended a colourless suffocating fog of loneliness.

Suddenly, in his despair, Edmund thought of Queenie. Queenie was a girl of whom he had seen much when, twenty years before, he had first lived in London. Even at that period, though fortified with a private income which sufficed, he had been commonly unsuccessful in reaching the hearts of the girls who really appealed to him; and in retrospect he perceived that Queenie had much in common with Teddie. He had been fond of her, and she had been more than fond of him. In those days Edmund's remarkable linguistic aptitude had served to make smooth the highways of the continent, instead of as now merely bringing him an undependable stipend as a translator; and Queenie had travelled many of the highways with him. She was well formed, and had been carefully nurtured (her baptismal name was Estelle; Queenie had attached itself to her at Newnham, reflection, perhaps, of something within her); and Edmund might well in the end have married her, had not ruin supervened. In fact she had married a man much older than herself, who had almost immediately afterwards fallen into invalidism. During the previous summer, in Victoria Street, Edmund had walked into an old friend of Queenie's named Sefton, a civil servant. They had not met for many years, and their only common subject of conversation was Queenie. Sefton told Edmund that Queenie's husband was now dead, and Edmund wrote down her new address and telephone number.

That number he now dialled for the first time.

'Who is it?' There had been no sound of ringing. The enquiry seemed to come immediately Edmund had dialled the last figure. The voice sounded warm and eager. It surpassed Edmund's recollection.

'You'll be surprised. It's Edmund. How are you, Queenie?'

'Edmund! Edmund St Jude?' It was delightful. There was real joy in her voice.

'I am glad you sound pleased. I wasn't sure . . .'

'You don't know how lonely I've been. No one knows.' Her voice had a slight throb in it which was charming, and also new.

Edmund's own recent experience made it impossible for him to offer easy commiseration. Instead he offered specific aid. 'I want you to dine with me on Christmas Day.'

'Are you giving a party?'

'I meant to originally. But I've thought better of it. Just the two of us, Queenie. If you will.'

She said nothing. Edmund could hear a light intermittent humming on the wire, like the sound of a very distant multitude. He spoke again. 'Please come, Queenie. I'm living in a friend's studio, and—'

She had apparently been gathering resolution, because now she burst out, 'I'm not Queenie.'

Edmund's heart would have fallen further than it did, had it not already premonished him.

'Then I should certainly apologise.'

'For asking me to Christmas Dinner?'

'Yes.'

'To dinner, perhaps. Surely *Christmas* Dinner's entirely different?'

The implication was perhaps too blatant, but Edmund was desperate, and, blatant or not, she sounded pleasant.

'In that case, will you come? Perhaps you would accompany Queenie, if she's not otherwise engaged?'

'Queenie *is* otherwise engaged.'

'Oh.' Edmund was not sure whether to feel disappointed. 'In that case—'

'I'd love to. But I can't.'

'Are you engaged too?'

'Not engaged. I just can't.' There was something a little hysterical about the way she made this plain statement. The humming sound had stopped. No less hysterically she added, 'I'm very sorry . . . Please don't ring off.'

'I'm sorry too,' said Edmund.

'Don't ring off,' she said again. 'I really am sorry.'

'Prove it by coming some other time,' suggested Edmund. 'What about tomorrow night?'

'You've never seen me. You don't know what I look like.'

'I can hear you,' replied Edmund, smiling into the telephone. 'Your voice speaks for you.' He hoped it did.

She made no reply, but suddenly began to sob. There was no doubt about it. Edmund could hear each separate gulping intake of breath. It seemed an unusually good line.

'Well, come some time,' said Edmund, embarrassed and slightly raising his voice.

'I may never be able to.'

It seemed unwise to probe. But Edmund thought that she would continue and explain.

'You've been so kind to me. May I ring you up again?'

'Of course.' Edmund gave her his number, but she seemed too overwrought particularly to take note of it.

'You'll really let me?' Her gratitude was embarrassing, but somehow not ridiculous.

'I might even ring *you*,' Edmund said gallantly.

'No. Just let *me*.'

'What about Christmas Day?'

'Oh *yes*.' She sounded like a schoolgirl.

The humming had resumed.

'And what about Queenie?'

She said something which he could not distinguish.

'Sorry. This humming noise.'

It was now quite loud. He realised that she was gone.

The afternoon post brought a still further rejection of Edmund's hospitality. Face to face with the unpleasing prospect of spending Christmas Day entirely alone, he again dialled the number which Sefton had given him. He reflected that Queenie might have returned by now, or that he might at least find out where she was from her curious friend. This time the bell began to ring at once. It continued to ring. Edmund let it ring for an interminable time before he capitulated. Then he rang up Sefton at his Ministry.

'I haven't actually seen her myself since her husband became so bad. In fact I can't have seen her for more than three years. To tell you the truth, I only got her address off another mutual friend. I meant to look her up, but you know what happens.'

'She doesn't answer the telephone.'

'Christmas, I expect. You know what it is. Sorry I can't help, but if you'll excuse me, I must go to a meeting.'

Civil servants at least have 'meetings', thought Edmund. The pink and blue children on the walls smiled at his plight, winsomely, cheekily, plethorically, according to character. Edmund settled to translating the first chapter of a Dutch work on the technological revolution of our time.

Christmas Day was the first of the many days which Edmund spent waiting for the telephone to ring. The morning post had brought a woolly scarf from his aunt (she had gone to the trouble of procuring one in his college colours), two Christmas cards, and a cablegram from Teddie: LOVELY XMAS HERE ALL LAID ON STOP HAPPIEST GREETINGS DARLING STOP CAN'T WAIT FOR CHRISTMAS NEXT YEAR. After that there was nothing except to attend upon the horrid little bell.

The fact that Edmund was far from sure that it would ring at all made the waiting much worse. He had several times attempted to telephone Queenie's number, but there was never a reply. The worst thing of all was the dreary knowledge that he who had dined tête-à-tête with Fritzi Massary, and been accounted a man of insight and judgement in certain high affairs, was now wholly preoccupied with and dependent upon the favours of an unknown with whom he had upon one single occasion exchanged some unintended remarks upon the telephone. He was fond of Teddie, but no more; and the thousands of miles which separated her from him tended also, to his real regret, to obliterate her as a living image in his thoughts. The unrest which the voice on the telephone had certainly created within him seemed to prove both the tenuousness of poor Teddie's hold on him and the general aridity of his days. It was absurd and out of proportion, but certainly true that the unknown, and the doubt whether he would hear from her again, had affected his nerves and further diminished his already sketchy appetite. On Christmas Day systematic translation seemed impossible. Edmund found it difficult to settle to occupation of any kind, and constantly caught his attention wandering into the evolution of persuasive verbal gambits. Before it was time for lunch, he was wondering whether his Christmas malaise would have been any worse if he had never heard from her at all.

She telephoned just when the fleeting and dreamlike December day had finally subsided into darkness. Although their conversation was disturbed by various cracklings and rumblings on the line, Edmund was astonished to notice, when it was over, that it had continued for at least half an hour. During this period, Edmund and she seemed to discover several points of sympathy. For example, when she said that her name was Nera Condamine, Edmund became certain that she belonged to the ancient and distinguished family of that name, and that she had descended in the world as he had. She took a critical and informed but appreciative interest in his remarks upon the eighteenth-century English poets, about whom he was an authority, and who entered the conversation when he quoted topically from Thomson's 'The Seasons'. Above all, Edmund felt, they had loneliness in common: each of them (he deprecatingly, she eagerly) seemed to throw out feelers of interrogation at which the other clutched. Only questions which were direct and personal she refused to answer: where she lived or why she must remain inaccessible. At the first sign of persistence on Edmund's part, she became hysterical.

'Please don't ask me. Please. Please.'

'Naturally I understand if you'd rather not tell me. I only thought—'

'I'll have to ring off if you ask me.'

'Then I'll certainly not ask you.'

In the end, however, she did let fall one minor fact.

'Of course I understand that very well,' she said. 'Because I'm a painter.'

'Do I know your work?' asked Edmund. All the children on the walls looked interrogative.

'I only paint for myself. There used to be others, but now there's only me.' The telephone croaked in mournful confirmation. Edmund dared not ask what had happened to the others.

By the end of their talk, in fact, a curious change had taken place. Originally it had been Nera, as Edmund at her request had begun to call her, who had repeatedly besought him not to ring off; now the fear lest they stop talking seemed to be primarily his. He perceived the change before he could think about it and account for it. On the whole, by the end of their talk, he was delighted with her.

'I'm glad we have made one another's acquaintance.' (He had almost said 'found one another'.) 'You have transformed Christmas Day for me.'

'We have a lot to say yet,' she replied lightly. 'But we've both time to burn.'

There was a click; without a farewell she was gone; and the Exchange was speaking: 'What number do you want?'

'That same number again,' replied Edmund with unusual resourcefulness.

'What number was it?' asked the Exchange, not

without petulance.

'I'm afraid I don't know. Can't you please trace it? I'd be most obliged if you could.'

'Sorry you've been troubled,' replied the Exchange.

Edmund looked at the electric clock, then sat for a long time staring at the small square electric heater. Thinking it over, he was unable to determine very clearly what indeed they had said to each other which had consumed so much time. There had been the eighteenth-century English poets (it was remarkable indeed to make a casual acquaintance who knew Addison's *Cato*); but otherwise there seemed to have been little but an interchange of remarks which barely amounted to conversation, because his preoccupation had been curiosity, hers a seemingly almost desperate reaching out for a response, for friendship. Edmund was not one of the many men whose response to an emotional need is inversely proportionate to the degree of that need. On the contrary, he tended by temperament to fall in with any demand made upon him. For this among other reasons, he now felt that, despite the queer circumstances, a new and important factor had entered his life. He had certainly been swept and ready . . .

At this time the oddness of the circumstances seemed to Edmund to come within the probable boundaries of such familiar concepts as 'discretion', 'gaining time', or even 'coquetry'. It was not until a later call that Nera's mysterious elusiveness began significantly to perturb him. Because during this particular conversation, in the course of which she took a clearer initiative than before, she stated, most unmistakably, that she loved him; and he, instead of proceeding as if he thought her remark was meant partly or mainly in jest, replied almost seriously, 'I think I love you too.' And when after that, and after sundry strange endearments between these lovers who had never set eyes upon one another and who often found themselves at cross purposes on the telephone, she still refused to say where she lived, Edmund was naturally aghast. He was able to notice, however, that whereas previously his more direct approaches had made her hysterical, she now refused him quite tranquilly.

'Am I, then, never to see you?' he cried.

'I haven't said that.'

'But when?'

'Wait until you can't live without me.'

Edmund checked himself from replying to that.

'Can I ring you?'

'No. No. No. But I'll ring you.'

'When?'

'Whenever I can, darling. Trust me.'

After that there was nothing for Edmund to do but translate from the Dutch, buy his food, and wait for the telephone. The call which had brought about such a striking alteration in the terms of his association with Nera had taken place on the Sunday after Christmas, but on Christmas Day she had not forewarned him, and now she had virtually stated her inability in future ever to do so. None the less, Edmund had something of emotional content to think about and to fill his life: for despairing inertia he had substituted dreams of desire; and for listlessness, eager and unresting expectancy. But there was something else. Edmund could never forget that he had not looked upon the being who so agitated his mind and heart; and never was able altogether to disregard the peril possibly implicit in her reluctance to let him look upon her. Simple sameness of days, therefore, had now for him been replaced by a difficult and intense inner combat.

When next he heard from Nera, however, she so enchanted him with tender words and a previously undisclosed richness of expression that the conflict within him began thereafter to abate, and the telephone more and more to become a simple instrument of bliss, like the soup kitchen to the outcast, or the syringe to the drug addict. When the first defences of convention and restraint had been penetrated, it was surprisingly easy to be intimate into the telephone, very intimate indeed . . .

Inevitably Edmund's various employers began to complain of late deliveries. In one case a decline in standard was also alleged – which was ominous because Edmund knew that few publishers and editors can afford to care much about the quality of a translation. The complaint probably implied some different, unnamed complaint in the background. On the other hand, Edmund now spent less time and money shopping; although previously he had contrived to continue gratifying some few of his more refined and expensive tastes, he now fed more and more on bread, potatoes, and the wholly flavourless 'luncheon meat' which a shop in the next street seemed always to conjure up in Ali Baba-like quantities.

Always it was impossible to tell when Nera would ring next. She might ring at any hour of the twenty-four, although in the main she seemed to favour the early evening or the early hours of the morning. Edmund would sit all day waiting for her, unable to work or eat; then, after she had telephoned at six or seven o'clock, find himself so nervously exhausted by the wasted hours that still he was unable to settle himself and concentrate. And things were, of course, made worse at such times by the complete uncertainty as to when he would hear from her again. For a long time a bad sleeper, he now hardly slept at all; so that when the bell rang at three or four in the morning, he was already taut and wakeful, and rose to answer like an opium-eater going to his brew and knowing as he goes that he is making worse tension for himself in the future.

A minor nuisance was the shortness of the flex. Unlike most women, Teddie had not provided for the telephone to stand by her bed. It stood at the other end of the studio, under the big window, and therefore nearly on the floor. The most inconvenient place possible, Edmund had thought soon after he took possession; especially in that the hanging of Teddie's pictures made it difficult to reposition the bed.

On one occasion Nera suggested an application for a longer flex.

'Don't suppose they'd give me one.'

'I got a longer flex years ago. Do try, darling.' But Edmund did nothing. One reason was that he feared lest Nera ring up while the flex purveyor was in the studio, so that his end of one of their strange indispensible conversations would be overheard and questioned. A worse possibility was that the fitting of the flex might involve the temporary disconnection of the telephone, so that he might miss a call altogether. He was at all times haunted by the possibility that if he were to miss one of Nera's calls, there might never be another one.

He found it impossible to communicate to her such fears as these. He had tried never to let her know even that he waited for hours, in fact all day and all night, for her calls, but sought to leave with her the presumption that it was by happy accident alone that so far she had always found him in. For whereas his attendance was incessant, her calls were remarkably undependable, and, all things considered, not particularly frequent. It was, in fact, this irregularity and infrequency which especially made Edmund shrink from disclosing his servitude to the little black instrument. Against Nera's refusal of information surely essential, he maintained this fiction of freedom.

Somewhere about the end of February began the intrusion of the Chromium Supergloss Corporation. For some reason the telephone began to ring several times a day (on some days as much as twelve or fifteen times), and when Edmund lifted the receiver it was almost always to discover the caller was dialling for the Corporation. Often when he ventured out in quest of his unappetising food, he would hear his telephone ringing from the bottom of the staircase to the studios. The studios were on the fourth floor of the block, with flats below; and had it been a still higher block, Edmund would not have been there, for he much feared heights. He would race up the eight flights of stone steps, his heart beating even more from warring emotions than from the ill-alimented exertion, collapse on the floor under the big window, and find only a customer for the Corporation, peevish at having reached the wrong number. These numerous strangers, Edmund noticed, regularly, when they got that far in their demands, asked for Extension 281. Edmund felt that this extension must be a busy one, but he knew that the Corporation was a large and multifunctional organisation, as was confirmed by the fact that calls for it (commonly still for Extension 281) not infrequently reached him after office hours, and indeed throughout the night.

The incessant 'wrong number' calls tended to convert Edmund from a passive into an active servitor of the telephone. After some weeks of it, he did write a strong letter to the Supervisor; and then, ten days later, received a courteous acknowledgement, printed in a carefully chosen type-face, and with a handwritten postscript, difficult to read but apparently conveying an assurance that this complaint was 'under investigation'. The calls continued as before. This development in Edmund's relationship with the telephone helped to conceal from him for some time that Nera's calls were becoming slowly but markedly fewer than ever.

One morning he noticed that there were buds on the plane trees beneath the studio window, and realised that, although the telephone bell seemed seldom to stop ringing, he had not heard from Nera for a week. Instantly his concentration upon the telephone leapt to and remained at a new intensity. As the tender tide of spring trickled round the grey rocks of London, Edmund became a man eviscerated and absorbed by the squat black monster tethered by its stubby flex.

As soon as possible, he challenged Nera. 'Wrong number' calls had been coming in all that day, varied by one call which was not a wrong number but informed Edmund that he would not be wanted to translate the Italian book on the eighteenth century in England after all. Nera came through at 11:25 P.M. precisely. She was as alluring as ever; roses in Edmund's horizonless desert. Never in retrospect could he at all determine what it was about those bare words of hers, intensified by no accessory charm beyond her attractive voice, which so moved him that he had become as one of Odysseus's sailors. Now he remonstrated and begged.

At first she made light of her remissness and little of Edmund's trouble. He noticed, however, that she did not, as she had originally seemed to do, claim that she had been *unable* to telephone. Convinced that she was tiring of their inadequate and unsatisfying association, he found himself pleading desperately.

'I can't live without you.' The rags and bones of his pride had hitherto prevented him from admitting so much as long as she persisted without explanation in standing so far off.

'Oh,' she said. 'Then it's time for me to come and see you.' Her voice was soft as grass new sprung from the seed.

This fulfilment of her previous vague promise was the last thing that Edmund had expected. He looked round the room for his reflection, but Teddie had managed to smash the mirror on the day she left, and Edmund had not replaced it.

'Yes,' he said in a low voice. 'Any time. When?'

'Very soon. Wait for me. Goodbye.'

After that Nera stopped telephoning Edmund altogether; but the telephone itself began to behave more and more strangely. The calls for the Corporation came as frequently as before; but now there were other calls which were wholly inexplicable. Believing that Nera would surely ring him up to tell him when she was coming, Edmund became more frightened than ever lest he miss a single one of them. He renewed efforts, suspended as unavailing during the first week of his tenancy, to arrange for food to be delivered at his door, but with no more success than then. Now, moreover, his money was fast running out, and the reservoir was by no means being replenished. He tried to arrange credit with the shop in the next street, but was no more successful than when he tried to persuade them to deliver. Edmund had never been apt with shop assistants, and now he felt that he was being eyed with positive hatred. There was a long London heat-wave, premature, opaque, and damp; through which Edmund sat seeing almost nobody, eating almost nothing, and no longer waiting for, but increasingly ministering to the telephone.

Sometimes now he would lift the receiver and hear only a crescendo of terrifying abuse and curses; at other times, groans and screams, as of the dying or the damned. Sometimes unknown voices would conduct hectoring or wheedling conversations with him; and, when he questioned them upon the number they wanted, persist that they wanted his. If he rang off, they would often ring again; threatening, or breaking down. Sometimes there was a cat's-cradle of confused noises, in part, it seemed to Edmund, mechanical, in part simply disembodied and without significance. Several times there was laughter on the line; and once an enormous voice which plunged through Edmund's head, then diminished before plunging again. It was like overhearing an immense ram as it battered its way through mighty resistances and defences. It was even more frightening than the confused noises.

One day the studio bell rang. It was the first occasion for weeks. Edmund, supposing that the shop in the next street might have changed its mind, opened the door. It was Teddie's friend Toby.

'Didn't recognise you, St Jude. It's that beard . . .'

He was inside the studio before Edmund could stop him.

'Sorry to butt in when you're not dressed.'

He looked round for Edmund to offer him a cigarette.

'When's Teddie coming back? Do you hear from

her?' He barely attempted even the surface of politeness.

'I see that you do.' He picked up a heap of air mail
envelopes which stood on Teddie's Benares table.

'Unopened, by God.' Toby was staring at Edmund.
He was now by the window. Edmund was at the door,
willing him to go.

The telephone rang.

Toby lifted the receiver.

'Miss Taylor-Smith's studio.'

Edmund was upon him, fighting like a starving
animal.

'What the hell—'

Toby's free arm wheeled round, pushed rather than
struck: and Edmund was on the floor.

'It's a bloke called Sefton.' Toby was holding out the
receiver. He seemed to bear no malice, but instead of
going, he seated himself in Teddie's big armchair and
found a cigarette of his own.

Sefton was speaking. 'I say, is everything all right?'

'Of course.' Edmund was picking himself up.

'Then in that case I can only say there's something
wrong with your line. I've been trying to get you for
days. I should report it to the Supervisor.'

'I'm sorry.'

'It's all right. But I've got some bad news. Did you
know that Queenie's dead?'

'No, I didn't. When did it happen?'

'I've only just heard about it. From another mutual
friend, you know. But it seems she died about six

months ago. Same trouble as her husband, I understand. It must have been about the time we last met. Strange how small the world is. I just thought I'd let you know, in case you hadn't heard.'

'Thank you,' said Edmund. 'I suppose you don't know who's now got her telephone number?'

'I don't,' said Sefton. 'If it matters, I should ask the Exchange.'

Toby didn't move when Edmund rang off. 'Still having trouble with the telephone?' he asked, filling the stuffy air with cigarette smoke and crossing his legs. 'It was going on when I came here before. Remember?'

'What makes you think—' began Edmund.

'I overheard your friend Sefton. I'm used to the telephone, you know. You're not.'

Edmund was now waiting for it to ring again.

'Things mechanical are like the ladies,' continued Toby. 'You need to understand their ways. If you understand them, they'll do what you want from the start. If you don't, they've got you. And then God help you.'

'Would you mind going?' said Edmund.

'I'll go,' said Toby. 'But first let me get the Supervisor for you.' He rose, returned to the telephone, and dialled o. Edmund, wrought up because the line was again being occupied, would have liked to stop him, but could not see how.

'Get me the Supervisor.'

There was a pause, but only a short one.

Toby gave the number. 'There've been a lot of complaints about delays in getting through. Look into it, will you, and report back as soon as possible?'

Clearly the answer was deferential.

'That's all.' He was about to ring off, but Edmund stopped him.

'I've got something to say myself.'

'Hold on.' Toby handed over the receiver.

'Would you mind leaving me?'

'OK. I'll be back. About Teddie, you know.' His glance was on the heap of unopened letters. 'I happen to love that girl, St Jude.' He went. This time he even shut the door.

'Hullo,' said Edmund.

'Do you wish to make a complaint?' enquired the voice at the other end, fretful with waiting.

'No. I just want to know who's got a certain number.' He mentioned the number which Sefton had given him, and which he would never forget.

'We're not supposed to give information like that,' snapped the voice. 'But hold on.' Plainly some part of Toby's aura remained.

There was a long wait.

'That number's dead.'

'I rang up. And someone answered.'

'Oh, you often get an answer on a dead number.'

'How can that be?'

'Dead person, I suppose.' Whether or not this was meant for facetiousness was unsure because the voice then rang off. Toby would never have been so treated.

None the less, the telephone now ceased to ring, as

had happened on the previous occasion when Edmund had grappled with the Exchange. Instead the studio was filled by day and night with a silent hot airlessness into which the children on the walls stared with assertive insignificance. There were no more callers, no more money, and, Edmund realised, no more letters from Teddie. After a week of silence, Edmund brought himself to tear open the last of the heap. The contents appalled him. Alarmed by his long-continued failure to write, Teddie was on her way home. She had left the New Mexico sanatorium in defiance of a united medical commination. Edmund looked at the date. Clearly she might arrive at any moment.

He dialled the familiar number. One or another kind of climax was inevitable. He could hear the telephone ringing, but faintly and distantly, as if at the end of a very long corridor. Then, although the bell continued dimly audible, he heard a voice.

'At last, darling, at last.'

'Nera! Where have you been?'

'There are terrible difficulties. We have to find a channel, you know.'

'We?' Edmund could still hear the bell, far off and minute. It was as if cushioned by a very thick fog.

'I've been trying to reach you, darling, ever since you came here. Didn't you know?' She laughed coquettishly. 'But here I am! You can ring off.'

As she spoke, the bell stopped ringing, and the line went quite silent.

'The line's gone dead.'

'Already?' She seemed unconcerned.

'Where are you?'

'What frightful-looking children? Put back the receiver, darling. You said the line was dead.'

Edmund's arm slowly dropped, lowering the receiver to his waist, as he fell back against the window. 'Where are you?'

'As the line's already dead, I suppose it doesn't matter whether you put back the receiver or not.' The worst thing was that her voice still sounded exactly as it had sounded over the telephone; attractive though it was, it retained the effect of having been filtered through the Exchange. Edmund let fall the receiver. It crashed to the floor.

'For God's sake, where are you?'

'I'm *here*, darling.' The voice, slightly dehumanised, seemed to come from no particular point. 'You said you couldn't live without me.'

'I can't see you.' The breakfast-food faces of the children smiled brightly at him through the sunshine.

'Not yet, darling. You said you couldn't live without me.'

'What do you mean?'

'Darling, you said you couldn't live without me.' It was exactly like one of the telephone's standard locutions: 'Sorry you've been troubled,' or 'Number, please.'

Edmund placed his hands before his eyes.

'Now there's no need to live without me. Don't you understand? Darling, just look behind you. Over your shoulder.'

Edmund stood rigid.

'Just one look, darling.'

Edmund was trembling all over with hunger and loneliness and terror.

'You must look, you know, darling.' The puppet-like voice seemed nearer. 'If you knew how hard it's been to reach you—'

Edmund was groping for his last charges of will-power.

'Now turn your head, darling.'

There was a rat-tat-tat at the door. Edmund clenched his fists and leapt towards it. He was sobbing as he flung it open.

'Bread.'

The shop in the next street had taken pity on him.

When Teddie arrived home, full of evil surmises, she duly found that Edmund was not only in hospital but on the danger-list. Immediately she put on her pinkest Transatlantic frock, and, accompanied by Toby, a note from whom, left in the studio against her arrival, had given her the news, went to visit him. She found him unbelievably thin, and his face a cadaverous dirty yellow, but immediately she approached, he clutched her hand and croaked, 'I love you, Nera. Forgive me, Nera. Please, please forgive me.'

Teddie withdrew her hand. The nurse was looking at her penetratingly.

Toby shrugged, as if he had known all the time. 'Name mean anything to you?'

'A little,' said Teddie, and changed the subject. Edmund said nothing further, but lay glazed and panting.

'I think you'd better go now, Miss Taylor-Smith. You have your own health to take care of.' Toby must have told her.

'He looks like a poet,' said Teddie. 'Will he get better?'

'Naturally we shall do all we can.'

'No, Toby. It's quite impossible. She can't even paint. Not even as well as me.' All the children smiled benignly; Toby did not care how well or badly Teddie painted.

'Nothing like that's impossible. Particularly not with a cove like St Jude.'

'Well, *this* is impossible.' She thought for a moment. 'Look, Toby. If you still doubt me, I'll introduce you.'

'OK by me. I'm only trying to save you from making a big mistake.'

'She's always at home in the evening.'

On the way to Nera Condamine's flat, which was in another part of London, he put his arm round her.

'Of course I know she was lonely.'

'There you are.'

'She used to ring me up at all hours. She always wanted me to ring her back. Where she worked. Some number or other – Extension 281.'

'Now that does cut out St Jude. Never known a chap so scared of the telephone.'

Teddie wriggled herself free for the moment. 'I'm going to introduce you anyway. You were at the hospital, and this must be stopped.'

'What's that on the floor?'

They had been standing for several minutes in the dim passage, unavailingly manipulating Miss Condamine's small brass knocker. The design was a jester's head.

'Telephone Directory,' reported Toby. 'A to D volume with her in it. Issued in July.'

They looked at one another.

'They bring it round, you know. If there's no answer, they leave it.'

Teddie raised the flap of the letter-box.

'Toby!' Now she clutched his arm.

Toby squared up to the door. 'Shall I?'

Teddie was coughing. But she nodded emphatically.

Both door and lock were cheap and nasty; and Toby was through in a minute. Inside the sun came mistily through the drawn magenta blinds. It was simpler to switch on the light.

The details it revealed were most horrible. Dressed in decaying party pyjamas of cerise satin, and regarded by several academic but aphrodisiac studies of the nude, lay on a chaise-longue the elderly body of Miss Condamine, a bread knife in one mouldering, but still well-shaped hand. With the knife she appeared for some reason to have amputated the telephone from the telephone system; but none the less the unusually long flex was wound tightly round her again and again and again from neck to ankles.

Growing Boys

What, you deny the existence of the supernatural, when there is scarcely a man or
woman alive who has not met with some
evidence for it!

Lucien

It is, indeed, singular that western man,
while refusing to place credence in anything he cannot see, while rejecting absolutely omens, prophecies, and visions,
should at the same time, as he so often
does, deny the evidence of his own eyes.

Osbert Sitwell

The first time it occurred to poor Millie that something
might really be wrong was, on the face of it, perfectly
harmless and commonplace.

Uncle Stephen, the boys' great-uncle, had found the
words, conventional though the words were. 'You're
much too big a boy to make messes like that, Rodney.
And you too, of course, Angus.'

'Angus wasn't making a mess,' Rodney had retorted.
'There's no need to bite his head off too.'

'Keep quiet, boy, and clean yourself up,' Uncle

Stephen had rejoined, exactly as if he had been father to the lads, and a good and proper father also.

In reality, however, Uncle Stephen was a bachelor.

'I'll take you up to the bathroom, Rodney,' Millie had intervened. 'If you'll excuse us for a few moments, Uncle Stephen.'

Uncle Stephen had made no effort to look pleasant and social. Rather, he had grated with irritation. When Millie took Rodney out of the room, Uncle Stephen was glaring at her other son, defying him to move, to speak, to breathe, to exist except upon sufferance.

It was certainly true that the boys lacked discipline. They were a major inconvenience and burden, over-shadowing the mildest of Millie's joys. Even when they were away at school, they oppressed her mind. There was nowhere else where they were ever away, and even the headmaster, who had been at London University with Phineas, declined to accept them as boarders, though he had also declined to give any precise reason. When Millie had looked very pale, he had said, as gently as he could, that it was better not to enter into too much explanation: experience had taught him that. Call it an intuition, he had experienced. Certainly it had settled the matter.

She had supposed that, like so many things, the head-master's decision might have related to the fact that the boys were twins. Twins ran in her family, and the two other cases she knew of, both much older than she was, did not seem to be happy twins. None the less, until the coming of Rodney and Angus, and though she would have admitted it to few people, she had always wished she had a twin herself: a twin sister, of course. Mixed twins were something especially peculiar. She had never herself actually encountered a case, within the family, or without. She found it difficult to imagine.

Now, Millie no longer wished for a twin. She hardly knew any longer what she wished for, large, small or totally fantastic.

All that notwithstanding (and, of course, much, much more), Millie had never supposed there to be anything very exceptional about her situation. Most mothers had troubles of some kind; and there were many frequently encountered varieties from which she had been mercifully spared, at least so far. Think of Jenny Holmforth, whose Mikey drank so much that he was virtually unemployable! Fancy having to bring up Audrey and Olivia and Proserpina when you had always to be looking for a part-time job as well, and with everyone's eyes on you, pitying, contemptuous, no longer even lascivious!

But upstairs in the bathroom, it came to Millie, clearly and consciously for the first time, that the boys were not merely too big to make messes: they were far, far too big in a more absolute sense. Rodney seemed almost to fill the little bathroom. He had spoken of Uncle Stephen biting his head off. That would have been a dreadful transaction; like . . . But Millie drew back from the simile.

Of course, for years no one could have failed to notice that the boys were enormous; and few had omitted to refer to it, jocularly or otherwise. The new element was the hypothesis that the irregularity went beyond merely social considerations. It existed in a limbo where she and her husband, Phineas, might well find themselves virtually alone with it, and very soon.

Millie had read English Language and Literature and knew of the theory that Lady Wilde and her unfortunate son had suffered from acromegaly. That appeared to have been something that ran in Lady Wilde's family, the Elgees; because Sir William had been quite stunted. But of course there were limits even to acromegaly. About Rodney and Angus, Millie could but speculate.

When all the clothes had been drawn off Rodney, she was appalled to think what might happen if ever in the future she had to struggle with him physically, as so often in the past.

Re-entering the drawing room, Rodney pushed in ahead of her, as he always did.

Angus seized the opportunity to charge out, almost knocking her down. He could be heard tearing upstairs: she dreaded to think for what. It mattered more when her respected Uncle Stephen was in the house.

She looked apologetically at Uncle Stephen and managed to smile. When her heart was in it, Millie still smiled beautifully.

'Rodney,' roared Uncle Stephen, 'sit down properly, uncross your legs, and wait until someone speaks to you first.'

'He'd better finish his tea,' said Millie timidly.

'He no longer deserves anything. He's had his

chance and he threw it away.'

'He's a very big boy, Uncle Stephen. You said so your-self.'

'*Too* big,' responded Uncle Stephen. 'Much *too* big.'

The words had been spoken again, and Millie knew they were true.

Uncle Stephen and Millie talked for some time about earlier days and of how happiness was but a dream and of the disappearance of everything that made life worth living. They passed on to Phineas's lack of prospects and to the trouble inside Millie that no doctor had yet succeeded in diagnosing, even to his own satisfaction. Millie offered to show Uncle Stephen round the garden, now that it had almost stopped raining.

'It's quite a small garden,' she said objectively.

But Uncle Stephen had produced his big, ticking watch from his waistcoat pocket, which sagged with its weight. There was this sagging pocket in all his waist-coats. It helped to confirm Uncle Stephen's identity.

'Can't be done, Millie. I'm due back for a rubber at six and it's five-eleven already.'

'Oh, I'm terribly sad, Uncle Stephen. Phineas and I have raised the most enormous pelargoniums. Mainly luck, really. I should so much like you to see them.' Then Millie said no more.

'My loss, Millie dear. Let me embrace my sweet girl before I go.'

He crushed her for a minute or two, then stepped back, and addressed Angus.

'Stand up and give me your hand.'

Angus soared upwards but kept his hands to himself.

'I mean to shake your hand,' bawled Uncle Stephen, in his quarter-deck manner; even though he had never mounted a quarter-deck, except perhaps on Navy Day.

Angus extended his proper hand, and Uncle Stephen wrenched it firmly.

When Millie and he were for a moment alone together in the little hall, something that could not happen often, Uncle Stephen asked her a question.

'Have you a strap? For those two, I mean.'

'Of course not, Uncle Stephen. We prefer to rely on persuasion and, naturally, love.'

Uncle Stephen yelled with laughter. Then he became very serious. 'Well, get one. And use it frequently. I've seen what I've seen in this house. I know what I'm talking about. Get two, while you're about it. The Educational Supply Association will probably help you.'

'Phineas will never use anything like that.'

'Then you'd better consider leaving him, Millie dear, because there's trouble coming. You can always make a home with me and bring the boys with you. You know that, Millie. There's a welcome for you at any time. Now: one more kiss and I must vamoose.'

As soon as the front door shut, Angus, who had been watching and listening to the scene through the hole the twins had made in the upstairs woodwork, almost fell on her in every sense.

Back in the drawing room she saw that Rodney, released from thrall, had resumed his tea, and had already eaten everything that had been left. Noting this, Angus began to bawl.

It might be all right later, but at that hour Millie was afraid lest the neighbours intervene: Hubert and Morwena Ellsworthy, who were ostentatiously childless.

'Don't cry, Ang,' said Rodney, putting his arm tightly round Angus's shoulder. 'Uncle Stephen always hogs the lot. You know that.'

Angus's rage of weeping failed to abate.

Rodney gave him a tender and succulent kiss on the cheek.

'We'll go to the Lavender Bag,' he said. 'I'm still hungry too. I think I've got the worms. I expect you have as well. Race you. Ready. Steady . . . Go.'

As the race began on the spot, the picking up and clearing up for Millie to do were not confined to the tea things.

The Lavender Bag was a café at the other end of The Parade. It was run by the Misses Palmerston, four of them. It was a nice enough place in its way, and useful for the release through long lunchtimes and teatimes of high spirits or low spirits, as the case might be. Millie went there often, and so did her friends, though soon she would have no friends. Some of them distrusted her already because they knew she had a degree.

Now Millie suddenly set down the cake tray she was holding. She took care not to let the large crumbs fall to the carpet.

'Oh God,' gulped Millie, sinking to the edge of the settee and almost to her knees. 'God, please, God. What have I done to be punished? Please tell me,

God, and I'll do something else.'

Only some outside intervention could possibly avail.

She had never been very good at having things out with anyone, not even with girl friends, and Phineas had undoubtedly weakened her further. All the same, something simply had to be attempted, however recurrent, however foredoomed.

To make a special occasion of it, she put on a dress, even though it had to be a dress that Phineas would recognise: at least, she supposed he must. The boys were still rampaging about at the Lavender Bag, which in the summer remained open for light snacks until 8 P.M. They liked to run round the tables wolfing everything that others had left on plates and in saucers. The Misses Palmerston merely looked on with small, lined smiles. Simultaneously the boys were normal children and flashing young blades.

'Why *should* you feel at the end of your tether?' enquired Phineas. 'After all, every day's your own. Certainly far more than my days are mine.'

If only one could give him a proper drink before one attempted to talk seriously with him; that is, to talk about oneself!

'It's the boys, Phineas. You don't know what it's like being at home with them all day.'

'The holidays won't last for ever.'

'After only a week, I'm almost insane.' She tried to rivet his attention. 'I mean it, Phineas.'

Millie knew extremely well that she herself would be

far more eloquent and convincing if Phineas's abstinence had not years ago deprived her too, though with never the hint of an express prohibition, but rather the contrary. When she was reading, she had learned of the Saxons never taking action unless the matter had been considered by the council, first when sober and then when drunk. It was the approach that was needed now.

'What's the matter with the boys this time?' asked Phineas.

Millie twitched. 'They're far too tall and big. How long is it since you looked at them, Phineas?'

'Being tall's hardly their fault. I'm tall myself and I'm their father.'

'You're tall in a different way. You're willowy. They're like two great red bulls in the house.'

'I'm afraid we have to look to *your* family for that aspect of it. Consider your Uncle Nero, if I may venture to mention him.'

'I don't like him being called that.'

'But you can't deny he's bulky. There's no one of his build anywhere up my family tree, as far as I am aware. For better or for worse, of course. There are more troublesome things than sturdiness, especially in growing boys.'

Millie did not have to be told. She had often reflected that Phineas, seeping tiredly over the settee at the end of the day's absence, was like an immensely long anchovy, always with the same expression at the end of it; and in the next bed it was, of course, far worse.

'Then you're not prepared to help in any way?

Suppose I have a breakdown?'

'There's be no danger of that, Millie, if only you could persuade yourself to eat more sensibly.'

'Perhaps you could persuade your sons of that?'

'I shall try to do when they are older. At present, they are simply omnivorous, like all young animals. It is a stage we go through and then try to pass beyond.'

'Then you do admit that they *are* like animals?'

'I suppose it depends partly upon which animals.'

Millie knew perfectly well, however, that for her they were not like animals, or not exactly; and despite what she had said to Phineas. They were like something far more frightening.

'Uncle Stephen was very upset by them before you came home.'

Phineas merely smiled at her. He had all but finished the lactose drink which he consumed every evening before their meal.

'Uncle Stephen said we ought to see what discipline could do.'

'Discipline would hardly prevent the boys growing up,' observed Phineas.

And it was still a matter of hours before it was even sunset.

The boys could be heard approaching in what had become their usual way. They stumbled in through the open French window.

'Got any good grub in your pockets, Dad?' shouted Rodney.

With a smile, Phineas produced a dun-coloured bag

of huge, gluey toffees; something he would never have put into his own mouth.

The boys fell into chairs and began to pass the bag from hand to hand.

'Mum going to cook supper soon?'

'I expect so, Angus.'

'What's it going to be, Dad?'

'Better ask her, Rodney.'

It was not, as he knew, that he aimed to instil manners. It was merely that he could not care less.

One thing Millie had particularly resented was that every single evening she had to produce two very different meals, and then be silently sneered at if she herself chose the more exciting one, or consumed any scrap of it.

Now Millie was past resentment. Panic had taken its place.

'We need food, Dad. You don't want us to outgrow our strength.'

'Besides, we're twins,' said Angus.

It was hard to see where that came in, but Millie knew quite well that somewhere it very much did.

Everything was fundamentally her own fault. She was perfectly well aware of that. Everything always is one's own fault.

'Our reports come yet, Dad?'

'I don't think so, Rodney.'

'You can't put them on the fire this time, because it's summer, but you *will* put them down the *topos*?'

'Unopened, Dad?' put in Angus. He was half on his

feet again, and redder than ever.

'*Unopened*, Dad,' insisted Rodney, though perhaps more calmly.

'Torn up, if you like,' said Angus.

'We shall have to see,' said Phineas. 'Shan't we? When the time comes, that is.'

He rose from the settee and walked quietly from the room.

'Oh Mum,' said Rodney, jumping up and down. 'Do get on with it.'

The patience of the young is soon exhausted.

'We're hungry,' Angus confirmed. 'Remember, we only had salad for lunch. Muck, we called it.'

It had been a cut-up which Phineas had not eaten the previous evening. One could not simply throw it away; and Phineas would never accept such things unless they were completely fresh. It was the trouble with food of that kind that no one ever wanted it all, and it then became useless. Nor was the household made of money. Phineas not only lacked prospects: he lacked a suitable income also. Unhappily, Phineas was an intellectual without either creativity or judgement. Millie had realised it even during those early days in the Camargue, when Rodney and Angus were being conceived.

In the kitchen, she was shaking so much she gashed the index finger of her left hand. It would, of course, have mattered more if she had been lefthanded, as were Phineas and the boys; but it was a nasty enough cut, which bled far too much, so that fair-sized gouts fell on the newly prepared vegetable matter, which thereupon

157

had to be slowly picked over a further time. Blood oozed through Millie's handkerchief and spotted the dress she had specially put on.

At the same time, the big fry-up for the boys was beginning to run out of fat.

In the end, they came charging in. Millie was weeping, of course, and in more and more of a muddle. Once, she had never muddled things, but quite the contrary: perhaps that was why she wept now.

'For God's sake, Mum! We're hungry. We told you.'

'Hungry as hunters.'

What had that originally meant? A kind of horse? A kind of tiger? A kind of man?

'What is it, Mum? What are we getting?'

'Chops and liver and bacon and things,' replied Millie in a very low voice, possibly inaudible above the sizzle. 'I've hurt my finger.'

'We could eat the entire animal,' said Angus.

Phineas always lay on his bed while a major meal was in preparation, and Millie had to ascend and summon him, because the boys simply did not do it, however often she asked them.

Four days later, Millie's finger was as bad as ever, and her left hand almost unusable. She knew that incurable illness often first manifested itself through minor injuries which failed to clear up.

'Oh Mum, do get better!' admonished Angus at breakfast when she let slip the teapot.

'It's entirely a matter of eating the right things,' observed Phineas mildly, 'though, naturally, it'll take some months before you can expect to enjoy the benefits.'

Phineas himself was eating a small quantity of muesli in skim milk. He always used a tiny teaspoon for such purposes.

The flap of the front-door letter-box was heard: presage everywhere of Charon's final shoulder-tap, bone against bone.

The boys made a dash, as they did each day; but this time Millie had reached the door of the room before them. She stood there facing them.

'We're going for the post, Mum.'

'I'm going for it this morning. You both sit down, please.'

'It may be our reports, Mum.'

'I'm going this morning, Angus.'

They were only a foot or two away, but before they could lay hands on her, she had not merely whipped open the door but also snatched the key out of the lock, flashed from the room, and managed to lock the door on the other side: all this with the real use of one hand only.

For the moment she had proved as effective as she used to be, but there had been something strange about the incident; which had all begun with a vivid dream she had had the previous night, so vivid that she remembered it (or imagined it) still, and in detail: a small dream really, but prophetic.

For the moment Phineas had been left to manage the two roaring boys. The French window was in the drawing room, but soon the boys would be out through the dining-room casements and making mischief of some kind. Happily, the big drawing-room window was never opened until after breakfast. The boys had never as yet intentionally smashed their way in or out, but Millie dreaded to see their huge faces gazing at her, diminishing her, from the world outside.

None the less, Millie paused for a moment, and quite consciously.

Much was at stake if her dream could be taken at all seriously.

It could. Millie had advanced into the hall and the delivery had proved to consist of two accounts rendered and a packet with the school crest upon the envelope.

Millie went back into the drawing room, and, sitting down, even straightened the crease in her jeans. Then, while in the locked room the abominable hubbub raged on, she calmly opened the boys' reports.

Reports they had been in her dream, and dire ones: at once a burden, but also, in certain ways, a release, or a faint hope of release. The actual packet proved, however, simply to contain a letter, together with some appeal forms for reconditioning the school chapel. The letter, addressed to Phineas, was from the deputy headmaster. Millie read it.

Dear Mr Morke,

I know you will forgive my writing on behalf of the Headmaster, who has unfortunately been in Hospital since the middle of the Spring Term, as you may possibly have heard from your Sons.

I very much regret to tell you that the Trustees, to whom the matter has been referred in the absence of the Headmaster, take the view that no useful purpose would be served by the return of your Sons to the School at the commencement of the Term now ahead, that is to say, the Autumn Term.

It is the view of the Trustees, in which I am bound to say I fully concur, that the Boys are too physically mature to benefit from the ordinary course of Tuition in Class, however excellent. Perhaps they may be regarded as outside and beyond the normal school disciplines.

In the circumstances, there would seem no advantage to our delivering the usual Reports upon the conduct of the Boys during the Summer Term, just past. Doubtless you will have drawn your own conclusions from the Reports relating to previous Terms, and will scarcely be surprised by the Decision which the Trustees have reached.

It is the custom of the School to extend Best Wishes to all its Old Boys when finally they move towards New Fields of Endeavour; and I am sure that the Headmaster, with whom, as I understand, you are on terms of long-standing and personal friendship, would wish me to make no exception in the present cases.

May I venture to remind you of the Outstanding Account in respect of the Boys' attendance during the Summer Term, and including a number of important Extras? The Bursar requests me to take this opportunity of remarking that he would be most grateful for a settlement during the next seven days, as he is keeping his Books open for this single item, and is being pressed by the School's Honorary Accountants. I am sure you will understand.

Yours sincerely,
PHILIP DE SODA
(REVD MA, BD)

Millie rose, unlocked the door, and re-entered the dining room, holding the letter high above her head.

'There are no reports, Phineas. 'They've been expelled.'

When the boys had been much younger, it might have availed to hold the letter up there, but now it was pointless, because they were far taller than she was, as well as in every way more brawny. The letter was out of her hands in a flash.

It was very unlikely that they could understand it, and doubtful if they could even read all of it, but she herself had provided the clue, and at least they could take in the signature.

'It's the Sod!' cried Angus. 'The Sod wrote it.'

'Give it here,' commanded Rodney. Within seconds the floor was littered with tiny scraps of paper, and the boys were standing shoulder to shoulder against the world, completely obscuring the framed photograph of their mother on a horse.

'What are you going to do now, Phineas?' enquired Millie.

Phineas was, as always, making a point of being undisturbed. He continued to chase the last particles of saturated muesli with his toy teaspoon.

'Well?' enquired Millie. 'Our sons have been expelled from their school. You'll have to do something with them.'

'Was the term *expulsion* actually employed in the letter?'

'Of course not. Schoolmasters don't use it nowadays. They're afraid of libel actions.'

'Well then, we mustn't exaggerate. It's not at all uncommon for a headmaster to reach the view that a boy would fare better in some other school. Nowadays, there's no question of a stigma at all. The change in itself is often entirely beneficial.'

He drew a crispbread from the packet, broke it in half, returned one half to the packet, and began to break up the other into reasonably symmetrical pieces on his plate.

Each of the boys now had his arm round the other's shoulder, in the style of Tweedledum and Tweedledee. But they had no other resemblance to Tweedledum and Tweedledee

'If you don't do something, Uncle Stephen will,' said Millie.

The boys extended their thick red tongues at her, but Phineas's eye was glancing at the *Guardian* which lay on the table for him alone to read and take to work.

Millie went upstairs, locked the door of the bedroom, and began looking through her old address book. It had little to offer, apart from varying shades and intensities of nostalgia and regret.

She lay down on her unmade bed, turning her back on Phineas's unmade bed.

She could not think while the boys were in the house, or, for different reasons, Phineas either.

She could hear birds singing, and, from the next house, screeching music for early housewives. She knew that they were supposed to choose the records for themselves.

Then, duly, there was a din of the boys leaving. At the moment their craze was to do something with dogs in the local wood – any dogs, as she understood it.

She had no idea what it was that they did, nor did she wish to know. The wood was of course deserted on a weekday morning, apart from the usual misfits straying about, and unlikely to present much of a problem to boys such as Rodney and Angus.

Millie gave it a little longer, lest she walk into Phineas then she unlocked the door and went down.

Phineas had departed for work, with all the others. She had feared that the letter from Mr de Soda might have held him back. She began to collect the torn pieces into a small plastic bag that was lying about, because she proposed to keep them. It was a surprisingly long job: she could not but remember that the mills of God tear exceeding small. Then she began to clear up, and, later, to wash up. She could count on a little tranquillity until the boys returned, raging for their midday meal.

But the bell rang, and then there was that same flop from the letter-box: somewhat less menacing, however, when it is presumably a matter not of a postal delivery, but more probably of a harmless circular.

Millie went out quite calmly. Duly, it was a publicity leaflet, a throwaway.

Your Fortune is in your Hands
Consult
Thelma Modelle

NOW

Modern Palmistry
Absolutely Private and Confidential
Normally no need for an appointment
Nothing spooky   Nothing embarrassing

4 The Parade

'There is no reason why the human hand
should not provide as good a guide to
individual destiny as any other.'

The concluding quotation was unascribed. Millie fancied that it came from Aldous Huxley. She seemed to remember encountering something of the kind when trying to read one of Huxley's works at Oxford. The leaflet was inexpensively produced in simple black on simple white. It was quite small.

Millie had almost finished her immediate chores.

There was little incentive to embellish the tasks. She stuffed the bag of torn-up paper into her handbag, because she could think of nothing else to do with it at the moment and set forth for 4 The Parade. Reason and careful thought had proved alarmingly unfruitful. The moment had come to give the subliminal a trial; if that was the applicable word. An omen was an omen, and there were few of them.

Number 4 The Parade was her own fish shop, selling rough vegetables and packet cheese as well. She had never previously had occasion to heed the number. Upstairs had lived the rheumatism lady, who went round all the old folk in her little car. Millie was aware that lately the rheumatism lady had moved to a proper clinic, paid for by the ratepayers, because everyone was talking about it. Now at the foot of the stairs there was an arrow, with a curious curve in it pointing upwards, and the name THELMA MODELLE newly painted at the heart of it in grey. Plain THELMA would, perhaps, have been too much like an unregulated fairground; and changing times were rendering the title 'Madame' obsolete even in such cases as this. There was nothing to do but ascend.

Thelma Modelle came out on to the little landing. Her jeans were pale green and she wore a sleeveless grey jumper which looked as if it were woven from used raffia. As promised, there was to be no attempt at formality or mystification.

Thelma Modelle had a smooth dark brown mop, fall-

ing over one side of her angular, sallow face; and the
enormous, rather empty eyes of the seer or pythoness.

Indeed, at first she stared at Millie for a perceptibly
long time without uttering a word.

'Well, come in,' she said at last, as if there had been
some demur.

They were in the rheumatism lady's small sitting
room, though already it looked much more run down.
The rheumatism lady's little water-colours had been replaced by wall cards bearing emblems of the zodiac;
somewhat stained, and by no means a complete set.
There was a round black table in the centre of things,
with two black composition chairs opposite one another.

'Sit down,' said Thelma Modelle, still a little petulantly, 'and call me Thelma.'

Millie sat, as one does at such times; but Thelma continued to stand. She was observing Millie.

'Would you prefer to smoke?'

'I've given it up. My husband made me stop it.'

'Then why are you carrying a packet of Players in
your handbag?'

Millie felt that she had turned pale and puce at the
same time.

'It's an unopened packet. I suppose you can see that
too.'

'One thing I can't see is why you're here. What are
you looking for?'

'Your leaflet came through my door. Just this moment, in fact. So will you please read my palm, or

whatever it is you do?' Millie extended her hand across the table.

'That's the wrong one,' said Thelma. 'But never mind. It would be no good with you in any case. I'll see what the cards have to say.'

She picked up a working pack from the mantel behind her. Millie would have supposed there would be shuffling, perhaps cutting, certainly a careful and symmetrical laying out. But all Thelma did was chuck six or seven apparently random cards across the surface of the table.

'You're in trouble right enough,' said Thelma.

'What sort of trouble?' asked Millie steadily.

'You'll know the details best.'

'What's going to happen about it?'

'It's going to get worse.'

'Yes, I suppose it's bound to do that.'

'I should try running away, if I were you. Hide. Change your name. Change your appearance. Change everything.'

'Join the raggle-taggle gypsies, in fact?' After all, one must at times seek some proportion in things.

'Please!' exclaimed Thelma. 'I *am* a gypsy.'

'I'm so sorry.' But that was wrong too. 'I wasn't meaning to be rude.'

'The gypsies wouldn't *have* you.'

'Why ever not?' But Millie was by now hardly surprised, hardly capable of surprise.

'You're marked.'

'In what way? How am I marked? You don't mean

168

that lacrosse accident?'

'No. Not that.'

Millie reflected silently for a moment. If Thelma Modelle would sit down, as consultants normally do, it could be that much easier.

Millie spoke again. 'Please tell me more.'

'The cards won't go any further.'

'Well, something else then.' After all, there was a crystal on the mantel too, though Millie had never seen one in her life before (it was smaller than she had supposed); and some sort of large, shapeless thing leaning against the wall.

'If you want to know more, it will have to be sex.'

Millie had heard at Oxford of 'sex magic' and its alleged dangers.

'I don't think I want that,' she said.

'That's quite all right,' said Thelma rather nastily. 'I shouldn't advise you to find out more anyway.'

'Why ever not? Is it really as terrible as all that?'

'It might make you mad.'

The familiar Shakespearian phrase was really too much. Millie rose to her feet.

'How much do I owe you?'

Thelma's expression had become very odd.

'No money. Just look in again. While you still have time of your own.'

'You've made a mistake there,' said Millie. 'The boys aren't going back. They've been expelled.'

'I've never claimed to be right every time.'

Millie managed to smile a little. 'Please take some

money. I have profited by your frankness.'

'Not from you,' said Thelma. 'I've told you what you can do.'

'I'll think about it,' said Millie.

'You can come and live here if you've nowhere else to go.'

'I can go to my Uncle Stephen. Actually he's pressing me.'

'You can do whatever you like,' said Thelma.

There was a scuffing up the stairs, and another client appeared. It was Dawn Mulcaster, mature, frustrated, and twittery as ever. She and Millie exchanged very faint smiles but no words. Millie sped downwards.

The curious thing was that, though nothing could have been more depressing and foreboding than Thelma's insights, yet Millie felt noticeably more buoyant than on her outward journey. As in the matter she had last night dreamed of, the burden was at the same time a release, or a faint hope of release. She was even able to muse smilingly upon a fortune-teller's obvious need of a receptionist; and upon the positively comical discrepancy between this particular fortune-teller's publicity and her performance. Perhaps the discrepancy was mainly in tone. All the same, surely the interview had been 'spooky' in the extreme? Dawn Mulcaster would certainly be finding it so. Millie felt that she had done better than Dawn was likely to be doing. In fairness to Thelma Modelle's publicity person, Millie had to acknowledge that she did not feel in the least 'embarrassed'.

She stopped in the street for a moment. A more precise thought had struck her. Her cut finger was completely healed. Somehow she had even parted with the unpleasant bandage. She smiled, and continued homewards.

The boys stormed back, wolfed their food without a word to Millie, and stormed out again.

Millie washed up after the three of them; circulated round The Parade and The Avenue, shopping, meditating; put together two totally different evening meals; and then went upstairs to lie on her bed, in order to prepare for another confrontation with Phineas. She must keep up the pressure or go mad, as Thelma Modelle had predicted.

Indeed, when Millie fell asleep, she found she was dreaming of Thelma's establishment, where she, Millie, now appeared to have a job of some kind, as she was seated at the toilet table in what had been the rheumatism lady's bathroom, and sorting through hundreds, perhaps thousands, of invoices in the desperate hope of finding her own. The invoices were on paper of different sizes and textures, and in many different handwritings, mostly illegible. Millie was amazed by the mental processes that must lie behind the ways in which many of the bills were laid out. Only those which had been drafted by Uncle Stephen were fully orderly. When Millie awoke, it occurred to her to wonder whether Thelma herself could write at all, or whether she relied mainly on bluff, as did Rodney and Angus though no one ever dared to mention it.

There was the noise of creeping about downstairs. Then Phineas's voice floated up the stairwell: 'Millie!' She shrivelled. 'Millie, where are you?'

It was far, far too early for his return. Could he have lost his job? That might be yet another burden which was not a burden entirely, but very faintly a forerunner.

Millie threw off the eiderdown, pulled on a jacket, and sauntered downstairs.

Phineas was positively prancing from room to room. It was impossible that he could have been promoted, because, in his position, there was no real promotion. His step seemed light and gay, as with the man in the ballad.

'I've been adopted!' cried Phineas, unable to contain himself until she had reached the ground floor, terra firma.

'Whatever for?'

'As Liberal candidate, of course. At North Zero.'

'Where's that?'

'It's in Cornwall and Andrew MacAndrew says I should have every chance.'

She had been perfectly well aware that Phineas was frequenting the local Liberal Association and bringing their literature home. It was one of various activities of his that resulted in her being so often alone with the boys.

'Does the Party find the money for your deposit, or do you have to do it?'

'I haven't the slightest idea. I haven't thought about it.'

'Perhaps the boys can go down and canvass for you?'

'They're too young, as you can perfectly well imagine for yourself. I'm afraid I shall have to sacrifice much of my family life, and leave the boys more in the hands of their mother. I notice that you haven't congratulated me, Millie.'

'If it's what you want, I'm pleased for you, Phineas. Provided, that is, that you find a new school for the boys before you set out.'

'I haven't been able to think much about that, as you can imagine. I feel it is something their mother can perfectly well do for them, if the necessity should arise.'

'I can and shall do nothing of the kind, Phineas. Finding a school for boys like that is the father's job. I mean it, Phineas.'

She was almost glowing with resolution. She realised that to display moral qualities demands practice, just as much as intellectual and manual qualities. She had never really attended when, down the years, such truths had been hammered into her. But she also knew that much of her relied upon the boys being out of the house.

'I had hoped you might be pleased for me,' said Phineas, entering the sitting room, and draping himself. 'Could I have my lactose, please?'

'It's too early. It's only just past teatime.' Phineas eschewed tea, because of the tannin, which affected both his colon and his autonomic structure.

'I'm going to get myself a cup of tea,' said Millie. 'And then I want to go on talking seriously.'

In her heart, she was not in the least surprised to find, when she returned, that Phineas had taken himself off. Perhaps he had gone out to look for the boys. He liked to delude himself that he could 'join in' their play, though Millie knew better, knew that he was accepted on the very thinnest of sufferance, for short periods only, and only for ulterior reasons. In the boys' eyes, there was very little to choose between Phineas's status and hers. She knew that, even if he did not.

Millie took her little tray upstairs, locked the bedroom door, took off her jacket once more, and wriggled beneath the eiderdown. She had brought up the Family Size packet of Playmate biscuits, really meant for the boys.

But, contrary to expectation, Phineas drifted back in no time. Elation at the thought of the new and more fulfilling life that lay before him had probably made him restless. Soon, he was tapping at their bedroom door.

'Let me in, please.'

'I'm having a rest. I'll come out when it's time for your supper.'

'Where are the boys?'

'In the wood with the dogs, as far as I know.'

'It might be better if they were encouraged to stay more in their own home.'

'That's their father's job.'

'Millie, what are you doing in there?'

'I'm lying down, and now I'm going back to sleep.' She knew that by now there was not a hope of it, though she had spoken as positively as she could.

So positively, indeed, that there was quite a pause. Then Phineas said, 'I might as well have my lactose now.

I've had a lot to think about today.'

Grumpily, Millie emerged. Rest and peace had gone, as well as slumber.

'Let me carry the tray,' said Phineas. 'It's right that I should do these things when I'm here.'

He was not at all used to the work, and had to descend the stairs very slowly, like a stick-insect.

'What is going to happen to your job?' asked Millie, as soon as the tray was on the sink-surround, more or less in safety.

'That must come second. In life, one has to make such decisions.'

'Meanwhile, what pays the boys' school fees? They won't have them at the ordinary local school. You know that.'

'I shall have my Parliamentary salary in the end, and shall of course make you an allowance for things of that kind. Could I please have my lactose?'

'So you propose quite calmly to live entirely on me. On my little income from Daddy's estate?'

'Not if you do not wish it. You and the boys can do that, if necessary; and lucky we are that it should be so. I myself can apply for a maintenance grant.'

'Do you mean the dole?'

'Of course not. I refer to the Applecroft Fund for supporting Liberal candidates. I did not intend to approach them but I always can if you lack all interest in your husband's career in life.'

'Phineas!' Millie tried to sound positively menacing. 'I tell you again that I accept no responsibility for the future of the boys, financial or otherwise. They are out of my hands.'

'Well, Millie, in the very, very last resort, that's a matter for the common law, is it not? But there is no need at all for it to come to that.'

'It would be bad for your chances, if it did.'

'Not nowadays. Your notion of the world often seems antediluvian, Millie dear.'

'The boys neither love nor want me. Not that they love or want you either.'

Quite unself-consciously, Phineas smiled. 'What boys feel for their father is something a woman cannot understand, not even their mother. It's something that really is antediluvian, Millie.'

'If you had any understanding whatever of what goes on around you, you'd know better than to talk such rubbish.'

'No one is more concerned than I am about what goes on everywhere in the world.'

His eyes were filled with a need for his mission to be understood and appreciated; for the lactose that by now really was due.

Millie set about preparing it.

'Where are the boys?' asked Phineas, as the sun sank in unnoticed glory.

'I expect they're at the Lavender Bag, as they were last night.' Millie looked at her watch; the boys having stopped the clock so often that it no longer seemed to her worth paying for repairs. 'No. The Lavender Bag will have shut some time ago.'

'Perhaps it's some kind of special evening?'

'They would have come here and gorged themselves and then gone back.'

'Well, what *are* we to think, Millie? It really might be better if you took more interest in what your sons do. I shan't be able to give so much time to it in the future. You must understand that.'

Millie went to the record-player and put on Honegger's *Pacific 231*. The next piece on the record was Mossolov's factory music. Before the record could reach Gravini's *Homage to Marinetti*, Millie turned the machine off.

'Would you like your supper? I should like mine.'

'I shall have to take more care over what I eat now that I have so much greater responsibility.'

But when, shortly afterwards, the moment came, he seemed to pick and niggle very much as usual. Her own appetite was undoubtedly the more disturbed of the two.

In the end, the police arrived, though not until it was quite dark. Most unusually, it was Phineas who unwound himself and let the man in. For this reason, Millie did not learn his rank: lacked the opportunity to glance at his official card. The man was not in his blues, but dressed overall by a multiple outfitter.

'Good evening, madam. Do either of you know anything of two men named Angus Morke and Rodney Morke? They've given this address.'

'They are our two sons, officer,' said Phineas.

'Indeed, sir? I should hardly have thought it. Certainly not in your case, madam. These two are fully grown men. In fact, rather more than that.'

'Don't be ridiculous, officer,' said Phineas. 'They are our sons, and we know exactly how big they are.'

'I wonder if you altogether do, sir. If you don't mind my saying so, madam. It took a whole squad to get them under any kind of control. And, even then, there are some very nasty injuries which the Court will be hearing about tomorrow, in addition to the other charges. The Sergeant is worried about whether the cells will hold them. The station isn't Parkhurst Prison. It's only intended for quiet overnight cases. But I mustn't do all the talking. I've only come to make the usual routine enquiries. The two men – boys, if you prefer, madam – do really reside here, then?'

'Of course they do,' said Phineas. 'This is their home.'

'If you say so, sir. Now, how old would each of them be?'

'They are twins. Surely you must have realised that? As far as I recall, they are rising sixteen.'

'You mean that they're fifteen, sir?'

'Yes, I think that's right. Fifteen.'

'It's incredible, if you don't mind my saying so, madam.'

'In the course of your work,' said Phineas, 'you must have realised that some boys grow faster than some other boys.'

It was high time for Millie to speak. 'What have

the two of them done?'

'What are they *alleged* to have done?' Phineas corrected. 'If anything, of course.'

The officer made it clear that from now on, and
whatever the rule book might say, he preferred to deal
with Millie.

'I'm afraid the charges are rather serious, madam. In
fact, we've never before had anything to compare with
it since the station first opened, which of course was
when most of the houses like this one were being built.
We haven't had much violence in the suburb, *serious* violence that is; though of course it's growing fast pretty
well everywhere in the world.'

'What have they done, officer? Please tell me. I'm
perfectly able to face it.' Again, the additional burden
that could at the same time be a further remote prospect
of freedom!

'Remember,' put in Phineas, 'that it's still only mere
allegation. It is well known that the police exaggerate;
sometimes very greatly. I speak as an adopted Parliamentary candidate.'

'Do you indeed, sir? For somewhere round here, that
is?'

'No, not locally. But it makes no difference.'

'Well, madam,' said the officer, with professional
quietness, 'as for the charges, they include a long list
of assaults, fifteen at least so far, and we are expecting
more. Some of those we already have are very serious
indeed. Not what we're used to round here, as I have remarked. More like the Glasgow docks in the old days,

I should have said. Then there's a lot of damage to property. A lot of damage to a lot of property, I should have put it. Doors stove in and roofs ripped about and ornaments smashed. There are a couple of attempted rapes expected to be reported soon, from what the other officers say. A couple at least.'

'In these times, there's no such thing as *attempted* rape,' objected Phineas. 'It's a rape, or it isn't a rape, and most people are very doubtful about it even if it's supposed to be proved.'

'And that's not to mention the injuries inflicted on the officers, which we don't like at all, madam, especially in a quiet district like this.'

'No,' said Millie soberly, 'I'm sure not.'

'Now, if I could have a few details of the education these lads have had? Supposing them to have had any, of course. But it's no matter for joking, all the same. It's an offence too, not to educate a child.'

Millie realised that the night air was coming in through the front door which Phineas had left open: the night air of a hot summer. Phineas made no move, and Millie did not care to leave him just then even for a single moment. Besides, closing the outer door might lead to new suspicions.

By the end of it, and indeed long before that, Millie knew perfectly well that Phineas should have produced the whisky, but that, thanks to Phineas, there was no whisky in the house. Most assuredly she could not be absent long enough to make tea, even supposing the officer to be interested in tea at that hour.

'If the accused really are what the law calls minors,' said the officer, 'then a parent will be required to attend the Court.'

'Of course my husband will attend the Court,' said Millie.

'Perhaps you too, madam? A mother can often influence the Justices more than a father.'

Millie smiled. 'I shall remember that, officer.'

'Not that a case of this kind is likely to remain with Petty Sessions for long. It will be simply a matter of a quick committal, as far as I can see.'

'I'm sure you are once more greatly exaggerating, officer,' said Phineas, smiling in his turn.

'You'll be there to hear for yourself, sir,' replied the officer, entirely reasonable.

When he had gone, Millie found it almost impossible even to speak to Phineas.

'I'm not sharing a room with you,' she managed to say.

'Please yourself,' said Phineas. 'After today's news, I've still a great deal to think about and plan, as anyone but you would see at once.'

Next morning, and really quite early next morning, the childless Hubert Ellsworth was the first with the local news; or with a bit of it.

In his old yachting jumper, with part of the club name still on it, and shapeless grey bags splashed with oil from his garden workshop, he stood there trying to arrange his scattered locks.

'I thought I ought to tell you first, Phineas, as, after all, we are neighbours. I've heard that there are two sex maniacs on the loose. Apparently, the authorities feel we should warn one another to keep everything bolted and barred. What times we live in! Eh, Phineas?'

Millie, who had overheard this in her nightdress, could already see, from the bathroom window, Morwena Ellsworthy sealing every aperture with passepartout, despite the season, and even pulling down blinds.

The next arrival was young Graham, the local weekly's cub reporter, as people described him, and the only one who left the office very often. Girls tended to tell him that they liked the name Graham.

That time, Millie opened the door.

'May I come in for a few moments, Mrs Morke? It's really rather important.'

Millie had never before spoken to him, though, like everyone else, she knew who he was. He was a nice young lad, everyone said. In any case, he was by now sufficiently practised in his profession never to take even the hint of a negation as an answer.

'Well, what is it?' asked Millie. 'Do sit down.'

Phineas, having dealt with Hubert Ellsworthy, had gone back to bed. In the marital bedroom: Millie had spent the night on the lounge sofa-convertible which, at the time of hire-purchase, she had, consciously or subconsciously, made sure really was long enough and wide enough to live up to its brochure.

'You've heard the news, Mrs Morke?'

'What news in particular?'

'The police station in The Approach has been completely wrecked. I've never seen anything like it,' said young Graham very seriously.

'Well, what can I do? Would you like a cup of coffee?'

'Not just at the moment, Mrs Morke, though thanks all the same. The thing is that the Station Inspector tipped us the wink that your two boys were being held for all that damage last night. And now, presumably, they've made a getaway. Would you care to give me a statement?'

'No,' said Millie.

'Are the boys here, Mrs Morke? After all, it's their home.'

'I have nothing to say,' said Millie, hoping she had the formula right.

'Then, presumably, they *are* here? Don't worry, I shan't give them away. Nor do *you* have to give them away. You can just say whatever comes into your head. It doesn't much matter what it is, really.'

Millie could see that he was only trying to be kind.

'Nothing. So would you please go? I'm sorry to turn you out, but I'm sure you'll understand.'

'Rum tykes, aren't they? Sorry, I suppose that's not a very nice way of talking to their mother. My kid brother told me about the month or whatever it was they spent in the under-seven. They made a mark there all right, from what Matheson had to say. Marked everyone, in fact. Do please give me a statement of some kind, Mrs Morke. Anything you like. Just anything.'

'I'm sorry,' said Millie. 'I really am. I know you're only doing your job.'

'Well, I suppose there's not much more I can do this time, but you're famous now, Mrs Morke, and there'll be others coming fast in my footsteps. Not that I've missed a scoop. Not personally, that is. I don't suggest that.'

'I'm glad,' said Millie, meeting his generosity at least halfway.

'And I'm sorry you're in trouble, Mrs Morke. I really am. You're still a very nice-looking girl. If I may put it that way.'

'I don't see why you shouldn't,' said Millie. 'Well, that's it, wouldn't you say?'

Millie opened her handbag and carefully combed her hair. She went upstairs.

Phineas lay there, reading Minutes.

'Phineas! I'm leaving you.'

'Oh, please calm down, and let's have breakfast.'

'Get it yourself. I'm packing and going. I'll collect the rest of my things as soon as I can. The things that are left. Before the boys smash them too.'

'Millie!' cried Phineas, while she bustled around with a quiet efficiency she had not known for years. 'Millie, don't you realise that this is the moment in all their lives when our sons are likely to need their mother most? Surely you must see that for yourself? The moment in their lives when *I* need you most too?'

'I've done all I can,' said Millie. 'You're full of educational theories. Now's the time for you to give them a real trial. You. Not me.'

'At least come with me to the Court? Let's have breakfast quietly and consider what line to take. I'm sure the whole thing is quite grossly exaggerated. The police do that, you know. I keep saying so.'

'It would be quite difficult to exaggerate in any way about the boys.'

'But you're their mother, Millie!'

'Perhaps that's how I know. You learn nothing.'

Replete and bursting though it was, she shut her suit-case with new strength. It still bore her maiden name: MELANIE PIGOTT. Why should she not return to that? When in due course she had left Uncle Stephen's abode and started a life of her own? The green suitcase had been a joint present from her parents on her twenty-first birthday. At the time, she had wondered how long the family name would still be hers; but now it might be hers once more, and for a very indefinite period. When empty, the suitcase was delightfully weightless; when full, delightfully substantial.

'I'm not going to bother with goodbye,' said Millie.

Phineas clutched at her physically. His overlong arm was as the tentacle of an undernourished octopus.

'Millie, do at least try to be sensible. Just get break-fast, and we'll talk it all over as much as you like.'

She threw his elongated hand back on the bedspread.

As she bore her packed suitcase briskly up The Drive, she reflected that two days ago she could hardly have lifted the thing from the bedroom floor.

She wondered how long it would be before the inevitable reaction and collapse.

Uncle Stephen saw to it that Millie wanted for nothing.

Every morning he brought her the loveliest, most fragrant breakfast in bed. Every evening he lingered in her room, tucking her in, adjusting the ventilation and positioning of the curtains, putting away any clothes she had left about, gossiping about the small events of the day, taking away her shoes in order to give them a rub.

He prepared most of the other meals too. As he pointed out, he would have had to feed himself in any case, and having to feed her too made the whole thing into a work of joy. He had many outside engagements: bridge, bowls, the rifle and revolver ranges, the committee of the small amateur soccer club, the British Legion, the Skeleton ARP, the Patriotic Alliance (which was often in a state of inner schism, and therefore particularly demanding); but Millie could never for one moment doubt that she constituted the primary demand both upon his heart and even upon his time. The undiagnosed trouble inside Millie had ceased even to demand diagnosis.

'You do spoil me, Uncle Stephen. It's lovely.' She lay on the settee in lounging pyjamas and matching surtout (as the manufacturers termed it). She had never been able to bother with garments of that kind before, but now Uncle Stephen had bought them for her at Katja's in the new Vanity Market, and she had helped to choose them too. She had rather looked down on such shops and on such clothes, but that had been ignorance and the wrong kind of sophistication. It was almost impossible to believe that Phineas lived only eleven and a half miles away as the crow flew, if any crow should be so misdirected.

'I like being spoilt, Uncle Stephen,' said Millie.

'I love to do it, girl. You're all I have, you know that, and always have been.'

That must have been what Phineas would have called an exaggeration, but it was true that Uncle Stephen, so far as was known, had at all times 'looked after himself'. Now he had a thick mop of silky white hair, like a wise old lion, and the same green eyes as his sister, Millie's mother, and as Millie herself.

'All the same, I can't stay for ever,' said Millie coyly.

'Why on earth not? First, *I'll* look after *you*, and do it with love in my heart. Then, when I'm past it, *you'll* look after *me* – well, some of the time. In the end, I'll leave you all I've got. I've no one else. Remember that. It's not much. But it will be enough.'

'I'll remember, Uncle Stephen, and thank you. All the same, a woman nowadays is expected to lead a life of her own. I was all set to do it.'

'You've tried that sort of thing once, girl, and you've seen what happened.' Uncle Stephen's eye wandered away from her, which was unusual. 'I wish I could put a hand to one of the rattans I used to have.'

'What are they, Uncle Stephen?' asked Millie, though really she knew fairly well.

'Disciplinary instruments, my love. Disciplinary

instruments. Never had one out of my right hand during all the years I was in the Archipelago.'

'I wonder if anything's happened by now?' Millie spoke a little drowsily. The wine at dinner had been South African, and she had fallen badly out of practice.

'You let sleeping dogs lie. Never trouble trouble until trouble troubles you.'

She smiled at him. It would be absurd to argue about anything.

'Carry me to bed, Uncle Stephen.'

She dreamt that she and Thelma Modelle were climbing Everest together. They were both garbed in the latest chic, waterproof, windproof, coldproof clothing, and carried little axes, silvery in the sun. Thelma, the gypsy, was deputising as a Sherpa. It was all exceedingly enjoyable, and not at all too steep for Millie's new energies. The summit lay straight ahead. They might have tea when they arrived there; or Thelma might have to have ideas of her own about a suitable gypsy celebration.

How many months later was it when Millie opened the *Daily Telegraph* and saw the familiar headline: LIBERAL LOSES DEPOSIT? Apparently the sitting member for North Zero had fallen over a cliff, or at least been discovered by children dashed to pieces on the rocks below. The coroner had returned an open verdict, and a by-election had followed. Previously Millie's eyes must have glided over these events.

Uncle Stephen brought her the *Daily Telegraph* or

the *Sunday Telegraph* with her early-morning tea; and *The Imperialist* every time there was a new issue. That day, when a little later he came up with her breakfast, two small, heavenly-smelling kippers and the perfect toast upon which she could always rely, she was pensive.

'Uncle Stephen, tell me. Did they ever catch those boys? I suspect you know all the time.'

'I know nothing that you don't know, little girl.'

She eyed him. 'What exactly does that mean? Do you know the answer to the question I asked?' She spoke quite roguishly.

'I do not. I know what my answer would be if I only had the chance. Now eat your scrap of porridge, or it'll go cold. I'll sugar it for you.'

Millie dragged herself upwards. She really preferred to eat in a sprawling position, but Uncle Stephen liked to see more of her.

'Tell me, Uncle Stephen, have there been any more happenings? Like the one on the night before I left. I simply don't read the reports of things like that.'

'That's the self-protective instinct, my little love, and you could do with more of it, not less.'

'But have there, Uncle Stephen? I'd rather like to know.'

'Nothing that anyone could get a grip on. Or nothing that's come my way. I don't spend all day reading the newspapers. It can get hold of you as poisonously as the television, if you once let it.'

'You're hiding something, Uncle Stephen.'

'That I am not. There are these violences all over the world every minute of the day. Everyone's a villain without proper discipline. I haven't noticed the names of your two lads in particular.'

'And you haven't heard anything locally either?'

'Not a word. I'd be out in no time if I had, after what's been done.'

The last words very nearly convinced Millie.

'Let me pour your chocolate,' said Uncle Stephen.

But immediately he spoilt it all by speaking further.

'They'll have shot up a lot further by this time,' he observed. His eyes were searching round the room, as they always did when the subject of the boys arose.

'Thank you, Uncle Stephen,' said Millie, as he stopped pouring. 'It's a beautiful breakfast. When I've finished it, I'd like to sleep a little more. Then I'll come down and give you a hand.'

He took the hint quite quietly. He merely said, 'I see now that you're looking pale. Don't you worry about helping me. I can easily bring up your little lunch when the time comes.'

'You *are* good to me, Uncle Stephen.'

But, as soon as he had left the room and closed the door, Millie began to heave; and in no time, while trying to muffle the noise, she was being copiously sick into the article provided in well-found houses for that and other purposes: as sick as she had been, without cessation as it had seemed, during the long months before the two boys were born.

*

Really there could be no question of Millie even attempting to lead a life of her own as, like so many women, she had originally, in a vague way, intended. She was afraid to leave the house, and even more so after what Uncle Stephen had so casually said.

That she had good reason to lie low was confirmed by the episodes that followed.

It was more than a year after Millie had left Phineas, and the gold of summer was fast dissolving into the copper of autumn, when one night Millie stirred in her sleep to see a big face pressed against the panes of her first-floor bedroom window. Whether it was Angus's face or Rodney's face, which of their faces, she would probably not by now have known in any case. It was an unseemly blot on the October moonlight, then it ducked.

What was more, her window was open, as at night it always was. The boy was far too big to climb right in, but he could easily have inserted a huge arm, perhaps reached to the bed, and then strangled or humiliated her. Millie had realised from the first that the boys must have a perfectly clear idea of where she was, even though she emerged so seldom, and Uncle Stephen never recommended otherwise. What had decided the boys to re-enter her life now? She had seen only one of them, but was sure that the other was there also, because the other always was. She suspected that by now their combined strength could throw down the entire house. And very possibly they were growing still. Boys by no means always cease to grow at sixteen or seventeen.

She drew on her kimono and ran to Uncle Stephen's room. She knocked at his door, as she had done before when hungry during the night, or when merely lonely.

'Come in, girl. Come in.'

'Uncle Stephen. The boys are back. One of them has just looked through my window in the moonlight. I think I'm going to be sick again.'

'Come in with me, little love. I'll look after you and protect you. That's what I'm doing in your life. That's what I'm here for. You know that.'

Fortunately, it was a very large bed. Uncle Stephen had brought it back from the East; from gorgeous, sanctified Goa, now for ever lost.

'When I was young, I could never in my life have even imagined anything so frightening,' said Millie. 'Not until the boys were born. Or actually a little before that. When Phineas and I were on our honeymoon. In France, and then in the marshes behind Ariano. I never dared to read horror stories and ghost stories.' She snuggled towards Uncle Stephen.

'No man and no woman knows anything of the troubles they are going to meet with in life. Or I take it they'd succeed in dodging them,' said Uncle Stephen. 'They're supposed to be sent to form and mould us, but my idea is to form and mould *them* whenever possible. Remember that.'

'You're the most wonderful uncle,' Millie murmured, though she was still shivering and gulping.

'I'll stay with you ten minutes while you calm down and arrange your pinafore, and then I'm going hunting.'

'No, Uncle Stephen! It's too dangerous. They're watching the house. They're *immense*.'

'Many times in my life I've been under siege. Each time, in the end, I burst out and destroyed everything in sight. I'm hard to hold, Millie.'

'Things have changed since those days, Uncle Stephen. It's sad, but it's true. Even *The Imperialist* admits it. That was the bit I read you, when you ordered me to stop. There's nothing for either of us to do nowadays but escape. A fortune-teller told me that last year, and now it's come true.'

'I know all about times changing, none better,' said Uncle Stephen, holding her close. 'The fact remains that *I* have *not* changed. I am older, unfortunately, but otherwise exactly the same. Also I have weapons, I have strategy and tactics, and I have experience. I am going to give those cubs the lesson they've needed since their first birthday. I learned, my little love, to deal with growing boys in a harder school than Eton and Harrow or any of those places.'

'I'm not going to let you try. You're over-confident. Those two are like children of the future.' She was appalled. 'Perhaps they *are* children of the future?'

'I'll admit that they're too big for their boots,' said Uncle Stephen drily.

'If you go anywhere near them they'll harm you. We're just going to wait for the daylight. I'll stay with you if you'll let me. Then we'll steal away somewhere for a bit. Somewhere nice. You've always said you could afford it, if only circumstances had been different. Well,

193

circumstances *are* different, whether we like it or not. We could go and stay in an hotel at Southampton and you could look at the different ships going to places. You would like that, wouldn't you?'

'And if everyone behaved in that way?' enquired Uncle Stephen. 'If everyone did, what would become of our country? Things are rough enough already. You're as bad as that so-called man of yours, Millie.' But he spoke affectionately, none the less, cuddling and caressing her, not meaning his comparison very seriously.

'Uncle Stephen, don't be silly. They're not ordinary boys you can either pamper or stand in the corner. They're *enormous*. I told you what the man from the police station said. They're quite beyond handling by any single individual.'

'All I know is that they're boys, and that's enough. I don't want to leave you alone, as you know perfectly well, my little pet, but I'm going. You just lie in my bed until I'm back. And don't worry. I'm here to keep you from all harm. And I have weapons. Remember that.'

He squeezed her hand, and clambered out into the night.

Soon he was on the roof, directly above her. She could hear the slotting of iron into iron, or was it nowadays steel into steel? When she had lived beside the Heath as a small child during the Second World War, the ATS girls operating the anti-aircraft unit concealed among the evergreen gorse had made that noise all day as they took the long guns to pieces and put them together again. Uncle Stephen possessed artillery of his own. It was included in the weapons he had mentioned; nor did it consist in a couple of squat, serio-comic muzzle-loading Peninsular War mortars, looking like pugs. On the contrary, Uncle Stephen could mount at least three quite modern-looking pieces, painted not black but dark green as gorse and palpably requiring expert knowledge to discharge satisfactorily; the kind of knowledge that the girls on the Heath had been acquiring during the daytime. He had explained to Millie that these guns were designed by the authorities primarily for withstanding a concerted rush. She wondered when he had managed to dismantle at least one of them in the room downstairs and reassemble it on the roof of the house without her hearing or noticing a thing. She might have been impressed by his foresight, but instead resurrected her suspicions that Uncle Stephen had all along known something that he had failed to pass on.

There was a flash and a crash: quite startlingly like 6:30 or 7:30 P.M. when Millie had been but a tot.

Another and another. Millie fully realised that this could not continue for long; not in the modern world. Somehow it would be stopped, however justified it might be, even by the narrowest legalistic standard of self-defence and of protecting an unarmed mother.

Concurrently, Millie was subdued by a confused mêlée of feeling about Angus and Rodney; even though she had never been able within herself to accept that they were authentically her own offspring.

A shadow passed between the moon and the casement. Surely the boys should have been intelligent enough to take cover? How, without doing so, had either of them survived Uncle Stephen's cannonade? Uncle Stephen was the least likely of men to aim and then miss. He kept in continual practice, as in so many directions.

Another flash and crash: though this time in the latter was a curious rending sound, as if the gun barrel were about to burst asunder. Millie had heard of guns soldering up through being fired continuously day and night. Probably Uncle Stephen's gun had not of late been fired often enough to be in prime condition. Millie realised the danger that Uncle Stephen might be running from the gun exploding within itself and shattering into smithereens, as she understood that guns not infrequently did.

But by now the official legions were massing. Millie could hear outerspace blastings of fire engines, of ambulances, of police cars; and between them the insect whinings of television vans and radar. It was much as the moment when an escape from a concentration camp is first notified. She ran to the window.

Functionaries were swarming over and around machines to make sure that nothing remained unaccounted for in the designated area, except criminally. It was an ideal spot for such an operation, as Uncle Stephen's house stood in comparative isolation at a corner of the woods; a public open space owned by the Council.

Millie ran back to her own room. It would be most unwise to turn on a light, and possibly the current had already been chopped at the main. In any case, public lights were beginning to range: brutal searchlights, and the torture-chamber arc lights necessary for television.

Millie tore off her nightdress. She plunged into her jeans and a thick sweater which Uncle Stephen had bought for her at the supply stores where he bought many of his own garments. She had lost her handkerchief and took out a clean one.

For these simple actions the case was cogent enough. But Millie then hesitated. Uncle Stephen had stopped firing, and Millie could but speculate upon the exact reason. She could not possibly bring herself to desert Uncle Stephen, but the thing of which she was most certain was that the two of them could not win. She suspected that Uncle Stephen really knew that as well as she did. So what then?

Cautiously, she re-entered Uncle Stephen's bedroom. The beam of light which now filled it illuminated nothing human or real. In her short absence, the room had been killed.

Millie realised that Uncle Stephen was in difficulties. The gun was refusing to fire, as cars sometimes refuse to start. Uncle Stephen was tinkering with it, bashing it, cursing it. Soon, in the nature of things, the functionaries would close in finally, nor would it be a concerted attack of the kind which the gun was designed to ward off. It would be more a matter of irresistible infiltration, worked out long before in every detail, standard practice, precluding all possibility of topographical variation.

Millie ascended the attic ladder to the rooftree.

'Uncle Stephen!' she called down to him.

Absorbed though he was in his male task, he looked up at once.

'Go back,' he cried out. 'Go back, little Millie.'

'What's up, Uncle Stephen? What's gone wrong?' Nothing else was possible than to enter into things as he saw them.

'The boys have won this round, Millie. We must admit that. They've put the gun right out of action.'

'But how, Uncle Stephen?'

'It's some kind of schoolboy muck. They dropped a whole gob of it into the breech. Clever monkeys, we must admit.'

Millie had almost forgotten the boys; incredible though that seemed.

'Where are they now?'

'I'll bet they've made off. They don't have much more to do, just at this moment.'

Millie glanced anxiously round amid the confused and inhuman lights. But she knew that for a second she had almost wished the boys had still been there; as some kind of reassurance against all that was developing.

'I said I was here to protect you,' affirmed Uncle Stephen, 'and I shall do it still. I have always won the last battle. Always and always.'

'Come away with me, Uncle Stephen, while there's time.'

He went through burlesque bristling motions. 'You don't suppose I shall knuckle down to a couple of schoolboys with their pockets full of gum.' He expressed it facetiously, but of course he meant it, could hardly have meant it more.

Now that the firing had ceased for some time, the encircling host had begun to relax. Cups of tea were being consumed; ambulance workers were chatting to firemen on familiar subjects, their respective rates of pay and conditions of employment, their pension prospects, the maladies of their dear ones.

'Oh come on, Uncle Stephen. If the boys have gone, we can go too.'

To her consternation, he was not to be budged. 'No, girl,' he said. 'This is my home, my castle, as we used to say; and perhaps by now it's your home and castle too. Wouldn't you say that's very nearly true, Millie?' He had given up fiddling with the gun, and was addressing himself to something even more important.

'The boys will return,' she said. 'When all the people have gone. And you'll be in endless trouble for firing that gun in any case, even though I know you did it for my sake.'

'All my guns are licensed, Millie. I'm a registered holder of firearms. And as for the boys, let them come. I want nothing better. They've won a battle. They won't win the war. They're hulking brutes, but they're still only schoolboys. Look at this.' Uncle Stephen displayed the mess on his hands and combat suit.

'We shan't feel the same about the house ever again, Uncle Stephen. You must know that.'

'If we were all to let ideas of that kind govern our lives, we'd all be homeless.' Uncle Stephen sat back on the semi-dismantled gun. 'You mustn't suppose, girl, that I don't know what you mean. It's simply that not one thing in life is ever gained by running away. This is our home, yours and mine, and here we stay.'

'I'm afraid of the boys coming back,' said Millie. 'I'm terrified.'

The big lights were being turned out, one after another. It is often noticeable that they are in use only for a few minutes. By now Millie was unsure whether she preferred the crude glare or the deep darkness.

Someone was hammering at the front door. It was of course inevitable, sooner or later. Probably it had been going on at a lesser intensity for some time.

Millie dropped down the attic ladder and flitted through the dark house like a noctambule. She was not going to wait for any nonsense from Uncle Stephen about taking no notice. All the same, at the foot of the stairs she stood and called out. After all, it might conceivably be the boys.

'Who's there?' In the hall, the trophies were shaggy as a tropical forest.

'I'm a police officer, madam. Kindly open the door.'

She knew the voice. She slipped the chain and drew the big bolts in a trice.

'We're old friends, officer.'

All the same, he showed his card, and said, 'Detective-Sergeant Meadowsweet.' Millie smiled. 'May we have some light on the scene, madam?'

'Would that be safe?'

'Safe as could be, madam. The two men have been

sighted miles away, and we're closing in steadily.'

'Oh!' gasped Millie. 'So you know?'

'Of course we know, madam. What else did you think we were doing here. Now, I just want you to tell me all that's taken place. After that, I must have a word with the gentleman upstairs who's been treating himself to a little pistol practice.'

'I hope he's not done any damage.'

'No particular damage that we know of, but that's more by luck than judgement, wouldn't you say?'

'He's got all the necessary licences.'

'We know that, madam, but he happens not to have a licence to fire at intruders, because no such licence exists. Jobs of that kind must be left to the police. It sometimes causes hardship, but it's the law, and a gentleman with all those different licences knows better than most what they permit him to do and what not.'

'Perhaps I should say,' put in Millie, 'that the gentleman's my uncle. He kindly took me in after the trouble we had a year ago. A little *more* than a year, actually.'

'I could see at the time that your husband wasn't much help,' said Detective-Sergeant Meadowsweet in his inimitable way; and then duly added, 'If you don't mind my saying so, madam.'

'Oh no, I don't mind,' said Millie. 'Phineas was utterly wet from first to last. The whole thing was the biggest mistake I ever made. Not that "mistake" is quite a strong enough word. But do sit down, Sergeant.'

'I take it,' said the Detective-Sergeant as he did so, 'that the two men were attempting to force an entrance? Tonight, I mean.'

'They're really only boys,' said Millie, 'absurd though it seems.'

'I don't think we need to go over that ground again, madam. If you remember, we covered it fully when Mr Morke was there. So the two of them were attempting to force an entrance?'

'Well, not exactly, as I have to admit. What happened was simply that I saw one of them out on the lawn and rather lost my head. You know what they look like, Sergeant? How enormous they are?'

'Yes, we know very well, madam. Don't you worry about that. The approved school couldn't hold them for a week. The Tower of London would be more the thing, I'd say. So what happened then?'

'They're so strong too. I admit that I'm frightened to think about it. But of course you know about that too.'

The Sergeant nodded. He had settled himself on a big black stool from somewhere in French West Africa. Millie had been given to understand that, before the French came, the potentate whose official seat it had been (perhaps even throne) had at times waded through blood almost to the knees. She had difficulty in remembering which of the different regions the different things came from; especially as Uncle Stephen had shifted in mid-career from the fairly Far East to Africa, and then back to the East. The legs of the stool were decorated with small projecting bones and teeth, inserted into the woodwork. Above the Detective-Sergeant's head flapped a faded rushwork curtain originally intended, Uncle Stephen had said, to deter the flesh-eating birds and bats from entering one's room during the night.

'So what happened then, madam?'

'I admit that I completely lost my head, and ran in to my uncle, who took steps to defend me. No more than that.'

Another voice broke in. 'I take full responsibility, officer.'

Uncle Stephen had appeared at the top of the stairs. He had changed into his usual sharply pressed trousers and camel-hair jacket. 'The situation was extremely menacing. I was protecting my own flesh and blood against a couple of thugs.'

'Yes, sir, they're a nasty enough pair, according to all the evidence. The police are fed to the teeth with them, I can tell you that.'

'Very good of you to confirm what I say, officer. I am sorry I had to take the law into my own hands, but you'll agree that I had every justification. I've spent most of my life in places where you have to think quickly the whole time, or you find yourself dead. Worse than dead. May I suggest that we say no more about it? Let me give you a stiff whisky before you go?'

'We're not supposed to drink while we're on duty, sir.'

'Of course not,' said Uncle Stephen. 'I have served with the police myself. In several different parts of the globe.'

A little later, when the three of them were sitting amicably together, Millie began to feel intensely sad.

'I cannot help feeling partially responsible,' she blurted out. 'Do you think, Sergeant, there's anything to be done? Anything, even in theory, that *I* could do? Any possibility?'

At once Uncle Stephen shouted out, 'Clap them in irons, I should hope. Use straitjackets, if necessary. Though you'd have to have them specially made big enough. And then you've got to lay hold of the boys first. Eh, officer? They won the first round against *me*, you know.'

'We'll manage that all right, sir,' replied Detective-Sergeant Meadowsweet. 'The police don't fancy having the mickey taken out of them by two overgrown kids. Which is what you and Mr Morke both said they were, madam.'

'But what can be done *then*?' persisted Millie, though somewhat against the grain, as she was perfectly well, although confusedly, aware. 'Is there *anything* that I could do?'

'All I am permitted to say is that it will then be a matter for the proper authorities.' The Detective-Sergeant thought for a few seconds and, in his characteristic way, he added, 'I wish them the best of British luck with it.'

Unfortunately, it soon proved that the Detective-Sergeant had been mistaken at the precise point where he had shown most confidence: his conviction that Angus and Rodney would be finally apprehended in virtually no time.

A week passed and there was no hint or rumour of an

arrest. On the other hand, Uncle Stephen had no further trouble with the authorities. There were questions at the next two Parish Council meetings, but nothing was permitted to come out of them. As for the two young giants themselves, they appeared to have gone into hiding, difficult though that must have been; or perhaps it was that they were passing almost unnoticed amidst the freaks and zanies that people urban and suburban areas in the later part of the twentieth century. Millie, however, remembering the pair, found that hard to believe; and shivered when recollection fell for a while into full focus.

None the less, she had begun to go out once more: shopping, visiting the library, even attending a lecture on Criminology by an Austrian refugee. Uncle Stephen was fiercely opposed to all these excursions, and, to please him (as she would have expressed it to a confidante), she gave two undertakings: that she would never be parted from a tiny gun he lent her; and that for any longer journey she would take his car and not lightly step out of it or turn off the engine. Before she was married, Millie had driven all the time. Uncle Stephen's car was a beautiful old Alvis. Millie loved muffling herself up in order to drive it; and it had the advantage that then she was not easily identifiable. The gun went into the pocket of her jeans, where it was no more noticeable than a compact. It fired special tiny bullets which, as Uncle Stephen confided, were, strictly speaking, illegal: a steady stream of them, if necessary; and it fired them almost silently. Uncle Stephen was at his best when instructing Millie on mid-week mornings in the small orchard.

These things were advances, and Millie had no doubt about how much Uncle Stephen loved and needed her; but the whole thing amounted to little more than a half-life, when all was said and done. Millie had no very precise idea of what the other half might consist in, still less of how best to go after it; but she missed it none the less, as people do. In the end, she decided finally that there was no sensible alternative to a further consultation with Thelma Modelle.

She had, of course, been aware of this for some time, and had continued to dream about Thelma quite frequently, but it meant returning to the other suburb, the suburb where she had lived for years with Phineas and the boys; so that she had hesitated and hesitated. Uncle Stephen would have had a fit if he had known what she was proposing.

Then one morning it became unbearable, as things suddenly do. It was a premonition or other compulsion.

She tied up her hair in a dark-green scarf, donned heavy-duty garments, and tucked in the ends of her knotted, paler green muffler; all without a word to Uncle Stephen except to the effect that she wanted some different air and would very likely die without it. It was not a very gracious thing to say but it was essential to seem adamant.

'Drive fast,' said Uncle Stephen anxiously. 'Never slow down unless you absolutely have to. And be ready for anything.'

She knew by now what that meant.

'Of course, Uncle Stephen,' she said. 'I'll be fine.'

'I ought by rights to come with you, and look after you, but it's not safe to leave the house on its own. You know how it is, Millie.'

'I know.'

'Luckily, I went over the car this morning while you were sleeping. She'll go like the wind. See to it that she does. There's a girl.'

'That's what I'm going to do.' She was tying an *eau-de-Nil* silk scarf round the lower part of her face.

'Goodbye, my sweet.'

Through the tight scarf, Uncle Stephen kissed her lips.

She roared away, but really there was a traffic light round the first bend, and always it was red. Uncle Stephen must have known that even better than she knew it.

None the less, she had a perfectly authentic disinclination to linger; and as the other suburb came nearer, one of her hands dropped half-consciously from the wheel and rested for longer and longer periods upon the reassuring object in her pocket.

The Parade, once again; the Lavender Bag; the fish shop! The fish shop was now even more diversified in its wares than when she had seen it last: now there was hardly a fish in sight. Millie felt no nostalgia; nothing but nausea.

She brought the Alvis to rest as unobtrusively as possible with such a machine and darted upstairs in her full rig. She had no more made an appointment than on the previous occasion.

But this time the visionary did not greet her upon the landing, and the door of the sanctum, once the rheumatism lady's little sitting room, was shut.

Millie hesitated for some time. After all, she was presumably hidden from observation, and could give a moment or two to thinking and deciding. Most probably, Thelma's practice had grown since those first days, so that by now a client would have to be specially fitted in. Alternatively, Thelma might have failed and gone. Or gone, anyway. Communities are full of neat or braggart labels referring to vanished enterprises.

Millie timidly tapped.

'What is it?' The voice was Thelma's.

How could Millie explain? It was best to open and enter.

Thelma sat on the floor by the rheumatism lady's miniature gas fire. The black table, with its attendant black chairs, had been pushed into a corner. The zodiacal wall cards hung at madder angles than ever. Thelma herself wore what looked like the same green jeans, though they also looked a year and more older; and a battle-dress tunic, dyed dark blue by the authorities. It could be deduced that business was less than brisk.

'Oh, it's you.'

Thelma did not get up, and this time it was Millie who stood.

'Yes, it's me. I want to know what's happening now.

Exactly, please. What's happening at this very moment, if possible.'

'Well, in that case you'd better shut the door.'

Millie complied. She perceived that she should have done it in the first place. At least Thelma had not specifically demurred.

'And you'd better take off your clothes.'

'Some of them,' said Millie, smiling.

She had unwound the silk scarf from her face before entering. Now she climbed out of the heavy-duty garments and threw them on the floor, where they lay like prehistoric monsters, alive or dead, as the case might be. The rheumatism lady had presumably arranged to take away her carpets since Millie had last been there, because now the boards were bare. They were also mottled, but that happens soon and mysteriously in almost any house.

'Leave that,' said Thelma sharply, as Millie was about to unwind the dark green scarf which confined her locks.

Millie desisted. Her brow was moist.

'Take off your sweater if you're too hot,' said Thelma.

Millie shook her head.

'This time I shall need your money,' said Thelma. 'You can't depend entirely on my good will. I might need a new dress. Have you thought of that?'

'How much money?' asked Millie, still on her feet.

'How much have you got with you?'

'Can't you see without asking me?'

'Yes,' said Thelma. 'Forty pounds in fivers, and ten

single pounds. You must want to know badly.'

'I do,' said Millie calmly. For some reason, Thelma, no matter what her words or deeds, never upset her, as so many people did, even when saying or doing very little. Thelma was like Uncle Stephen in that.

'I'll take forty-nine pounds of it. You may need a pound suddenly when you leave.' Millie had noticed before that Thelma was surprisingly well-spoken in her own way.

'Only if you tell me what I've asked you to tell me and tell me the truth and the whole truth.'

Thelma shot Millie a confusing glance. Though intense, it was not necessarily hostile.

Then she arose from the floor and drew the curtains across the single window. They were not the rheumatism lady's pretty chintz, but heavy, dun, and unshaped. As they were touched and moved, they smelt. It was as if old clothes were being draped before the fairy windows of a wagon.

Thelma locked the door.

'I'm not locking you in. You can leave any time you like.'

And Millie could indeed see that the key was still there.

Thelma lifted the crystal and placed it on the floor. Sure enough, it was much smaller than Millie had always supposed such gadgets to be. Perhaps they came in different sizes, according to the purchaser's needs and resources?

The only light was from under the door and from the

small yellow gas fire. The room was odorous as well as stuffy.

Thelma signalised this fact by throwing off her dark-blue tunic. Beneath it she wore a fragile pinkish garment with big rents in it, through which her brown skin could be seen by what light there was. Her mop of hair was uncombed and uneven in length.

'Do what I am doing,' directed Thelma; and added, 'If you really must go on with this.'

When Millie made no answer, Thelma wriggled down on the floor until she lay at full length upon her front with the crystal about two inches before her eyes.

She looked ridiculous; or any other woman in her position would have looked ridiculous. Millie had supposed that crystal-gazing was done seated at a table. Moreover, a very suitable table was in the room with them.

'I advised you to take off your sweater,' said Thelma. 'Why not be more friendly?'

Millie continued calm. Upon the passage to truth, crosscurrents are to be expected.

'I'm all right,' she said, and lay down upon her front on the diametrical other side of the small crystal. She rested her chin upon her two hands, as Thelma was doing. At these close quarters, Thelma's lupine aroma was very pungent. Millie tried to concentrate upon gazing into the crystal. She assumed that to be the right thing to do. If only the crystal had been proportioned for a mature woman instead of for a waif!

But that matter began to adjust itself, and before

Millie had had time even to begin feeling physically uncomfortable. As she gazed through the crystal at Thelma's rock-pool eyes, the yellow light from the gas fire turned blue; and the circumference of the crystal expanded and expanded, as did Thelma's orbs on the other side of it. Indeed, Millie realised quite clearly that it must always have been impossible for her to have seen Thelma's eyes *through* the actual crystal. All anyone could really have seen *through* it, would have been Thelma's nose and a small distance on either side of it.

Incandescent with darting blue lights, the crystal grew until it filled the room, until it *was* the room, and Thelma's eyes were no longer there, as if her face had split vertically down the middle and her eyes had rolled away round the polished sphere, each in a different direction.

But by now Millie was in a room no longer. Nor was she lying inconveniently upon her front. On the contrary, she was in a small woodland clearing and was observing with perfect ease what therein transpired.

The two boys were sitting, rather absurdly jammed together, on a tree trunk. It was not a whole fallen giant of the forest, but a neatly sawn-off section, awaiting the arrival of the timber float and its tractor, or perhaps left there by intention as a nature seat for wooers, an accessory to picnics. In fact, the boys, ravenous as ever, were at that moment engaged upon a picnic of their own.

Each boy held in his hand a very large, very red bone,

from which he was gnawing in the frenzied manner that Millie remembered so well.

On the worn, wintry grass before them lay what was left of a human body.

The boys had already eaten their way through most of it, so that it could not even be described as a skeleton or semi-skeleton. The disjoined bones were everywhere strewn about at random, and only the top part of the frame, the upper ribs, remained in position, together with the half-eaten head.

It was Phineas's head.

Things swam.

Millie felt that her soul was rushing up a shaft at the centre of her body. She knew that this is what it was to die.

But she did not die.

She realised that now she was lying on her back in the still-darkened room. Thelma must have moved her. The gas fire was as yellow as before, no doubt because there was something wrong with it; and Thelma in her pink rags and dirty jeans was standing before her, even looking down at her.

'You've been out a long time.'

'I wish I were still out.'

'*You* may, but I don't. I've things to do. You forget that.'

Millie hesitated.

'Did you see them too?'

'Of course I saw them. Remember, I asked you whether you really had to go on with it.'

'What else could I do?'

'I don't know. I'm not your nursemaid.'

Millie sat up. 'If you pass me my handbag, I'll pay you.'

Thelma passed it. It did not seem to have been rifled during Millie's anaesthesia.

'Perhaps we could have a little more light?' suggested Millie.

Thelma threw on her tunic and, without fastening it, began to draw back or take down the window coverings. Millie did not examine which it was.

She rose to her feet. Had Thelma been behaving differently, she, Millie, would have been shaking all over, still prostrate. She seated herself on one of the dusty black chairs. She counted out forty-nine pounds on to the black table in the corner. Then she gazed for a moment straight into Thelma's vatic eyes. At once the sensations of a few moments before (or of what seemed a few moments) faintly recurred. Millie felt dragged out of herself, and turned her face to the dingy wall.

'You can stay if you wish. You know that.' Thelma made no attempt to take up the money; though Millie could be in small doubt that the sum would make a big difference for Thelma, at least temporarily.

'You can't expect me to keep open house for you always.'

Millie turned a little and, without again looking at Thelma, attempted a smile of some kind.

'I shan't be around much longer,' said Thelma.

'Surely you can see that?'

Millie stood up. 'Where will you go?'

'I shall go back to decent people. I should never have left them.'

'What made you?'

'I killed a girl.'

'I see.'

'I did right.'

There was a pause: a need (perhaps on both sides) for inner regrouping. It was a metaphor that Uncle Stephen might have approved.

Millie gathered herself together. 'Is that the sort of thing *I* ought to do?'

'How can I tell? Why ask *me*? You must decide for yourself.'

Millie gathered herself together a second time. It was difficult to petition. The forty-nine pounds still lay untouched on the hocus-pocus table. 'You *can* tell, Thelma. I know you can. They're obscene, monstrous, all those words. You know as well as I do. You're the only one who does. I feel responsible for them. Is that what I ought to do? Tell me.'

Thelma seemed actually to reflect for a moment; instead of darting out a reply like the double tongue of a snake, the flick of a boxing second's towel, as she usually did.

'You're not the kind,' said Thelma. 'It would be beyond you.'

'Then what? Help me, Thelma. Please, please help me.'

'I told you before. Run away.'

Millie stared blankly at the entire, round, empty world.

'Be more friendly and you can lie up with *me*. I keep saying so. But soon I shan't be here. I have debts.'

Millie wondered with what currency Thelma proposed to settle.

'Hurry up and put the money away somewhere,' Millie said.

But Thelma again spoke to the point: 'I'll place my right hand on your heart and you'll place your on mine. Then we'll be friends.'

Millie glanced at Thelma's ragged pink garment, but all she said was, 'It wouldn't be fair.' Then she added, 'Thank you all the same.' What a depraved, common way to express gratitude, she thought.

There was a tapping at the locked door.

'Who's that?' asked Millie, as if she really did live there.

Thelma had leapt upon the money like a cheetah and shoved it hugger-mugger into her jeans.

'It's Agnes Waterfield. She comes every day at this hour.'

'God! I don't want to meet *her*,' cried Millie.

'Well, you'll have to,' said Thelma, and unlocked the door on the instant.

Millie could only snatch her garments and scuttle away like a cat, hoping that Agnes might be too involved in her own troubles and preoccupations to recognise her, though not really believing it.

Outside, it had begun to snow. The big open car was spattered with separate flakes.

Millie sped away. Soon the suburb which had once been home was miles behind.

The straggling and diminishing woodlands touched the road at several places before one reached the main section in which lay Uncle Stephen's house. The ground was hummocky here, and nowadays the road ran through several small cuttings, ten or twelve feet high, in order to maintain a more or less constant level for the big lorries, and to give the tearaway tourists an illusion for a minute or two that they were traversing the Rocky Mountains. There were even bends in the road which had not yet been straightened, and all the trees in sight were conifers.

Thinking only of sanctuary, Millie tore round one of these bends (much too fast, but almost everyone did it, and few with Millie's excellent reason); and there were the two boys blocking the way, tall as Fiona Macleod's lordly ones, muscular as Gogmagog, rising high above the puny banks of earth. It was a busy road and they could only a moment before have dropped down into it. Beneath the snow patches on their clothing, Millie could clearly see the splashes of blood from their previous escapade. The boys were so placed that Millie had to stop.

'Got any grub, Mum?'

Quite truthfully, she could no longer tell one twin from the other.

'That's all we ask, Mum,' said the other twin. 'We're hungry.'

'We don't want to outgrow our strength,' said the first twin, just as in the old days.

'Let's search,' cried the second twin. Forbearance was extinguished by appetite.

The two boys were now on the same side of the car.

Millie, who had never seen herself as a glamorous mistress of the wheel, managed something that even Uncle Stephen might have been proud of in the old, dead days at Brooklands. She wrenched the car round on to the other side of the highway, somehow evaded the towering French truck charging towards her, swept back to her proper lane and was fast on her way.

But there was such a scream, perhaps two such screams, that, despite herself, she once more drew up.

She looked back.

The snow was falling faster now; even beginning to lie on the car floor. She was two or three hundred yards from the accident. What accident? She had to find out. It would be better to drive back rather than to walk: even in the modern world, the authorities would not yet have had time to appear and close the road. Again Millie wheeled.

The two vast figures lay crushed on the highway. They had been standing locked together gazing after her, after the car in which there might have been sweets or biscuits; so that in death, as in life, they were not divided. They had been killed by a police vehicle: naturally one of the heavier models. Millie had underestimated the instancy of modernity. The thing stood there, bluely lighted and roaring.

'It was you we were after, miss,' remarked the police officer, as soon as Millie came once more to a standstill. All the police were ignoring the snow completely. 'You were speeding. And now look what's happened.'

'If you ask Detective-Sergeant Meadowsweet, he will explain to you why I was going fast.' Millie shivered. 'I have to go fast.'

'We shall make enquiries, but no individual officer is empowered to authorise a breach of the law.'

By the time the usual particulars had been given and taken, the ambulance had arrived, screaming and flashing with determination; but it was proving impossible to insert the two huge bodies into it. The men were doing all they could, and the police had surrounded the area with neat little objects, like bright toys; but anyone not immediately involved could see that the task was hopeless.

The snow was falling more heavily every minute, so that by the time Millie was once more left alone among the traffic surging round the frail barrier, the two boys were looking like the last scene in *Babes in the Wood*, except that the babes had changed places, and changed roles, with the giants.

The Fetch

In all that matters, I was an only child. There was a brother once, but I never saw him, even though he lived several years. My father, a Scottish solicitor or law agent, and very much a Scot, applied himself early to becoming an English barrister, and, as happens to Scots, was made a Judge of the High Court, when barely in middle age.

In Court, he was stupendous. From the first, I was taken once every ten days by Cuddy, my nurse, to the public gallery in order to behold him and hearken to him for forty minutes or so. If I made the slightest stir or whimper, it was subtly but effectively repaid me; on those and all other occasions. Judges today are neither better nor worse than my father, but they are different.

At home, my father, only briefly visible, was as a wraith with a will and power that no one available could resist. The will and power lingered undiminished when my father was not in the house, which, in the nature of things, was for most of the time. As well as the Court, and the chambers, there were the club and the dining club, the livery company and the military historical society, all of which my father attended with dedication and sacrifice. With equal regularity, he pursued the cult of self-defence, in several different branches, and with little heed for the years. He was an elder of a Scottish church in a London suburb, at some distance from where we lived. He presided over several successive Royal Commissions, until one day he threw up his current presidency in a rage of principle and was never invited again. After his death I realised that a further centre of his interest had been a club of a different kind, a very expensive and sophisticated one. I need not say how untrue it is that Scots are penny-scraping in all things.

I was terrified of my father. I feared almost everything, but there was nothing I feared more than to encounter my father or to pick up threads from his intermittent murmurings in the corridors and closets. We lived in a huge house at the centre of Belgravia. No Judge could afford such an establishment now. In addition, there was the family home of Pollaporra, modest, comfortless, and very remote. Our ancestry was merely legal and commercial, though those words have vastly more power in Scotland than in England. In Scotland, accomplishments are preferred to graces. As a child, I was never taken to Pollaporra. I never went there at all until much later, on two occasions, as I shall unfold.

I was frightened also of Cuddy, properly Miss Hester MacFerrier; and not least when she rambled on, as Scottish women do, of the immense bags and catches ingathered at Pollaporra by our ancestors and their like-minded acquaintances. She often emphasised how cold the house was at all times and how far from a 'made road'. Only the elect could abide there, one gathered;

but there were some who could never bear to leave, and who actually shed tears upon being compelled by the advancing winter to do so. When the snow was on the ground, the house could not be visited at all; not even by the factor to the estate, who lived down by the sea loch, and whose name was Mason. Cuddy had her own methods for compelling the attention of any child to every detail she cared to impart. I cannot recall when I did not know about Mason. He was precisely the man for a Scottish nursemaid to uphold as an example.

My father was understood to dislike criminal cases, which, as an advanced legal theorist and technician, he regarded with contempt. He varied the taking of notes at these times by himself sketching in lightning caricature the figures in the dock to his left. The caricatures were ultimately framed, thirty or forty at a time; whereafter Haverstone, the odd-job man, spent upwards of a week hanging them at different places in our house, according to precise directions written out by my father, well in advance. Anybody who could read at all could at any time read every word my father wrote, despite the millions of words he had to set down as a duty. Most of the other pictures in our house were engravings after Landseer and Millais and Paton. Generations of Scottish aunts and uncles had also contributed art works of their own, painstaking and gloomy.

I was afraid of Haverstone, because of his disfigurements and his huge size. I used to tiptoe away whenever I heard his breathing. I never cared or dared to ask how he had come to be so marked. Perhaps my idea of his bulk was a familiar illusion of childhood. We shall scarcely know; in that Haverstone, one day after my seventh birthday, fell from a railway bridge into the main road beneath and was destroyed by a lorry. Cuddy regarded Haverstone with contempt and never failed to claim that my father employed him only out of pity. I never knew what he was doing on the railway bridge, but later I became aware of a huge mental hospital near by and drew obvious conclusions.

My mother I adored and revered. For better or for worse, one knows the words of Stendhal: 'My mother was a charming woman, and I was in love with my mother . . . I wanted to cover my mother with kisses and wished there weren't any clothes . . . She too loved me passionately. She kissed me, and I returned those kisses sometimes with such passion that she had to leave me.' Thus it was with me; and, as with Stendhal, so was the sequel.

My mother was very dark, darker than me, and very exotic. I must suppose that only the frenzy of Scottish lust brought my father to marrying her. At such times, some Scots lose hold on all other considerations; in a way never noticed by me among Englishmen. By now, my father's fit was long over. At least he did not intrude upon us, as Stendhal's father did. I am sure that jealousy was very prominent in my father, but perhaps he scorned to show it. He simply kept away from his wife entirely. At least as far as I could see. And I saw most things, though facing far from all of them, and acknowledging none of them.

223

Day after day, night after night, I lay for hours at a time in my mother's big bed, with my head between her breasts, and my tongue gently extended, as in infancy. The room was perfumed, the bed was perfumed, her nightdress was perfumed, she was perfumed. To a child, it set the idea of Heaven. Who wants any other? My mother's body, as well as being so dark, was softer all over than anyone else's, and sweeter than anything merely physical and fleeting, different and higher altogether. Her rich dark hair, perfumed of itself, fell all about me, as in the East.

There was no social life in our home, no visiting acquaintances, no family connections, no chatter. My father had detached himself from his own folk by his marriage. My mother loved no one but me. I am sure of that. I was in a position to know. The only callers were her hairdresser, her dressmaker, her maker of shoes and boots, her parfumier, her fabricator of lingerie, and perhaps one or two others of the kind. While she was shorn, scented, and fitted, I sat silently in the corner on a little grey hassock. None of the callers seemed to object. They knew the world and what it was like: and would soon enough be like for me. They contained themselves.

I was there whatever my mother did; without exception.

Cuddy dragged me off at intervals for fresh air, but not for very long. I could see for myself that Cuddy, almost familiar with my father, was afraid of my mother. I never knew why, and am far from certain now, but was glad of the fact. It was the key circumstance that transformed the potential of utter wretchedness for me into utter temporary bliss.

My mother taught me all I know that matters; smiling and laughing and holding me and rewarding me, so that always I was precocity incarnate; alike in concepts, dignity, and languages. Unfortunately, my mother was often ill, commonly for days, sometimes for weeks; and who was there to care, apart from me, who could do nothing – even if there was something that others could have done? My lessons ceased for a spell, but as soon as possible, or sooner, were bravely resumed.

Later, I strayed through other places of education, defending myself as best I could, and not unsuccessfully either; and, of what I needed, learning what I could. It was not my father who dispatched me. He regarded me without interest or expectation. To him I was the enduring reminder of a season's weakness. The ultimate care of me lay with Trustees, as often in Scotland; though only once did I see them as individuals, and hardly even then, because the afternoon was overcast, and all the lights were weak, for some reason that I forget.

Before all that formal education, I had encountered the woman on the stairs. This brief and almost illusory episode was the first of the two turning points in my life and I suspect the more important.

I had been playing on the landing outside the door of my mother's room. I do not know how long she had been ill that time. I feared to count the days, and never did so. I am sure that it was longer than on various previous occasions. I was alarmed, as always; but not especially alarmed.

My mother had been instrumental in my being given a railway, a conjuring outfit, and a chemical set: those being the things that small boys were supposed to like. My father should have given me soldiers, forts, and guns; possibly a miniature, but accurate, cricket bat; but he never once gave me anything, or spoke at all in our house if he could avoid it – except, on unpredictable occasions, to himself, memorably, as I have hinted.

I mastered the simple illusions, and liked the outfit, but had no one to awe. Even my mother preferred to hug me than for me to draw the ace of spades or a tiny white rabbit from her soft mouth. The chemical effects, chlorine gas and liquid air, I never mastered at that time, nor wished to. The railway I loved (no other word), though it was very miniature: neither 1 gauge (in those days) nor o gauge, but something smaller than oo. The single train, in the Royal Bavarian livery of before the First World War, clinked round a true circle; but en route it traversed a tunnel with two cows painted on top and one painted sheep, and passed through two separate stations, where both passengers and staff were painted on the tin walls, and all the signs were in Gothic.

That day, I had stopped playing, owing to the beating of my heart; but I had managed to pack everything into the boxes. I needed no bidding to do that, and never had done. I was about to lug the heap upstairs, which by then I could perfectly well do. I heard the huge clock in the hall strike half past three. The clock had come from Pollaporra, and reached the ceiling. I looked at my watch, as I heard it. I was always doing that. It was very late autumn, just before Christmas, but not yet officially winter. There is nothing in this world I know better than exactly what day of the year it was. It is for ever written in the air before me.

My ears were made keen by always listening. Often, wherever I was, even at the top of the house, I waited motionless for the enormous clock to strike, lest the boom take me by surprise. But the ascending woman was upon me before I had heard a footfall. I admit that all the carpets were thickest Brussels and Wilton. I often heard footfalls, none the less, especially my father's strangely uneven tread. I do not think I heard the woman make a sound from first to last. But last was very close to first.

She had come up the stairs, beyond doubt, even though I had neither heard nor seen anything; because by the time I did observe her, she was still two or three steps from the top of the flight. It was a wide staircase, but she was ascending in a very curious way, far further from the rail than was necessary and far nearer to the wall, and with her head and face actually turned to the wall.

At that point, I did hear something. I heard someone shut the front door below; which could not be seen from where I stood. I was surprised that I had not heard the door being opened, and the words of enquiry and caution. I remember my surprise. All these sounds were unusual in our house at that time.

I felt the cold air that the woman had brought in with her from the December streets and squares, and a certain cold smell; but she never once turned towards me. She could easily have been quite unaware of me; but I was watching her every motion. She had black hair, thin and lank. She was dressed in a dirty red and blue plaid of some kind, tightly wound. I was of course used to pictures of people in plaids. The woman's shoes were cracked and very unsuited to the slush outside. She moved with short steps, and across the carpet she left a thin trail of damp, though I knew that it was not raining. It was one of the things I always knew. Everything about the woman was of a kind that children particularly fear and dislike. Women, when frightening, are to children enormously more frightening than any man or men.

I think I was too frightened even to shrink back. As the woman tottered past, I stood there with my boxes beside me. My idea of her motion was that she had some difficulty with it, but was sustained by extreme need. Perhaps that is a fancy that only came to me later.

I never had any doubt about where the woman was going but, even so, I was unable to move or to speak or to do anything at all.

As she traversed the few yards of the landing, she extended her right arm and grimy hand from out of her plaid, the hand and arm nearer to me, still without in any degree turning her head. In no time at all, and apparently without looking, she had opened the door of my sweet mother's room, had passed within, and had shut the door behind her.

I suppose it is unnecessary for me to say that when my mother was ill, her door was never locked; but perhaps it is not unnecessary. I myself never entered at such times. My mother could not bear me to see her when she was ill.

There was no one sympathetic to whom I could run crying and screaming. In such matters, children are much influenced by the facilities available. For me, there was only my mother, and, in fact, I think I might actually have gone in after the woman, though not boldly. However, before I was able to move at all, I heard Cuddy's familiar clump ascending the stair behind me as I gazed at the shut door.

'What are you doing now?' asked Cuddy.

'Who was that?' I asked.

'Who was who?' Cuddy asked me back. 'Or what?'

'The woman who's gone in there.'

'Whist! It's time *you* were in bed with Christmas so near.'

'It *wasn't* Father Christmas,' I cried.

'I daresay not,' said Cuddy. 'Because it wasn't anybody.'

'It was, Cuddy. It *was*. Go in and look.'

It seems to me that Cuddy paused at that for a moment, though it may only have been my own heart that paused.

It made no difference.

'It's bed for you, man,' said Cuddy. 'You're over-excited and we all know where that ends.'

*

Needless to say, it was impossible for me to sleep, either in the dark or in the light: the choice being always left to me, which was perhaps unusual in those days. I heard the hours and the half hours all through the night, and at one or two o'clock my father's irregular step, always as if he were dodging something or someone imperfectly seen, and his periodical mutterings and jabberings as he plodded.

All was deeply upsetting to a child, but I must acknowledge that by then I was reasonably accustomed to most of it. One explanation was that I had no comparisons available. As far as I knew, all people behaved as did those in my home. It is my adult opinion that many more, in fact, do so behave than is commonly supposed, or at least acknowledged.

Still, that night must have proved exceptional for me; because when Cuddy came to call me in the morning, she found that I was ill too. Children, like adults, have diseases that it is absurd to categorise. Most diseases, perhaps all, are mainly a collapse or part-collapse of the personality. I daresay a name for that particular malady of mine might in those days have been brain fever. I am not sure that brain fever is any longer permitted to be possible. I am sure that my particular malady went on for weeks, and that when I was once more deemed able to make sense out of things, I learned that my mother was dead, and, indeed, long buried. No one would tell me where. I further gathered that there was no memorial.

About four weeks after that, or so it now seems to

me, but perhaps it was longer, I was told that my father was proposing to remarry, though he required the consent of the Trustees. A Judge was but a man as far as the Trustees were concerned, a man within the scope of their own settlement and appointment. Thus it was that I acquired my stepmother; *née* Miss Agnes Emily Fraser, but at the moment a widow, Mrs Johnny Robertson of Baulk. To her the Trustees had no objection, it seemed.

I still have no idea of why my father married Agnes Robertson, or why he remarried at all. I do not think it can have been the motive that prompted his earlier marriage. From all that, since his death, I have learned of his ways, the notion would seem absurd. It was true that the lady had wealth. In the end, the Trustees admitted as much; and that much of it was in Burmah Oil. I doubt whether this was the answer either. I do not think that more money could have helped my father very much. I am not sure that by then anything could have helped him. This is confirmed by what happened to him, conventional in some ways though it was.

Moreover, the marriage seemed to me to make no difference to his daily way of life: the bench, the chambers, the club, the dining club, the livery company, the military historical society, the self-defence classes, the kirk; or, I am sure, to those other indulgences. On most nights, he continued to ponder and by fits and starts to cry out. I still tiptoed swiftly away and, if possible, hid myself when I heard his step. I seldom set eyes upon my stepmother, though of course I am not saying that I never did. I took it for granted that her attitude to me was at least one thing that she shared with my father. That seemed natural. I found it hard to see what else she had any opportunity of sharing. It had, of course, always been Cuddy to whom I was mainly obliged for information about my father's habits and movements, in so far as she knew them. Cuddy was much less informative about my stepmother.

One new aspect of my own life was that my lessons had stopped. I believe that for more than a year I had nothing to do but keep out of the way and play, as far as was possible. Now, there seemed to be no callers at all, and assuredly not parfumiers and designers of lingerie. No doubt my stepmother's circle was entirely in Scotland, and probably to the north of the Forth and Clyde Canal. She would not have found it easy to create an entirely new circle in Belgravia. I suppose there were two reasons why I suffered less than I might have done from the unsatisfactory aspects of my situation. The first was that I could hardly suffer more than I was suffering from my sweet mother's death. The second reason was my suspicion that any other life I might be embarked upon would be even more unsatisfactory.

In the end, the Trustees intervened, as I have said; but, before that, Cuddy had something to impart, at long last, about my stepmother. She told me that my stepmother was drinking.

It debarred her, Cuddy informed me in a burst of gossip, from appearing in public very often. That was exactly how Cuddy expressed it; with a twinkle or a glint or whatever may be the Scottish word for such extra intimations. I gathered that my stepmother seldom even dressed herself, or permitted herself to be dressed by Cuddy. One thing I was not told and do not positively know is whether or not the poor lady was drinking as hard as this before her second marriage. It is fair to her to say that the late Johnny Robertson was usually described as a scamp or rogue. Certainly my stepmother's current condition was something that would have had to be concealed by everyone as far as possible at that time in Belgravia, and with her husband a High Court Judge.

In any case, after the Trustees had taken me away and sent me to an eminent school, I began to hear tales. At first, I knocked about those who hurled and spat them at me. I discovered a new strength in the process; just as the grounding (to use the favoured word) provided by my mother enabled me to do better than most in class, not so much by knowing more as by using greater imagination and ingenuity, qualities that tell even in rivalry among schoolboys. The jibes and jeers ceased, and then I began cautiously to enquire after the facts. The school was of the kind attended by many who really know such things. I learned that my father too had long been drinking; and was a byword for it in the counties and the clubs. No doubt in the gaols also, despite my father's dislike of criminal jurisdiction.

One morning, Jesperson, who was the son of a Labour ex-minister and quite a friend of mine, brought me *The Times* so that I could see the news before others did. I read that my father had had to be removed from his Court and sent for treatment. *The Times* seemed to think that if the treatment were not successful, he might feel it proper to retire. There was a summary of the cases over which he had presided from such an unusually early age (some of them had been attended by me, however fleetingly); and a reference to his almost universal popularity in mainly male society.

I was by then in a position at school to take out any chagrin I might feel upon as many other boys as I wished, but I was too introspective for any such easy release, and instead began for the first time to read *The Divine Comedy*.

There was nothing particularly unusual in what had happened to my father so far, but the treatment seems, as far as one can tell, to have been the conclusive ordeal, so that he died a year later in a mental hospital, like poor Haverstone, though not in the same one. My father returned in spirit to his sodden, picturesque wilderness, and is buried in the kirkyard four or five miles by a very rough road from Pollaporra. It was the first instruction in his will, and the Trustees heeded it, as a matter of urgency, to the last detail.

I could not myself attend the funeral, as I was laid low by a school epidemic, though by then in my last term, and older than any of my confrères. My stepmother also missed the funeral, though she had returned to Scotland as soon as she could. She had resolved to remain there, and, for all I know, she is there still, with health and sobriety renewed. Several times I have looked her up in directories and failed to find her, despite reference to all three of her known surnames; but I reflect that she may well have married yet again.

My father had left her a moiety of his free estate, in equal part with the various organisations he wished to benefit, and which I have already listed. She possessed, as I have said, means of her own. My father left me nothing at all, but he lacked power, Judge though he was, and a Scots solicitor also, to modify the family settlement. Therefore, I, as only surviving child, inherited a life interest in Pollaporra, though not in the house in Belgravia, and a moderate, though not remarkable, income for life. Had my brother survived, he would have inherited equally. Thinking about him, I wondered whether the demon drink, albeit so mighty among Scotsmen, had not rather been a symptom of my father's malady than the cause of it. Thinking of that, I naturally then thought about my own inwardness and prospects. Eugene O'Neill says that we become like our parents of the same sex, even when we consciously resolve not to. I wept for my mother, so beloved, so incomparable.

II

Immediately, the question arose of my going to a university. The idea had of course been discussed before with the Trustees, but I had myself rejected it. While my father had been alive, my plan had been simply to leave the country as soon as I could. Thanks to my mother,

I had made a good start with two European languages, and I had since advanced a little by reading literature written in them: *Die Räuber* and *Gerusalemme liberata*. The other boys no longer attacked or bullied me when they found me doing such things; and the school library contained a few basic texts, mostly unopened, both in the trade sense and the literal sense.

Now I changed my mind. The Trustees were clamant for Edinburgh, as could be expected; but I scored an important victory in actually going to Oxford. Boys from that school did not proceed to Edinburgh University, or did not then. It had never been practicable to send me to Fettes or Loretto. My friend, Jesperson, was at Oxford already. Oxford was still regarded by many as a dream, even though mainly in secret and in silence.

I read Modern Languages and Modern History, and I graduated reasonably, though not excitingly. I surprised myself by making a number of friends. This brought important benefits, in the short term and the long.

I now had no home other than Pollaporra, which, as will be recalled, could not always be visited during the winter, in any case. I spent most of the vacations with new friends; staying in their homes for astonishingly generous periods of time, or travelling with them, or reading with them. With the Second World War so plainly imminent and so probably apocalyptic, everyone travelled as much as he could. I met girls, and was continually amazed by myself. My closest involvement was with a pretty girl who lived in the town; who wrote poetry that was published; and who was almost a cripple. That surprised me most of all. I had learned something about myself, though I was unsure what it was. The girl lived, regardless, at the top of the house, which taught me something further. Her name was Celia. I fear that I brought little happiness to her or to any of the others, do what I would. I soon realised that I was a haunted man.

As for the main longer-term benefit, it was simple enough, and a matter of seemingly pure chance. My friend, Jack Oliver, spoke to his uncle, and as soon as I went down, modestly though not gloriously endorsed, I found myself en route to becoming a merchant banker. I owe Jack a debt that nothing can repay. That too is somehow a property of life. Nothing interlocks or properly relates. Life gives, quite casually, with one hand, and takes away rather more with the other hand, equally unforeseeably. There is little anyone can do about either transaction. Jack Oliver was and is the kindest man I have known, and a splendid offhand tennis player. He has a subtle wit, based on meiosis. From time to time, he has needed it. I have never climbed or otherwise risen to the top of the banking tree, but the tree is tall, and I lived as a child in a house with many stairs.

It was Perry Jesperson who came with me on my first visit to Pollaporra. He had borrowed one of his father's cars.

Even on the one-inch map, the topography was odd. It had struck me as odd many years before. I had always thought myself good with maps, as solitary children so often are; but now that I had been able to travel frequently, I had come to see that one cannot in every case divine from a map a feature of some kind that seems central when one actually arrives and inspects. In that way, I had made a fool of myself on several occasions, though sometimes to my own knowledge only. When it comes to Scotland, I need hardly say that many one-inch maps are sometimes needed for a journey from one place to another, and that some of the maps depict little but heaving contours and huge hydroelectric installations.

Pollaporra stood isolated amid wild altitudes for miles around. Its loneliness was confirmed by its being marked at all. I knew very well that it was no Inveraray or even Balmoral. It stood about three and a half miles from the sea loch, where Mason lived. That of course was as the crow flies, if crows there were. I had miled out the distance inaccurately with thumb and forefinger when I had still been a child. I had done it on many occasions. The topographical oddity was that the nearest depicted community was eight miles away in the opposite direction, whereas in such an area one would expect it to be on the sea, and to derive its hard living therefrom. It was difficult to think of any living at all for the place shown, which was stuck down in a hollow of the mountains, and was named Arrafergus. An uncoloured track was shown between Pollaporra and Arrafergus; the rough road of which I had heard so much, and along which my father's corpse had passed a few years before. One could see the little cross marking the kirk and kirkyard where he lay. It was placed almost halfway between the two names, which seemed oddest of all. For much of the year, no congregation could assemble from either house or village. A footpath was shown between Pollaporra and the sea loch, but one could hardly believe in more than a technical right of way, perhaps initiated by smugglers and rebels.

I had commented upon all this to Jesperson before we left. He had said, 'I expect it was an effect of the clearances.'

'Or of the massacres,' I had replied, not wishing to become involved in politics with Jesperson, even conversationally.

The roads were already becoming pretty objectionable, but Jesperson saw it all as progress, and we took it in turns to drive. On the third morning, we were advancing up the long road, yellow on the map, from the dead centre of Scotland to little Arrafergus. By English standards, it should not have been shown in yellow. Even Jesperson could hardly achieve more than a third of his normal speed. We had seen no other human being for a very long time, and even animals were absent, exactly as I had expected. Why was Arrafergus placed where it was, and how could it survive? Long ago the soaking mist had compelled us to put up the hood of the roadster. I admit that it was April.

In the early afternoon, the road came to an end. We were in a deep cleft of the rock-strewn hills, and it would have been impossible for it to go further. There was a burn roaring, rather than gurgling, over the dark stones. There was no community, no place, not even a road sign saying where we were or prohibiting further progress, not a shieling, not a crow. I speculated about what the funeral cortège could have done next.

'Do you want to get out and look for the foundations?' enquired Jesperson. 'There's probably the odd stone to be found. The landlords razed everything, but I'm told there are usually traces.'

'Not for the moment,' I said. 'Where do you suppose is the track to Pollaporra?'

'Up there,' said Jesperson immediately, and pointed over my head.

How had I missed it? Despite the drizzle, I could now see it quite plainly. Nor must I, or anyone, exaggerate. The track was exceedingly steep and far from well metalled, but, apart from the angle of incline, hardly worse to look at than the yellow road. Obviously, it must be difficult to keep the maps up to date, and in certain areas hardly worth while at present prices.

'Are we game?' I asked Jesperson. 'It's not your car, and I don't want to press.'

'We've got to spend the night somewhere,' said Jesperson, who had not even stopped the engine.

After that, all went surprisingly well. Cars were tougher and more flexible in those days. We ascended the mountain without once stopping, and there were no further major gradients until we came within sight of Pollaporra itself. I had feared that the track would die out altogether or become a desert of wiry weeds such as spring up vengefully on modern roads, if for a moment neglected.

The little kirk was wrapped in rain which was now much heavier. There were a few early flowers amidst and around the crumbling kirkyard walls. By June there would be more.

Jesperson drew up and this time stopped the engine reverently.

'It's all yours,' he said, glancing at me sideways.

I stepped out. The huge new monument dominated the scene.

I scrambled across the fallen stones.

My father's full name was there, and his dates of birth and death. And then, in much smaller lettering, A JUST MAN A BRAVE MAN AND A GOOD. That was it, the commemorated was no one's beloved husband or beloved father; nor were any of his honours specified; nor was confident hope expressed for him, or, by implication, for anyone, he having been so admirable.

Around were memorials, large and small, to others among my unknown ancestors and collaterals; all far gone in chipping, flaking, and greening, or all that I studied. Among us we seemed to cram the entire consecrated area. Perhaps the residue from other families had no mementoes. I was aware of the worms and maggots massed beneath my feet; crawling over one another, as in a natural history exhibit. At any moment, the crepe rubber soles of my shoes might crack and rot. Moreover, did the Church of Scotland ritually consecrate any place? I did not know. I turned round and realised that in the distance I could see Pollaporra also.

The house, though no more than a grey stone,

slate-roofed rectangle, neither high nor particularly long, dominated the scene from then on, probably because it was the only work of man visible, apart from the bad road. Also it seemed to stand much higher than I had expected.

Jesperson wisely refused to set his father's car at the final ascent. We went up on foot. From the ridge we could make out the sea loch, green and phantasmal in the driving drizzle.

Cuddy was living in the house now; virtually pensioned off by the Trustess, and retained as caretaker: also as housekeeper, should the need arise, as it now did, almost certainly for the first time.

'Cuddy,' I cried out in my best English university style, and with hand outstretched, as we entered. It was desirable to seem entirely confident.

'Brodick,' she replied, not familiar perhaps, but independent.

'This is Mr Jesperson.'

'It's too late for the shooting and too early for the fishing,' said Cuddy. I think those were her words. I never quite remember the seasons.

'Mr Leith has come to take possession,' said Perry Jesperson.

'It's his for his life,' said Cuddy, as if indicating the duration of evening playtime.

'How *are* things?' I asked in my English university way. I was trying to ignore the chill, inner and outer, which the place cast.

'Wind and watertight as far as this house is concerned. You can inspect it at once. You'll not find one slate misplaced. For the rest you must ask Mr Mason.'

'I shall do so tomorrow,' I replied. 'You must set me on the way to him.'

'It is a straight road,' said Cuddy. 'You'll not go wrong.'

Of course it was not a road at all, but a scramble over rocks and stones all three miles; slow, slippery, and tiring. I could see why Mason spent little of his time visiting. None the less, the way was perfectly straight to the sea; though only from the top could one discern that. Jesperson had volunteered to look for some sport. Cuddy had been discouraging, but the house was as crammed with gear as the kirkyard with ancestral bones.

Mason lived in a small, single-storeyed house almost exactly at the end of the path, and at the edge of the sea. The local letter-box was in his grey wall, with a single collection at 6:30 A.M. each day, apart from Saturdays, Sundays, and Public Holidays. There were a few other small houses, too small for the map but apparently occupied, and even a shop, with brooms in the window. The shop was now closed, and there was no indication of opening hours. A reasonably good, though narrow, road traversed the place, and in both directions disappeared along the edge of the loch. It ran between the path from Pollaporra and Mason's house. There was no detectable traffic, but there was a metal bus-stop sign, and a time-table in a frame. I looked at it. If Jesperson's father's car were to break up, as seemed quite likely,

243

we should need alternative transport. I saw that the bus appeared at 7:00 A.M. on the first Wednesday in each month between April and September. We had missed the April bus. I persisted and saw that the bus returned as early as 4:30 P.M. on the same day, and then went on to Tullochar at the head of the loch. Despite the length of the inlet, the waves were striking the narrow, stony beach sharply and rapidly. A few small broken boats were lying about, and some meshes of sodden net, with shapeless cork floats. There was even a smell of dead crustaceans.

I realised that all these modest investigations were being observed by Mason himself. He had opened the faded brown door of his house and was standing there.

'Brodick Leith,' he said, in the Scottish manner.

'Mr Mason,' I replied. 'I am very glad to meet you. I have heard about you all my life.'

'Ay,' said Mason, 'you would have. Come indoors. We'll have a drop together and then I'll show you the books. I keep them to the day and hour. There's not as much to do as once there was.'

'That was in my father's time?'

'In the Judge's time. Mr Justice Leith. Sir Roderic Leith, if you prefer. A strong man and a mysterious.'

'I agree with what you say.'

'Come inside,' said Mason. 'Come inside. I live as an unmarried man.'

Mason opened a new bottle, and before I left, we had made our way through all of it, and had started on the remains of the previous one. Though I drank appreciably less than half, it was still, I think, more spirit than I had drunk on any previous occasion. The books were kept in lucid and impersonal handwriting, almost as good as my father's, and were flawless, in so far as I could understand them; my career in banking having not yet begun. Mason left me to go through them with the bottle at my elbow, while he went into the next room to cook us steaks, with his own hands. I could see for myself that the amounts brought out as surplus or profit at the end of each account were not large. I had never supposed they would be, but the costs and responsibilities of land ownership were brought home to me, none the less. Until then, I had been a baby in the matter, as in many others. Most people are babies until they confront property ownership.

'I know you attended my father's funeral, Mr Mason,' I said. 'How was it? Tell me about it.' The steak was proving to be the least prepared that I had ever attempted to munch. No doubt the cooking arrangements were very simple. I had not been invited to inspect them.

'Ay,' said Mason, 'and the funeral was the least of it.' He took a heavier swig than before and stopped chewing altogether, while he thought.

'How many were there?' I had always been curious about that.

'Just me, and Cuddy MacFerrier, and the Shepstones.'

The Shepstones were relatives. I had of course never set eyes upon even one of them. I had never seen a likeness. Millais had never painted a single Shepstone, and if one or more of them had appeared upon a criminal charge, my father would hardly have been the Judge.

'How many Shepstones?' I asked, still essaying to devour.

'Just the three of them,' replied Mason, as if half-entranced. I am making little attempt to reproduce the Scottishness of his speech, or of anyone else's. I am far from being Sir Walter or George Douglas.

'That is all there are?'

'Just the three. That's all,' said Mason. 'Drink up, man.'

'A minister was there, of course?'

'Ay, the minister turned out for it. The son was sick, or so he said.'

'I am the son,' I said, smiling. 'And I *was* sick. I promise you that.'

'No need to promise anything,' said Mason, still motionless. 'Drink up, I tell you.'

'And no one else at all?' I persisted.

'Maybe the old carlin,' said Mason. 'Maybe her.'

For me that was a very particular Scottish word. I had in fact sprung half to my feet, as Mason spoke it.

'Dinna fash yoursel'. She's gone awa' for the noo,' said Mason.

He began once more to eat.

'I saw her once myself,' I said, sitting right down again. 'I saw her when my darling mother died.'

'Ay, you would,' said Mason. 'Especially if maybe you were about the house at the time. Who let her in?'

'I don't know,' I replied. 'Perhaps she doesn't have to be let in?'

'Och, she does that,' said Mason. 'She always has to be let in.'

'It was at the grave that you saw her?'

'No, not there, though it is my fancy that she was present. I saw her through that window as she came up from the sea.'

I know that Mason pointed, and I know that I did not find it the moment to look.

'Through the glass panes or out on the wee rocks you can view the spot,' said Mason. 'It's always the same.' Now he was looking at nothing and chewing vigorously.

'I saw no face,' I said.

'If you'd seen that, you wouldn't be here now,' said Mason. He was calm, as far as I could see.

'How often have you seen her yourself?'

'Four or five times in all. At the different deaths.'

'Including at my mother's death?'

'Yes, then too,' said Mason, still gazing upon the sawn-up sections of meat. 'At the family deaths she is seen, and at the deaths of those, whoever they be, that enter the family.'

I thought of my brother whom I had never known. I wasn't even aware that there had been any other family deaths during Mason's likely lifetime.

'She belongs to those called Leith, by one right or another,' said Mason, 'and to no one at all else.'

As he spoke, and having regard to the way he had put it, I felt that I saw why so apparently alert a man seemed

247

to have such difficulty in remembering that I was presumably a Leith myself. I took his consideration kindly.

'I didn't see anyone when the Judge died,' I remarked.

'Perhaps in a dream,' said Mason. 'I believe you were sick at the time.'

That was not quite right of course, but it was true that I had by no means been in the house.

We dropped the subject, and turned once more to feu duties, rents, and discriminatory taxes; even to the recent changes in the character of the tides and in the behaviour of the gannets.

I have no idea how I scrambled back to dismal Pollaporra, and in twilight first, soon in darkness. Perhaps the liquor aided instead of impeded, as liquor so often in practice does, despite the doctors and proctors.

III

After the war, Jack Oliver was there to welcome me back to the office off Cornhill. He was now a colonel. His uncle had been killed in what was known as an incident, when the whole family house had been destroyed, including the Devises and De Wints. The business was now substantially his.

I found myself advanced very considerably from the position I had occupied in 1939. From this it is not to be supposed, as so many like to suppose, that no particular aptitude is required for success in merchant banking. On the contrary, very precise qualities both of mind and of temperament are needed. About myself, the conclusion I soon reached was that I was as truly a Scottish businessman as my ancestors in the kirkyard, whether I liked it or not, as O'Neill says. I should have been foolish had I *not* liked it. I might have preferred to be a weaver of dreams, but perhaps my mother had died too soon for that to be possible. I must add, however, that the business was by no means the same as when I had entered it before the war. No business was the same. The staff was smaller, the atmosphere tenser. The gains were illusory, the prospects shadowy. One worked much less hard, but one believed in nothing. There was little to work for, less to believe in.

It was in the office, though, that I met Shulie. She seemed very lost. I was attracted by her at once.

'Are you looking for someone?' I asked.

'I have just seen Mr Oliver.' She had a lovely voice and a charming accent. I knew that Jack was seeking a new secretary. His present one had failed to report for weeks, or to answer her supposed home telephone number.

'I hope that all went well.'

Shulie shook her head and smiled a little.

'I'm sorry about that.'

'Mr Oliver had chosen a girl who went in just before me. It always happens.'

'I'm sure you'll have better luck soon.'

She shook her head a second time. 'I am not English.'

'That has advantages as well as disadvantages,' I replied firmly.

It struck me that she might be a refugee, with behind her a terrible story. She was small, slender, and dark, though not as dark as my mother. I could not decide whether or not she looked particularly Jewish. I daresay it is always a rather foolish question.

'No advantages when you are in England,' she said. 'Can you please tell me how to get out of this place?'

'I'll come with you,' I said. 'It's difficult to explain.'

That was perfectly true. It matters that it was true, because while we were winding through the corridors, and I was holding swing doors, I was successful in persuading Shulie to have lunch with me. Time was gained for me also by the fact that Shulie had a slight limp, which slowed her down quite perceptibly. I am sure she was weary, too, and I even believe that she was seriously underfed, whatever the exact reason. I perceived Shulie as a waif from the start; though also from the start I saw that it was far from the whole truth about her. I never learned the whole truth about her. Perhaps one never does learn, but Shulie refused, in so many words, to speak about it.

It was February, and outside I could have done with my overcoat. Jack Oliver still went everywhere in a British warm. He had several of them. There was snow on the ground and on the ledges. We had been under snow for weeks. Though do I imagine the snow? I do not imagine the cold. Shulie, when the blast struck her, drew into herself, as girls do. She was certainly not dressed for it; but few girls then were. The girlish image was still paramount. I myself actually caught a cold that day, as

I often did. I was laid up for a time in my small flat off Orchard Street, and with no one in any position to look after me very much. Later, Shulie explained to me that one need never catch cold. All that is necessary is a firm resolution against it: faith in oneself, I suppose.

On most days, Jack and I, together or apart, went either to quite costly places or to certain pubs. That was the way of life approved, expected, even enforced; and, within the limits of the time, rewarded. I, however, had kept my options more open than that. I took Shulie to a nearby tea shop, though a somewhat superior tea shop. We were early, but it was filling fast. Still, we had a table to ourselves for a time.

'What's your name?'

'Shulie.'

Her lips were like dark rose petals, as one imagines them, or sometimes dreams of them.

I have mentioned how lamentably sure I am that I failed to make Celia happy; nor any other girl. During the war, I had lived, off and on, with a woman married to another officer, who was never there when I was. I shall not relate how for me it all began. There was a case for, and a case against, but it had been another relationship inconducive to the ultimate happiness of either party.

When I realised that I was not merely attracted by Shulie, but deeply in love with her, and dependent for any future I might have upon marrying her, I applied myself to avoiding past errors. Possibly in past circumstances, they had not really been errors; but now they might be the difference between life and death. I decided that, apart from my mother, I had never previously and properly loved anyone; and that with no one else but my mother had I been sufficiently honest to give things a chance. When the time came, I acted at once.

Within half an hour of Shulie tentatively accepting my proposal of marriage, I related to her what Mason had told me, and what I had myself seen. I said that I was a haunted man. I even said that she could reverse her tentative decision, if she thought fit.

'So the woman has to be let in?' said Shulie.

'That's what Mason told me.'

'A woman who is married does not let any other woman in, except when her husband is not there.'

'But suppose you were ill?'

'Then you would be at home looking after me. It would not be a time when you would let in another woman.'

It was obvious that she was not taking the matter seriously. I had been honest, but I was still anxious.

'Have you ever heard a story like it before?'

'Yes,' said Shulie. 'But it is the message that matters more than the messenger.'

After we married, Shulie simply moved into my small flat. At first we intended, or certainly I intended, almost immediately to start looking for somewhere much larger. We, or certainly I, had a family in mind. With Shulie, I wanted that very much, even though I was a haunted man, whose rights were doubtful.

But it was amazing how well we seemed to go on living exactly where we were. Shulie had few possessions to bring in, and even when they were increased, we still seemed to have plenty of room. It struck me that Shulie's slight infirmity might contribute to her lack of interest in that normal ambition of any woman: a larger home. Certainly, the trouble seemed at times to fatigue her, even though the manifestations were very inconspicuous. For example, Jack Oliver, at a much later date, denied that he had ever noticed anything at all. The firm had provided me with a nice car and parking was then easier than it is now. Shulie had to do little walking of the kind that really exhausts a woman; pushing through crowds, and round shops at busy hours.

As a matter of fact, Shulie seldom left the flat, unless in my company. Shulie was writing a book. She ordered almost all goods on the telephone, and proved to be skilful and firm. She surprised me continually in matters like that. Marriage had already changed her considerably. She was plumper, as well as more confident. She accompanied me to the Festival Hall, and to picnics in Kew Gardens. The picnics were made elegant and exciting by her presence, and by her choice of what we ate and drank, and by the way she looked at the flowers, and by the way people and flowers looked at her. Otherwise, she wrote, or mused upon what she was about to write. She reclined in different sets of silk pyjamas on a bright-blue daybed I'd bought for her, and rested her square, stiff-covered exercise book upon her updrawn knees. She refused to read to me what she had written, or to let me read it for myself. 'You will know one day,' she said.

I must admit that I had to do a certain amount of explaining to Jack Oliver. He would naturally have preferred me to marry a woman who kept open house and was equally good with all men alike. Fortunately, business in Britain does not yet depend so much upon those things as does business in America. I was able to tell Jack that setting a wife to attract business to her husband was always a chancy transaction for the husband. For better or for worse, Jack, having lately battled his way through a very complex divorce, accepted my view. The divorce had ended in a most unpleasant situation for Jack financially, as well as in some public ridicule. He was in no position even to hint that I had married a girl whom he had rejected for a job. His own wife had been the daughter of a baronet who was also a vice-admiral and a former Member of Parliament. Her name was Clarissa. Her mother, the admiral's wife, was an MFH.

After my own mother's death, I should never have thought possible the happiness that Shulie released in me. There was much that remained unspoken to the end, but that may have been advantageous. Perhaps it is always so. Perhaps only madmen need to know everything and thus to destroy everything. When I lay in Shulie's arms, or simply regarded her as she wrote her secret book, I wished to know nothing more, because more would diminish. This state of being used to be known as connubial bliss. Few, I believe, experience it. It is certainly not a matter of deserts.

Shulie, however, proved to be incapable of conception. Possibly it was a consequence of earlier sufferings and endurances. Elaborate treatments might have been tried, but Shulie shrank from them, and understandably. She accepted the situation very quietly. She did not seem to cease loving me. We continued to dwell in the flat off Orchard Street.

I asked Shulie when her book would be finished. She replied that the more she wrote, the more there was to be written. Whenever I approached her, she closed the excercise book and lifted herself up to kiss me. If I persisted at all, she did more than kiss me.

I wanted nothing else in life than to be with Shulie, and alone with her. Everything we did in the outside world was incorporated into our love. I was happy once more, and now I was happy all the time, even in the office near Cornhill. I bought a bicycle to make the journey, but the City men laughed, and nicknamed me, and ragged me, so that Jack Oliver and the others suggested that I give it up. Jack bought the bicycle himself, to use at his place in the country, where, not necessarily on the bicycle, he was courting the divorced daughter of the local High Sheriff, a girl far beyond his present means. She was even a member of a ladies' polo team, though the youngest. When one is happy oneself, everyone seems happy.

Our flat was on the top floor in a small block. The block had been built in more spacious days than the present, and there were two lifts. They were in parallel shafts. Above the waistline, the lifts had windows on three sides; the gate being on the fourth. They were large lifts, each *Licensed to carry 12 people*; far more than commonly accumulated at any one time. The users worked the lifts themselves, though, when I had first taken the flat, the lifts in Selfridges round the corner had still been worked by the famous pretty girls in breeches, among whom an annual competition was held. The two lifts in the flats were brightly lit and always very clean. Shulie loved going up and down in them; much as she loved real traffic blocks, with boys ranging along the stationary cars selling ice cream and evening newspapers. None the less, I do not think she used the lifts very much when I was not there. Travelling in them was, in fact, one tiny facet of our love. When Shulie was alone, I believe she commonly used the stairs, despite her trouble. The stairs were well lit and well swept also. Marauders were seldom met.

Tenants used sometimes to wave to their neighbours through the glass, as the two lifts swept past one another, one upwards, one downwards. It was important to prevent this becoming a mere tiresome obligation. One morning I was alone in the descending lift. I was on my way to work: Bond Street Underground station to Bank Underground station. There had been a wonderful early morning with Shulie, and I was full of joy; thinking about nothing but that. The other lift swept upwards past me. In it were four people who lived in the flats, three women and one man; all known to me by sight, though no more than that. As a fifth, there was the woman whom I had seen when my mother died.

Despite the speed with which the lifts had passed, I was sure it was she. The back was turned to me, but her sparse hair, her dirty plaid, her stature, and somehow her stance, were for ever unmistakable. I remember thinking immediately that the others in the lift must all be seeing the woman's face.

Melted ice flowed through me from the top of my head to the soles of my feet. There was a device for stopping the lift: *To be used only in Emergency.* And of course I wanted to reverse the lift also. I was so cold and so shaky that I succeeded merely in jamming the lift, and neatly between floors, like a joke in *Puck* or *Rainbow*, or a play by Sartre.

I hammered and raved, but most of the tenants had either gone to work or were making preparations for coffee mornings. The other lift did not pass again. As many as ten minutes tore by before anyone took notice of me, and then it was only because our neighbour, Mrs Delmer, wanted to descend from the top, and needed the lift she always used, being, as she had several times told us, frightened of the other one. The caretaker emerged slowly from his cubicle and shouted to me that there was nothing he could do. He would have to send for the lift company's maintenance men. He was not supposed to be on duty at that hour anyway, he said. We all knew that. Mrs Delmer made a detour as she clambered down the staircase, in order to tap on the glass roof of my lift and give me a piece of her mind, though in refined phrases. In the end, I simply sank upon the floor and tried to close myself to all thought or feeling, though with no success.

I must acknowledge that the maintenance men came far sooner than one could have expected. They dropped from above, and crawled from below, even emerging from a trap in the lift floor, full of cheerful conversation, both particular and general. The lift was brought slowly down to the gate on the floor immediately below. For some reason, that gate would not open, even to the maintenance men; and we had to sink, slowly still, to the ground floor. The first thing I saw there was a liquid trail in from the street up to the gate of the other lift. Not being his hour, the caretaker had still to mop it up, even though it reeked of seabed mortality.

Shulie and I lived on the eighth floor. I ran all the way up. The horrible trail crossed our landing from the lift gate to under our front door.

I do not know how long I had been holding the key in my hand. As one does at such times, I fumbled and fumbled at the lock. When the door was open, I saw that the trail wound through the tiny hall or lobby and entered the living room. When the woman came to my mother, there had been a faint trail only, but at that time I had not learned from Mason about the woman coming from the sea. Fuller knowledge was yielding new evidence.

I did not find Shulie harmed, or ill, or dead. She was not there at all.

Everything was done, but I never saw her again.

IV

The trail of water soon dried out, leaving no mark of any kind, despite the rankness.

The four people whom I had seen in the lift, and who lived in the flats, denied that they had ever seen a fifth. I neither believed nor disbelieved.

Shulie's book was infinitely upsetting. It was hardly fiction at all, as I had supposed it to be, but a personal diary, in the closest detail, of everything we had done together, of everything we had been, of everything she had felt. It was at once comprehensive and chaste. At one time, I even thought of seeking a publisher for it, but was deterred, in an illogical way, by the uncertainty about what had happened to Shulie. I was aware that it had been perfectly possible for her to leave the building by the staircase, while I had been caged between floors in the lift. The staircase went down a shaft of its own.

The book contained nothing of what had happened to Shulie before she met me.

Shulie's last words were, 'So joyful! Am I dreaming, or even dead? It seems that there is no external way of deciding either thing.' Presumably, she had then been interrupted. Doubtless, she had then risen to open the door.

I had been married to Shulie for three years and forty-one days.

I wrote to the Trustees suggesting that they put Pollaporra on the market, but their law agent replied that it was outside their powers. All I had done was upset both Cuddy and Mason.

I sold the lease of the flat off Orchard Street, and bought the lease of another one, off Gloucester Place.

I settled down to living with no one and for no one. I took every opportunity of travelling for the bank, no matter where, not only abroad, but even to Peterhead, Bolton, or Camborne. Previously, I had not wished or cared to leave Shulie for a single night.

I pursued new delights, such as they were, and as they came along. I joined a bridge club, a chess club, a mahjong society, and a mixed fencing group. Later, I joined a very avant-garde dance club, and went there occasionally.

I was introduced by one of the people in my firm to a very High Anglican church in his own neighbourhood, and went there quite often. Sometimes I read one of the lessons. I was one of the few who could still do that in Latin.

Another partner was interested in masonics, but I thought that would be inconsistent. I did join a livery company: it is expected in the City.

I was pressed to go in for regular massage, but resisted that too.

I was making more paper money than I would ever have thought possible. Paper money? Not even that. Phantom wealth, almost entirely: taxes took virtually the whole of it. I did not even employ a housekeeper. I did not wish for the attentions of any woman who was not Shulie. All the same, I wrote to Celia, who replied at once, making clear, among very many other things, that she was still unmarried. She had time to write so long and so prompt a letter. She had hope enough to think it worth while.

It is amazing how full a life a man can lead without for one moment being alive at all, except sometimes when sleeping. As Clifford Bax says, life is best treated as simply a game. Soon enough one will be bowled middle stump, be put out of action in the scrum, or ruled offside and sent off. As Bax also says, it is necessary to have an alternative. But who really has?

None the less, blood will out, and I married again. Sometime before, Shulie's death had been 'presumed'. Mercifully, it was the Trustees who attended to that.

I married Clarissa. I am married to her now.

The Court had bestowed upon Clarissa a goodly slice of Jack's property and prospects, and Jack was recognised by all as having made a complete fool of himself, not only in the area of cash; but Clarissa never really left at all. Even though Jack was now deeply entangled with Suzanne, herself a young divorcée, Clarissa was always one of Jack's house party, eager to hear everything, ready to advise, perhaps even to comfort, though I myself never came upon her doing that. She might now be sleeping in the room that had once been set aside for the visits of her sister, Naomi, but of course she knew the whole house far more intimately than Jack did, or than any normal male knows any house. She continued being invaluable to Jack; especially when he was giving so much of his time to Suzanne. One could not know Jack at all well, let alone as well as I knew him, without continuing to encounter Clarissa all the time.

The word for Clarissa might be deft – the first word, that is. She can manage a man or a woman, a slow child or a slow pensioner, as effortlessly as she can manage everything in a house, at a party, in a shop, on a ship. She has the small but right touch for every single situation – the perfect touch. Most of all, she has the small and perfect touch for every situation, huge or tiny, in her own life. Few indeed have *that* gift. No doubt Clarissa owes much to her versatile papa. On one occasion also, I witnessed Clarissa's mother looking after a difficult meet. It was something to note and remember.

Clarissa has that true beauty which is not so much in the features and body, but around them: nothing less than a mystical emanation. When I made my proposal to Clarissa, I naturally thought very devoutly of Shulie. Shulie's beauty was of the order one longs from the first to embrace, to be absorbed by. Of course, my mother's dark beauty had been like that also. Clarissa one hardly wished or dared to touch, lest the vision fade. A man who felt otherwise than that about Clarissa would be a man who could not see the vision at all. I imagine that state of things will bear closely upon what happens to Clarissa. There is little that is mystical about Clarissa's detectable behaviour, though there must be *some* relationship between her soul and the way she looks. It is a question that arises so often when women as beautiful as Clarissa materialise in one's rose garden. I myself have never seen another woman as beautiful absolutely as Clarissa, or certainly never spoken to one.

Clarissa has eyes so deep as to make one wonder about the whole idea of depth, and what it means. She has a voice almost as lovely as her face. She has a slow and languorous walk: beautiful too, but related, I fear, to an incident during her early teens, when she broke both legs in the hunting field. Sometimes it leads to trouble when Clarissa is driving a car. Not often. Clarissa prefers to wear trousers, though she looks perfectly normal in even a short skirt, indeed divinely beautiful, as always.

I fear that too much of my life with Clarissa has been given to quarrelling. No one is to blame, of course.

There was a certain stress even at the proposal scene, which took place on a Saturday afternoon in Jack's house, when the others were out shooting duck. Pollaporra and its legend have always discouraged me from field sports, and all the struggling about had discouraged Clarissa, who sat before the fire, looking gnomic.

But she said yes at once, and nodded, and smiled.

Devoted still, whether wisely or foolishly, to honesty, I told her what Mason had told me, and what I had myself seen on two occasions, and that I was a haunted man.

Clarissa looked very hostile. 'I don't believe in things like that,' she said sharply.

'I thought I ought to tell you.'

'Why? Did you want to upset me?'

'Of course not. I love you. I don't want you to accept me on false pretences.'

'It's got nothing to do with my accepting you. I just don't want to know about such things. They don't exist.'

'But they do, Clarissa. They are part of me.'

From one point of view, obviously I should not have persisted. I had long recognised that many people would have said that I was obsessed. But the whole business seemed to me the explanation of my being. Clarissa must not take me to be merely a banker, a youngish widower, a friend of her first husband's, a faint simulacrum of the admiral.

Clarissa actually picked up a book of sweepstake tickets and threw it at me as I sat on the rug at her feet.

'There,' she said.

It was a quite thick and heavy book, but I was not exactly injured by it, though it had come unexpectedly, and had grazed my eye.

Clarissa then leaned forward and gave me a slow and searching kiss. It was the first time we had kissed so seriously.

'There,' she said again.

She then picked the sweepstake tickets off the floor and threw them in the fire. They were less than fully burnt ten minutes later, when Clarissa and I were more intimately involved, and looking at our watches to decide when the others were likely to return.

The honeymoon, at Clarissa's petition, was in North Africa, now riddled with politics, which I did not care for. For centuries, there has been very little in North Africa for an outsider to see, and the conformity demanded by an alien society seemed not the best background for learning to know another person. Perhaps we should have tried Egypt, but Clarissa specifically demanded something more rugged. With Shulie there had been no honeymoon.

Before marrying me, Clarissa had been dividing her life between her flat and Jack's country house. Her spacious flat, very near my childhood home, was in its own way as beautiful as she was, and emitted a like glow. It would have been absurd for me not to move into it. The settlement from Jack had contributed significantly to all around me, but by now I was able to keep up, or nearly so. Money is like sex. The more that everyone around is talking of little else, the less it really accounts for, let alone assists.

Not that sex has ever been other than a problem with Clarissa. I have good reason to believe that others have found the same, though Jack never gave me one word of warning. In any case, his Suzanne is another of the same kind, if I am any judge; though less beautiful, and, I should say, less kind also. Men chase the same women again and again; or rather the same illusion; or rather the same lost part of themselves.

Within myself, I had of course returned to the hope of children. Some will say that I was a fool not to have had that matter out with Clarissa before marrying her, and no doubt a number of related matters also. They speak without knowing Clarissa. No advance terms can be set. None at all. I doubt whether it is possible with any woman whom one finds really desirable. Nor can the proposal scene be converted into a businesslike discussion of future policy and prospects. That is not the atmosphere, and few would marry if it were.

With Shulie, the whole thing had been love. With Clarissa, it was power; and she was so accustomed to the power being hers that she could no longer bother to exercise it, except indirectly. This was and is true even though Clarissa is exceedingly good-hearted in many other ways. I had myself experienced something of the kind in reverse with poor Celia, though obviously in a much lesser degree.

Clarissa has long been impervious to argument or importunity or persuasion of any kind. She is perfectly equipped with counterpoise and equipoise. She makes discussion seem absurd. Almost always it is. Before long, I was asking myself whether Clarissa's strange and radiant beauty was compatible with desire, either on her part or on mine.

There was also the small matter of Clarissa's black maid, Aline, who has played her little part in the immediate situation. On my visits to the flat before our marriage, I had become very much aware of Aline, miniature and slender, always in tight sweater and pale trousers. Clarissa had told me that Aline could do everything in the place that required to be done; but in my hearing Aline spoke little for herself. I was told that often she drove Clarissa's beautiful foreign car, a present from Jack less than a year before the divorce. I was also told, as a matter of interest, that Jack had never met Aline. I therefore never spoke of her to him.

I was telling him much less now, in any case. I certainly did not tell him what I had not previously told myself: that when I was away for the firm, which continued to be frequently, Aline took my place in Clarissa's vast and swanlike double bed. I discovered this in a thoroughly low way, which I do not propose to relate. Clarissa simply remarked to me that, as I knew, she could never sleep well if alone in the room. I abstained from rejoining that what Clarissa really wanted was a nanny; one of those special nannies who, like dolls, are always there to be dominated by their charges. It would have been one possible rejoinder.

Nannies were on my mind. It had been just then that the Trustees wrote to me about Cuddy. They told me that Cuddy had 'intimated a wish' to leave her employment at Pollaporra. She wanted to join her younger sister, who, I was aware, had a business on the main road, weaving and plaiting for the tourists, not far from Dingwall. I could well believe that the business had become more prosperous than when I had heard about it as a child. It was a business of the sort that at the moment did. The Trustees went on to imply that it was my task, and not theirs, to find a successor to Cuddy. They reminded me that I was under an obligation to maintain a property in which I had merely a life interest.

It was a very hot day. Clarissa always brought the sun. She had been reading the letter over my shoulder. I was aware of her special nimbus encircling my head and torso when she did this. Moreover, she was wearing nothing but her nightdress.

'Let's go and have a look,' she said.

'Are you sure you want to?' I asked, remembering her response to my story.

'Of course I'm sure. I'll transform the place, now I've got it to myself.'

'That'll be the day,' I said, smiling up at her.

'You won't know it when I've finished with it. Then we can sell it.'

'We can't,' I said. 'Remember it's not mine to sell.'

'You must get advice. Jack might be able to help.'

'You don't know what Pollaporra's like. Everything is bound to be totally run down.'

'With your Cuddy in charge all these years, and with nothing else to do with herself? At least, you say not.'

I had seen on my previous visit that this argument might be sound, as far as it went.

'You can't possibly take on all the work.'

'We'll have Aline with us. I had intended that.'

By now, I had seen for myself also that Aline was indeed most competent and industrious. It would have been impossible to argue further: Clarissa was my wife and had a right both to accompany me and to take someone with her to help with the chores. If I were to predecease her, she would have a life interest in the property. Moreover, Clarissa alone could manage very well for us when she applied herself. I had learned that too. There were no sensible, practical objections whatever.

'Aline will be a help with the driving as well,' added Clarissa.

There again, I had seen for myself how excellent a

driver little Aline could be. She belongs to just the sort of quiet person who in practice drives most effectively on the roads of today.

'So write at once and say we're arriving,' said Clarissa.

'I'm not sure there's anyone to write to,' I replied. 'That's the point.'

I had, of course, a set of keys. For whatever reason, I did not incline to giving Mason advance notice of my second coming, and in such altered circumstances.

'I'm not sure how Aline will get on with the Highlanders,' I remarked. There are, of course, all those stories in Scotland about the intrusion of huge black men, and sometimes, I fancy, of black females. They figure in folklore everywhere.

'She'll wind each of them three times round each of her fingers,' replied Clarissa. 'But you told me there *were* no Highlanders at Pollaporra.'

Clarissa, when triumphing, looks like Juno, or Diana, or even Minerva.

Aline entered to the tinkling of a little bell. It is a pretty little bell, which I bought for Clarissa in Sfax; her earlier little bell having dropped its clapper. When Aline entered in her quiet way, Clarissa kissed her, as she does every morning upon first sighting Aline.

'We're all three going into the wilderness together,' said Clarissa. 'Probably on Friday.'

Friday was the day after tomorrow. I really could not leave the business for possibly a week at such short notice. There was some tension because of that, but it could not be helped.

*

When we did reach Pollaporra, the weather was hotter than ever, though there had been several thunderstorms in London. Aline was in her element. Clarissa had stocked up the large car with food in immense quantity. When we passed through an outlying area of Glasgow, she distributed two pounds of sweets to children playing in the roads of a council estate. The sweets were melting in their papers as she threw them. The tiny fingers locked together.

When we reached the small kirkyard, Clarissa, who was driving us along the rough road from Arrafergus, categorically refused to stop.

'We're here to drive the bogies out,' she said, 'not to let them in.'

Clarissa also refused to leave the car at the bottom of the final slope, as Perry Jesperson had done. My friend Jesperson was now a Labour MP like his father, and already a Joint Parliamentary Secretary, and much else, vaguely lucrative and responsible. Clarissa took the car up the very steep incline as if it had been a lift at the seaside.

She stood looking at and beyond the low grey house. 'Is that the sea?' she asked, pointing.

'It's the sea loch,' I replied. 'A long inlet, like a fjord.'

'It's a lovely place,' said Clarissa.

I was surprised, but, I suppose, pleased.

'I thought we might cut the house up into lodges for the shooting and fishing,' said Clarissa. 'But now I don't want to.'

'The Trustees would never have agreed,' I pointed out. 'They have no power to agree.'

'Doesn't matter. I want to come here often. Let's take a photograph.'

So, before we started to unpack the car, Clarissa took one of Aline and me; and, at her suggestion, I took one of Aline and her. Aline did not rise to the shoulders of either of us.

Within the house, the slight clamminess of my previous visit had been replaced by a curiously tense airlessness. I had used my key to admit us, but I had not been certain as to whether or not Cuddy was already gone, and Clarissa and I went from room to room shouting for her, Clarissa more loudly than I. Aline remained among the waders and antlers of the entrance hall, far from home, and thinking her own thoughts. There was no reply anywhere. I went to the door of what I knew to be Cuddy's own room, and quietly tapped. When there was no reply there either, I gently tried the handle. I thought the door might be locked, but it was not. Inside was a small unoccupied bedroom. The fittings were very spare. There were a number of small framed statements on the walls, such as *I bow before Thee*, and *Naught but Surrender*, and *Who knows All* without a mark of interrogation. Clarissa was still calling from room to room. I did not care to call back but went after her on half-tiptoe.

I thought we could conclude we were alone. Cuddy must have departed some time ago.

Dust was settling everywhere, even in that remote

spot. The sunlight made it look like encroaching fur. Clarissa seemed undeterred and undaunted.

'It's a lost world and I'm queen,' she said.

It is true that old grey waders, and wicker fish baskets with many of the withies broken, and expensive guns for stalking lined up in racks, are unequalled for suggesting loss, past, present, and to come. Even the pictures were all of death and yesterday – stags exaggeratedly virile before the crack shot; feathers abnormally bright before the battue; men and ancestors in bonnets before, behind, and around the ornamentally piled carcases, with the lion of Scotland flag stuck in the summit. When we reached the hall, I noticed that Aline was shuddering in the sunlight. I myself had never been in the house before without Cuddy. In practice, she had been responsible for everything that happened there. Now I was responsible – and for as long as I remained alive.

'We'll paint everything white and we'll put in a swimming pool,' cried Clarissa joyously. 'Aline can have the room in the tower.'

'I didn't know there was a tower,' I said.

'*Almost* a tower,' said Clarissa.

'Is there anything in the room?' I asked.

'Only those things on heads. They're all over the walls and floor.'

At that, Aline actually gave a little cry. Perhaps she was thinking of things on walls and floors in Africa.

'It's all right,' said Clarissa, going over to her. 'We'll throw them all away. I promise. I never ask you to do anything I don't do myself, or wouldn't do.'

But, whatever might be wrong, Aline was uncomforted. 'Look!' she cried, and pointed out through one of the hall windows, all of them obstructed by stuffed birds in glass domes, huge and dusty.

'What have you seen this time?' asked Clarissa, as if speaking to a loved though exhausting child.

At that moment, it came to me that Clarissa regularly treated Aline as my mother had treated me.

Aline's hand fell slowly to her side, and her head began to droop.

'It's only the car,' said Clarissa. '*Our* car. You've been driving it yourself.'

I had stepped swiftly but quietly behind the two of them. I admit that I too could see nothing but the car, and, of course, the whole of Scotland.

I seldom spoke directly to Aline, but now was the moment.

'What was it?' I asked, as sympathetically as I could manage. 'What did you see?'

But Aline had begun to weep, as by now I had observed that she often did. She wept without noise or any special movement. The tears just flowed like thawing snow; as they do in nature, though less often on 'Change.

'It was nothing,' said Clarissa. 'Aline often sees nothing, don't you, Aline?' She produced her own handkerchief, and began to dry Aline's face, and to hug her tightly.

The handkerchief was from an enormous casket of objects given us as a wedding present by Clarissa's grandmother (on the mother's side), who was an invalid, living in Dominica. Clarissa's grandfather had been shot dead years before by thieves he had interrupted.

'Now,' said Clarissa after a few moments of tender re-assurance. 'Smile, please. That's better. We're going to be happy here, one and all. Remember. Happy.'

I suppose I was reasonably eager, but I found it difficult to see how she was going to manage it. It was not, as I must in justice to her make clear, that normally I was unhappy with Clarissa. She was too beautiful and original for that to be the word at any time. The immediate trouble was just Pollaporra itself: the most burdensome and most futile of houses, so futile as to be sinister, even apart from its associations, where I was concerned. I could not imagine any effective brightening; not even by means of maquillage and disguise: a pool, a disco-thèque, a sauna, a black-jack suite. To me Pollaporra was a millstone I could never throw away. I could not believe that modern tenants would ever stop there for long, or in the end show us a profit. For all the keep nets and carcase sleighs in every room, I doubted whether the accessible sport was good enough to be marketed at all in contemporary terms. Nor had I started out with Clarissa in order that we should settle down in the place ourselves. When I can get away from work, I want somewhere recuperative. About Pollaporra, I asked the question all married couples ask when detached from duties and tasks: what should we do all day? There was nothing.

'I have never felt so free and blithe,' said Clarissa later

that evening, exaggerating characteristically but charmingly. She was playing the major part in preparing a quite elaborate dinner for us out of tins and packets. In the flat, Aline had normally eaten in her own pretty sitting room, but here she would be eating with us. Clarissa would be tying a lace napkin round her neck, and heaping her plate with first choices, and handing her date after date on a spike. Employees are supposed to be happier when treated in that way, though few people think it is true, and few employees.

'We'll flatten the roof and have li-los,' said Clarissa, while Aline munched with both eyes on her plate, and I confined myself to wary nibblings round the fringe of Rognons Turbigo, canned but reinvigorated. The plates at Pollaporra depicted famous Scots, such as Sawney Bean and Robert Knox, who employed Burke and Hare, the body-snatchers. Mr Justice Leith, who despised the criminal law, had never been above such likenesses, as we know; nor had he been the only sporting jurist in the family, very far from it.

'I think to do that we'd have to rebuild the house,' I remarked.

'Do try not to make difficulties the whole time. Let yourself go, Brodick.'

It is seldom a good idea, according to my experience, and especially not in Scotland, but of course I could see what Clarissa meant. There was no reason why we should not make of the trip as much of a holiday as was possible. It would be a perfectly sensible thing to do. If Clarissa was capable of fun at Pollaporra, I was the last person with a right to stand in her way.

'We might build a gazebo,' I said, though I could feel my heart sinking as I spoke.

Aline, with her mouth full of prunes (that day), turned her head towards me. She did not know what a gazebo was.

'A sort of summerhouse,' explained Clarissa. 'With cushions and views. It would be lovely. So many things to look at.'

I had never known Clarissa so simple-minded before; in the nicest sense, of course. I realised that this might be a Clarissa more real than the other one. I might have to consider where I myself stood about that. On the other hand, Pollaporra, instead of bringing out at long last the real woman, might be acting upon her by contraries, and have engaged the perversity in her, and to no ultimately constructive end. I had certainly heard of that too, and in my time seen it in action among friends.

'I don't want to look,' said Aline, expelling prune stones into spoons.

'You will by tomorrow. You'll feel quite different. We're going to drive all the banshees far, far away.'

I am sure that Aline did not know what a banshee was either, but Clarissa's general meaning was clear, and the word has an African, self-speaking sound in itself, when one comes to think about it. Words for things like that are frightening in themselves the world over.

Only Clarissa, who believed in nothing she could not see or imagine, was utterly undisturbed. I am sure that must have played its part in the row we had in our room that night.

There were small single rooms, of course, several of them. There were also low dormitories for body servants and sporting auxiliaries. All the rooms for two people had Scottish double beds. Clarissa and I had to labour away in silence making such a bed with sheets she had brought with us. Blankets we should have had to find in drawers and to take on trust, but on such a night they were unnecessary. Aline, when not with Clarissa, always slept in a striped bag, which that night must have been far too hot. Everything, everywhere, was far too hot. That contributed too, as it always does. Look at Latin America!

I admit that throughout the evening I had failed to respond very affirmatively to Clarissa's sequence of suggestions for livening up the property and also (she claimed) increasing its market value; which, indeed, cannot, as things were and are, be high. I could see for myself how I was leading her first into despondency, then into irritation. I can see that only too well now. I was dismayed by what was happening, but there was so little I could conscientiously offer in the way of encouragement. All I wished to do with Pollaporra was patch up some arrangement to meet my minimum obligations as a life tenant, and then, if possible, never set eyes upon the place again. One reason why I was cast down was the difficulty of achieving even a programme as basic as that. I daresay that Clarissa's wild ideas would actually be simpler to accomplish, and conceivably cheaper also in the end. But there is something more than reason that casts me down at Pollaporra. Shall I say that the house brings into consciousness the conflict between my heraditament and my identity? Scotland herself is a land I do well to avoid. Many of us have large areas of danger which others find merely delightful.

There was no open row until Clarissa and I went upstairs. One reason was that after doing the washing-up, Aline had come into the sitting room, without a word, to join us. I was not surprised that she had no wish to be alone; nor that she proved reluctant to play a game named Contango, of which Clarissa was very fond, and which went back to her days with Jack, even though Jack had always won, sometimes while glancing through business papers simultaneously, as I had observed for myself. Both Clarissa and Aline were wearing tartan trousers, though not the same tartan. I had always been told by Cuddy that there was no Leith tartan. I have never sought further to know whether or not that is true.

As soon as we were in bed, Clarissa lay on her front, impressing the pillow with moisture from her brow, and quietly set about me; ranging far beyond the possibilities and deficiencies of Pollaporra. Any man – any modern man – would have some idea of what was said. Do the details matter? I offered no argument. At Pollaporra, I spoke as little as I could. What can argument achieve anywhere? It might have been a moment for me to establish at least temporary dominance by one means or another, but Pollaporra prevented, even if I am the man to do it at any time. I tried to remember Shulie, but of course the circumstances left her entirely unreal to me, together with everything else.

And, in the morning, things were no better. I do not know how much either of us had managed to sleep. For better or worse, we had fallen silent in the heat long ago. In the end, I heard the seabirds screaming and yelling at the dawn.

Clarissa put on a few garments while I lay silent on the bed and then told me that as there was nothing she could do in the house, she was departing at once.

'I should leave Aline behind, but I need her.'

'I quite understand,' I said. 'I advised you against coming in the first place. I shall go over to see Mason and try to arrange with him for a caretaker. It won't take more than a day or two.'

'You'll first need to change the place completely. You are weak and pigheaded.'

'They sometimes see things differently in Scotland. I shall come down as soon as I can.' I might have to hire a car to some station, because I did not think Mason owned one, or anyone else in his small community. That was a trifle; comparatively.

'No hurry. I shall use the time deciding what to do for the best.' She was combing her mass of hair, lovely as Ceres' sheaf. The comb, given her by the Aga Khan, was made of ebony. The air smelled of hot salt.

I suppose I should have begged her pardon for Pollaporra and myself, and gone back to London with her, or to anywhere else. I did not really think of it. Pollaporra had to be settled, if at all possible. I might never be back there.

In a few moments, Clarissa and I were together in the hall, the one high room, and I saw Aline silently standing by the outer door, as if she had stood all night; and the door was slightly open. Aline was in different trousers, and so was Clarissa.

'I can't be bothered to pack up the food. You're welcome to all of it.'

'Don't go without breakfast,' I said. 'The lumpy roads will make you sick.'

'Breakfast would make me sick,' said Clarissa.

Clarissa carried very few clothes about. All she had with her was in the aircraft holdall she clutched. I do not know about Aline. She must have had something. I cannot remember.

'I don't know when we'll meet again,' said Clarissa.

'In two or three days,' I said. 'Four at the most.' Since I had decided to remain, I had to seem calm.

'I may go and stay with Naomi. I want to think things out.'

She was wearing the lightest of blouses, little more than a mist. She was exquisite beyond description. Suddenly, I noticed that tears were again streaming silently down Aline's face.

'Or I may go somewhere else,' said Clarissa, and walked out, with her slight but distinctive wobble.

Instead of immediately following her, as she always did, Aline actually took two steps in my direction. She looked up at me, like a rococo cherub. Since I could not kiss Clarissa, I lightly kissed Aline's wet lips, and she kissed me.

I turned my back in order not to see the car actually depart, though nothing could prevent my hearing it. What had the row been really about? I could surmise and guess, but I did not know. I much doubted whether Clarissa knew. One could only be certain that she would explain herself, as it were to a third party, in a totally different way from me. We might just as well belong to different zoological species, as in the Ray Bradbury story. The row was probably a matter only of Clarissa being a woman and I a man. Most of all, rows between the sexes have no more precise origin; and, indirectly, many other rows also.

I think I stood for some time with my back to the open door and my face to the picture of an old gillie in a tam, with dead animals almost to his knees. It had been given us by the Shepstones. It was named *Coronach* in Ruskinian letters, grimly misapplied. Ultimately, I turned and through the open door saw what Aline may have seen. The auld carlin was advancing across the drive with a view to entering.

Drive, I have to call it. It was a large area of discoloured nothingness upon which cars stood, and before them horses, but little grew, despite the lack of weeding. Needless to say, the woman was not approaching straightforwardly. Previously, I had seen her only when she had been confined to the limits of a staircase, albeit a wide one, a landing, and, later, a lift. If now she had been coming straight at me, I might have had a split second to see her face. I realised that, quite clearly, upon the instant.

I bounded forward. I slammed the door. The big key was difficult to turn in the big lock, so I shot the four rusty bolts first. Absurdly, there was a 'chain' also and, after I had coped with the stiff lock, I 'put it on'.

Then I tore round the house shooting other bolts; making sure that all other locks were secure; shutting every possible window and aperture, on that already very hot early morning.

It is amazing how much food Clarissa laid in. She was, or is, always open-handed. I am sure that I have made that clear. Nor of course does one need so much food – or at least want so much – in this intense heat. Nor as yet has the well run dry. Cuddy refused to show me the well, saying the key was lost. I have still not seen either thing.

There is little else to do but write this clear explanation of everything that has happened to me since the misfortune of birth. He that has fared better, and without deceiving himself, let him utter his jackass cry.

Not that I have surrendered. There lies the point. Pollaporra is not on the telephone, nor ever could be, pending the 'withering away of the State'; but before long someone may take note that I am not there. The marines may descend from choppers yet. Clarissa may well have second thoughts. Women commonly do, when left to themselves. She loves Pollaporra and may well devise a means of wrestling my life interest away from me, and welcome. I don't know where Aline would enter into that hypothesis. Possibly I made a mistake in not writing to Mason that I was coming. But I doubt whether in such personal matters his time-scale is shorter than months.

Off and on, I see the woman at one window or another; though not peeking through, which, as will have been gathered, is far from her policy. At least twice, however, it has been at a window upstairs; on both occasions when I was about to undress for some reason, not necessarily slumber, of which I have little. At these times, her slimy-sleek head, always faceless, will tip-tap sharply against the thick glazing bars. The indelicacy, as Jack might put it (I wonder how Cuddy would put it?), set me upon a course of hard thinking.

So long as I keep myself barred up, she can achieve nothing. Mason seemed quite certain of that, and I accept it. But what does the woman aim to do to me? When she appeared to me before, my poor mother soon passed away. When she appeared to me a second time, my dear, dear Shulie vanished from my life. It is not to be taken for granted that either of these precise fates is intended for me. I am not even ill or infirm. There may be a certain room for manoeuvre, though I can foresee no details.

More often, I see the woman at corners of what used to be the lawn and garden, though never in my time. It lies at the back of the house, and far below lies the loch. Sometimes too, the creature perches on the ornaments and broken walls, like a sprite. Such levitations are said to be not uncommon in the remoter parts of Scotland. Once I thought I glimpsed her high up in a bush, like dirty rags in a gale. Not that so far there has been any gale, or even any wind. The total silent stillness is one of the worst things. If I die of heat and deoxygenation, it will be one solution.

Yes, it is a battle with strong and unknown forces that I have on my hands. 'But what can ail all of them to bury the old carlin in the night time?' as Sir Walter ventures to enquire; in *The Antiquary*, if I remember rightly.

The Inner Room

It was never less than half an hour after the engine stopped running that my father deigned to signal for succour. If in the process of breaking down, we had climbed, or descended, a bank, then first we must all exhaust ourselves pushing. If we had collided, there was, of course, a row. If, as had happened that day, it was simply that, while we coasted along, the machinery had ceased to churn and rattle, then my father tried his hand as a mechanic. That was the worst contingency of all; at least it was the worst one connected with motoring.

I had learned by experience that neither rain nor snow made much difference, and certainly not fog; but that afternoon it was hotter than any day I could remember. I realised later that it was the famous Long Summer of 1921, when the water at the bottom of cottage wells turned salt, and when eels were found baked and edible in their mud. But to know this at the time, I should have had to read the papers, and though, through my mother's devotion, I had the trick of reading before my third birthday, I mostly left the practice to my younger brother, Constantin. He was reading now from a pudgy volume, as thick as it was broad, and resembling his own head in size and proportion. As always, he had resumed his studies immediately the bumping of our almost springless car permitted, and even before motion had ceased. My mother sat in the front seat inevitably correcting pupils' exercises. By teaching her native German in five schools at once, three of them distant, one of them fashionable, she surprisingly managed to maintain the four of us, and even our car. The front offside door of the car leaned dangerously open into the seething highway.

'I say,' cried my father.

The young man in the big yellow racer shook his head as he tore by. My father had addressed the least appropriate car on the road.

'I say.'

I cannot recall what the next car looked like, but it did not stop.

My father was facing the direction from which we had come, and sawing the air with his left arm, like a very inexperienced policeman. Perhaps no one stopped because all thought him eccentric. Then a car going in the opposite direction came to a standstill behind my father's back. My father perceived nothing. The motorist sounded his horn. In those days, horns squealed, and I covered my ears with my hands. Between my hands and my head my long fair hair was like brittle flax in the sun.

My father darted through the traffic. I think it was the Portsmouth Road. The man in the other car got out and came to us. I noticed his companion, much younger and in a cherry-coloured cloche, begin to deal with her nails.

'Broken down?' asked the man. To me it seemed obvious, as the road was strewn with bits of the engine and oozy blobs of oil. Moreover, surely my father had explained?

'I can't quite locate the seat of the trouble,' said my father.

The man took off one of his driving gauntlets, big and dirty.

'Catch hold for a moment.' My father caught hold.

The man put his hand into the engine and made a casual movement. Something snapped loudly.

'Done right in. If you ask me, I'm not sure she'll ever go again.'

'Then I don't think I'll ask you,' said my father affably. 'Hot, isn't it?' My father began to mop his tall corrugated brow, and front-to-back ridges of grey hair.

'Want a tow?'

'Just to the nearest garage.' My father always spoke the word in perfect French.

'Where to?'

'To the nearest car repair workshop. If it would not be troubling you too much.'

'Can't help myself now, can I?'

From under the backseat in the other car, the owner got out a thick, frayed rope, black and greasy as the hangman's. The owner's friend simply said, 'Pleased to meet you,' and began to replace her scalpels and enamels in their cabinet. We jolted towards the town we had traversed an hour or two before; and were then untied outside a garage on the outskirts.

'Surely it is closed for the holiday?' said my mother. Hers is a voice I can always recall upon an instant: guttural, of course, but beautiful, truly golden.

''Spect he'll be back,' said our benefactor, drawing in his rope like a fisherman. 'Give him a bang.' He kicked three times very loudly upon the dropped iron shutter. Then without another word he drove away.

It was my birthday, I had been promised the sea, and I began to weep. Constantin, with a fretful little wriggle, closed further into himself and his book; but my mother leaned over the front seat of the car and opened her arms to me. I went to her and sobbed on the shoulder of her bright red dress.

'Kleine Lene, wir stecken schön in der Tinte.'

My father, who could pronounce six languages perfectly but speak only one of them, never liked my mother to use her native tongue within the family. He rapped more sharply on the shutter. My mother knew his ways, but, where our welfare was at stake, ignored them.

'Edgar,' said my mother, 'let us give the children presents. Especially my little Lene.' My tears, though childish, and less viscous than those shed in later life, had turned the scarlet shoulder of her dress to purple. She squinted smilingly sideways at the damage.

My father was delighted to defer the decision about what next to do with the car. But, as pillage was possible, my mother took with her the exercises, and Constantin his fat little book.

We straggled along the main road, torrid, raucous, adequate only for a gentler period of history. The grit and dust stung my face and arms and knees, like granulated glass. My mother and I went first, she holding my hand. My father struggled to walk at her other side, but for most of the way, the path was too narrow. Constantin mused along in the rear, abstracted as usual.

'It is true what the papers say,' exclaimed my rather. 'British roads were never built for motor traffic. Beyond the odd car, of course.'

My mother nodded and slightly smiled. Even in the lineless hopsacks of the twenties, she could not ever but look magnificent, with her rolling, turbulent, honey hair, and Hellenic proportions. Ultimately we reached the High Street. The very first shop had one of its windows stuffed with toys; the other being stacked with groceries and draperies and coal-hods, all dingy. The name POPULAR BAZAAR, in wooden relief as if glued on in building blocks, stretched across the whole front, not quite centre.

It was not merely an out-of-fashion shop, but a shop that at the best sold too much of what no one wanted. My father comprehended the contents of the Toy Department window with a single, anxious glance, and said, 'Choose whatever you like. Both of you. But look very carefully first. Don't hurry.' Then he turned away and began to hum a fragment from 'The Lady of the Rose'.

But Constantin spoke at once. 'I choose those telegraph wires.' They ranged beside a line of tin railway

289

that stretched right across the window, long undusted and tending to buckle. There were seven or eight posts, with six wires on each side of the post. Though I could not think why Constantin wanted them, and though in the event he did not get them, the appearance of them, and of the rusty track beneath them, is all that remains clear in my memory of that window.

'I doubt whether they're for sale,' said my father. 'Look again. There's a good boy. No hurry.'

'They're all I want,' said Constantin, and turned his back on the uninspiring display.

'Well, we'll see,' said my father. 'I'll make a special point of it with the man . . .' He turned to me. 'And what about you? Very few dolls, I'm afraid.'

'I don't like dolls any more.' As a matter of fact, I had never owned a proper one, although I suffered from this fact when competing with other girls, which meant very seldom, for our friends were few and occasional. The dolls in the window were flyblown and detestable.

'I think we could find a better shop from which to give Lene a birthday present,' said my mother, in her correct, dignified English.

'We must not be unjust,' said my father, 'when we have not even looked inside.'

The inferiority of the goods implied cheapness, which unfortunately always mattered; although, as it happened, none of the articles seemed actually to be priced.

'I do not like this shop,' said my mother. 'It is a shop that has died.'

Her regal manner when she said such things was, I think, too Germanic for my father's Englishness. That, and the prospect of unexpected economy, perhaps led him to be firm.

'We have Constantin's present to consider as well as Lene's. Let us go in.'

By contrast with the blazing highway, the main impression of the interior was darkness. After a few moments, I also became aware of a smell. Everything in the shop smelt of that smell, and, one felt, always would do so, the mixed odour of any general store, but at once enhanced and passé. I can smell it now.

'We do not necessarily want to buy anything,' said my father, 'but, if we may, should like to look round?'

Since the days of Mr Selfridge the proposition is supposed to be taken for granted, but at that time the message had yet to spread. The bazaar keeper seemed hardly to welcome it. He was younger than I had expected (an unusual thing for a child, but I had probably been awaiting a white-bearded gnome); though pale, nearly bald, and perceptibly grimy. He wore an untidy grey suit and bedroom slippers.

'Look about you, children,' said my father. 'Take your time. We can't buy presents every day.'

I noticed that my mother still stood in the doorway.

'I want those wires,' said Constantin.

'Make quite sure by looking at the other things first.'

Constantin turned aside bored, his book held behind his back. He began to scrape his feet. It was up to me to uphold my father's position. Rather timidly, I began to peer about, not going far from him. The bazaar keeper silently watched me with eyes colourless in the twilight.

'Those toy telegraph poles in your window,' said my father after a pause, fraught for me with anxiety and responsibility. 'How much would you take for them?'

'They are not for sale,' said the bazaar keeper, and said no more.

'Then why do you display them in the window?'

'They are a kind of decoration, I suppose.' Did he not know? I wondered.

'Even if they're not normally for sale, perhaps you'll sell them to me,' said my vagabond father, smiling like Rothschild. 'My son, you see, has taken a special fancy to them.'

'Sorry,' said the man in the shop.

'Are you the principal here?'

'I am.'

'Then surely as a reasonable man,' said my father, switching from superiority to ingratiation.

'They are to dress the window,' said the bazaar man. 'They are not for sale.'

This dialogue entered through the back of my head as, diligently and unobtrudingly, I conned the musty stock. At the back of the shop was a window, curtained all over in grey lace: to judge by the weak light it offered, it gave on to the living quarters. Through this much-filtered illumination glimmered the façade of an enormous dolls' house. I wanted it at once. Dolls had never been central to my happiness, but this abode of their was the most grown-up thing in the shop.

It had battlements, and long straight walls, and a variety of pointed windows. A Gothic revival house, no doubt; or even mansion. It was painted the colour of stone; a grey stone darker than the grey light, which flickered round it. There was a two-leaved front door, with a small classical portico. It was impossible to see the whole house at once, as it stood grimed and neglected on the corner of the wide trestle-shelf. Very slowly I walked along two of the sides; the other two being dark against the walls of the shop. From the first-floor window in the side not immediately visible as one approached, leaned a doll, droopy and unkempt. It was unlike any real house I had seen, and, as for dolls' houses, they were always after the style of the villa near Gerrard's Cross belonging to my father's successful brother. My uncle's house itself looked much more like a toy than this austere structure before me.

'Wake up,' said my mother's voice. She was standing just behind me.

'What about some light on the subject?' enquired my father.

A switch clicked.

The house really was magnificent. Obviously, beyond all financial reach.

'Looks like a model for Pentonville Gaol,' observed my father.

'It is beautiful,' I said. 'It's what I want.'

'It's the most depressing-looking plaything I ever saw.'

'I want to pretend I live in it,' I said, 'and give masked

balls.' My social history was eager but indiscriminate.

'How much is it?' asked my mother. The bazaar keeper stood resentfully in the background, sliding each hand between the thumb and fingers of the other.

'It's only second-hand,' he said. 'Tenth-hand, more like. A lady brought it in and said she needed to get rid of it. I don't want to sell you something you don't want.'

'But suppose we *do* want it?' said my father truculently. 'Is nothing in this shop for sale?'

'You can take it away for a quid,' said the bazaar keeper. 'And glad to have the space.'

'There's someone looking out,' said Constantin. He seemed to be assessing the house, like a surveyor or valuer.

'It's full of dolls,' said the bazaar keeper. 'They're thrown in. Sure you can transport it?'

'Not at the moment,' said my father, 'but I'll send someone down.' This, I knew, would be Moon the seedman, who owned a large canvas-topped lorry, and with whom my father used to fraternise on the putting green.

'Are you quite sure?' my mother asked me.

'Will it take up too much room?'

My mother shook her head. Indeed, our home, though out of date and out at elbows, was considerably too large for us.

'Then, please.'

Poor Constantin got nothing.

Mercifully, all our rooms had wide doors, so that Moon's driver, assisted by the youth out of the shop, lent specially for the purpose, could ease my birthday present to its new resting place without tilting it or inflicting a wound upon my mother's new and self-applied paint. I noticed that the doll at the first-floor side window had prudently withdrawn.

For my house, my parents had allotted me the principal spare room, because in the centre of it stood a very large dinner table, once to be found in the servants' hall of my father's childhood home in Lincolnshire, but now the sole furniture our principal spare room contained. (The two lesser spare rooms were filled with cardboard boxes, which every now and then toppled in heart-arresting avalanches on still summer nights.) On the big table the driver and the shop boy set my house. It reached almost to the sides, so that those passing along the narrow walks would be in peril of tumbling into a gulf; but, the table being much longer than it was wide, the house was provided at front and back with splendid parterres of deal, embrocated with caustic until they glinted like fluorspar.

When I had settled upon the exact site for the house, so that the garden front would receive the sun from the two windows, and a longer parterre stretched at the front than at the back, where the columned entry faced the door of the room, I withdrew to a distant corner while the two males eased the edifice into exact alignment.

'Snug as a bug in a rug,' said Moon's driver when the perilous walks at the sides of the house had been made straight and equal.

'Snugger,' said Moon's boy.

I waited for their boots, mailed with crescent silvers of steel, to reach the bottom of our creaking, coconut-matted stair, then I tiptoed to the landing, looked, and listened. The sun had gone in just before the lorry arrived, and down the passage the motes had ceased to dance. It was three o'clock, my mother was still at one of her schools, my father was at the rifle range. I heard the men shut the back door. The principal spare room had never before been occupied, so that the key was outside. In a second, I transferred it to the inside, and shut and locked myself in.

As before in the shop, I walked slowly round my house, but this time round all four sides of it. Then, with the knuckles of my thin white forefinger, I tapped gently at the front door. It seemed not to have been secured, because it opened, both leaves of it, as I touched it. I pried in, first with one eye, then with the other. The lights from various of the pointed windows blotched the walls and floor of the miniature Entrance Hall. None of the dolls was visible.

It was not one of those dolls' houses of commerce from which sides can be lifted in their entirety. To learn about my house, it would be necessary, albeit impolite, to stare through the windows, one at a time. I decided first to take the ground floor. I started in a clockwise direction from the front portico. The front door was still open, but I could not see how to shut it from the outside.

There was a room to the right of the hall, leading into

two other rooms along the right side of the house, of which, again, one led into the other. All the rooms were decorated and furnished in a Mrs Fitzherbert-ish style; with handsomely striped wallpapers, botanical carpets, and chairs with legs like sticks of brittle golden sweetmeat. There were a number of pictures. I knew just what they were: family portraits. I named the room next the Hall, the Occasional Room, and the room beyond it, the Morning Room. The third room was very small: striking out confidently, I named it the Canton Cabinet, although it contained neither porcelain nor fans. I knew what the rooms in a great house should be called, because my mother used to show me the pictures in large, once-fashionable volumes on the subject which my father had bought for their bulk at junk shops.

Then came the Long Drawing Room, which stretched across the entire garden front of the house, and contained the principal concourse of dolls. It had four pointed French windows, all made to open, though now sealed with dust and rust; above which were bulbous triangles of coloured glass, in tiny snowflake panes. The apartment itself played at being a cloister in a Horace Walpole convent; lierne vaulting ramified across the arched ceiling, and the spidery Gothic pilasters were tricked out in mediaeval patchwork, as in a Puseyite church. On the stout golden wallpaper were decent Swiss pastels of indeterminate subjects. There was a grand piano, very black, scrolly, and, no doubt, resounding; four shapely chandeliers; a baronial fireplace with a mythical blazon above the mantel; and eight dolls, all of them female, dotted about on chairs and ottomans with their backs to me. I hardly dared to breathe as I regarded their woolly heads, and noted the colours of their hair: two black, two nondescript, one grey, one a discoloured silver beneath the dust, one blonde, and one a dyed-looking red. They wore woollen Victorian clothes, of a period later, I should say, than that when the house was built, and certainly too warm for the present season; in varied colours, all of them dull. Happy people, I felt even then, would not wear these variants of rust, indigo, and greenwood.

I crept onwards; to the Dining Room. It occupied half its side of the house, and was dark and oppressive. Perhaps it might look more inviting when the chandelier blazed, and the table candles, each with a tiny purple shade, were lighted. There was no cloth on the table, and no food or drink. Over the fireplace was a big portrait of a furious old man: his white hair was a spiky aureole round his distorted face, beetroot-red with rage; the mouth was open, and even the heavy lips were drawn back to show the savage, strong teeth; he was brandishing a very thick walking stick, which seemed to leap from the picture and stun the beholder. He was dressed neutrally, and the painter had not provided him with a background: there was only the aggressive figure menacing the room. I was frightened.

Two rooms on the ground floor remained before I once more reached the front door. In the first of them a lady was writing with her back to the light and therefore to me. She frightened me also; because her grey hair was disordered and of uneven length, and descended in matted plaits, like snakes escaping from a basket, to the shoulders of her coarse grey dress. Of course, being a doll, she did not move, but the back of her head looked mad. Her presence prevented me from regarding at all closely the furnishings of the Writing Room.

Back at the north front, as I resolved to call it, perhaps superseding the compass rather than leading it, there was a cold-looking room, with a carpetless stone floor and white walls, upon which were the mounted heads and horns of many animals. They were all the room contained, but they covered the walls from floor to ceiling. I felt sure that the ferocious old man in the Dining Room had killed all these creatures, and I hated him for it. But I knew what the room would be called: it would be the Trophy Room.

Then I realised that there was no kitchen. It could hardly be upstairs. I had never heard of such a thing. But I looked.

It wasn't there. All the rooms on the first floor were bedrooms. There were six of them, and they so resembled one another, all with dark ochreous wallpaper and narrow brass bedsteads corroded with neglect, that I found it impracticable to distinguish them other than by numbers, at least for the present. Ultimately I might know the house better. Bedrooms 2, 3 and 6 contained two beds each. I recalled that at least nine people lived in the house. In one room the dark walls, the dark floor, the bed linen, and even the glass in the window were splashed, smeared, and further darkened with ink: it seemed apparent who slept there.

I sat on an orange box and looked. My house needed painting and dusting and scrubbing and polishing and renewing; but on the whole I was relieved that things were not worse. I had felt that the house had stood in the dark corner of the shop for no one knew how long, but this, I now saw, could hardly have been true. I wondered about the lady who had needed to get rid of it. Despite that need, she must have kept things up pretty thoroughly. How did she do it? How did she get in? I resolved to ask my mother's advice. I determined to be a good landlord, although, like most who so resolve, my resources were nil. We simply lacked the money to regild my Long Drawing Room in proper gold leaf. But I would bring life to the nine dolls now drooping with boredom and neglect . . .

Then I recalled something. What had become of the doll who had been sagging from the window? I thought she must have been jolted out, and felt myself a murderess. But none of the windows was open. The sash might easily have descended with the shaking; but more probably the poor doll lay inside on the floor of her room. I again went round from room to room, this time on tiptoe, but it was impossible to see the areas of floor just below the dark windows . . . It was not merely sunless outside, but heavily overcast. I unlocked the door of our principal spare room and descended pensively to await my mother's return and tea.

Wormwood Grange, my father called my house, with

penological associations still on his mind. (After he was run over, I realised for the first time that there might be a reason for this, and for his inability to find work worthy of him.) My mother had made the most careful inspection on my behalf, but had been unable to suggest any way of making an entry, or at least of passing beyond the Hall, to which the front doors still lay open. There seemed no question of whole walls lifting off, of the roof being removable, or even of a window being opened, including, mysteriously, on the first floor.

'I don't think it's meant for children, Liebchen,' said my mother, smiling her lovely smile. 'We shall have to consult the Victoria and Albert Museum.'

'Of course it's not meant for children,' I replied. 'That's why I wanted it. I'm going to receive, like La Belle Otero.'

Next morning, after my mother had gone to work, my father came up, and wrenched and prodded with his unskilful hands.

'I'll get a chisel,' he said. 'We'll prise it open at each corner, and when we've got the fronts off, I'll go over to Woolworths and buy some hinges and screws. I expect they'll have some.'

At that I struck my father in the chest with my fist. He seized my wrists, and I screamed that he was not to lay a finger on my beautiful house, that he would be sure to spoil it, that force never got anyone anywhere. I knew my father: when he took an idea for using tools into his head, the only hope for one's property lay in a scene, and in the implication of tears without end in the future,

301

if the idea were not dropped.

While I was screaming and raving, Constantin appeared from the room below, where he worked at his books.

'Give us a chance, Sis,' he said. 'How can I keep it all in my head about the Thirty Years War when you haven't learned to control your tantrums?'

Although two years younger than I, Constantin should have known that I was past the age for screaming except of set purpose.

'You wait until he tries to rebind all your books, you silly sneak,' I yelled at him.

My father released my wrists.

'Wormwood Grange can keep,' he said. 'I'll think of something else to go over to Woolworths for.' He sauntered off.

Constantin nodded gravely. 'I understand,' he said. 'I understand what you mean. I'll go back to my work. Here, try this.' He gave me a small, chipped nail file.

I spent most of the morning fiddling very cautiously with the imperfect jemmy, and trying to make up my mind about the doll at the window.

I failed to get into my house, and I refused to let my parents give me any effective aid. Perhaps by now I did not really want to get in, although the dirt and disrepair, and the apathy of the dolls, who so badly needed plumping up and dispersing, continued to cause me distress. Certainly I spent as long trying to shut the front door as trying to open a window or find a concealed spring (that idea was Constantin's). In the end I wedged the two halves of the front door with two halves of match; but I felt that the arrangement was makeshift and undignified. I refused everyone access to the principal spare room until something more appropriate could be evolved. My plans for routs and orgies had to be deferred: one could hardly riot among dust and cobwebs.

Then I began to have dreams about my house, and about its occupants.

One of the oddest dreams was the first. It was three or four days after I entered into possession. During that time it had remained cloudy and oppressive, so that my father took to leaving off his knitted waistcoat; then suddenly it thundered. It was a long, slow, distant, intermittent thunder; and it continued all the evening, until, when it was quite dark, my bedtime and Constantin's could no longer be deferred.

'Your ears will get accustomed to the noise,' said my father. 'Just try to take no notice of it.'

Constantin looked dubious; but I was tired of the slow, rumbling hours, and ready for the different dimension of dreams.

I slept almost immediately, although the thunder was rolling round my big, rather empty bedroom, round the four walls, across the floor, and under the ceiling, weighting the black air as with a smoky vapour. Occasionally, the lightning glinted, pink and green. It was still the long-drawn-out preliminary to a storm; the tedious, imperfect dispersal of the accumulated energy of the summer. The rollings and rumblings entered my dreams, which flickered, changed, were gone as soon as come, failed, like the lightning, to concentrate or strike home, were as difficult to profit by as the events of an average day.

After exhausting hours of phantasmagoria, anticipating so many later nights in my life, I found myself in a black wood, with huge, dense trees. I was following a path, but reeled from tree to tree, bruising and cutting myself on their hardness and roughness. There seemed no end to the wood or to the night; but suddenly, in the thick of both, I came upon my house. It stood solid, immense, hemmed in, with a single light, little more, it seemed, than a night-light, burning in every upstairs window (as often in dreams, I could see all four sides of the house at once), and illuminating two wooden wedges, jagged and swollen, which held tight the front doors. The vast trees dipped and swayed their elephantine boughs over the roof; the wind peeked and creaked through the black battlements. Then there was a blaze of whitest lightning, proclaiming the storm itself. In the second it endured, I saw my two wedges fly through the air and the double front door burst open.

For the hundredth time, the scene changed, and now I was back in my room, though still asleep or half-asleep, still dragged from vision to vision. Now the thunder was coming in immense, calculated bombardments; the lightning ceaseless and searing the face of the earth. From being a weariness the storm had become an ecstasy. It seemed as if the whole world would be in dissolution before the thunder had spent its impersonal, unregarding strength. But, as I say, I must still have been at least half-asleep, because between the fortissimi and the lustre I still from time to time saw scenes, meaningless or nightmarish, which could not be found in the wakeful world; still, between and through the volleys, heard impossible sounds.

I do not know whether I was asleep or awake when the storm rippled into tranquillity. I certainly did not feel that the air had been cleared; but this may have been because, surprisingly, I heard a quick soft step passing along the passage outside my room, a passage uncarpeted through our poverty. I well knew all the footsteps in the house, and this was none of them.

Always one to meet trouble halfway, I dashed in my nightgown to open the door. I looked out. The dawn was seeping, without effort or momentum, through every cranny, and showed shadowy the back of a retreating figure, the size of my mother but with woolly red hair and long rust-coloured dress. The padding feet seemed actually to start soft echoes amid all that naked woodwork. I had no need to consider who she was or whither she was bound. I burst into the purposeless tears I so despised.

In the morning, and before deciding upon what to impart, I took Constantin with me to look at the house. I more than half expected big changes; but none was to be seen. The sections of match-stick were still in position, and the dolls as inactive and diminutive as ever, sitting with their backs to me on chairs and sofas in the Long Drawing Room; their hair dusty, possibly even mothy. Constantin looked at me curiously, but I imparted nothing.

Other dreams followed; though at considerable intervals. Many children have recurring nightmares of oppressive realism and terrifying content; and I realised from past experience that I must outgrow the habit or lose my house – my house at least. It is true that my house now frightened me, but I felt that I must not be foolish and should strive to take a grown-up view of painted woodwork and nine understuffed dolls. Still it was bad when I began to hear them in the darkness; some tapping, some stumping, some creeping, and therefore not one, but many, or all; and worse when I began not to sleep for fear of the mad doll (as I was sure she was) doing something mad, although I refused to think what. I never dared again to look; but when something happened, which, as I say, was only at intervals (and to me, being young, they seemed long intervals), I lay taut and straining among the forgotten sheets. Moreover, the steps themselves were never quite constant, certainly too inconstant to report to others; and I am not sure that I should have heard anything significant if I had not once seen. But now I locked the door of our principal spare room on the outside, and altogether ceased to visit my beautiful, impregnable mansion.

I noticed that my mother made no comment. But one day my father complained of my ingratitude in never playing with my handsome birthday present. I said I was occupied with my holiday task: *Moby-Dick*. This was an approved answer, and even, as far as it went, a true one, though I found the book pointless in the extreme, and horribly cruel.

'I told you the Grange was the wrong thing to buy,' said my father. 'Morbid sort of object for a toy.'

'None of us can learn except by experience,' said my mother.

My father said, 'Not at all,' and bristled.

All this, naturally, was in the holidays. I was going at the time to one of my mother's schools, where I should stay until I could begin to train as a dancer, upon which I was conventionally but entirely resolved. Constantin went to another, a highly cerebral co-educational place, where he would remain until, inevitably, he won a scholarship to a university, perhaps a foreign one. Despite our years, we went our different ways dangerously on small dingy bicycles. We reached home at assorted hours, mine being the longer journey.

One day I returned to find our dining-room table littered with peculiarly uninteresting printed drawings. I could make nothing of them whatever (they did not seem even to belong to the kind of geometry I was – regretfully – used to); and they curled up on themselves when one tried to examine them, and bit one's finger. My father had a week or two before taking one of his infrequent jobs; night work of some kind a long way off, to which he had now departed in our car. Obviously the drawings were connected with Constantin, but he was not there.

I went upstairs, and saw that the principal spare room door was open. Constantin was inside. There had, of course, been no question of the key to the room being removed. It was only necessary to turn it.

'Hallo, Lene,' Constantin said in his matter-of-fact way. 'We've been doing axonometric projection, and I'm projecting your house.' He was making one of the drawings; on a sheet of thick white paper. 'It's for homework. It'll knock out all the others. They've got to do their real houses.'

It must not be supposed that I did not like Constantin, although often he annoyed me with his placidity and precision. It was weeks since I had seen my house, and it looked unexpectedly interesting. A curious thing happened: nor was it the last time in my life that I experienced it. Temporarily I became a different person; confident, practical, simple. The clear evening sun of autumn may have contributed.

'I'll help,' I said. 'Tell me what to do.'

'It's a bore I can't get in to take measurements. Although we haven't *got* to. In fact, the Clot told us not. Just a general impression, he said. It's to give us the *concept* of axonometry. But, golly, it would be simpler with feet and inches.'

To judge by the amount of white paper he had covered in what could only have been a short time, Constantin seemed to me to be doing very well, but he was one never to be content with less than perfection.

'Tell me', I said, 'what to do, and I'll do it.'

'Thanks,' he replied, sharpening his pencil with a special instrument. 'But it's a one-man job this. In the nature of the case. Later I'll show you how to do it, and you can do some other building if you like.'

I remained, looking at my house and fingering it, until Constantin made it clearer that I was a distraction. I went away, changed my shoes, and put on the kettle against my mother's arrival, and our High Tea.

When Constantin came down (my mother had called for him three times, but that was not unusual), he said, 'I say, Sis, here's a rum thing.'

My mother said, 'Don't use slang, and don't call your sister Sis.'

He said, as he always did when reproved by her, 'I'm sorry, Mother.' Then he thrust the drawing paper at me. 'Look, there's a bit missing. See what I mean?' He was showing me with his stub of emerald pencil, pocked with toothmarks.

Of course, I didn't see. I didn't understand a thing about it.

'After Tea,' said my mother. She gave to such familiar words not a maternal but an imperial decisiveness.

'But Mum—' pleaded Constantin.

'Mother,' said my mother.

Constantin started dipping for sauerkraut.

Silently we ate ourselves into tranquillity; or, for me, into the appearance of it. My alternative personality, though it had survived Constantin's refusal of my assistant, was now beginning to ebb.

'What is all this that you are doing?' enquired my mother in the end. 'It resembles the Stone of Rosetta.'

'I'm taking an axonometric cast of Lene's birthday house.'

'And so?'

But Constantin was not now going to expound immediately. He put in his mouth a finger of rye bread smeared with homemade cheese. Then he said quietly, 'I got down a rough idea of the house, but the rooms don't fit. At least, they don't on the bottom floor. It's all right, I think, on the top floor. In fact that's the rummest thing of all. Sorry, Mother.' He had been speaking with his mouth full, and now filled it fuller.

'What nonsense is this?' To me it seemed that my mother was glaring at him in a way most unlike her.

'It's not nonsense, Mother. Of course, I haven't measured the place, because you can't. But I haven't done axonometry for nothing. There's a part of the bottom floor I can't get at. A secret room or something.'

'Show me.'

'Very well, Mother.' Constantin put down his remnant of bread and cheese. He rose, looking a little pale. He took the drawing round the table to my mother.

'Not that thing. I can't understand it, and I don't believe you can understand it either.' Only sometimes to my father did my mother speak like that. 'Show me in the house.'

I rose too.

'You stay here, Lene. Put some more water in the kettle and boil it.'

'But it's my house. I have a right to know.'

My mother's expression changed to one more familiar. 'Yes, Lene,' she said, 'you have a right. But please not now. I ask you.'

I smiled at her and picked up the kettle.

'Come, Constantin.'

I lingered by the kettle in the kitchen, not wishing to give an impression of eavesdropping or even undue eagerness, which I knew would distress my mother. I never wished to learn things that my mother wished to keep from me, and I never questioned her implication of 'all in good time'.

But they were not gone long, for well before the kettle had begun even to grunt, my mother's beautiful voice was summoning me back.

'Constantin is quite right,' she said, when I had presented myself at the dining-room table, 'and it was wrong of me to doubt it. The house is built in a funny sort of way. But what does it matter?'

Constantin was not eating.

'I am glad that you are studying well, and learning such useful things,' said my mother.

She wished the subject to be dropped, and we dropped it.

Indeed, it was difficult to think what more could be said. But I waited for a moment in which I was alone with Constantin. My father's unhabitual absence made this difficult, and it was completely dark before the moment came.

And when, as was only to be expected, Constantin had nothing to add, I felt, most unreasonably, that he was joined with my mother in keeping something from me.

'But what *happened*?' I pressed him. 'What happened when you were in the room with her?'

'What do you think happened?' replied Constantin, wishing, I thought, that my mother would re-enter. 'Mother realised that I was right. Nothing more. What does it matter anyway?'

That final query confirmed my doubts.

'Constantin,' I said. 'Is there anything I ought to do?'

'Better hack the place open,' he answered, almost irritably.

But a most unexpected thing happened, that, had I even considered adopting Constantin's idea, would have saved me the trouble. When next day I returned from school, my house was gone.

Constantin was sitting in his usual corner, this time absorbing Greek paradigms. Without speaking to him (nothing unusual in that when he was working), I went straight to the principal spare room. The vast deal table, less scrubbed than once, was bare. The place where my house had stood was very visible, as if indeed a palace had been swept off by a djinn. But I could see no other sign of its passing: no scratched woodwork, or marks of boots, or disjoined fragments.

Constantin seemed genuinely astonished at the news. But I doubted him.

'You knew,' I said.

'Of course I didn't know.'

Still, he understood what I was thinking.

He said again, 'I didn't know.'

Unlike me on occasion, he always spoke the truth.

I gathered myself together and blurted out, 'Have they done it themselves?' Inevitably I was frightened, but in a way I was also relieved.

'Who do you mean?'

'They.'

I was inviting ridicule, but Constantin was kind.

He said, 'I know who I think has done it, but you mustn't let on. I think Mother's done it.'

I did not again enquire uselessly into how much more he knew than I. I said, 'But *how*?'

Constantin shrugged. It was a habit he had assimilated with so much else.

'Mother left the house with us this morning and she isn't back yet.'

'She must have put Father up to it.'

'But there are no marks.'

'Father might have got help.' There was a pause. Then Constantin said, 'Are you sorry?'

'In a way,' I replied. Constantin with precocious wisdom left it at that.

When my mother returned, she simply said that my father had already lost his new job, so that we had had to sell things.

'I hope you will forgive your father and me,' she said. 'We've had to sell one of my watches also. Father will soon be back to Tea.'

She too was one I had never known to lie; but now I began to perceive how relative and instrumental truth could be.

I need not say: not in those terms. Such clear concepts, with all they offer of gain and loss, come later, if they come at all. In fact, I need not say that the whole of what goes before is so heavily filtered through later experience as to be of little evidential value. But I am scarcely putting forward evidence. There is so little. All I can do is to tell something of what happened, as it now seems to me to have been.

I remember sulking at my mother's news, and her explaining to me that really I no longer liked the house and that something better would be bought for me in replacement when our funds permitted.

I did ask my father when he returned to our evening meal, whistling and falsely jaunty about the lost job, how much he had been paid for my house.

'A trifle more than I gave for it. That's only business.'

'Where is it now?'

'Never you mind.'

'Tell her,' said Constantin. 'She wants to know.'

'Eat your herring,' said my father very sharply. 'And mind your own business.'

And, thus, before long my house was forgotten, my occasional nightmares returned to earlier themes.

It was, as I say, for two or three months in 1921 that I owned the house and from time to time dreamed that

314

creatures I supposed to be its occupants had somehow invaded my home. The next thirty years, more or less, can be disposed of quickly: it was the period when I tried conclusions with the outer world.

I really became a dancer; and, although the upper reaches alike of the art and of the profession notably eluded me, yet I managed to maintain myself for several years, no small achievement. I retired, as they say, upon marriage. My husband aroused physical passion in me for the first time, but diminished and deadened much else. He was reported missing in the late misguided war. Certainly he did not return to me. I at least still miss him, though often I despise myself for doing so.

My father died in a street accident when I was fifteen: It happened on the day I received a special commendation from the sallow Frenchwoman who taught me to dance. After his death my beloved mother always wanted to return to Germany. Before long I was spiritually self-sufficient enough, or said I was, to make that possible. Unfailingly, she wrote to me twice a week, although to find words in which to reply was often difficult for me. Sometimes I visited her, while the conditions in her country became more and more uncongenial to me. She had a fair position teaching English Language and Literature at a small university; and she seemed increasingly to be infected by the new notions and emotions raging around her. I must acknowledge that sometimes their tumult and intoxication unsteadied my own mental gait, although I was a foreigner and by no means of sanguine temperament. It is a mistake to think that all professional dancers are gay.

Despite what appeared to be increasing sympathies with the new régime, my mother disappeared. She was the first of the two people who mattered to me in such very different ways, and who so unreasonably vanished. For a time I was ill, and of course I love her still more than anybody. If she had remained with me, I am sure I should never have married. Without involving myself in psychology, which I detest, I shall simply say that the thought and recollection of my mother lay, I believe, behind the self-absorption my husband complained of so bitterly and so justly. It was not really myself in which I was absorbed but the memory of perfection. It is the plain truth that such beauty, and goodness, and depth, and capacity for love were my mother's alone.

Constantin abandoned all his versatile reading and became a priest, in fact a member of the Society of Jesus. He seems exalted (possibly too much so for his colleagues and superiors), but I can no longer speak to him or bear his presence. He frightens me. Poor Constantin!

On the other hand, I, always dubious, have become a complete unbeliever. I cannot see that Constantin is doing anything but listening to his own inner voice (which has changed its tone since we were children); and mine speaks a different language. In the long run, I doubt whether there is much to be desired but death; or whether there is endurance in anything but suffering. I no longer see myself feasting crowned heads on quails.

So much for biographical intermission. I proceed to

the circumstances of my second and recent experience of landlordism.

In the first place, I did something thoroughly stupid. Instead of following the road marked on the map, I took a short cut. It is true that the short cut was shown on the map also, but the region was much too unfrequented for a wandering footpath to be in any way dependable, especially in this generation which has ceased to walk beyond the garage or the bus stop. It was one of the least populated districts in the whole country, and, moreover, the slow autumn dusk was already perceptible when I pushed at the first, dilapidated gate.

To begin with, the path trickled and flickered across a sequence of small damp meadows, bearing neither cattle nor crop. When it came to the third or fourth of these meadows, the way had all but vanished in the increasing sogginess, and could be continued only by looking for the stile or gate in the unkempt hedge ahead. This was not especially difficult as long as the fields remained small; but after a time I reached a depressing expanse which could hardly be termed a field at all, but was rather a large marsh. It was at this point that I should have returned and set about tramping the winding road.

But a path of some kind again continued before me, and I perceived that the escapade had already consumed twenty minutes. So I risked it, although soon I was striding laboriously from tussock to brown tussock in order not to sink above my shoes into the surrounding quagmire. It is quite extraordinary how far one can stray from a straight or determined course when thus preoccupied with elementary comfort. The hedge on the far side of the marsh was still a long way ahead, and the tussocks themselves were becoming both less frequent and less dense, so that too often I was sinking through them into the mire. I realised that the marsh sloped slightly downwards in the direction I was following, so that before I reached the hedge, I might have to cross a river. In the event, it was not so much a river as an indeterminately bounded augmentation of the softness, and moistness, and ooziness: I struggled across, jerking from false foothold to palpable pitfall, and before long despairing even of the attempt to step securely. Both my feet were now soaked to well above the ankles, and the visibility had become less than was entirely convenient.

When I reached what I had taken for a hedge, it proved to be the boundary of an extensive thicket. Autumn had infected much of the greenery with blotched and dropping senility; so that bare brown briars arched and tousled, and purple thorns tilted at all possible angles for blood. To go further would demand an axe. Either I must retraverse the dreary bog in the perceptibly waning light, or I must skirt the edge and seek an opening in the thicket. Undecided, I looked back. I realised that I had lost the gate through which I had entered upon the marsh on the other side. There was nothing to do but creep as best I could upon the still treacherous ground along the barrier of dead dog-roses, mildewed blackberries, and rampant nettles.

But it was not long before I reached a considerable

gap, from which through the tangled vegetation seemed to lead a substantial track, although by no means a straight one. The track wound on unimpeded for a considerable distance, even becoming firmer underfoot; until I realised that the thicket had become an entirely indisputable wood. The brambles clutching maliciously from the sides had become watching branches above my head. I could not recall that the map had showed a wood. If, indeed, it had done so, I should not have entered upon the footpath, because the only previous occasion in my life when I had been truly lost, in the sense of being unable to find the way back as well as being unable to go on, had been when my father had once so effectively lost us in a wood that I have never again felt the same about woods. The fear I had felt for perhaps an hour and a half on that occasion, though told to no one, and swiftly evaporating from consciousness upon our emergence, had been the veritable fear of death. Now I drew the map from where it lay against my thigh in the big pocket of my dress. It was not until I tried to read it that I realised how near I was to night. Until it came to print, the problems of the route had given me cat's eyes.

I peered, and there was no wood, no green patch on the map, but only the wavering line of dots advancing across contoured whiteness to the neck of yellow road where the short cut ended. But I did not reach any foolish conclusion. I simply guessed that I had strayed very badly; the map was spattered with green marks in places where I had no wish to be; and the only question was in which of those many thickets I now was. I could think of no way to find out. I was nearly lost, and this time I could not blame my father.

The track I had been following still stretched ahead, as yet not too indistinct; and I continued to follow it. As the trees around me became yet bigger and thicker, fear came upon me, though not the death fear of that previous occasion, I felt, now that I knew what was going to happen next; or, rather, I felt I knew one thing that was going to happen next, a thing which was but a small and far from central part of an obscure, inapprehensible totality. As one does on such occasions, I felt more than half outside my body. If I continued much further, I might change into somebody else.

But what happened was not what I expected. Suddenly I saw a flicker of light. It seemed to emerge from the left, to weave momentarily among the trees, and to disappear to the right. It was not what I expected, but it was scarcely reassuring. I wondered if it could be a will-o'-the-wisp, a thing I had never seen, but which I understood to be connected with marshes. Next a still more prosaic possibility occurred to me, one positively hopeful: the headlights of a motor car turning a corner. It seemed the likely answer, but my uneasiness did not perceptibly diminish.

I struggled on, and the light came again: a little stronger, and twisting through the trees around me. Of course another car at the same corner of the road was not an impossibility, even though it was an unpeopled area. Then, after a period of soft but not comforting dusk, it came a third time; and, soon, a fourth. There was no sound of an engine: and it seemed to me that the transit of the light was too swift and fleeting for any car.

And then what I had been awaiting happened. I came suddenly upon a huge square house. I had known it was coming, but still it struck at my heart.

It is not every day that one finds a dream come true; and, scared though I was, I noticed details: for example, that there did not seem to be those single lights burning in every upstairs window. Doubtless dreams, like poems, demand a certain licence; and, for the matter of that, I could not see all four sides of the house at once, as I had dreamed I had. But that perhaps was the worst of it: I was plainly not dreaming now.

A sudden greeny-pink radiance illuminated around me a morass of weed and neglect; and then seemed to hide itself among the trees on my right. The explanation of the darting lights was that a storm approached. But it was unlike other lightning I had encountered: being slower, more silent, more regular.

There seemed nothing to do but run away, though even then it seemed sensible not to run back into the wood. In the last memories of daylight, I began to wade through the dead knee-high grass of the lost lawn. It was still possible to see that the wood continued, opaque as ever, in a long line to my left; I felt my way along it, in order to keep as far as possible from the the house. I noticed, as I passed, the great portico, facing the direction from which I had emerged. Then, keeping my distance, I crept along the grey east front with its two tiers of pointed windows, all shut and one or two broken; and reached the southern parterre, visibly vaster, even in the storm-charged gloom, than the northern, but no less ravaged. Ahead, and at the side of the parterre far off to my right, ranged the encircling woodland. If no path manifested, my state would be hazardous indeed; and there seemed little reason for a path, as the approach to the house was provided by that along which I had come from the marsh.

As I struggled onwards, the whole scene was transformed: in a moment the sky became charged with roaring thunder, the earth with tumultuous rain. I tried to shelter in the adjacent wood, but instantly found myself enmeshed in bines and suckers, lacerated by invisible spears. In a minute I should be drenched. I plunged through the wet weeds towards the spreading portico.

Before the big doors I waited for several minutes, watching the lightning, and listening. The rain leapt up where it fell, as if the earth hurt it. A rising chill made the old grass shiver. It seemed unlikely that anyone could live in a house so dark; but suddenly I heard one of the doors behind me scrape open. I turned. A dark head protruded between the portals, like Punch from the side of his booth.

'Oh.' The shrill voice was of course surprised to see me.

I turned. 'May I please wait until the rain stops?'

'You can't come inside.'

I drew back; so far back that a heavy drip fell on the back of my neck from the edge of the portico. With absurd melodrama, there was a loud roll of thunder.

'I shouldn't think of it,' I said. 'I must be on my way the moment the rain lets me.' I could still see only the round head sticking out between the leaves of the door.

'In the old days we often had visitors.' This statement was made in the tone of a Cheltenham lady remarking that when a child she often spoke to gypsies. 'I only peeped out to see the thunder.'

Now, within the house, I heard another, lower voice, although I could not hear what it said. Through the long crack between the doors, a light slid out across the flagstones of the porch and down the darkening steps.

'She's waiting for the rain to stop,' said the shrill voice.

'Tell her to come in,' said the deep voice. 'Really, Emerald, you forget your manners after all this time.'

'I *have* told her,' said Emerald very petulantly, and withdrawing her head. 'She won't do it.'

'Nonsense,' said the other. 'You're just telling lies.' I got the idea that thus she always spoke to Emerald.

Then the doors opened, and I could see the two of them silhouetted in the light of a lamp which stood on a table behind them; one much the taller, but both with round heads, and both wearing long, unshapely garments. I wanted very much to escape, and failed to do so only because there seemed nowhere to go.

'Please come in at once,' said the taller figure, 'and let us take off your wet clothes.'

'Yes, yes,' squeaked Emerald, unreasonably jubilant.

'Thank you. But my clothes are not at all wet.'

'None the less, please come in. We shall take it as a discourtesy if you refuse.'

Another roar of thunder emphasised the impracticability of continuing to refuse much longer. If this was a dream, doubtless, and to judge by experience, I should awake.

And a dream it must be, because there at the front door were two big wooden wedges; and there to the right of the Hall, shadowed in the lamplight, was the Trophy Room; although now the animal heads on the walls were shoddy, fungoid ruins, their sawdust spilled and clotted on the cracked and uneven flagstones of the floor.

'You must forgive us,' said my tall hostess. 'Our landlord neglects us sadly, and we are far gone in wrack and ruin. In fact, I do not know what we should do were it not for our own resources.' At this Emerald cackled. Then she came up to me, and began fingering my clothes.

The tall one shut the door.

'Don't touch,' she shouted at Emerald, in her deep, rather grinding voice. 'Keep your fingers off.'

She picked up the large oil lamp. Her hair was a discoloured white in its beams.

'I apologise for my sister,' she said. 'We have all been so neglected that some of us have quite forgotten how to behave. Come, Emerald.'

Pushing Emerald before her, she led the way.

In the Occasional Room and the Morning Room, the gilt had flaked from the gingerbread furniture, the family portraits stared from their heavy frames, and the striped wallpaper drooped in the lamplight like an assembly of sodden, half-inflated balloons.

At the door of the Canton Cabinet, my hostess turned. 'I am taking you to meet my sisters,' she said.

'I look forward to doing so,' I replied, regardless of truth, as in childhood.

She nodded slightly, and proceeded. 'Take care,' she said. 'The floor has weak places.'

In the little Canton Cabinet, the floor had, in fact, largely given way, and been plainly converted into a hospice for rats.

And then, there they all were, the remaining six of them thinly illumined by what must surely be rushlights in the four shapely chandeliers. But now, of course, I could see their faces.

'We are all named after our birthstones,' said my hostess. 'Emerald you know. I am Opal. Here are Diamond and Garnet, Cornelian and Chrysolite. The one with the grey hair is Sardonyx, and the beautiful one is Turquoise.'

They all stood up. During the ceremony of introduction, they made odd little noises.

'Emerald and I are the eldest, and Turquoise of course is the youngest.'

Emerald stood in the corner before me, rolling her dyed-red head. The Long Drawing Room was raddled with decay. The cobwebs gleamed like steel filigree in the beam of the lamp, and the sisters seemed to have been seated in cocoons of them, like cushions of gossamer.

'There is one other sister, Topaz. But she is busy writing.'

'Writing all our diaries,' said Emerald.

'Keeping the record,' said my hostess.

A silence followed.

'Let us sit down,' said my hostess. 'Let us make our visitor welcome.'

The six of them gently creaked and subsided into their former places. Emerald and my hostess remained standing.

'Sit down, Emerald. Our visitor shall have *my* chair as it is the best.' I realised that inevitably there was no extra seat.

'Of course not,' I said. 'I can only stay for a minute. I am waiting for the rain to stop,' I explained feebly to the rest of them.

'I insist,' said my hostess.

I looked at the chair to which she was pointing. The padding was burst and rotten, the woodwork bleached and crumbling to collapse. All of them were watching me with round, vague eyes in their flat faces.

'Really,' I said, 'no, thank you, It's kind of you, but I must go.' All the same, the surrounding wood and the dark marsh beyond it loomed scarcely less appalling than the house itself and its inmates.

'We should have more to offer, more and better in every way, were it not for our landlord.' She spoke with bitterness, and it seemed to me that on all the faces the expression changed. Emerald came towards me out of her corner, and again began to finger my clothes.

But this time her sister did not correct her, and when I stepped away, she stepped after me and went on as before.

'She has failed in the barest duty of sustentation.'

I could not prevent myself starting at the pronoun. At once, Emerald caught hold of my dress, and held it tightly.

'But there is one place she cannot spoil for us. One place where we can entertain in our own way.'

'Please,' I cried. 'Nothing more. I am going now.'

Emerald's pygmy grip tautened.

'It is the room where we eat.'

All the watching eyes lighted up, and became something they had not been before.

'I may almost say where we feast.'

The six of them began again to rise from their spidery bowers.

'Because *she* cannot go there.'

The sisters clapped their hands, like a rustle of leaves.

'There we can be what we really are.'

The eight of them were now grouped round me. I noticed that the one pointed out as the youngest was passing her dry, pointed tongue over her lower lip.

'Nothing unladylike, of course.'

'Of course not,' I agreed.

'But firm,' broke in Emerald, dragging at my dress as she spoke. 'Father said that must always come first.'

'Our father was a man of measureless wrath against a slight,' said my hostess. 'It is his continuing presence about the house which largely upholds us.'

'Shall I show her?' asked Emerald.

'Since you wish to,' said her sister disdainfully.

From somewhere in her musty garments Emerald produced a scrap of card, which she held out to me.

'Take it in your hand. I'll allow you to hold it.'

It was a photograph, obscurely damaged.

'Hold up the lamp,' squealed Emerald. With an aloof gesture her sister raised it.

It was a photograph of myself when a child, bobbed and waistless. And through my heart was a tiny brown needle.

'We've all got things like it,' said Emerald jubilantly. 'Wouldn't you think her heart would have rusted away by now?'

'She never had a heart,' said the elder sister scornfully, putting down the light.

'She might not have been able to help what she did,' I cried.

I could hear the sisters catch their fragile breath.

'It's what you do that counts,' said my hostess, regarding the discoloured floor, 'not what you feel about it afterwards. Our father always insisted on that. It's obvious.'

'Give it back to me,' said Emerald, staring into my eyes. For a moment I hesitated.

'Give it back to her,' said my hostess in her contemptuous way. 'It makes no difference now. Everyone but Emerald can see that the work is done.'

I returned the card, and Emerald let go of me as she stuffed it away.

'And now will you join us?' asked my hostess. 'In the inner room?' As far as was possible, her manner was almost casual.

'I am sure the rain has stopped,' I replied. 'I must be on my way.'

'Our father would never have let you go so easily, but I think we have done what we can with you.'

I inclined my head.

'Do not trouble with adieux,' she said. 'My sisters no longer expect them.' She picked up the lamp. 'Follow me. And take care. The floor has weak places.'

'Goodbye,' squealed Emerald.

'Take no notice, unless you wish,' said my hostess.

I followed her through the mouldering rooms and across the rotten floors in silence. She opened both the outer doors and stood waiting for me to pass through. Beyond, the moon was shining, and she stood dark and shapeless in the silver flood.

On the threshold, or somewhere on the far side of it, I spoke.

'I did nothing,' I said. 'Nothing.'

So far from replying, she dissolved into the darkness and silently shut the door.

I took up my painful, lost, and forgotten way through the wood, across the dreary marsh, and back to the little yellow road.

Never Visit Venice

Travel is a good thing; it stimulates the imagination. Everything else is a snare and a delusion. Our own journey is entirely imaginative. Therein lies its strength.

Louis-Ferdinand Céline

I

Henry Fern was neither successful in the world's eyes nor unsuccessful; partly because he lived in a world society in which to be either requires considerable craft. Fern was not good at material scheming. His job stood far below his theoretical capacities, but he had a very clear idea of his own defects, and was inclined inwardly to believe that but for one or two strokes of sheer good fortune, he would have been a mere social derelict. He did not sufficiently understand that it has been made almost impossible to be a social derelict.

Not that Fern was adapted to that status any better than to the status of tycoon. Like most introverts, he was very dependent upon small, minute-to-minute comforts, no matter whence they came. Fern's gaze upon life was very decisively inwards. He read much. He reflected much. One of his purest pleasures was an entire day in bed; all by himself, in excellent health. He lived in a quite pleasant surburban flat, with a view over a park. Unfortunately, the park, for the most part, was more beautiful when Fern was not there; because when he was there, it tended to fill with raucous loiterers and tiny piercing radios.

Fern was an only child. His parents were far off and in poorer circumstances than when he had been a boy. He had much difficulty, not perhaps in making friends, but in keeping up an interest in them. There seemed to be something in him which made him different from most of the people he encountered in the office or in the train or in the park or at the houses of others. He could not succeed in defining what this difference was, and he simultaneously congratulated and despised himself for having it. He would sincerely have liked to be rid of it, but at the same time was pretty sure it was the best thing about him. If only others were interested in the best!

One thing it plainly did was hold Fern back in what people called his career. Here it did damage in several different ways. That it disconnected him from the network of favour and promotion was only the most obvious. Much worse was that it made favour and promotion seem to Fern doubtfully worth while. Worse still was that it made him see through the work he had to do: see that, like so much that is called work, it was little more than protective colouration; but see also that the blank disclosure of this fact would destroy not merely the work itself and his own income, but the hopes of the many who were committed to at least a half-belief in its importance, even when they chafed against it. Worst of all probably was the simple fact that this passionate division inside him ate up his energy and sent it to waste. Fern would have liked to be an artist, but seemed to himself to have little creative talent. He soon realised that it has become a difficult world for those who possibly are artists only in living. There is so little scope for practice and rehearsal.

Nor could Fern find a woman who seemed to feel in the least as he did. Having heard and read often that it is useless to seek for one's ideal woman, that the very fancy of an ideal woman is an absurdity, he at first made up his mind to concentrate upon the good qualities that were actually to be found, which were undoubtedly many, at least by accepted standards. He even became engaged to be married on two occasions; but the more he saw of each fiancée, despite her beauty and charm of character, the more he felt himself an alien and an imposter. Unable to dissemble any more, he had himself broken off the engagement. He had felt much anguish, but it was not, he felt, anguish of the right kind. Even in that he seemed isolated. The women must have realised something of the truth, because though both, when he spoke, expressed aggressive dismay, since marriage is so much sought after for itself, they soon went quietly, and were heard of by Fern no more. Now he was nearing forty: not, he thought, unhappy, when all was considered; but he could not do so much considering every day, and often he felt puzzled and sadly lonely. Things could be so very much worse, and that very easily, as none knew better than Fern; but this reflection, well justified though it was, did not prevent Fern from thinking, not infrequently, of suicide, or from letting the back of his mind dwell pleasurably and recurrently upon the thought of Death's warm, white, and loving arms.

One thing about which Fern felt true anguish was the problem of travel, or, as others put it, his 'holidays'.

Here the shortage of money really mattered. 'Why do I not go out for more?' he asked himself.

He had no difficulty in answering himself. Apart from the obvious doubt as to whether it was a good bargain to sell himself further into slavery in order to receive in return perhaps seven more days each year for travel and enough extra money to travel a little (a very little) more comfortably, he saw well that even these rewards might be vitiated by the extra care that would probably travel with the recipient of them. He realised early that, except for a few natural bohemians, travel can be of value only when based upon private resources: hence the almost universal adulteration of travel into organised tourism, an art into a science, so that the shrinking surface of the earth, in its physical aspect as in its way of life, becomes a single place, not worth leaving home to see. Fern saw this very clearly, but it was considerably too wide and theoretical a consideration to deter one so truly a traveller but who had yet travelled so little as Fern. What really held Fern back from travel, as from much else, was the lack of a fellow-traveller, remembering always that this fellow-traveller had to comply pretty nearly with an ideal which Fern could by no means define, but could only sense and serve, present or (as almost always) absent beyond reasonable hope.

He had shared a holiday with both his fiancées – one holiday in each case. Much the same things had happened each time; doubtless because men notoriously involve themselves (even when they do it half-heartedly) with the same woman in different shapes, or, perhaps, as Lord Chesterfield says, because women are so much more alike than are men. On each occasion, it had been two or three weeks of differing objectives, conscious and unconscious, at all levels, and, especially, of utterly different responses to everything encountered; but a matter also of determined and scrupulous effort on both sides not only to understand but to act upon and make allowances for the other's point of view. All these things had made of the holiday a reproduction or extension of common life, which was not at all what Fern had in mind. Both parties had, in the American formula, 'worked at' the relationship, worked as hard as slaves under an overseer; but the produce was unmarketable. 'You're too soulful about everything,' complained one of the girls. She spoke quite affectionately, and truly for his own good, as the world goes, and as Fern perceived. None the less, he came to surmise that for him travel might be a mystical undertaking. He had some time read of Renan's concept that for each man there is an individual 'means to salvation': for some the ascent to Monsalvat, for some alcohol or laudanum, for some wenching and whoring, for some even the common business of day-to-day life. For Fern salvation might lie in travel; but surely not in solitary travel. And how much more difficult than ever this new consideration would make finding a companion! Almost, how impossible! Fern felt his soul (as the girl had called it) shrink when he first clearly sensed the hopeless conflict between deepest need and inevitable absence of response; the conflict which makes even men and women who are capable of better things live as they do. He and the girl were on a public seat in Bruges at the time; among the trees along the Dyver, looking at the swans on the canal.

At least politeness had been maintained on these trips; from first to last. It was something by no means to be despised. Moreover, when Fern had travelled with others, with a man friend, or with a party, he had fared considerably worse. Then there had been little in the way of manners and no obligation even to essay mutuality. In the longer run, therefore, Fern had travelled little and enjoyed less. This in no way modified his unwordly attitude to travel. He knew that few people do enjoy it, despite the ever-increasing number who set forth; and resented the fact that actual experience of travel had seemed, for practical purposes, to put him among the majority – of them, but not with them, as usual. Nor could he see even the possibility of a solution. Not enough money. Not enough time. And no intimates, let alone initiates. It had been quite bad enough even when he had only been twenty-five.

Fern began to have a dream. Foreshadowings or intimations came to him first; thereafter, at irregular

335

intervals, the whole experience (in so far as it could be described as a whole), or bits or scraps of it, portions or distortions. There seemed to be no system in its total or partial recurrence. As far as Fern was concerned, it merely did not come often enough. He felt that it would be unlucky (by which he meant destructive) to note too precisely the dates of the dream's reappearances. But Fern was soon musing about the content of the dream during waking hours; sometimes even by policy and on purpose. To the infrequent dream of the night, he added an increasing habit of deliberate daydreaming; a pastime so disapproved of by the experts.

Fern's dream, though glowing, was simple.

He dreamed that he was in Venice, where he had never been. He was drifting in a gondola across an expanse of water he had read about, called the Lagoon. Lying in his embrace at the bottom of the boat was a woman in evening dress or party dress or gay dress of some kind. He did not know how he had met her: whether in Venice or in London. Conceivably, even, he knew her already, outside the dream; had long known her, or at least set eyes on her. When he awoke, he could never remember her face with sufficient clarity; or perhaps could remember only for a moment or two after waking, in the manner of dreams. It was a serious frustration, because the woman was very desirable, and because between Fern and her, and between them only as far as Fern was concerned, was understanding and affinity. Such understanding could not last, Fern realised even in the dream: it might not last beyond that one night; or it might last as long as six or seven days. Fern could always remember the woman's dress: but it was not always the same dress; it was sometimes white, sometimes black, sometimes crimson, sometimes mottled like a fish. Above the boat, were always stars, and always the sky was a peculiarly deep lilac, which lingered with Fern and which he had never seen in the world exterior to the dream. There was never a moon, but behind the gondola, along some kind of waterfront, sparkled the raffish, immemorial, and evocative lights of Fern's hypothetical Venice. Ahead, in contrast, lay a long, dark reef, with occasional and solitary lights only. There were tiny waves lapping round the gondola, and Fern was in some way aware of bigger waves beating slowly on the far side of the reef. He never knew where the two of them were going, but they were going somewhere, because journeys without destination are as work without product: the product may disappoint, but is indispensible and has to be borne. Fern wished that he could enter the dream at an earlier point, so that he might have some idea of how he had met thewoman, but always when awareness began, the pair of them were a long way out across the water with the string of gaudy lights far behind. For some reason, Fern had an idea that he had met the woman by eager but slightly furtive arrangement, outside an enormous hotel, very fashionable and luxurious. The gondolier was always vague: Fern had read and been told that, since the advent of powered craft, gondoliers were costly and difficult. (None the less, this one seemed, whatever the

337

explanation, to be devoted and amenable.)

The beginning and the end of the dream were lost in the lilac night. The beginning, Fern thought, the beginning of the whole, wonderful experience might have been only a few hours earlier. The end he hesitated to speculate about. Nor could he even, upon waking, remember anything that he and the woman had said to one another. A curious, disembodied feeling came back with him, however, and remained with him until the demands of the day ahead dragged him within minutes into full consciousness. He felt that his personal identity had been in partial dissolution, and that in some measure he had been also the night, the gondola, and even the woman with him. This sense of disembodiment he could even sometimes recapture in his daydreams, when circumstances permitted sufficient concentration. Above all, the dream, possibly more tender than passionate, brought a boundless feeling of plain and simple relief. Fern could not conceive of the world's cares ever diminishing to permit so intense a relief in waking life.

By day, more and more often, Fern saw himself in Venice. By night – on *those* nights – he was in Venice.

It had begun happening years ago, and he had still never been to Venice. The impact of Fern's dream upon waking existence seemed confined to the fact that when men and women spoke of their goals in life, as men and women occasionally do, referring to a sales managership or a partnership or a nice little cottage in the country or a family of four boys and four girls, Fern at once saw that lilac sky, heard the lapping of those tiny waves, felt a deep, obscure pain, and sensed an even greater isolation than usual.

He supposed that the dream was fragile. If thought about too practically, if analysed too closely, it might well cease to recur. The dream was probably best left in the back of the mind, at the edges of the mind; within that mental area which comes into its own between waking and sleeping – and, less happily, between sleeping and waking.

Possibly, therefore, the dream had the effect of actually deterring Fern from looking out much more practical knowledge about Venice. All he knew about the place was scrappy, uncoordinated stuff ingathered from before the time when the dream had first visited him: for example, he had read a steam-rollered abridgement of Arthur Machen's Casanova translation, and, long before that, a costumed legend of Venice in the Renaissance by Rafael Sabatini, which belonged to his mother. Fern fully realised that, even geographically, the real Venice could hardly be much like his dream. And it scarcely needs adding that the woman in the dream seemed outside the bounds of possibility, let alone the money to pay for her and the gondola. Just as the real Venice could not resemble the dream Venice, so real life could not resemble life in the dream.

For years, then, Fern teetered along the tightrope between content and discontent; between mild self-congratulation and black frustration; between the gritty disillusionments of human intimacy and travel (for Fern the two became more and more inseparable), and the truth and power of his dream. It might be a twilight tightrope, but twilight was not an hour which Fern despised.

So when trouble was added unto Fern in the end, he failed for a long time to be aware of it. Then one spring day, and what was more, in the office, he suddenly realised that his dream had not returned for a long time. He thought that it must have been months since it had last visited him; perhaps more than a year. And, in consequence, he perceived that the dream of the day, always so much paler, of course, but normally, and given even reasonably right circumstances, almost summonable at will, had become totally bloodless and faintly hysterical. Instead of advancing to meet him halfway when he felt the need of it, it was more and more requiring to be conjured, even compelled. It had become much like an aspirin: an anodyne strictly exterior, and so a deceiver. Fern soon came to see that for months he had been standing naked against life's stones and spears without knowing it.

Even though it was the spring, always the most difficult season of the year, he looked himself over, confirmed that he was surviving, and seemed to inaugurate an inner change. This was perhaps the moment, which comes to so many, when Fern simultaneously matured and withered. He became more practical, as people call it; less demanding of life.

He was sincerely astonished when during that same summer he was given significant promotion in his work. In due course, he was equally surprised to find that the additional responsibilities of his new position by no means outweighed the advantage of the greater pay, as he had always supposed they would; the truth being that the tendency is for all to carry the same responsibility, so that soon all will receive the same reward, if reward will any longer be the word. People felt vaguely but approvingly that Fern had taken more of a grip on himself. Fern, cheated of his dream, sometimes even felt something of the kind himself. Two or three years passed, while the land steadily receded beneath Fern's tightrope.

When the dream snapped off (as seemed to Fern to have happened, so abrupt had been discovery), its place was taken in the back and the edges of Fern's mind by the sentiment of death. 'God!' he had thought earlier, feeling pierced by a sword through the stomach, as, at that moment, we all do; 'God! I am going to have to die.' But in those days, with the rest of us, he had thought of it only occasionally. Now the thought was no longer an infrequent, stabbing shock. It was a soft-footed, never-absent familiar; neither quite an enemy to him nor quite a friend. The thought was steadily making Fern dusty, mangy, less visible; all in the midst of his perceptibly greater successfulness.

And it was almost as if it were these two things in conjunction, the new practicality and the faint, ever-spinning sentiment of death, that brought about Fern's ultimate decision actually to see Venice; as if he had abruptly said out loud, 'After all, a man should visit Venice before he dies.' With departure in sight, and

341

upon the advice of an older man, he read the Prince of Lampedusa's *Gattopardo* in an English paperback. 'It happens to be about Sicily,' observed Fern's friend, 'but it applies to the whole of Italy, and it's concerned with the only thing that matters there, unless you're an actual archaeologist.' Fern gathered that the only thing which mattered was that Italy had undergone a great change.

II

Despite his ruminations and his hopes, Fern had never before travelled beyond France, the Low Countries, and Scandinavia, to all of which regions he considered himself comparitively acclimatised and much attached. By the time he found himself, as will shortly be seen, thinking once more about his dream, he had been in and around Venice for seventeen days, and they had been days of surprise, horror, fantasy, and conflict.

He could find kinship with no one. There was something terrifyingly insane about the total breakdown of the place: the utter discrepancy between the majesty and mystery of the monuments and the tininess of all who dwelt around them or came supposedly to gaze upon them. Fern looked upon these mighty works and despaired. Now he sat on an eighteenth-century stone bollard at the tip of the Punta di Salute, and summed it all up.

Many times Fern had read or been told that the great trouble with Venice was the swarm of visitors. You could hardly see the real people, he had always been informed. Indeed, the real people were often said to be dying out.

But by now it was the visitors who seemed to him a mere mist: a flutter of small, anxious sparrows, endlessly twittering, whether rich or poor, about 'currency' (Fern could fully understand only those who twittered in English); endlessly pecked and gashed by the local hawks; endlessly keeping up with neighbours at home, who were as unqualified to visit Venice as themselves. All visitors had at once too little time and too much. As he wandered down a *calle* or through a palazzo, he perceived that very few indeed of the visitors visited anything beyond the cathedral and seat of the former rulers; or saw much even of these, if only because of the crowd inside and the shouting of the guides, as mechanical and stereotyped as the swift mutterings of the priests.

The visitors sat about the Piazzo San Marco, proclaimed by so many wise voices as the world's most beautiful work of men (though infested with pigeons, shot or mutilated elsewhere in Italy), in a constant stew, rich or poor, about the prices: a preoccupation which was thoroughly justified. The women took off their shoes because they had walked a few hundred yards. They stuck out their poor legs, and, to do them justice, endeavoured intermittently but with pathetic unproficiency, to catch a life as it passed, to utter the right cries. If life, their faces enquired, could not be caught in Venice, where could it be caught? For a few, right back at home, Fern felt; for the majority, no longer

343

anywhere. Of the men, most were past even making the attempt. They sat looking foolish, fretful, bored, insufficiently occupied, and, above all, out of place. Nor could Fern but agree it was hard that one could not buy an aniseed or a cup of coffee in a place so beautiful without the beauty being tarnished by the price – a price probably unavoidable from the caterer's point of view, because of forces as uncontrollable by him as by Fern . . . And, of course, there were other visitors, mainly English, who despised the great and ancient monuments, structures on so different a scale from themselves, and spent their time poking their noses into what they conceived to be the 'real living and working conditions' of the Venetians.

It was not so much the visitors, with their fleeting passage, their phantom foreign money, that startled Fern, but these same Venetians. So far from the place being half empty, as he had been led to expect, it was swarming from edge to edge; and it swarmed with sentimental, self-satisfied philistines, more identical and mass-produced than he would have thought possible, inescapable except inside the faded, ill-kept palazzi where one had to pay to enter. Those among the Venetians who were not leeching on the visitors seemed to be industrial workers from the vast plants lined up across the water at Mestre; labour force to the war machines of a new invader holding the city under siege of modernity and required merely to await the inevitable self-induced collapse, much as the Turks waited for Byzantium to destroy itself.

The human din in Venice cancelled the quiet which might have been expected from the absence of Motor Moloch. It continued throughout the twenty-four hours, merely becoming after midnight more sinister, shrill, and unpredictable. Every night, gangs of youths screamed their way through the alleys. Folding iron shutters crashed like cannon through the early watches. Altercations, sexual or political, continued fortissimi in male voices for fifty minutes at a time. Fern, in his pension attic, would look at his watch and see it was two o'clock, three o'clock, four o'clock. The noise would diminish, he would fall asleep, and then there would be more screaming boys, more clanging shutters. It was a highly traditional uproar perhaps, but Venice seemed to have an unhappy aptitude for combining only the worst of past society with the society of today. What might once have been falcons, had become hawks, and were now carrion crows.

Fern went to hear *Rigoletto* at the Fenice and to hear a concert with a famous conductor and a famous soloist: both occasions were more than half empty, and such people as were there were either elderly Americans doing their duty by a dead ideal (often at the behest of their hotel porters) and intermittently slumbering, or dubious Italian youths, palpably with free seats and very concerned to make clear that fact to the fools who had paid. The performances in themselves seemed to Fern good, but that only made it worse. They seemed to be provided for a bygone generation, a bygone species of man, a world that had been

345

laughed out of life and replaced by nothing.

Fern wandered through the shouting, pushing crowds, more and more sick at heart. As, at the concert, the beauty of the performance only made more poignant the entire absence of an audience, so, in the city at large, the incomparable magnificence and grace of the structures only made more dispiriting the entire absence of these qualities in the beholders. The stripped palaces, indifferently maintained even when a few rooms were 'open to the public', failed even to evoke their past. They would appeal only to those ultimate playboys who positively prefer their roses or their canals to be dead.

Fern found only one place that satisfied when regarded even as a ghost, and as thus offering life of a kind and in a degree. This was a suite of comparatively small bedrooms and dressing rooms and powder rooms high up in one of the remoter palaces, all fragile woodwork in faded green, red, and gold, with elaborate Murano looking-glasses; tender, canopied beds; and flowery dressing-tables. These small, fastidious, flirtatious rooms, alone in all Venice, vouchsafed that frisson which is history. Obviously, few came near them, other than an occasional perfunctory cleaner, from year's end to year's end. This might spare the delightful rooms for their proper wraiths, but it also pointed to an insoluble dilemma.

In most of the palazzi, Fern could spend a morning or afternoon and see only a handful of his kind in the whole building, and all of them rushing through in twenty minutes. Nor could this be sensibly objected to: with the destruction of their owners the palazzi had been destroyed also. It was offensive to pretend that these corpses still lived; odious to seek profit from their corruption.

Between the beauty of Venice and the people there was no link: not even of ignorant awe; perhaps that least of all. Much as the folk had pillaged the Roman villas, so Venice was being pillaged now; and Fern sensed that the very fact of the pillage being often called preservation implied that total dissolution was in sight. Venice was rotted with the world's new littleness. To many her beauty was actually antagonistic, as imposing upon them a demand to which they were unable to rise. Soon the Lagoon would be 'reclaimed' and the Venetian dream submitted to a new law of values; a puritan law antithetical to the law of pleasure that had prevailed there for so long; the terrain applied to the uses of the post-Garibaldian mass, existing only in its own expansion. Mestre and multiplication would compel unconditional surrender. The state of affairs that Fern now looked upon was more of a pretence, more of a masquerade than anything even in Venice's past. It was perhaps proper that Venice should end with a divertissement, but Fern felt that the fires of dawn were visible through the holes in the scenery; the decapitation overdue.

The Venetian dream?

Perched on his bollard, Fern realised with a start that he had been in Venice seventeen days, and not given a thought to his own dream.

During those seventeen days, he had not spoken to a single person except in the ways of triviality and cross-purposes. He never struck up acquaintance easily, but the conflictual impact of Venice, at once so lovely and so appalling, had transfixed him into even more of a trance than usual. He had wandered with a set stare; lost in a dream of another kind, a seemingly impersonal dream in which the dreamer had been the shadow. Big ships were passing quite frequently along the Canale della Giudecca to his left, into and out from the docks renewed by Mussolini. Unlike so much else, the ships were beautiful and alive at the same time. The scale of things contracted to the problems of one dreamer. Fern felt very lonely.

A manifest Englishman landed with an Italian youth from the *traghetto* at Fern's rear. He was bald and barrel-shaped. His large moustache and fringe of hair were ginger. He wore a brown tweed jacket buttoned across the stomach, dingy grey trousers, and an untidy shirt with a club tie. One might see him presiding know-ledgeably over a weekend rally of motor cars in Surrey or Hampshire.

He walked out at the end of the stone promontory, dragging the Italian boy (in open white shirt and tight, bright trousers) by the hand. The Italian boy was making a girlish show of reluctance. The Englishman, a few feet away from Fern's bollard, pointed with his free hand to some object in the distance; something about which it was inconceivable to him that no one else should care, let alone a person for whom he himself cared so much. All the same, the boy did not care at all. He was no longer going through the motions of petulance, but stood quite still, looking blank, bored, resistant of new knowledge, and professionally handsome.

'Damn it!' said the Englishman. 'You might show some interest.'

The boy said nothing. An expression of dreadful disappointment and wild rage transfigured the Englishman's unremarkable face. He said something in Italian which Fern took to be at once bitter and obscene. At the same time, he threw away the boy's hand as if it had turned glutinous in his grasp. He then strutted off by himself towards the Zattere.

The Italian still stood looking fixedly at the paving stones. Then he thrust one hand into the back pocket of his trousers and produced a neat pocketbook: possibly a gift from the Englishman. After examining the contents with almost comic care, he returned the pocketbook to its place and strolled off. In pursuit, Fern imagined; thought he did not turn round to see. Judging from many experiences since his arrival, he thought that were he to do so, the next approach might be to him. He had found it a situation that put him at a loss in all its aspects. He simply could not live up to what was expected of a lone Englishman in Italy.

By now he felt so alone that he almost wished that he could. Hitherto in Venice he had been neither happy nor unhappy but simply amazed; on occasion aghast.

Now the recollection of his dream had coincided with the rapid dissolution of the perambulating philosopher in him. Acclimatisation to Venice had set in with a rush. The September breeze blew gently up the Canale di San Marco in Fern's face; sweet and cool, as it sighed for the slow sickness of Venice's stifling summer. The flashy motor-boats cackled and yelped around him, driving the gondolas to their death. Fern, thrust back upon his own life, passed his hand over his legs, his arms, his shoulders. He felt a pain he had almost forgotten during the years he had walked his tightrope.

What could Venice do for him but sadden him further? Fern decided to go home the next day; if the owner of the pension would permit him to depart ahead of his time. He rose, extended and contracted his legs, stumped up and down a bit, gazed for the last time upon one particularly incomparable Venetian prospect, and felt quite equal to weeping, had it not been for the self-consciousness of solitude in a foreign land.

He walked away.

III

That evening, Fern pushed his way along the Molo. He wanted no more unsettled business in his heart.

The owner of the pension had indicated that for a room in modern Venice, as for so much else, there is always a queue. He tried to charge Fern up to the end of the week, but did not try to keep him. Fern had already suspected that in the campaign between the visitors and the Venetians there are few clear-cut victories on either side.

Fern had even an excuse for his promenade. It was to be his last night in Venice, and, as he might have put it in his manly and practical aspect, 'You can't leave Venice without ever having been in a gondola.' Gondolas may not last much longer, nor may people. But gondolas, being no longer very functional, are not much good without someone to love on the journey.

On the Molo, Americans stood about, japing one another uneasily or over-confidently; wondering how to fill in before flying on to Athens or back to Paris the next morning; questing for highballs or local vintages on the rocks. Uncontrolled Italian children and their plump, doting parents effortlessly dominated the prospect. Away to the south, over towards Chioggia, single lights gleamed romantically. The sky was turning to deep lilac and filling with festive, silvery stars.

Fern turned leftwards up an alley, where it was quieter, then wound about through dark courts and passages, like a beetle through a tomb. Immediately he was alone, or almost so, among the great dark buildings, his mind returned to those small, elegant bedrooms and boudoirs at the top of the palazzo he had visited. The recollection of them made him shiver with the pathos of something so hopelessly irrecoverable that was still so hopelessly necessary. Thinking about them, feeling still the intensity of their atmosphere, he could smell the perfume of the Venetian decadence; that long century when the lion drowsed, awaiting Napoleon, the city fell irrevocably to pieces, and all the fashionable wore curious, enveloping masks, so that they looked partly like strange animals, partly like comedians, and partly like ravishers and ravished.

There was such a figure standing before him; dark and motionless against the rail along the side of a canal, which edged the small piazzetta Fern entered; neither quite in the light from the one lamp in the piazzetta, nor quite out of it. Fern slipped into a shadowy doorway and stared, silent and listening to his heartbeat.

On the other side of the canal loomed a formless stone structure, from all the windows of which seemed to shine an even, pale light, something between pink and blue; and Fern, whose hearing was at all times excessively acute, thought he could detect the faint echo of music and revelry seeping through the thick walls and closed casements. Then he realised that the pale light was the reflection of the late evening sky on the glass, and that the sound was no more than the general cry of Venice. He drew himself together.

Almost in silence down the canal came a gondola. Fern, however sharp his ears, could hear only the softest plash, plash, plash. Then the *ferro* came into view, and the gondola stopped by the figure against the railing. The gondolier seemed to be dressed in black. But Fern's attention was concentrated upon the equally dark passenger; the person for whom the gondola had come.

At first, and in the most curious way, nothing more seemed to happen. The gondola just lay there in the faintly coloured dusk; with the gondolier almost invisible, and the presumed passenger still apparently waiting for someone or something, certainly making no motion to step aboard, indeed making no motion of any kind. Two middle-aged men, both dressed in light colours, crossed the piazzetta from the opposite corner, and proceeded in the direction from which Fern had come. They were talking loudly and simultaneously, in the usual way, and gave no sign of noticing the gondola and the figure by the railing. Of course, there was no reason why they should notice them. All the same, Fern felt that two or three minutes must have passed while the group remained motionless in dim outline against the vast stone building on the other side of the canal.

At least that length of time passed before it occurred to Fern that it might be for him they waited. He had set forth to destroy his dream (even though he had not expressed it quite like that) and thereby, as so often, might have wound up the mechanism for making it come true; because life goes ever crabwise, as the great Venetian, Baron Corvo, constantly proclaimed. Fern shrank back into his dark doorway. He feared lest the whiteness of his face give him away.

The strange set piece lingered for a few more moments. Then Fern realised that the figure which had been standing by the railings was now somehow in the gondola, and that the gondola was once more coming towards him. It glided down the side of the piazzetta, making only the ghost of a sound; the plash, plash, plash of the paddle might have been the wings of a night bird, or the trembling of Fern's own heart muscles. Five or six gay little children ran across the piazzetta in the line of the two men in grey. They were heavily preoccupied with abusing and hitting one another.

Peeping out, Fern saw that the passenger was still standing in the gondola, somewhat towards the bow. The whole course of events was too fanciful, so that Fern's only resolution was to withdraw. He was waiting until the disappearance of the gondola should make this possible. The gondola could hardly have taken more than a minute to pass, but before it had departed from Fern's view, as he hid in his doorway, the standing passenger made a slight movement; from within the dark hooded cloak a woman looked straight into Fern's pale face, and seemed to smile in welcome. In an instant, the gondola was gone.

A narrow *fondamenta* continued alongside the canal from out of the piazzetta. Fern ran to the corner and hastened after the vanishing boat, which seemed now to be travelling very much faster. As he sped on, his shoes clattering on the stones, he wondered if insidious Venice had promoted an insanity in him, a mad confusion between dream and dread. He was pretty sure that, if he should run at all, he should by rights run in the opposite direction. But having started to run, having begun such a disturbance of the night, he had to run on. He nearly managed to overtake the boat just as it was passing under the next bridge. One would have been convinced that the gondolier at least must have heard him and seen him, but the gondola slid on undeflected. Fern realised that beyond the bridge the *fondamenta* did not continue. He stood on the crest of the arch and watched. He did not care, had no title, to call after. The stones of Venice closed softly over the departing shadow.

And then, only twenty or thirty minutes later, something happened which explained these small but singular events.

Deep in thought, and troubled in soul, Fern strolled back to the wide promenade which faces the Canale di San Marco and is the principal waterfront of the city. The distance from the piazzetta of the odd events was not great, but in Venice, for better or for worse, one can seldom walk straight ahead and unobstructed for more than a few paces, and Fern, his mind in any case on other things, lost himself in a small way at least twice. In the end, he emerged on the Riva degli Schiavoni. Everything was brightly illuminated, the sky was perfect, and Fern reflected that, after all, Venice did look rather festive, even a trifle exalted, as she should do. But his mind was on his own loneliness, and on his dream: if, at this late hour, he had, after all, made a tiny concession to Venice, he wanted someone with whom to join hands on it, wanted that person badly. Even so, he stood still, uncertain whether to turn leftwards where it would be quieter, or rightwards where adventure was more likely. Now that the chance had gone, he very positively wished that he had spoken to the woman in the piazzetta. It could hardly have been a matter of life or death. Fern trembled slightly. He was indeed an irresolute creature. By now, reason told him, it could

355

hardly matter less which way he turned.

He simply lacked the heart, the energy, the curiosity to wander off towards the darker area to the left; to take a brisk solitary constitutional along the front, safe except perhaps from cutpurses, as his father would certainly do, and think nothing of it, indeed be all the better for it. Fern turned towards Danieli's (a line of American women leaned like beautiful wasting candles over the rail of the roof-garden, high above); towards the Piazza; towards life, in the commercial or Thomas Cook connotation of the word.

Within a minute or two, he thought he saw again the woman whose face he had seen so momentarily in the gondola.

She was standing by herself in much the same way at the edge of the canal, though this time it was the Canale di San Marco, almost the sea. She was still wearing the hooded black cloak, as in a picture by one of the Longhis, but was no longer so muffled in it. It looked to Fern that beneath it she was wearing a spreading, period dress. Despite the crowd, which had by no means ceased to push and bawl in his ears, he was really frightened. He did not put the thought into words within his head, but his thought was that this was an apparition, and that he was having a breakdown. The figure stood there so motionless, so detached from all those vulgar people, so spectrally apparelled; and, of course, so recurrent. As in the piazzetta, he stood and stared; not unlike a ghost himself. Everything faded but that single figure.

Then she walked steadily towards him, twenty or

thirty-five yards, and spoke.

'English?'

She really was dressed in an eighteenth-century style, and beneath her hood Fern could see piled-up hair.

'Yes,' said Fern. 'English.'

'The city of Venice would like to invite you for a gondola trip.'

Here indeed was an explanation: at least within limits. She was connected with 'publicity' and was merely dressing the part. It was an explanation all too consistent with what Fern had seen of the place. He laughed a little too brashly, a little too brusquely.

But no doubt she was accustomed professionally to all gradations of oafishness.

'Complimentary, of course,' she said.

That, thought Fern, was like the Venice he had so far seen.

The woman was an Italian and did not speak words such as 'complimentary' with ease.

'Are you alone?' asked the woman.

'Yes,' said Fern. 'Quite alone. You must invite someone else. I don't qualify.'

'But you do qualify,' said the woman. 'The city of Venice wants to help lonely visitors.'

It sounded ghastly, but the woman spoke with an aspect of sincerity that at least made it possible to reply with reasonable self-respect.

'Tell me more,' said Fern.

'We go in a gondola,' explained the woman, speaking carefully, in the way of professional guides, as if to a backward child, 'along the Grand Canal and across the Lagoon.'

It was not the manner in which Fern had visualised the realisation of his dream, but no doubt it was the dream which controlled the situation, and not he. Just then he could hardly be expected to think it all out.

'We?' enquired Fern. 'How many will there be?'

'Just you and I.' She said it with the dignity that certain Italian women can bring to statements that many other women can utter only with a blush and giggle or excessive explanation.

'And, of course, the gondolier,' she added with a beautiful smile.

'I shall be very pleased,' said Fern. 'Thank you.' He managed to accept with some degree of the same simplicity.

'There you are,' she said, using perhaps not quite the right idiom, and pointing to a gondola. Fern, even though apprehensive of capsizing the unknown craft, managed to hand her in as if to the manner born. They settled side by side on the cushions. Her cloak and wide skirt beneath spread themselves over his legs. She had neither spoken to the gondolier nor, as far as Fern had noticed, even looked at him. He cast off in silence, and they were out on the canal, with the other side, the Isola di San Giorgio Maggiore looking disproportionately nearer almost of the instant. Fern tried to squint backwards in order to examine the gondolier, but it was difficult to see more than his shoes.

Fern squinted backwards a second time. They were

not shoes. They were black feet.

But now there was nothing to worry about: indeed, when things were rightly conceived, there never had been anything to worry about. 'I think I saw you earlier this evening,' said Fern conversationally. 'On one of the narrower canals.'

'People often see me, but it is only a few that I can call,' she replied in her not quite perfect idiom.

She began to describe the sights they were passing. Fern knew most of them already, and more about them than the basic information deemed appropriate for Anglo-Saxon visitors. All the same, he liked listening to her deep voice and was often charmed by the way she put things. The effect of her simple tale was quite different when one was alone with her, he felt, than it would have been if she had been speaking to a crowd of tourists. They entered the Grand Canal. Just visible across the water to the left was the bollard on which that same afternoon Fern had summed up his conflictual condemnation; had sentenced Venice to depart from his life the next morning.

Fern continued listening respectfully, but by now he could feel the warmth of her body, and the spreading of her stiff skirt over his legs was delightful. It was difficult to listen indefinitely to such topographical platitudes when there was so much else that might be said, and doubtless a limit on the time.

He must have conveyed something of discontent to her because it seemed to him that her flow of facts (not all of them facts, either, he rather thought) began to falter. As they were traversing the few seconds of darkness under the Ponte dell'Accademia, she said, 'Perhaps you know Venice as well as I do?' Her tone was not peevish but friendly and solicitous, and Fern decided at once that it was a most unusual thing for a professional guide, always fearful of losing all justification for existence if any real knowledge on the part of the visitor is admitted. Fern's heart warmed to her further.

'I'm sure not,' he said. 'I've been here just over two weeks. Just long enough to know that two months are needed or perhaps two years.'

'If I go beyond the obvious things, I get into what you call deep waters.'

'I can well imagine,' replied Fern, not necessarily imagining very clearly. 'Let's stick to the obvious things.'

Fern, when he thought about it, could see and hear that the Canal Grande, most beautiful thoroughfare in the world (as so many have said), was its usual horrible self, loaded with roaring power-craft, congested with idiot tourists, lined with darkened palaces that should have been alive with lights; but he found that for once he was hardly thinking about it at all. He even reflected that he was glad the power-craft made his own progress slower; though it was, as ever in modern Venice, hard on the black gondolier.

'It was all so beautiful once.'

Fern could hardly believe his ears. He had so far found it a point of honour among Venetians not to admit that things had ever been better than they were now.

He believed, indeed, that most of them were quite sincerely unaware of the fact.

Fern took his companion's hand. It seemed a very soft and unprofessional hand, and she let it lie in his undisturbed.

She spoke again. 'There is a rich American woman further back who has collected all the ugliest things in the world. You could never believe how ugly and how many. She keeps them in a half-built palazzo, which she never finishes. I could not bring myself to spoil so nice an evening by pointing it out.'

'I know about her,' smiled Fern. 'I've been there.'

'Can such a woman be capable of love?'

They were slowly passing the Palazzo Rezzonico.

'Never the time and the place and the one capable of love, said the English poet.' Fern was rather surprised by himself.

A speed-boat full of white-shirted youths whizzed across their bows, almost capsizing them.

'It will be better out on the Lagoon,' said Fern's companion, drawing up her feet. 'Less interference and more real danger.'

Fern could not be sure what exactly she meant, but she seemed to find the prospect pleasurable, because her eyes gleamed for a second inside her hood as she spoke.

'Why danger?'

'At night there is always some danger out on the Lagoon.' She said it placidly, perhaps with a faint potentiality of contempt. Fern did not risk making the potential actual.

However curious Fern was about her, he asked no personal questions. He probably felt that they could elicit only inappropriate answers, but more important was the fact that he found the relationship easy and delightful, just as it was. Particularly unwise would have been any reference to the many others with whom she must have made this excursion, 'lonely people': Fern knew it was an odious cliché. It had never before occurred to Fern as possible that what was, after all, companionship on a business basis could so touch his real feelings. Least of all was it the way in which he had dreamed it.

But now she seemed to have shrunk away into the blackness. Fern still held her hand, but he felt that the racket around them, the emptiness of the palaces, spread a paralysing infection of disillusionment. He too began to long for the Lagoon.

He decided that sincerity was best.

'I really didn't mean to stop you talking. I was enjoying it.'

'I have nothing to tell which you do not know already.' Her voice was muffled by the black garment into which she had withdrawn.

'I used to have a dream,' said Fern in something of a rush. 'For years I dreamt that I was doing – exactly what I am doing now.'

'Venice is everyone's dream,' she replied. 'Venice *is* a dream.'

'With no reality?'

'The reality is what you call a nightmare.'

They were within two or three hundred yards of the

Rialto bridge, high and wide with the marble bowers of ancient jewellers and poison-sellers. Here the scene on both sides of the canal was more animated; people sat at waterside café tables; a barge ploughed up and down bearing massed singers of 'O Sole Mio' and 'Torna a Surriento.' Many people were at least attempting to enjoy themselves.

'The city fathers would hardly approve of your calling Venice a nightmare,' said Fern, pressing her hand.

'The city fathers, as you call them, are all dead. Everyone in Venice is dead. It is a dead city. Do you need to be told?'

Then Fern got it out; put it into words. 'I need you to love me.'

Amid the glare of the café lights, and the booming of the drum, he lifted himself on to his elbow and looked down at her elusive face, cased in its dark hood.

She said nothing.

'Make my dream come true. Love me.'

She still did not speak. Now they were actually abreast of the man with the vast drum. He shouted something light-hearted and scatological as the gondola toiled past the broken water. Boom, boom, boom, boom.

'Make my life worth while. Redeem me.'

From the depths of her black cloak she looked into his eyes.

'You said you dreamed no longer. Do you know why?'

'I think I began to despair of the dream coming true.'

'The dream stopped when you decided to visit

Venice. Never visit Venice.'

She stirred, withdrew her hand, and kissed him softly with cool lips.

'Set me free,' said Fern. 'Give me peace.'

In the long darkness beneath the Ponte di Rialto, he put his hand on the tight bodice over her breast. When they emerged, his arms were so fast around her that nothing could ever part them. The sorters in the Post Office on the Fondamenta dei Tedeschi perceived this and called shrilly. It was rare to see anyone in a gondola except the elderly and exhausted, with death making a busy third at the paddle.

There was no more for Fern to say except endearments. On and up past the dark palaces went the gondola, ploughing and labouring, tilting and rocking, as powered craft, large and small, shot past like squibs and rockets. The very extremity and eccentricity of the consequent, artificial motion added to the isolation as Fern made love on the deep, velvety cushions. Their black gondolier must have had the tirelessness of a demiurge, so regular and relentless was their advance.

'You are the moon and the stars,' said Fern. 'You are the apples on the tree, the gold of the morning, the desire of the evening. You are good, you are lovely, you are life. You are my heart's delight.'

The Palazzo Vendramin-Calergi came into sight.

'Isolde!' said Fern tenderly.

He had found a travelling companion.

'Tristan!' she replied, entering into the spirit of it.

'Perhaps that was when Venice died?' suggested Fern.

'When *Tristan and Isolde* was composed here.'

'If Venice every really lived!' she retorted.

But the gondolier changed the subject for them by turning off the Grand Canal on to the Rio di San Felice. They were bound for the wide waters of the Lagoon.

In the Sacca della Misericordia, the almost square bay on the Venetian north shore, all was silent. There are no footways and in the buildings was only an occasional dim light, suggesting a rogue tenant, even now up to no good.

'Is this where the danger begins?' asked Fern.

She made no reply, but drew even closer. Beneath the dim, lilac amphora of the sky, she was all black or white, like Pierrot. The gondolier, with strokes as strong and regular as if he were swinging a scythe, swept them forward to their consummation.

Here, to the north of Venice, the Lagoon was incandescent. It seemed to Fern, who had never seen it like this before, a nearer word than phosphorescent, because the light which gleamed from the water, faintly around the gondola, but in distant patches quite brightly, was multicoloured, blue, white, yellow, pink; and always with lilac in it too, from the infusion of the sky. There were small glittering waves, and vast, indefinite areas of coloured froth or scum, like torn lace. Already it was a little colder.

They approached an island. Fern saw the white shape of a Renaissance church and, extending from it along the entire shore, a high wall, as of a prison or asylum. Ranged in the small piazzetta before the church door was a line of figures, indistinct in respect of age, sex, or costume, but each bearing a lighted Venetian lantern, a decorated light on a decorated pole, a device, here, now, and always one of the distinctive splendours of Venice. The figures seemed to agitate the lanterns almost frenziedly, in welcome to Fern and his companion, but from the group Fern could hear no sound, though by now they were less than a hundred yards away, and the whiteness of the church behind them was luminous as a leper's face.

'Isn't it San Michele?' whispered Fern. 'The cemetery island, where at night no one stays?'

'The dead stay. By this time, no one knows how many of them. All who permit themselves to be taken from their beds, dressed in the streets, and buried.' She pressed her soft cool lips on his to dismiss the thought.

When Fern looked up once more, they were almost past the island. The lines of figures with the gorgeous lanterns lay far astern, though the lanterns were still tilting at odd, wild angles. It occurred to Fern that the figures were not expecting the gondola to stop, but had come out in order to speed it on its way, as it might be the barge of Bianca Capello. He saw that the lights were now higher in the air, as the poles were lifted joyously to their full length. But there was still no sound beyond the sounds of night and the sea.

Out here, while the small, scattered navigation lights flickered and bickered, Fern could see that, in places, the water was not merely faintly radiant but transparent right down to the wrack and garbage settled on the bottom from earliest times. In other places, it was opaque, sometimes as if great volumes of powder had been dissolved in it, and sometimes as if it were effervescent and gaseous. Every now and then Fern could see bones, human or animal, arranged in dead seaweed, or a hideous pile of discarded domesticities, or a small, vague underwater mountain, not quite mineral, not quite vegetable, not quite animal, but riddled and crawling with life of a kind, notwithstanding. Big lumpy fish and pale grey and pink serpentine creatures, elaborately devious in structure, glided in and out of the clear patches, sometimes seeming almost to gambol round the gondola, occasionally breaking surface for a second, with a gasp and croak. Everywhere was an entanglement of seadrift, rotted but constantly self-renewing. The north shore of Venice, always the dark side of the city, was now a necklace of single lamps round the throat of the night: the different floors and the buildings were levelled off by distance and amalgamated with the public lamp posts of the Fondamenta Nuove. Over on the left of the gondola, the ancient glassworks of Murano, working day and night to produce brittle joys for visitors, thrust quick swords of fire into the encroaching blackness.

Further than Murano it seemed impossible for even this gondolier to continue with so much power; but there was no sign of flagging.

'He is a strong man,' said Fern.

'Here there is a current,' replied his companion. 'Here the struggle ends.'

Fern perceived that they had indeed changed direction. Ahead lay a long dark shore, as in his dream. But he knew quite well what it was. It was the Litorale; the long, narrow, reef strengthened and sustained through the ages to prevent the high seas of the Adriatic from entering the Lagoon and eroding Venice; a reef penetrated by three gaps or *porti*, through which shipping passed, one of which, Fern knew, must be somewhere ahead, the Porto di Lido, standing at the north of that notorious wilderness of pleasure. He realised now where their journey would end. Where else could an official tour of Venice terminate but at Lido?

'We leave the Laguna Morta and enter the Laguna Viva,' said his guide.

Fern was not sure that this was exactly accurate; but it did not really matter, because the next thing she said was, 'This is the moment of love,' and because that, for some little time, was what it proved to be.

After so many mortal years, Fern's dream was proving more than true. Fern was proving himself right and the rest of the world wrong.

Now the sky was at last completely black, the stars gave little light, and the effulgent Lagoon was becoming the sombre sea. Upon all the black gondolier must have looked down, with more time to stare, now that his work was lighter, but about him it did not seem to Fern the moment to concern himself. To Fern, life had become an affair of moments only; a present without past, without future.

How long had passed by the hands of Fern's watch, he never knew, because when, somewhat later, he looked at his watch, he found that it had stopped.

IV

When first he stirred, he realised that a fairly stiff breeze was blowing round the little craft. The gondola was tossing and plunging quite seriously.

Fern drew himself up and looked round. There were biggish waves, and the scanty lighting at the northern, garrison end of Lido, instead of lying ahead, was distinctly to the leftward, the garish glow of the pleasure grounds completely out of sight: to all intents and purposes, Fern realised with a shock, the lights of the Lido pleasure area were *behind* them. It was somewhere in this watery region that on the Festa de Sensa the Doge at the prow of the *Bucentaur*, loveliest vessel in the world, each year married the sea. It startled him that his own strange marriage had found its culmination just there. This was when Fern looked at his watch.

Then he twisted right round, for the first time since he had entered the boat, and, kneeling on the keel, looked straight back to the gondolier. Then he had his third and greatest shock. There was no one there at all. The gondola was merely being swept out to sea on the current. It came to Fern that, even though there are said to be but small tides or no tides in the Mediterranean, yet the very expression 'Laguna Morta' referred to areas 'under water only at high tides'; and that now the Lagoon was emptying, pouring out through the relatively narrow breach ahead.

When Fern first roused himself after the moment of love, he had left his companion remuffled in her black cloak, soft, small, and silent. Now he turned to where she lay beside him. He could not decide what first to say. It seemed terrible to speak at once of the mere practical circumstances, and worse if the circumstances were of danger, as he could not doubt they were. He was appalled by the surmise that the gondolier, strong as he was, had been somehow swept from the boat, while the two of them had been lost in passion and the spell of the night. Gently, he put out his hand and drew away the black hood. Then, in the solitude of the sea and against the rising wind, Fern screamed out loud. Inside the black hood was a white skull; and an instantaneous throwing back of the entire black cloak, revealed inside it only an entire white skeleton.

V

At the Porto di Lido, the main entrance to the harbour of Venice, two very long stone breakwaters run far out to sea. There was no question for Fern of a storm having arisen, or of any serious change at all in the weather. The change was merely that brought about by leaving a more or less still and dead pool for the living, unpredictable ocean. Even the wind which so alarmed Fern was little more than the breeze encountered in almost all regions when one embarks seriously upon open waters. Between the Porto di Lido breakwaters, therefore, vessels passed in and out in fair numbers, hardly sentient of the racing ebb which for a single gondola was so formidable.

Fern, in fact, passed no fewer than four incoming ships; and two others overtook him. Some of them came far too close to his uncontrolled cockleshell, but his wild shouting and waving reached never a soul aboard any of them, so black was the night, so black his craft, in accordance with the decree of 1562. Between the long breakwaters, the passing ships were the obvious danger: it was certainly not rough, though it was reasonably unpleasant for a man pitching about in a vessel so small as a gondola. The possibility of the gondola, instead of being run down, sinking beneath him, did not, therefore, seriously occur to him until the real sea was drawing quite near.

He shrank forward to the peak of the vessel, so as to separate himself from his now terrible companion, and squatted before the tall iron *ferro*, only a few inches ahead. The *ferro* would surely drag the boat down all the faster when the moment came.

At the very end of the leftward or San Erasmo breakwater, the shorter of the two, Fern could just make out a large inscription daubed by supporters of the previous Italian regime, and never obliterated owing to difficulty of access – and perhaps other things. It was to the effect that a simple hour as a lion is to be preferred to a lifetime as an ass.

And now there was only the Lido breakwater and, afterwards, the turbulent, nocturnal Adriatic. The gondola sped on like a black leaf on a millstream.

Fern had proved his resolution to leave Venice before the morrow night.

371

Into the Wood

> At night those unfortunates who suffered
> from insomnia or nightmare used to
> wander about in the fields or the woods,
> trying to reach a pitch of exhaustion that
> would give them back the power of sleep.
> Among the afflicted creatures were people
> from the upper classes, well-educated
> women – why, there was even a parish
> priest!
>
> August Strindberg ('Inferno')

These areas are not uncommon if you know how (or
are compelled) to look for them. As men and women
work more and more against nature, nature works more
and more against men and women. All the same, a few
of the areas are of long acceptance; dating back to the
earliest memory of man, as the international lawyers put
it. Some of them, in the beginning, were probably holy
places of the pre-Christians; of whom a few even now
survive on our continent, if, once more, you know how
(or are driven) to look for them. Sometimes one is
amazed to discover how little that is real or true ever
finds its way into general knowledge: in so far, of course,
as general knowledge is still an expression with meaning.

'Harry and Molly Sawyer' was what they had printed on their Christmas Cards; with an address in a Cheshire town that was hardly a town any more, but a sprawling and sleeping area for Manchester. Harry Sawyer's business card indicated that he was an 'Earth Mover', though when one met him he seemed to have neither the back muscles of Atlas nor the mental leverage of Archimedes, nor yet the power to shake the world of Marx or Hitler; and when one saw his yellow, space -fiction machines on the move, each with SAWYER painted in black capitals on all four sides, each able to pulp a platoon of soldiers at a swing of the beam, one wondered how long he could possibly hope to keep them under control.

Margaret Sawyer saw as little of the yellow monsters as she could, and, with the other well-to-do Manchester wives, strove for domestic realisation among an ever-growing assembly of lesser monsters, all whirring, spinning, and chopping, in kitchen, washroom, and lounge. Among other things, the gadgets ('gadflies', she once thought) were supposed to give her more time for her children, two girls and a boy; but it seldom worked that way. Margaret could hardly hope to be happier than the other Manchester wives; but until one night in Sweden, she would have rejected the idea that she was positively unhappy. Nor was she: until that night she was insufficiently grown for happiness or unhappiness; might well have been among those who express doubt as to whether the words mean very much.

Sawyer had to visit Sovastad, on the eastern side of central Sweden; where a big, wide, dangerous, costly road was being built across the mountains into Norway. As he would have to stay there at least a week, the Swedes, hospitable ever, had suggested that he bring Margaret with him. Those of the Swedish wives who were not pursuing careers of their own, would be able to look after her during the day, and see that she had a good time. Margaret had acquiesced: one could not use a stronger word.

And so, on the whole, it had worked out. Margaret had never been so thoroughly and efficiently looked after in all her previous life; never had so concentrated a good time. There was a highpowered, unflagging, day-and-night cordiality among the richer Swedes, to which she was totally unaccustomed, and which by the end of the week, she found very exhausting, though she would have hesitated to say so, even to herself, because back in Cheshire, she had supposed it to be the very thing she wanted. Harry also grew quieter and quieter. He admitted to her that he found Swedish businessmen and business methods very hard going. 'Particularly the younger men,' he said. 'They're so keen and sharp, they take the skin off your hands, and then they turn round and deliver a lecture about British Imperialism and what's wrong with our hospitals. You can't tell where you stand at all.'

Nor, despite the social whirlwind, did Margaret find Sovastad a jocund town. It straggled along the shore of a vast, black lake, described as one of the biggest not only in Sweden but in Europe; and the high mountains to the west cut off the sun halfway through the day, darkened the streets, and made the water look like tar. The lake was said to be so deep as never to have been fathomed, and, as often in such cases, to harbour a creature of enormous bulk, terrifying aspect, species unknown to zoology, and origin unknown to all. There were many representations of this beast in the conscientious provincial museum, round which Margaret was conscientiously conducted by three Swedish ladies, all better dressed than she was and better preserved also, all erudite about the exhibits, in a manner unimaginable in Manchester. In late-mediaeval woodcuts, the creature appeared with protuberant eyes, a forked tongue, and a thick circle of whiskers like seaweed. In eighteenth-century guides to natural philosophy, it had quietened down into the likeness of a baroque ceiling embellishment. A century later, with the advance of the scientific attitude, the most barbaric devices had been constructed by the locals to trap and kill it. They were all faithfully exhibited, and the Swedish ladies explained in detail how they would have worked. Margaret was glad that there had been no occasion.

'So the creature's still in the lake?' she asked. She could not pronounce the Swedish name for the monster.

'The children think so,' replied the Swedish ladies.

The lake was, in fact, named after it, they explained: 'Lake Orm', meaning 'serpent'. It was one of the few Swedish words Margaret felt able more or less to manage. The high tessitura in which the language is spoken, the combination of breadth and altitude in the vowel sounds, were quite beyond her. All the same, a guide-book to the district which she came upon later, said that the name of the lake originated merely in its serpentine periphery, with long arms reaching into the mountains like tentacles.

Sovastad, Margaret decided, was a little too small for its pretensions. The Swedes made the very most of every urban feature, designing them splendidly, using them fully, but the population was not big enough to prevent the rocks struggling through in almost every street and prospect, and determining the prevailing ethos. By half past three in the afternoon, the feeling would set in that this was a community almost as in-volved in a ceaseless struggle with harsh natural forces as a colony of Esquimaux. There was every amenity, but they were a little like the comforts of an air force base with a bitter war on its hands. Not that Margaret could think of any better adaptation to the forbidding rocks and endless winter, to which much reference was made, jocular but surprisingly grim also. Beyond doubt, the Swedes had done wonders, but a feeling of strain was pervasive. Perhaps only a newcomer, a visitor from abroad, would be aware of it.

At the same time, there was always in Sovastad a faint mistiness, a clammy softness; or, when the sun was strik-ing directly down, an expectation of it. It too seemed to pervade the communal life; in the hectic quality of which was something almost Russian. When the sun did strike, the faint, vague mist seemed to make it still hotter. Then, very quickly, the high mountains would cut off the radiance, and within a quarter of an hour, Margaret would feel as chilled as previously she had felt warmed. She would have liked to wear trousers, but Henry implied that it would diminish their status, already none too secure. When Margaret pointed out how many of the Swedish women wore them, he inevitably replied that this was one of the very reasons why she shouldn't.

Henry's attitude, and the possibility of consequent dissension between them, was the main reason, as far as Margaret was concerned, for their going on Sunday for a drive through the mountains by car, instead of for a trek on foot, which the Swedes had suggested in the first place. She could hardly, she felt, go mountaineering in a two-piece from Kendall, Milnes and frail, almost cocktail-time shoes; especially when so many continentals tended to adopt near-battledress for even an afternoon walk. The Swedes would laugh at her, and, however she dealt with the situation, Henry would sulk. It was remarkable how deeply men seemed to feel such things when their attitude to the whole question of clothes was almost always so entirely negative.

Therefore they went, six of them, by car, higher and higher, along roads very unlike the ones which Henry was building to a scale that was not human. The conifers that cover so much of Sweden, the pools, quagmires, and small lakes that occupy so much of the land area, were sad, and, at the same time, slightly mysterious and equivocal, but Margaret became aware of a spell in the very monotony, even though she was seated in the back of the big Volvo with a married couple eager that she miss absolutely nothing. The spell lay perhaps in the monotony and the boundlessness combined: already she had seen much landscape like this on the way up from Stockholm, she knew that it extended all the way northwards to the commencement of the tundra, and she had become aware how different are Swedish distances from their aspect in the ordinary school atlas. There were no footpaths through the trees, such as still survive through most woodlands in England; no tracks; no apparent access to the woods at all except by struggle. It was not so much that these millions of conifers would be likely to conceal a huge, lost city or a race of pygmies, but rather that they might of themselves generate and diffuse forces quite outside their arboricultural aspects, forces which one might have to tramp far and long to sense, because it might take much time and distance to disengage oneself sufficiently from machines like Henry's, from life like that in the Cheshire subtopia.

They reached a high place. The car stopped and they got out. 'Don't leave the road,' said the Swedes. 'You'll sink above your ankles.' Margaret thought it was an exaggeration, but it was still odd that women were required to array themselves primarily as erotic objects, even on the most unsuitable occasions, even when they had passed forty, even when the last thing that men like Henry seemed to think of was eroticism, anyway where his wife was concerned. Moreover, there was a wind blowing with a filter of ice behind it, to which Margaret was unaccustomed in England.

Still she gazed around, conscious of the spell. From this height, there were dark-green trees to the edges of the earth. Directly below, like a big, irregular rent in the greenery, spread the Orm, all of it visible at once; the square miles of black pool beside which stood the puny town; the winding, octopus arms stretching towards her. Sovastad looked like a cluster of limpets on the hard rock; or like the first town that men had built. The line of the new road made another tear in the woodlands, but outside Sovastad there was hardly a building to be seen in the entire panorama.

When, however, in a few steps they reached the top of the ridge, with a similar vast expanse of green to the west, Margaret saw that on this side a single structure rose fairly near at hand from the trees on the westward side of the mountains. It was a sizeable, wooden edifice, painted white, and with a slate roof.

'Who lives there?' asked Margaret, making conversation.

'It is the Kurhus. A sanatorium,' said one of the Swedish wives.

'It is not only for the sick,' explained the other Swedish wife.

'It is a place where people stay, but where there is treatment too, if you want it.'

'What you call a rest cure,' added one of the Swedish husbands.

From what Margaret had seen of Swedish life, she

was not surprised.

'It has fallen out of fashion,' observed the second Swedish husband. 'People have no time for rest cures today.'

'Your country has the reputation of having more welfare than anywhere else,' Margaret could not help observing.

'Welfare is not rest,' replied the Swede; speaking quite severely.

'The Kurhus would do better to move with the times and become a motel,' said the other Swede. 'Businessmen today often prefer to sleep outside the city, provided there is a good road.'

'It must have a wonderful view, and the afternoon sun and the sunset too,' remarked Margaret. In Sovastad, there were no sunsets.

'That is true,' said one of the Swedish women seriously. 'The Kurhus sees the sinking sun. It is appropriate.'

No more was said on the subject, but, after they had gone for a little walk along the ride (Margaret would gladly have continued much further), they drove a short distance along the western flank of the mountain before returning to Sovastad, and actually passed the Kurhus portal. Flowers hung from baskets and a number of people were sitting about at tables on a terrace. To Margaret, it did not look in the least out of fashion or unsuccessful. Indeed, she liked the look of it very much: especially the contrast between the small but elegant sophistications of decor and the immense wild prospect extending north, south, and west under the warm sun. The new road had not yet reached this side of the mountains, and Margaret had no idea whether it ever would. Since they had come to Sweden, Henry seemed to experience such difficulty in holding on to the the various rights and duties of his position that he had never found breathing-space to go into such geographical particulars with her.

Two days later, in fact, things rose to a crisis. In the middle of the morning, Henry routed Margaret out of a *konditori*, where she was consuming successive cups of excellent but expensive coffee, and told her that he would have to go back for the next two nights to Stockholm, and that their departure for England would have to be postponed until at least two days after that. 'I shall be obliged to come back here again, dammit,' said Henry. 'I must make sure that they really understand what Stockholm has decided.'

'What a pest for you!' said Margaret.

'Will you come to Stockholm with me, or would you prefer to stay here till I come back? I'm sure the Larssons and the Falkenbergs will give you a good time.'

'I don't want much more good time just for the present. May I go and stay at the Kurhus?'

Henry looked doubtful. 'They said it wasn't up to much.'

'That might mean it's quiet. Of course, I mustn't keep the room in the hotel here at the same time, but I'm sure you can arrange something.'

'Never mind about that,' said Henry generously. 'If

you want a change, of course you must have it.'

'If you're not going to be here,' said Margaret, 'I want some more of the sun. If you'll tell me when you'll be back, I'll be here again waiting for you.'

'A completely new girl,' said Henry, and kissed her.

At the Kurhus next midday, Margaret was given the most beautiful room: large, with a view from the windows extending for miles, charmingly furnished, and with no fewer than three long rows of assorted books in at least four languages. Margaret, who read books, looked at this small library with considerable curiosity. As far as she could tell, the volumes seemed even to have been chosen with care, and to be by no means mere left-behinds or the bedtime reading one might expect – if one could in an hotel expect anything of that kind at all. But immediately it had occurred to Margaret that these were not books of the sort that most people would read to induce slumber, she observed that the next work on the shelf was a substantial tome named *Die Schlaflosigkeit*, which she suspected might mean 'Insomnia'. She put it back in a hurry. Margaret made a point of sleeping like a top and believed that insomnia was largely a matter of suggestion. She wanted to know nothing about it. The next book was Daudet's *Sappho*. If she had been there to improve her French instead of to have a rest, that might have been well worth struggling with.

After she had said goodbye to Henry, and before leaving Sovastad, Margaret had braved the language barrier in order to buy herself a pair of sober green trousers, dark as the conifers; a coffee-coloured shirt, a lighter green anorak, and a pair of tough shoes. Into this costume she now changed. Probably she was too old for it, at least by British standards; but she intended her standard, for these two days, to be that of the woods and rocks and mountains, rather than that of the neighbours at home. Feeling almost a girl again, she fell on the huge double bed and, splaying out her legs, wrote a joyful postcard to each of her three children at their respective boarding schools. Then, to her intense surprise, she found that in the full flood of the mountain sun she was falling uncontrollably asleep.

When she woke up, she had, to say the least of it, missed luncheon. It was really rather queer. She had slept the night before, as long and as well as she always did, even though in the next bed Henry had probably tossed and turned as usual. She could not remember when last she had fallen asleep in the middle of the day: hardly, she thought, since she had been made to have a daily rest as a child. As far as she could recall, she had not dreamed. It was simply as if two hours or more of her proper life had been stolen from her, arbitrarily cancelled. 'It's the relaxation,' she thought; not quite daring to think, 'It's the relief' . . . 'It's the beautiful big bed.' (Henry always insisted on single beds, because he slept so badly; and it was a long time since she had slept in – or even on – anything else.) 'It's my new clothes' . . . 'It's the sun, the mountain air.'

She was not exactly hungry, but felt that if she didn't

eat *something* at this accustomed hour, she would regret it. Also she had to buy some stamps. She drew up the zip of her anorak, arranged her shirt collar outside it, put on some lipstick, and descended, feeling strange in every way, but not unpleasantly so. Architecturally, the hotel really was rather fine in its period manner: a wide staircase, with brass wood-nymphs holding up the baluster, wood-nymphs that were half trees; a square hall with tall, thin, Gothic windows, and more wood-nymphs in the stained glass.

From experience of other continental hotels, Margaret had rather expected that someone would enquire solicitously, or pester (according as one saw it), about her lunch – for which she (or Henry) would be, in any case, paying, in accordance with Henry's usual rule. But no one did. In fact, there was no one about at all; not even behind the hotel desk. Nor was there a sound; not even of birds without. The big front door stood wide open and the hall was like a temple into which sunlight streamed through every aperture, strewing the stained-glass nymphs across the white-tiled floor. Margaret reflected that even if she had been set on lunch, she would hardly have got it. At the thought, she felt quite empty.

She imagined that people would be sitting about on the terrace, as she had seen them when she had driven past; but there proved to be no one. She stood by the balustrade, enthralled, though a little oppressed also, by the immensity of sunlit green. The sun was almost directly overhead and really hot. Margaret took off her anorak, and sat down on one of the brightly coloured terrace chairs, uncertain what to do next. She noticed that almost every window in the hotel seemed to be wide open; possibly a consequence of the hotel's sanatorium function. She noticed also that below the terrace on this side, the opposite side from the road (itself a minor one), ran a path. It emerged from the woodland on her right and entered the woodland on her left.

For some reason, it made her think of the track along which the figures pass when a mediaeval cathedral clock strikes the hour. She expected to see a red-eyed dragon emerge from one of the green tunnels, with a jewelled St George in pursuit; and disappear into the other tunnel, eternally unconquered, though hourly beset. Or perhaps it might be a procession of twelve wise virgins; or of six pilgrims and six temptations. She herself sat at a higher level, observant of all, like the Madonna. It was along tracks such as the one below that all creation ran from darkness to darkness, everything from the stars to the rabbits in the corner of an altarpiece; until Copernicus, and Kepler and Brahe, and Galileo began upsetting things. One of the hospitable Swedes had shown her a big illustrated book about Brahe, translating all the captions into better English than the English speak. The Swedish family had not appeared to doubt that Brahe and his kind were advantageous.

Out of the forest, as Margaret sat in the hot sun, came not St George, but a bustling grey-haired woman in a red dress and carrying illustrated papers. Obviously a hotel resident, she ascended the steps to the terrace.

'Good afternoon,' she said to Margaret, staring at her clothes. 'You are a newcomer.' The woman could not have been anything but a lady from England. 'It is unfortunate that I cannot in all honesty wish you a happy stay.' Margaret supposed that she was a trifle eccentric, as the English abroad are so often said to be.

'I'm only here for two nights,' she said smiling.

'Really!' exclaimed the English lady, apparently much surprised. 'A casual. We get very few casuals nowadays. So much the worse, perhaps. But it's connected with changing tastes. There's nothing to do here, you know. Absolutely nothing. What made you come here?'

'I drove past with some Swedish friends and liked the look of it.'

'A pity your Swedish friends didn't tell you that this is not an ordinary hotel. Some of them must have known perfectly well. Most people in Sweden know, and a good many elsewhere too.' She was standing with her hand on the back of the chair on the other side of the table from the chair on which Margaret was seated.

'But my friends did tell me,' said Margaret patiently. 'They warned me it was partly a sanatorium. As a matter of fact, they more or less advised me against coming here. I just didn't think their reasons were very good. As far as I was concerned anyway. I wanted the sun and I wanted not to have to wear my best clothes all the time. That was all. I wanted a rest. For two days, you know.'

'I see,' said the English lady.

'But won't you sit down?'

'Thank you,' said the English lady. 'I had better introduce myself. I am Sandy Slater. At least that is what I have always been called. No one has ever called me Alexandra. *Mrs* Slater, by the way; though my marriage was little more than a formality. I was born a Brock-Vere.'

'I am Margaret Sawyer. I have usually been called Molly, but I like it less than I did. Mrs, too. My husband is concerned with building the new road.'

'I understand that the new road will make little difference to the Jamblichus Kurhus. The authorities have taken care to keep us at a distance.'

'Is that a good thing? I imagine that the owners mightn't think so. One of my Swedish friends actually said that the Kurhus ought to go in more for attracting motorists.'

'He must have been a very ignorant man,' said Mrs Slater firmly. 'I notice that many of the Swedes are nowadays. If you will forgive my saying so about a friend of yours.'

'Oh, that's all right,' said Margaret. 'They're friends of my husband's really. Or not even that. More business acquaintances. Not that they haven't been very kind to us. They've been quite fantastic. Though that reminds me,' she continued. 'For some reason I fell asleep almost immediately I arrived here, which is something I never normally do, and in consequence I missed lunch, though it seems a silly thing to say. I'm beginning to feel rather hungry. Is it possible to attract some service?'

'Not until four o'clock,' said Mrs Slater.

'But it's not yet three!' exclaimed Margaret. 'This is

as bad as England. I shall be *paying* for lunch too, or at least my husband will. He *will* book everything, though I should often prefer to be less tied down.'

'Clearly,' said Mrs Slater in a calm voice, 'you have no idea what this place is. Why do you suppose it is called the *Jamblichus* Kurhus?'

'I didn't know it was until you just mentioned it. It doesn't seem to be put up anywhere. I suppose he was some nineteenth-century German doctor who invented a patent treatment? So many of them seem to have done it.'

'Jamblichus was the one among the seven sleepers who after they had slept for two centuries, went down into the town in order to buy food, tendered the obsolete coins, and found himself arrested. Don't you remember your Gibbon?' enquired Mrs Slater, even more unexpectedly.

'You mean the *Decline and Fall*? I'm afraid I've never had time for it. I have three children to look after, you know.'

Mrs Slater gazed at her. 'It's different here,' she said weightily. 'But I knew about Jamblichus before I came here. He's the only one of the seven sleepers whom most people *can* name. Anyway, places like this used often to be called Jamblichus Groves; even by the unsophisticated. This, my dear Mrs Sawyer (how odd that our husbands' names should be so alike), is an establishment for insomniacs. One can hardly call it an hotel, because hotels are primarily places to sleep in. Still less can one call it a cure, because there is no cure.'

'I noticed a book in my room—' began Margaret, then reflected. 'How terrible! Do you mean that *you* suffer from it?'

'Not as badly as some – including some who are here. I usually get a few hours in the course of a week. Some of the people here haven't slept for years.'

'But that's impossible!' cried Margaret. She recollected herself. 'But you mean that they haven't slept *regularly* for years?'

'I mean that for years they have not slept at all. Not at all. Never.' Mrs Slater seemed still to be speaking quite calmly.

'But surely,' enquired Margaret timidly, 'surely you can't *live* without *any* sleep?'

'You can,' replied Mrs Slater. 'In a way. You can live here.'

'What is there special about here, and why do people who have difficulty in sleeping have to live with other people who have difficulty in sleeping? I know very little about it, I'm afraid, because I seem always to have slept rather well, but I should have thought that living all together would be the very worst thing for them.'

'When the trouble passes a certain point – a point far short of never sleeping at all, I assure you – the victim is driven out. Sleepers cannot live for long with an insomniac. It is like living with something supernatural: people who are normal come to feel it as a shadow on their own lives. And they come to feel it quite soon. I speak from knowledge. I told you that my marriage was little more than a formality. I am sure you thought that I was born to be an old maid, as so many English-women are, in spite of all the pretences and defences. Whether I am one of that kind or not, it was my inability to sleep that ended my marriage. Marriage – anyway the usual kind of marriage – is one of the things that insomnia makes impossible. One of the many and important things.'

'I suppose I can imagine that,' said Margaret, 'or begin to imagine. But I still find it unbelievable. I'm glad to say I've always been a good sleeper myself – though, as a matter of fact, always a little afraid of not being – yet I've naturally known people who aren't. It's awful for them, as I quite see, but it doesn't have to be quite as bad as you say. I'm sure it doesn't.'

'That is the usual reaction,' replied Mrs Slater, still quite calmly. 'At least, the usual first reaction. The answer is that the people you have known aren't real insomniacs at all. They are just people who from time to time have difficulty in sleeping as much as they would like to, or think they ought to. It may be a matter of personal psychology, or temporary stress, or even digestion. But, in the very great majority of such cases, it is simply a matter of the person not really needing anything like as much sleep as he supposes – or, more usually, wants. People *want* sleep, just as they want love, or want what they call distractions, or even want death. In purely biological terms, most people sleep far more than they need to. Twice as much, or even more.'

Margaret felt that she herself was incriminated by her admissions and by Mrs Slater's didactic stare.

'The quantity of sleep required to eliminate the poisons from the blood stream is much less than people like to think,' continued Mrs Slater. She broke off. 'You do *know* that that is the physiological function of sleep?' she asked.

'I think I learnt it at school,' said Margaret, caring less and less for the conversation, feeling more and more aware of a threat, but unable to stop listening, or even asking, however empty her inside.

'As I say, much less sleep is required physiologically than people choose to think. In fact, it is perfectly possible to eliminate the poisons without sleeping at all. Some people, a few people, are built like that.'

Margaret, secure in her steady sleepiness and in all it stood for, had given so little conscious thought to the biology of it that she was in no position to argue.

'That', said Mrs Slater, 'is the plight of the true insomniac. He is one who has little need for sleep at any time; or none.'

'I suppose there might be certain *advantages*,' said Margaret.

'That is often the second reaction,' said Mrs Slater. 'There are no advantages; or at least not by the standard of the world outside. The man or woman who in the true sense cannot sleep is a kind of troll, as they call it here. Life is so made that without sleep only a troll can endure it. The sleepers have no alternative to driving us out.'

'I've heard the word, but I've never quite known what a troll is.'

'Those who are kept out. The unearthly and mysterious, as people say,' replied Mrs Slater. She seemed to speak with some slight relish.

'Is lack of sleep as disastrous as *that*?'

'Even the most normal people teeter all their lives along a narrow line between good and evil; between impulse and judgement, as we may say. Sleep does two things for the normal person. It gives him constant, long periods of respite from the conflict. It also enables his impulses to find a certain fulfilment in dreams, especially his most lawless impulses. You doubtless have dreams of that kind, Mrs Sawyer?'

'Sometimes,' said Margaret.

'Think for yourself what life must be like for one who has neither dreams nor tranquillity. Such a life is unendurable, and those condemned to it must become trolls, as I just said.'

Margaret produced a packet of cigarettes from the pocket of her trousers and offered one to Mrs Slater.

'No thank you,' said Mrs Slater. 'When we cannot sleep, the narcotics soon cease to have power over us. All of us here have to live with reality for twenty-four hours out of twenty-four . . . This is not a place for a holiday, Mrs Sawyer; still less for a rest. None the less, I so much hope you won't go.'

The smoke from Margaret's cigarette rose perpendicularly in the still, warm air. Through it, she had been quietly inspecting the aspect of Mrs Slater. Margaret could see neither horns nor tip of tail, neither exceptional wrinkles nor even unusually tragic eyes. Mrs

Slater's eyes were not happy eyes, but her total appearance, eyes included, was unreservedly typical of her age, type, and station. She might have been the Acting Vice-Chairman of a Woman's Institute in East Sussex.

'What is everyone doing now?' Margaret asked.

'They are resting,' said Mrs Slater. 'At night the insomniac is at his most active. No kind of repose is possible. But much rest is needed when you do not sleep, however hard it is to find. In the afternoon most of us can at least stop moving about. Some persuade themselves that this cessation of movement even amounts to a kind of sleep.'

'What about you?' asked Margaret. 'I'm not keeping you from your rest, am I?'

'No, Mrs Sawyer. I was restless this afternoon in any case. In so far as the idea of rest has any meaning for people like me, I have been restless all day.' Whatever Mrs Slater's plight, Margaret was, among other things, beginning to find her continuous self-pity as jarring as her paradoxes were unconvincing. She had noticed before that a person's troubles, the pity the person has for those troubles, and the pity a second person feels for the first person, are all independent from one another. 'Perhaps I have been restless today,' continued Mrs Slater, 'because I knew that a stranger was coming.'

'I shouldn't think that's very likely,' said Margaret.

'Many of us here acquire such foresight,' said Mrs Slater. 'It is likely that we should, when you think about it. It's another of the reasons why people dislike and fear us, and drive us out. All the same they're not above sneaking back to us when they're in trouble themselves. They creep back during the night in search of our guidance. I have always thought that the Witch of Endor was one of us.'

While Mrs Slater had been speaking, an elderly couple had come out of the building and sat down in silence at a table on the other side of the terrace. They were followed almost immediately by another similar couple, who seated themselves at the next table but one to that occupied by Margaret and Mrs Slater.

Margaret could not help asking a question.

'These couples . . . Are *both* of them sufferers?'

'Yes,' replied Mrs Slater; 'but they are not couples in the usual sense.' She spoke in a lowered voice, as if she had been intercepted in the drawing room of a private hotel at Eastbourne. 'They are merely unhappy people who have found another unhappy person. Most of us remain alone. It makes little difference really. Though now, of course, Mrs Sawyer, I have found *you*.' Mrs Slater did not smile. Margaret wondered whether it would have been any better if she had smiled.

'Even to a lost soul like me, it still means something to find another English gentlewoman.' Mrs Slater glanced again at Margaret's somewhat ungentle womanly costume. 'Most of the people here are, naturally, foreigners; people with whom one has merely this one, dreadful thing in common. The only other English at the moment are two very old women, so old that they are both more than a little dotty. As soon as it is four o'clock, you and I must have tea together, Mrs Sawyer.'

A young man in a black suit and wearing a black tie, had appeared; and then a dark, swarthy woman, who looked like a middle-aged stage gypsy. They had each taken up a table, so that five tables were now occupied, but in the manner of a continental café, there were still many more tables that were empty. Margaret noticed that none of the residents greeted any of the others – or, for that matter, acknowledged her own arrival. They all sat quite silent, and, it seemed to Margaret, almost motionless; though ideas of that sort, she at once reflected, were probably morbidity on her part.

'Thank you very much,' said Margaret to Mrs Slater. 'If you'll forgive me, I must first go and wash.' She rose and picked up her anorak.

'As you wish,' said Mrs Slater, in her tiresomely resigned way. 'I shall sit here and wait for you. It will be nice to talk about the London shops, which I shall never see again.'

'Actually, I live near Manchester.' It was doubtless silly to be unkind, but, whatever happened, Margaret did not intend her friendship with Mrs Slater to ripen.

Coming down the Kurhus steps was a girl who looked hardly more than a child. She was tiny and slender, with very pale, fair hair, hanging to her shoulders. She wore the simplest possible white cotton dress, without sleeves, and showing almost no figure. Her legs were bare, but white sandals were on her feet. As she descended, her eyes met Margaret's. They were exceedingly blue eyes, but singularly lifeless; more like screens than like pools. Margaret would have expected sleeplessness to manifest

395

most of all in the eyes, but these were the first unusual eyes she had seen in the Kurhus, and it was inconceivable that this very young girl could be among Mrs Slater's insomniacs; even if all the other people were, about which Margaret felt considerable doubt.

Margaret fancied that self-pity might not be Mrs Slater's only aberration – or, to say the least, hyperbole; but she knew with certainty that the Kurhus was now spoiled for her, Margaret, and that she wanted to escape from it. She wanted not least to escape from Mrs Slater personally.

The big hall was quite full of people, who seemed to be converging from all directions, but still without speaking. There were many assorted ages, and various palpable indicia of different nationalities. All the same, it was a perfectly commonplace group; seemingly re-markable only for its silence. The silence, however, chilled Margaret's nerves. Escape she must. The crowd rambled forward to the sunny terrace.

'I've decided to follow your example,' said a voice in Margaret's ear: actually a voice; but, unfortunately, it was the voice of Mrs Slater. 'I'm going to spruce myself up before we have tea together.'

Margaret could only nod. Mrs Slater passed her and ascended the staircase between the wood-nymphs that were half trees.

There was now a young Swede behind the hotel desk. It was he who had booked her in and taken away her passport when she arrived. He had fair hair with tight curls, and looked like a boxer or a bison.

Margaret decided not to beat about the bush. She told the hotel clerk that though she had known the Kurhus was partly a sanatorium, she had not realised that so many of the inmates would be patients rather than guests, and that she wanted to go elsewhere. This would surely be understood, though it might not be popular. She thought she would just make off in a taxi; and, if she could devise nothing better, merely return to the hotel in Sovastad.

The first difficulty proved to be that the reception clerk seemed to have very little English, so that he was unable properly to understand her. Margaret had met few Swedes with whom she had been so unable to communicate. But she recognised that her message was unusual and her request arbitrary. So she concentrated on the essential: immediate departure.

'Your passport,' said the clerk. 'It has gone. It will not be back until tomorrow. I told you.'

It was true that he had. It was the kind of thing that often happened in continental hotels, and Margaret, knowing that she was booked in for two days, had not worried about it.

'Where is it?' she asked the clerk.

'Gone. It has gone. I told you.' The clerk stared at her, faintly pugilistic, faintly bovine.

Margaret knew from experience what a hopeless morass this sort of thing could be, even at the best of times; even when it was only that Henry's business compelled the two of them suddenly to go elsewhere.

'I'm not leaving Sweden. I'll come back in a taxi and

collect my passport tomorrow. I want to go now just the same. I'm sorry about it, but all these sick people depress me. I quite understand that I shall have to pay. I am prepared to pay for the whole reservation now, if you'll get me a taxi.' She produced a wad of notes from her other trouser pocket. Suddenly her mountain costume, which for a brief time had meant so much to her, had become a middle-aged folly, and a conspicuous one. All the other, rather horrible people were dressed with utter conventionality.

'No taxi,' said the reception clerk, sulky but firm.

'What do you mean?' cried Margaret; less and less dignified, as she all too well knew.

'No taxi after four o'clock,' said the reception clerk.

'Why ever not?' cried Margaret; even while she knew it was not the way to put it if she wanted to get results.

'Not after four o'clock,' repeated the reception clerk.

Margaret began a foolish altercation; feeling all the time like an English innocent abroad in some banal farce. Quite protracted the dispute must have been, as well as foolish; because in the middle of it, Margaret realised, with something not far short of alarm, that Mrs Slater had reappeared on the staircase in a pink silk tea gown with polka dots; with too much rouge on her cheeks; and with her grey hair so frizzed up that it all stood on end.

'Mrs Slater, please,' shouted the reception clerk. 'Please explain to this lady—'

But Margaret was saved from final public shame. At this moment, a senior personage appeared from a room behind the desk. He was, like his subordinate, a noticeably muscular-looking man, but his thick black hair was greying, his face was still and worn.

'Forgive me, madam,' he said to Margaret, in more or less perfect English. 'I have been listening, and I have to give you my personal assurance that tonight nothing can be done.'

Mrs Slater had put her hand on Margaret's left elbow, and was standing expectantly. Margaret would not have hesitated to offend her, had there seemed any real prospect of departure from the Kurhus; but, as things were, she was rather glad that nothing the Manager had said, and that Mrs Slater could have heard, had been particularised.

'Come on and let's have our tea,' said Mrs Slater breezily.

Margaret could only turn away from the desk and follow her; quite unwashed.

Margaret had noticed on other occasions how differently one can feel about a group of people seated around a picturesque hotel terrace after one has come to learn a little more about them; after the hopeful, even happy, expectation one feels at first sight, has been tempered by some degree of real contact.

Emerging down the Kurhus steps, with Mrs Slater's red hand pressed lightly against her forearm as if to guide her, Margaret recollected that these were the people who had looked so gay when three days before she had sped past in the superlatively hospitable Volvo.

Mrs Slater guided her back to the same table; which she had 'reserved' by leaving copies of *Vogue* and *The Lady* lying about.

'Please call me Sandy,' said Mrs Slater.

There *was* something queer about the look of the people sitting on the terrace, though it was nothing obvious. To a passerby, they would still be a perfectly average assembly of respectable citizens. Their oddity lay in their quietness and aloofness. By now, some of them were occasionally exchanging a few words, but the words were palpably functional, connected with the tea, the coffee, the fluffy, flaky cream cakes, or the heat of the afternoon: Margaret felt that they had long ago said absolutely everything they could possibly say. She had a frightening glimpse into how long they had probably had in which to say it. In any case, most of them were solitaries, as Mrs Slater had remarked: scattered about one at a table, often with head sunk, and in no case making any attempt at communication or affability. An unusual proportion of the whole group was, however, reading, including, in several cases, two at the same table; and reading, almost always, not merely glossy ephemerae, as in Mrs Slater's case, but heavy, austerely bound volumes with many hundreds of pages. That was only to be expected, Margaret supposed, recollecting the remarkable little library in her own bedroom. There was more and more evidence that Mrs Slater had not drawn as long a bow as Margaret had assumed and hoped.

'Please call me Sandy,' said Mrs Slater a second time.

Margaret supposed she had again been rude in making no specific response.

'If you wish,' she said, trying to sound neither too ungracious nor too gracious. 'So long as you don't call me Molly.'

'Oh but I want to do that,' said Mrs Slater. The tips of all her red fingers were on the edge of the white, wooden table.

'You may call me Margaret.' It sounded feeble, but the right note was so difficult to strike.

'I have ordered a real English tea for both of us, Margaret. I have one every day. The two old ladies used to do the same, and we all had tea together, summer and winter; but now they don't come down until nightfall. I don't think they eat during the day any more.'

'You make them sound like vampires,' said Margaret. Really Mrs Slater had to be regulated.

'You are quite right, Margaret,' replied Mrs Slater seriously. 'I have often thought that the origin of the vampire belief lies in the insomniacs. There is something not quite nice about us, as I have told you.' Mrs Slater actually giggled. It was a most unusual thing to do on the Kurhus terrace.

A young waiter in a linen jacket arrived with a double English tea on a heavy brass tray; including sandwiches, near-Dundee cake, and even hot scones in a silver calabash, from which the sun glinted and sparkled, like a tiny display of white fireworks.

'Shall I be mother?' enquired Mrs Slater; already, however, in the act of pouring. The fluid streaming

401

from the long, thin, silver spout, looked very pale. Probably there were not enough tea-bags in the pot.

None of the others was consuming a meal like this, though most of them seemed to be consuming something. Margaret noticed that the small, slim girl in the white dress was merely absorbing a proportionately small tumbler of water. At least, it was presumably water. She lay back at a table by herself, facing the sun; almost staring at it with her blue eyes. She was so very exiguous that her white dress looked as if inside it were merely a few pieces of straw and cardboard; leaving her head, legs, and arms as the only parts that were what they seemed. Two young men were sitting, each by himself, at tables quite near her. One would have expected them to show at least covert interest, but Margaret could see no sign of it. One was eating äggöra and drinking coffee, but both seemed far gone in melancholy.

'That girl,' asked Margaret. 'Surely she is not here because she can't sleep?'

'That girl,' replied Mrs Slater, 'has never been asleep in her life.'

'I find it awfully hard to believe.'

'In England perhaps. Here they'd know at once what she was.'

Margaret looked up from her second scone.

'What do you mean by that? How would they know what?'

'They'd know she doesn't sleep,' said Mrs Slater in her calm, conclusive way. 'There are more people like that here than there are in England, and of course the population's much smaller, so everyone gets to know the signs. It's how woods like this began. But won't you take off your jacket again? You must be too hot, I'm sure.'

'No, I'm not too hot.'

'I expect you thought you were coming to some kind of skiing hotel?'

'Not exactly, in the middle of the summer.'

'I should be delighted to lend you a frock. We're much the same size and much the same age, so that the same style should suit us, and all my clothes come from England. We're quite a dressy party here at night.'

'Thank you very much, but I've got several dresses. I've been wearing them ever since I've been in Sweden,' Margaret added, unkindly once more. 'I hoped things up here would be more informal and that I should get two or three days of mountain walking.'

'Not days,' said Mrs Slater gently. 'It's by night that we walk the mountains here. We don't wear special clothes for it. It's our way of life, so to speak, our destiny. Nothing special about it for us. It's why the wood was put here in the first place.'

'What do you mean by "wood"?' asked Margaret. 'Which wood? There are trees as far as the eye can see, and almost all Sweden seems to be made up of them.'

'Round the Kurhus is a wood,' said Mrs Slater, 'with paths in it, paths everywhere, paths that have been there for hundreds of years. You saw me following one. It is a Jamblichus wood.'

'I'm sorry to be rude, but I think that name sounds

like *Alice in Wonderland.*'

Mrs Slater smiled faintly. 'I always thought it was more like Edward Lear,' she said.

'How can you tell, with all these trees, where your particular wood begins and ends?'

Mrs Slater looked down at the stone flooring of the terrace. 'If I were to suggest that, with all these trees, it perhaps has no beginning or ending – at least in your sense of the words – you wouldn't believe me.' Then Mrs Slater added softly, and as if interrogating her own heart, 'Would you?'

'It would mean an awful lot of walking, for some of these older people.'

'You are right,' said Mrs Slater, looking up at Margaret, and again speaking firmly. 'A time comes when people can go no further. In the end, the paths just lose themselves among the trees.'

Really it all *was* like the *Alice* books; the *Alice* books and no others. Margaret thought so more and more. It was one thought that helped to keep out other thoughts.

'I've eaten far too much tea.' Curiously enough, she had; despite everything. At least she had if life at the Jamblichus Kurhus (an unconvincing name in almost any language, she would have thought), if life at the Kurhus followed any sort of normal order. 'What time's dinner? I take it that there *is* dinner?'

'We follow the customary scheme of things. Perhaps we value it all the more,' said Mrs Slater, courageous to the last. 'Dinner is described as from eight, but most of us are very punctual. You are sure you have a frock? I hope you will share my table?'

'I should be delighted,' said Margaret. 'Thank you.'

Margaret wanted both to stretch her legs in the sunshine and mountain air and to examine for herself Mrs Slater's alleged wood, where she suspected she would find nothing very special. But she did not want Mrs Slater to come with her. In fact, a further thing she wanted very much, was simply to get away from Mrs Slater. She thought of escaping by going up to her room as an excuse, and then running off into the forest, but this might be made difficult by the fact that the only public exit from the Kurhus seemed to be that on to the terrace. Moreover, she felt in her bones that she would never evade Mrs Slater of all people, merely by dodging her round the bushes, as if they had been two schoolgirls. Mrs Slater would be the first to cry caught any day.

Mrs Slater insisted on showing Margaret some of the large dress illustrations in *Vogue*, making, on the different garments, comments which were detailed and long-winded, but which struck Margaret as academic, where Mrs Slater's own needs and circumstances were concerned, and as rather creepy when applied to her own supposed case.

'*You* would look *gorgeous* in *that*,' Mrs Slater would breathe out earnestly; pointing at something fleecy with her dark red forefinger and pushing the something almost into Margaret's face, while Margaret gazed out at the slopes of green descending from the terrace and ascending another mountain ridge, ten, twenty, or thirty miles off, it was hard to guess how many.

'If *I* lived *your* life, I'd always wear nice things,' said Mrs Slater. 'I have excellent taste.'

Margaret had often heard women of sixty or seventy talking for hours in just that way: weighing every detail; speculating, wistfully or cattily, about how this or that garment would suit this or that common acquaintance; at once identifying with and envying Margaret herself, when she happened to be at their disposal for the purpose. The half-dream, half-contest seemed to keep innumerable women not happy, but certainly alive, even through senility. It must serve a purpose, but Margaret did not find it even pathetic. She found it a spun-out makeshift (the very words were significant) which symbolised the worst aspect of being a woman. But everyone lived on makeshifts. Look at Henry, his lumbering toys and his social anxieties!

'What colour do you find suits you best?' asked Mrs Slater.

'This colour,' said Margaret, pointing to her legs. 'That colour': pointing to the wilderness of leaves.

The others on the terrace had stopped eating and drinking. In any other community, half of them would by now have fallen asleep.

'Forgive me, please,' said Margaret. 'I should like to wander about a little before dinner.' She rose. No one seemed to take any notice; even to glance at her.

'I'll show you round,' said Mrs Slater, scrambling together her papers. 'There are things that need to be explained.'

'It's very kind of you, but I'll take my chance.' Margaret had a bright idea. 'Like a famous Swede, I want to be alone.'

Mrs Slater was not to be silenced conclusively, 'Just as you like,' she said, 'but remember: it is not like going for a stroll in England.'

The differences, Margaret at first thought, were that here there were no litter, no structures, no advertisements, no noise of cars and aeroplanes and radios, and, above all, no people. Man had presumably planted these trees and tramped out these paths, but he had done nothing else. It was, indeed, very unlike a wood in Cheshire.

When Margaret had descended from the terrace, she had by instinct avoided the green tunnel from which Mrs Slater had originally emerged, and, crossing below the terrace, had entered the other one, which for a few yards ran beneath the wall of the Kurhus itself. Margaret could hear the swill and clatter of the kitchen; and as well as these things, the chatter of the staff, which harmonised with them. After the silent terrace, the cheerful sound came as a relief. But it was audible for only a minute or two; nor was the Kurhus building visible for longer than that through the forest.

And almost immediately, the fat, beaten path reached a nodule whence it unwound into a dozen or more rabbit-runs among the trees. It was as if at this point the withdrawal of man had left small animals to continue his work. The paths, though very narrow, seemed definite, but it was impossible to know which to choose. All were compelled to wind continuously, as they pressed forward through the irregularly planted trees. Already, after only a few hundred yards from the terrace, there was a real danger of being lost. It struck Margaret as an ideal area for going round and round in a hopeless circle, as the lost are well known to do, owing (she had heard) to almost everybody having one leg shorter than the other. It was not at all the sort of situation she had contemplated as having perhaps lain behind Mrs Slater's rejected offer of guidance. She had visualised something far more fanciful.

She selected a path almost at random, and began to weave about among the trees. The path, however narrow, was unobstructed: there was no question of pressing through bushes, or pushing aside branches. Even the surface was comparatively smooth. It was almost as if the vegetation had been cut back, but Margaret saw that there was no sign of this. It seemed rather as if it had never grown across the path; just as weeds never take root in water that is constantly traversed by boats. Margaret perceived at once what this implied: the little paths must be in continuous use, as Mrs Slater had said. It was a further confirmation of Mrs Slater's entire improbable thesis about the insomniacs.

Margaret stopped. There was a steady, rustling, pulsation in the thick undergrowth between the trees; and a whirring and flapping among the leaves overhead that would rise and fall suddenly, like a very irregular line on a graph. To judge by the sounds, there might have been condors among the branches and anacondas among the bushes. Margaret, in fact, was unsure what might not really be there: were there not still wolves and bears in Sweden, and, probably, many more varieties of reptile than in Britain? The brush was here as high as her elbows and dense enough to conceal anything short of an elephant. It was a second situation that she had not thought of when dismissing Mrs Slater's offer.

She walked on. The narrow shafts of sun struck down like spotlights in a theatre, she being the principal actress; the wider cataracts descended like a benediction in an Italian painting, she being the saint. But in many places the trees were so thick that the sunlight penetrated only as a flickering radiance, suggesting a different and brighter world above. After a time, and quite suddenly, the underbrush almost ceased and the little tracks traversed dunes of pine needles.

Tracks, not track. Even through the underbrush had run several transverse tracks. Out here, many intersecting paths could be seen simultaneously, which was reassuring, because, at the worst, and if one knew one's direction, one could cross the open ground, but disconcerting too, as suggesting that the entire forest was a maze.

Margaret was in many ways enjoying herself, but she realised that she would have to go back. She regretted that she had so little equipment for pathfinding. She had been feeling regrets of that kind almost since she had first arrived in Sweden. But it was so difficult to know what one could do. All the possibilities seemed ridiculous. Her mother had not let her even be a Girl Guide.

Margaret felt, in any case, that woodland techniques, though important in themselves, were very secondary to something else . . . She had words for it, she had long had them, though they were negative words: what was needed was the rejection of so many of the things that her husband, Henry, appeared to stand for. The thought had roamed about her brain and body for years, like a germ in the blood, always poisoning her content. In this Swedish forest, a far and lonely place by comparison with most other places she had known, the unrest flared up and momentarily put her off balance. She attempted to make her usual answer to herself: tried to enter into Henry's point of view, to make proper allowance for the fact that he was far from a free agent. He was hardly more a free agent than the people were at the Kurhus, according to Mrs Slater's tales, and according to the evidence of these teeming little rabbit-runs through the woods. All the same, she felt that it was up to a man to be more of a free agent than Henry was. It was not that she herself especially wanted to blaze trees and utter bird-calls. It was rather that the forest symbolised something that was outside life – certainly outside Henry's life and her own. And not part of Henry's inner life either, though it apparently was part of hers, if one could judge by what she felt now.

Margaret took a small pull on herself. Henry must be broadly right and she broadly wrong, or life would simply not continue as it did, and more and more the same everywhere. The common rejoinder to these feelings of rebellion was, as she knew well, that she needed a little more scope for living her own life, even (as a few Mancunians might dare to say) for self-expression. But that popular anodyne never, according to Margaret's observation of other couples, appeared in practice to work. Nor could she wonder. It reduced the self in one to the status and limits of a hobby. It offered one lampshade making, or so many hours a week helping the cripples and old folk, when what one truly needed was a revelation; was simultaneous self-expression and selfloss. And at the same time it corrupted marriage and cheapened the family. The rustling, sunny forest, empty but labyrinthine, hinted at some other answer; an answer beyond logic, beyond words, above all beyond connection with what Margaret and her Cheshire neighbours had come to regard as normal life. It was an answer different in kind. It was the very antithesis of a hobby, but not necessarily the antithesis of what marriage should be, though never was.

Margaret could again hear the sounds of the Kurhus kitchen. A girl there was singing. Margaret stopped and listened for a moment; which, as she reflected, she would probably not have done had she been able to understand the words. The song had some pure existence and beauty, which understanding of the words, while possibly bringing something else, would have destroyed. Listening to the talk in the intervals at Hallé concerts, Margaret had suspected that too much understanding of musical theory can be similarly destructive. And so often people said to her that when they travelled abroad they wanted really to meet and know the local population; in the same sort of way, as far as possible, as they met and knew their fellow English. They spent hard evenings learning languages for the purpose – or in the hope. Margaret realised that this was not her idea at all. The song of this girl was precisely akin to the song of the forest: if one worked at it, one would cease to hear it. In fact, now that Margaret came to think, she realised that she had been unconsciously disengaging the song from the loud clanging of pans in which, properly speaking, it was submerged. She had been hearing only the song, and nothing of the mechanism that, objectively, almost overwhelmed it; and assuredly put it in its place. So it had been in the forest. One had to lose the noise of the mechanism, not least the ever-deafening inner echoes of it. One had to dispel practicality. Then something else could be heard – if one was lucky, if the sun was shining, if the paths were well made, if one wore the right garments: and if one made no attempt at definition or popularisation.

Margaret perceived with surprise two practicalities: she had been walking for an hour and a half, far longer than she had supposed; and from the clear ground where the rabbit-runs were all visible at once, she had returned without giving a thought to her route. Blazing trees could not be the only ciphering. Losing one's way was largely an act of intention.

All the same, Margaret had virtually to scamper into her dress with the velocity of a child. Not only was the terrace deserted, but there was the beginning of a crowd in the hall, as she hastened through. They were arrayed in half-festivity; the counterpart of half-mourning. As usual, Mrs Slater had spoken aright. What was more, Margaret observed that her huge bed had not been 'turned down'. It was the first hotel of that standing where she had encountered such an omission.

Margaret stood for a moment naked in the evening sunlight, finding her silhouette more pleasing than she had found it for some time; then scrambled into a stone-coloured garment in hard silk, the best she could do for Mrs Slater, whom there could be no hope of eliminating.

'Look,' said Mrs Slater. 'There are the other two English-women.'

Few could have told to what nation they belonged. They resembled two very ancient, long-neglected, near-to-death bushes; which now put out each year only a few half-hearted leaves in the entire mass. One felt that at any moment, a branch might quietly drop off, or the entire bole split and subside.

'Mrs Total and Mrs Ascot,' expounded Mrs Slater. 'I used to be able to play games with them, but no more. I do wish you were here for longer, Margaret. You can imagine how alone I am.'

'Is there really nowhere else you could go?'

'The other places are even worse.'

There was more conversation at dinner, in a variety of tongues; and more at the end than at the beginning.

413

Undeniably it was as if they were all working up to something, even though they did it in a careful and hypochondriac way. None the less, those who had sat alone on the terrace, sat alone in the dining room also. It was merely that some of them spoke from time to time across a void, and that certain of the couples appeared more in touch. Also there were more people in the dining room than Margaret had until then seen in the Kurhus. Certainly the better spirits could not be attributed to liquor, because there was none. Margaret was accustomed to hotels where before one dined, one had several drinks at the bar, sometimes in advance of one's husband. Occasionally one met people there. Infrequently, they were quite interesting. She realised that here there was seldom anyone new to meet. She was surprised that no one other than Mrs Slater seemed concerned to meet *her*. Possibly it was the language difficulty.

'Drink is absolutely forbidden?' She feared that again she was tending merely to bait poor Mrs Slater.

'Nothing is *forbidden*,' replied Mrs Slater, in a very English way. 'If we don't smoke or drink, it's because we've all learnt better. When you can't sleep, the consequences of drinking are indescribable. You do know that the physiological function of alcohol if soporific? For us, it would be like an impotent man taking an aphrodisiac.'

Margaret especially disliked Mrs Slater's occasional shafts of modern frankness. Besides she had always understood that it was exactly what impotent men did do.

'Of course it's entirely different for you,' said Mrs Slater. 'I am sure that if you were to stay longer, something could be arranged with the doctors. I myself shouldn't mind your drinking all you wanted.'

'Doctors!' said Margaret. 'I hadn't realised that there were doctors.'

'Oh yes. Though of course they're no use to us. There's no cure for *our* condition.'

'Then why are they here?'

'Old people, like Mrs Total and Mrs Ascot, can't settle down unless there are doctors about. And I am sure it applies to foreigners too. Don't you think it applies to most people today, whatever their age? They must all have doctors, be the cost what it may.'

'I suppose I should have expected doctors,' said Margaret. 'Where are they now? Have we seen one?'

'The surgery is on the very top floor The *kirurgi*, as it's called in Swedish. There are two doctors on duty at all times, night and day, in case there's a crisis. You will help yourself to rödkål from the bowl?'

They were seated by a window, outside which summer night was falling.

'What sort of crisis is commonest?'

'I'm afraid our most frequent crises are sudden mania and sudden death. For this reason, the doctors have to be fairly young and strong. The same applies to the male staff in general, as you may have noticed. With insomnia, there is often a quick snap. The strain can be borne no longer. That is still another of the reasons why we have always been made to live apart. The provincial mental hospital finds many of its recruits here, but few of its so-called cures. You'd hardly believe it, but even *there* people like us don't sleep. And as for our dead, there is a special place for *them* in the wood: not easy to find unless you know where to look. Even after death, it's the same old story of exclusion. But I fear that all this is hardly the way to make you extend your visit. I know only too well that instead of arousing love and pity, as one might hope, the facts do just the opposite. We poor folk are doomed to eternal self-sufficiency, whether we like it or not. So eat up your mört, Margaret, and take no notice of all these gloomy thoughts.'

Margaret decided that, in fact, she did not feel as gloomy as she should have done. Mrs Slater still wallowed too much; and Margaret's main feeling about the Kurhus as a whole was acute and ever-growing curiosity, reprehensible though that might be. She felt mildly stimulated by a community so entirely novel and unpredictable, however unconvivial. Besides, her experience in what Mrs Slater called 'the wood', had perceptibly shifted the four points of her inner compass. Life's terms of reference had changed . . . Conceivably, she reflected, as Mrs Slater helped her to a crumbling wodge of efterrättstårta, the unaccustomed liberty and isolation would have gone a little to her head, wherever she had found herself; but the real wonder lay in taking only one short step and lighting upon an entire world so different. These people round her might, in a sense, be outcasts, as Mrs Slater said. Quite possibly, they suffered; looking at them, it was hard to be sure. What

Margaret did know was that the Kurhus had already recharged the battery of her life, rewound the spring. After long inertia, she was again, mysteriously, on the move.

'Cream?' enquired Mrs Slater, holding high a silver boat. 'Or as the Swedes call it, *grädde*?'

On the move once more, and so soon after starting, Margaret could not be expected to think about how to stop.

'Why do you smile?' asked Mrs Slater.

'I'm so sorry,' said Margaret. 'It must have been something in my own thoughts.'

'No, there's no coffee,' said Mrs Slater. 'As everybody knows, the physiological consequence of coffee is wakefulness. But in your case it may this time be just as well that there is none. Because if I were you, I should go straight to bed.'

'But I don't feel in the least like sleep.' Margaret spoke without thinking. At the Kurhus, even new clichés were needed. 'Oh, I've said the wrong thing. I do apologise.'

Mrs Slater gazed back with fishy eyes.

'Even if you don't sleep, stay in your room.'

'Why?'

'At night we walk. After dinner, we begin; and many of us walk till dawn. It is not a thing for you to see.'

'Mrs Slater,' began Margaret.

'Sandy, if you don't mind.'

'Sandy, of course,' Again Margaret smiled. 'Sandy, if

what you say is true, I'm very sorry for you all, but you can't suppose that I could come here, and listen to what you've told me, and not want to see for myself? It may be wrong of me, but I just can't help it.'

'I suppose it's natural,' said Mrs Slater, 'and I've known it often. With the world what it is today, I imagine we're lucky that people aren't brought in buses to stare at us, like they used to stare at the lunatics in Bedlam. I expect it will come to that in the end, though they won't get the local people to drive the buses for them. We're unlucky, and on the unlucky is a curse. I warn you, Margaret. The local people know and are right.'

Margaret looked down at the gay table mats.

'Since you're warning me, please tell me exactly what you're warning me of. What could happen to me?'

But Mrs Slater was entirely unspecific. 'Nothing good,' was all she said. 'Nothing that you would wish. I am speaking to you as a friend.'

It was very unconvincing. Margaret even wondered whether she was not being merely warned against making undesirable acquaintances. It was difficult to decide what to do.

The dining room was rapidly emptying. All seemed to be quiet once more. The diners were leaving in silence; almost stealthily, Margaret thought. It was nearly dark, but the air was still faintly crimson from reflections of the sunset.

'Tell me,' said Margaret, 'what happens in winter, when the snow is on the mountains? They talk a lot about that in Sovastad.'

418

'We suffer the more,' replied Mrs Slater. 'We sit all night and wait for the spring. What else could we do?'

'All right,' said Margaret. 'I'll stay in my room. And tomorrow I think I'd better go somewhere else.'

'Please don't go before you have to,' pleaded Mrs Slater. 'You'll be all right. You'll sleep since you've had no coffee. There is nothing to keep you awake. You'll have an excellent night.'

The big hall was lit, though only rather faintly, by pretty lamps, in which the brass nymphs on both sides of the staircase gleamed and flickered. A well-built elderly man whom Margaret had noticed dining by himself stood in a far corner, apparently musing. There was no one else to be seen. Mrs Slater once more put her hand on Margaret's arm.

'I'll see you to the door of your room,' said Mrs Slater.

'No,' said Margaret. 'Let's part here.'

Mrs Slater paused.

'You won't forget your promise?'

'It wasn't a promise,' said Margaret. 'But I'll not forget.'

Mrs Slater withdrew her hand, then held it out as if to bind Margaret in a pledge. But all she said was, 'Then, good night.' Bravely she added, 'Sleep well.'

'See you in the morning,' said Margaret, wondering if she would, and if these were appropriate words. Was it possible that at this moment Mrs Slater was preparing to 'walk'?

A middle-aged woman, perhaps eight or ten years older than Margaret, but still noticeably beautiful, descended the staircase in a costly-looking fur coat, although the evening was very warm, tap-tapped across the white, tiled floor, and went out into the darkness.

Mrs Slater went up the staircase without once looking back at Margaret. She disappeared down a corridor which was not Margaret's corridor.

Margaret had intended herself to go up almost immediately, having delayed for a moment only from anxiety to avoid a bedroom colloquy with Mrs Slater; but on the instant she was alone, the elderly man in the corner of the hall advanced towards her and said, 'Forgive me, but I was bound to overhear what Mrs Slater, a dear friend of us all, was saying to you. There is little conversation here, and most that is said is heard not by one alone. You would be mistaken altogether to accept Mrs Slater's sad view of our curious community. There is, I assure you, a different side to us. We are not sad all the time. You felt that yourself when you walked this evening in our wood.'

'Did you see me there?' asked Margaret. 'What you say is quite true.'

'Just as most of the things that are said to one are heard by many, so most of the things that each of us does are known to all.' 'Would you do me the honour of taking a cup of coffee with me?'

An elderly pair came down the stairs and went silently forth.

'Mrs Slater said there was no coffee. She also advised me against going out.'

'Mrs Slater, as you say in English, exaggerated, so let

us then have coffee. You will see.'

He pressed a bell on the reception desk. One of the white-jacketed waiters appeared. The elderly man gave the order in the most usual way.

A man of about forty, who had not changed from his light suit for dinner, walked straight from the dining room, across the hall, to the steps down to the terrace.

'Let me introduce myself. I am Colonel Adamski. You, I know, are Mrs Sawyer.'

For a member of a community that seemed so silent and so uninterested, it was amazing how much he knew.

They shook hands.

'The point that Mrs Slater overlooks is that only by great sacrifice can we poor human beings reach great truth.'

Margaret sat up straight. 'Yes,' she said. 'I understand. I really do.' She was astonished with herself.

'Of course you do,' said Colonel Adamski. 'The Italian man of the world, Casanova – if you'll forgive my mentioning such a scamp – remarks on the basis of unusually wide knowledge of the world that, in his ob-servation, only one human being in a hundred, or some such proportion, ever experiences the jolt that sets the faculty for truth in motion. Casanova's faculty was set in motion by freemasonry – though that is something else that, as a good Catholic, I should not bring into the con-versation, least of all with a charming lady. Nor is a jolt – a shock, a blow, a fatality – always necessary. I doubt whether you regard yourself as having suffered a jolt?'

'I think that what Mrs Slater had to say might have

been a jolt,' said Margaret. 'This afternoon, I mean.'

'You are right to name the time,' said Colonel Adamski, lightly pouncing. 'Already you understand much: so much more than you know. For the reason why Mrs Slater is so sad and so uncomprehending is that she walks in the afternoon instead of at night.'

'Does she not walk at night as well?'

'Seldom.' The Colonel broke off. 'But here is our coffee. Will you please pour? Alas, my hand is not steady.'

'I'm so sorry.'

'It was that terrible war we fought, where the powers of darkness were almost equally strong on both sides. Not a righteous war, not a necessary war, not a war in which victory was for one moment possible. You can see at once, I would suppose, that I take an unusual view for a Polish officer. It was towards the end of that war that I stopped sleeping – stopped entirely; and it has been here that I have seen the truth of things. Great sacrifice: great truth. It is something that Mrs Slater, who walks in the afternoon as if she were on holiday at Royal Leamington Spa or Royal Tunbridge Wells, does not understand.'

'Colonel Adamski,' said Margaret. 'I have to ask you whether you take milk?'

'No milk. It is black coffee, pure but strong, that fortifies against the powers of darkness with which the world is filled.'

All the time, people were passing through the hall in ones and twos, more commonly the former; and the night, now utterly black when viewed from the lamplight, was swallowing them. Warm though it had been, and in the Kurhus still was, Margaret was becoming aware of a little icy gust every time the door opened.

'A long war,' said Colonel Adamski. 'Those so-called concentration camps, of which we hear so much. A bad illness. A heartbreak that is without hope. The suffering that grows with religion. These are among the things that set the faculty for truth in motion. Or sleeplessness. Shakespeare complains often of not sleeping, but see how much he owes to it! Even the absurd local poet, Strindberg, would be still more grotesque if shafts of truth had not occasionally struck home as he lay wakeful; at one time in this very place. It would have been better by far if he had never left it. Then think of your own great statesman, Lord Rosebery: recognised by all as a man marked out, a man in a different mould from the pygmies who swarmed around his feet; though few of those who knew this could say why. Some of them even wrote books to explain how unable they were to account for Lord Rosebery's obvious greatness. Did you know, Mrs Sawyer, that for many years Lord Rosebery hardly slept at all?'

'I'm afraid he was rather before my time,' said Margaret.

'He would have understood well that we who live here are at once cursed as Mrs Slater says, but chosen also. He had the blue eyes that are commonest among our kind.'

'It seems to me that most of you *look* very much like the rest of the world.'

'We have the commonplace aspect of monks. Remove the distinguishing clothing, and many monks resemble Mrs Slater. If you will pardon the paradox.'

The hall was now quite quiet.

'May I give you some more coffee, Colonel Adamski?'

'If you please.'

She refilled both cups, and then sat thinking.

'Are there boundaries?' she asked, after a while. 'Or frontiers? To me it seemed that the wood, this special wood that you all speak of, was just part of the whole Swedish forest.'

'That is true,' said the Colonel. 'Every now and then one of us fails to return. Some find tracks into the further forest, and return never.'

'Perhaps they have merely decided to leave the Kurhus, and find that the simplest way of doing it? I can imagine that. I wanted to leave this afternoon, but it seemed almost impossible . . . I am glad now that I stayed,' she added, smiling, and unwrapping a lump of sugar from its paper.

The Colonel bowed gravely. 'They go,' he said, 'because they have reached their limit. For men and women there is to everything a limit, beyond which further striving, further thought, leads only to regression. And this is true even though most men and women never set out at all; possibly are not capable of setting out. For those who do set out, the limit varies from individual to individual, and cannot be foreseen. Few ever reach it. Those who do reach it are, I suspect, those who go off into the further forest.'

424

Margaret's eyes were shining. 'I know that you are right,' she cried. 'It is something I have long known, without finding the words.'

'We all know it,' said the Colonel. 'And we all fear it. Because beyond our limit is nothing. It is a little like the Italian parable of the onion: skin after skin comes away, until in the end there is nothing – nothing but a perfume that lingers a little, as the dead linger here a little after death, perfuming the air, and then are gone. Or, more grandly, it is like Nirvana, no doubt; though Nirvana is something no European can understand. For me, it is like a particular moment in the war; a moment when, having no weapons, I had to fight hand to hand. It was not a moment I care to recall, even when I walk in the wood. It is far from true, Mrs Sawyer, that we soldiers are men of strength and blood. New soldiers are like that in the least. But it was for me the moment when I stopped sleeping, stopped dreaming. Dreams, Mrs Sawyer, are misleading, because they make life seem real. When it loses the support of dreams, life dissolves. But perhaps we have spoken enough of this funny little group to which I have found my way? Even I who am one of them do not deceive myself that it is the whole world, and you are only a visitor among us, here today and gone tomorrow, as your idiom puts it?'

'I shall be sorry to be gone,' said Margaret matter-of-factly. She tilted the coffee pot, then lifted the lid. 'I'm afraid there's no more. In England the coffee's bad, but there's more of it. I expect that's symbolical too.'

The Colonel laughed politely.

'Should I enter the wood, Colonel Adamski? Now, I mean, when all of you are walking? Mrs Slater forbade me most strictly. What do you advise?'

'You will have realised by now that on many questions there is no one view amongst us. No more than in the rest of the world. No more than in a monastery, to return to that example. You might be surprised! I went to school with monks, and can assure you that they differ among themselves every bit as much as politicians or businessmen. Mrs Slater's view reflects Mrs Slater. When I was stationed for years in Britain with the Polish forces, waiting and learning, but mainly waiting, I learned that Britain's strength lay in women like Mrs Slater, cautious and unimpassioned. It would be wrong for me to argue with so excellent an example of your fellow-countrywomen.'

'But should I enter the wood, Colonel Adamski?'

'Why ever not, Mrs Sawyer, if you want to? Why ever not? Few of us night-walkers actually bite. And certainly we should never bite a lovely lady like you.'

He moved in his chair.

'Oh,' said Margaret, remembering. 'I do hope I haven't been keeping you?'

'But most agreeably.' The Colonel rose and faintly clicked his heels. 'Your husband is a fortunate man. I could only wish he didn't build roads.'

'Why?' asked Margaret.

The Colonel spread out his hands.

'The blood. The noise. The aggression and hostility.

The devastation and emptiness. The means with no ends. The first roads, the first roads like that, were built by Hitler. The place of war is now taken in society by motoring. I, a soldier, tell you that my trade has changed its shape. But these are not things I should disclose to a road-builder's wife, who has done me the honour of taking coffee with me after dinner. I apologise, Mrs Sawyer. I go.' The Colonel again made the faintest possible click with his heels, and went off up the stairs, stepping very silently for so well-built a man.

It seemed likely that all who meant to go out had now gone; possibly the entire guest-list, with the exceptions of Mrs Total and Mrs Ascot, Mrs Slater and Margaret herself. Margaret sat on in the silent hall with its scattered fairy lights, hardly in sum providing even illumination by which one wishing to could read. In the end, a single late-departer descended the staircase. It was the small, slim girl, who earlier had worn a white dress. Now she wore a dark garment (there was not enough light for Margaret to discern the exact colour); which fitted as a skin and as tightly as a young one. She tripped down the stairs, swiftly but not hurriedly; not only as if to be last was her proper place, but perhaps even as if aware that she was expected and awaited. She looked skinnier and frailer than ever: her legs attentuated rather than slender, her breasts almost invisible in the darkness of the fabric that covered them. As she walked past, she glanced at Margaret directly, for the first time: her big blue eyes seemed to flash for a half-second, as light caught them; and to Margaret it seemed that her tiny, almost wasted mouth smiled slightly though whether in recognition it was impossible to say. In any case, she was past in a moment, and, in another, out through the door on to the terrace, where the blackness covered and absorbed her instantly.

Margaret found that, without volition, she had risen to her feet and was staring out towards the night beyond the glass panels in the door. She walked down the hall and followed the girl on to the terrace.

It was quite unexpectedly cold: she had forgotten the contrast in temperature between the Swedish daylight and the Swedish darkness. Later in the year, as she understood, there would be no darkness at any time during the twenty-four hours, but now it was thick and moonless and starless, thick and icy. Shaking all over in her dinner dress (though she could recall that many of the other guests had not looked particularly wrapped up when they went forth) and with her teeth already chattering so badly that her head felt like a skull, Margaret none the less groped her way slowly along the dark terrace, trying to dodge round the almost invisible tables and chairs, and guiding herself by the dim, pale line of the stone balustrade to her left. In the end, she reached the few steps down to the transverse path along which Mrs Slater had so long before emerged; descending them with stress in her high-heeled shoes; and tottered off towards the wood she had entered that afternoon, the wood about which opinions seemed to differ so much, the wood where her own view of things had shifted perceptibly, as she knew quite well, and even though she had but dropped in as a foreign tripper, and but for a period of time to be counted more rationally in minutes than in hours, days, or years.

She went forward among the trees for perhaps fifty yards, then stopped. She had not even reached the nodule where the wider path untwined into the little rabbit-runs. She realised that if she went further, she would lose even the edgeless oval of something less than darkness behind her. Now there was no sound from the Kurhus kitchen, nor a light, visible through the foliage, in any part of the structure. It struck Margaret that the staff might go away each night to sleep. For the staff – the staff, of course, *slept*; and might well find the indulgence easier when uncontrasted with universal wakefulness. To Margaret, the cold was the strangest thing. In only a few minutes her body had become so cold that she no longer even suffered from the chill. It felt like a body packed in a single block of ice; serene, and no longer any responsibility of hers. She wondered whether if one really were packed in a block of ice, one still spent a third of one's life with one's eyes closed, sleeping.

She had ceased to shiver or to chatter. She stood still and, there being nothing at all to see, listened. The steady, slight rustling of the afternoon was still to be heard. It could then have been the small creatures of the day. Margaret supposed it could not be the small creatures of the night; even more numerous, she understood. Still it seemed unlikely that small creatures would continue the same noise – and the same *degree* of noise (so that only when one stopped making an unnecessary noise oneself could one hear it) – in light and in darkness. Then Margaret realised that this might be a wood in which *nothing* slept; perhaps not even the trees.

The soft rustling went on and on. Occasionally a black bird swooped down invisibly. Outside and beyond the clear ice that enfolded her, Margaret suddenly began to be afraid lest in the darkness one of the perambulant Kurhus guests brush past her. She doubted whether she could face such an occurrence.

Probably it was this comparatively trifling fear which tipped the scale. Probably everything in the world is decided by tiny last straws. Though she had no doubt that, for a little time to come, she would despise herself, Margaret resolved upon retreat, upon leaving it at that: she would return to the Kurhus at once; go to her room; rub the ice out of herself with the huge Swedish bath towel, have a hot bath, turn on the heater, if there was one; snuggle down, as the women's papers put it, in bed; aim to sleep, even pray to sleep, if she had to, though not once in her life hitherto had she found sleep to involve anything of the kind. And tomorrow, as would then be logical and necessary, she would return, having made herself as invisible as possible during the short remaining time at the Kurhus, to Sovastad, a day of her holiday lost, to say nothing of a day of Henry's money. Perhaps, she thought, she had reached her limit; considerably sooner than for a brief period that evening she had supposed, even taken for granted about herself.

As she picked her way out of the dark wood, she realised that she had begun to shiver again. Crossing

430

the silent hall, she wondered whether it would all end merely in a bad cold. It would be an appropriate sequel to her surrender. She despised herself for not changing her clothes and returning to the wood. She had not even confirmed that the people who had gone out through the Kurhus hall were in the wood at all. She was only sure that even in her thickest clothes she would find the wood almost as icy as if she were wearing nothing.

She rubbed herself down. She sank into steaming water. She went to bed. She felt self-betrayed, that she had behaved as an average woman would do; she had reached a point where she could be told little more and beyond which, if she went on, she would have to go alone, frozen and undefended; but she soon slept, and with no special measures.

When she woke to the morning sun (as high as this on the mountains the sun could shine at any hour), she knew that she would have to go at once. If a taxi could not be got, she would make her way on foot down the mountain to Sovastad, leaving her small luggage for Henry to go after when he returned. At one point she would not have wished that Henry should visit the Kurhus, but now it did not matter. She put on the dress in which she had arrived.

There was no demur. The hall was empty of guests, as it so often was, but the young Swede who looked like a boxer, was behind his desk, produced Margaret's passport, and said he would ring up for a taxi at once. He did enquire whether Margaret wanted breakfast, but seemed unsurprised when she declined. Margaret wanted to meet neither Mrs Slater nor Colonel Adamski, and did not know which, in their very different ways, she wanted to meet the less. Perhaps she wanted least of all to meet the frail-looking girl with bright blue eyes; whose resistance to cold, even in thin black tights, seemed to be so much greater than her own. The young reception clerk did not offer to abate half of Henry's liability; or seem to think that the matter called for reference.

Surprisingly soon, the taxi arrived and Margaret directed it back to the familiar hotel in Sovastad. She hoped that she would not find it full. Her present reservation began, of course, only on the night of the next day, when Henry would be back. Looking out of the taxi's rear window, she saw the white tables scattered about the deserted terrace, the bright flowers in hanging baskets, the vast sweep of green descending the side of the mountain, of which the lower part had not yet caught the morning sun. Presumably the regular inmates of the Kurhus were, in their own way, resting after the night's peregrinations. There was still so much that Margaret did not understand.

The hotel in Sovastad said it was already fully booked that night, and was none too polite about it either. Had it not been that she and Henry had just stayed in the establishment for a week, and had this not been emancipated Sweden, Margaret might have thought from the demeanour of the reception staff that a foreign woman travelling alone was not welcome as a guest. All three of them glowered at her, as if she were a complete stranger and an undesirable one. Moreover, the taxi-driver had brought her case into the hotel and was shifting about apparently almost as eager to be rid of her as were the hotel people.

'Can you recommend me somewhere else?'

'The Central.'

'You realise that I shall be returning here tomorrow?'

They simply stared back at her and said nothing. She imagined that they had not enough English to understand her.

The taxi-driver, with extreme grumpiness, took her to the Central.

The Central was apparently so fully booked that the elderly woman behind the desk did not even need to consult her record. In fact, she did not speak at all. She merely shook her head, on which the smooth grey hair surmounted the familiar Swedish bone structure. However, she shook it with great decisiveness.

'Can you recommend me somewhere else?'

This time Margaret seemed more or less to be understood.

'Krohn's.'

Sovastad was only a small town, despite its skilful graft of Scandanavian urbanity, and Margaret appreciated that as the quest continued, standards were bound to sink. Krohn's was a pension, basically, perhaps, for commercial travellers. None the less, it was clean, bright, and attractive.

It was also full up. This time the reception was in charge of a small boy, with a tousle of wild blond hair larger than his face, and curious, angular eyes. He wore an open white shirt, and a scarlet scarf round his neck. He could speak no English at all, so that it was useless even asking for a suggestion of somewhere else. Foreign visitors were unusual at Krohn's.

The boy stood behind a table (Krohn's did not rise to a formal reception desk) holding tight to the edge of it, and visibly wishing Margaret out of the place and far away. One might have thought he was quite frightened of her, and Margaret supposed it was only reasonable seeing that he was perhaps but ten or eleven, and with not a word he could share with her.

'Where now?' she asked the taxi-driver.

It was still only half past ten, but the situation was becoming disturbing. Margaret wondered if the taximan would by this time suggest that she return for the night to the Kurhus. She began to wish that she was not alone in Sovastad. She supposed that she could have recourse to Henry's Swedish friends, but it was the last thing she wanted (short of returning to Kurhus) and the last moment at which she would have wanted it. She would have such particularly difficult things to explain, and she was bound to be questioned with solicitous closeness, and probably reported back to Henry in the same spirit.

'Frälsningsarmén,' he said.

'What's that?'

'Frälsningsarmén,' he said again. 'It's all you'll get.'

This last could hardly be true, Margaret thought. Sovastad was not a large town, but she herself, during the previous week, had seen more than three places at which it seemed possible to stay. Possibly the taxi-driver knew that all were full. Possibly there was some big event in the town which had booked all the beds. She decided at least to have a look at the place the taxi-driver had suggested.

It proved to be a hostel of the Salvation Army.

'No, really,' said Margaret; but she was too late.

A woman officer had immediately appeared and was not so much welcoming her in, as drawing her in; pulling at her arm, gently but very firmly, as if already commencing the process of redemption, manifesting the iron goodness beneath the common flesh.

The place proved to look quite agreeable (as well as most astonishingly cheap, to judge from the prominently placed list of charges): more like a normal hotel, though simple and scrubbed, than like Margaret's idea of a Salvation Army hostel in England, concerning which *Major Barbara* was her most recent authority. Margaret's room contained a Bible, a book in Swedish expounding the Bible, a holy picture, and a selection of Swedish tracts; there seemed to be no reference to any more direct programme of observance in the establishment.

At one moment, however, when Margaret was lying down, there was a knock at the door, and the officer who had received her, handed her a tract in English. It was entitled 'Purification', and the woman passed it over un-smilingly. Margaret had realised already that the woman had very little English. Now Margaret got the impression that the English tract was the fruit of searching in cupboards and chests for something suitable for the visitor from abroad. She felt mildly appreciative of so much trouble on her behalf and smiled as gratefully as she could. The woman went silently away.

There seemed to be no further attempt at Margaret's conversion.

Indeed, she was perfectly free to go off into the town and eat there or go to the cinema. There was no real reason why she should not be, but she felt faintly surprised all the same. A more real difficulty was that she had already very much seen all there was to be seen in Sovastad, and also very much wanted not to meet at the moment anyone there whom she knew. She therefore read for much of the day and industriously washed things; lunched in the hotel or hostel or whatever it properly was (the food was primitive but good); and confined herself to sneaking out to dinner in a café she had not before entered. She did not read the tract on purification.

She found the café disappointing. She was hidden away in a corner and served with a rudeness and indifference she had not previously met with in Sweden – or perhaps elsewhere either. But Margaret had not travelled very much, and still less on her own. She knew that lone women were often said not to be popular with waiters, or even with restaurant managements. 'No wonder,' she thought, 'that, with one thing and another, women tend to retreat into their little nests.' Altogether, she reflected, her short period of time away from Henry might well, in one way and another, have been the most vivid and informative of her entire life. She tried to put away the thought. It might at all times be a mistake to know more than one's husband. She had never before noticed the Swedes as being so dour and unobliging, but that was doubtless something to be learnt too.

That night Margaret slept brokenly and badly. There was heavy traffic in the street outside. Margaret wondered how much worse it would be when Henry's road was completed; thought warmly of Colonel Adamski; and tried to deflect her mind, though, lying there awake, it was difficult. She explained to herself that she had, after all, consumed very little energy that day; done little but lie about and ruminate.

At some dark and unknown hour, there was a tap at the door. It actually woke Margaret up.

The woman officer entered. Could this be another, Margaret instantly thought, who did not sleep? It seemed very unlikely, despite Adamski's emphasis upon the all-sorts-to-make-a-world theme.

The woman was carrying a candle. She walked towards the bed and, without preliminary, asked in her strong accent, 'Would you like me to pray with you? I'm afraid I can pray only in Swedish.'

Margaret sat up, with a view to showing some kind of respect. Then she felt that the black nightdress, which Henry liked, might here be a mistake.

'It's very kind of you,' she replied uncertainly.

'Do not despair,' said the woman. 'There is pardon for all. For all who seek it on their knees.'

'But if I could not understand you—' said Margaret, trying to cover her unsuitable apparel with her arms.

It was neither a very ready nor a very gracious reply, but Margaret, newly awakened from scanty sleep, could think of nothing else.

The woman gazed at her from behind the candle in its cheap tin candlestick.

'We never force salvation upon any,' she said, after a longish pause. 'Those who are able to find it seek it on their own.'

It did seem to Margaret that the woman, having decided to appear at all, could have been more cordial; but she thought she had heard that something of what the woman had said was an item of Salvation Army philosophy.

The woman turned and walked away, shielding the candle-flame with her left hand, and quietly closing the door. Margaret felt that she herself would have been obscurely glad of something further; but had to admit that she had offered little encouragement. She returned to her disturbed and scrappy slumbers. The night seemed very long as well as shockingly noisy; and Margaret had troubled thoughts about the morrow.

In the morning, the woman officer was merely quiet and efficient, though still unsmiling, at least where Margaret was concerned. Margaret wished she could have eaten more of the pleasant breakfast, but found that her mind was too full of conflict. Henry was due to arrive before lunch, and in due course she set off for the railway station, this time carrying her own bag. The place where she had stayed seemed to think it the normal thing to do. They did not offer to send for a taxi, and Margaret felt one could hardly ask. Nor did she much care for the taxi-drivers of Sovastad. Perhaps her muscles had strengthened a little, as her vision, for better or for worse, had a little cleared.

'Had a good time?'

'Lovely.'

'You look a bit peeky.'

'I didn't sleep very well last night.'

'Missing me, I hope?'

'I expect so. How did you get on in Stockholm?'

'Bloody. These Swedes just aren't like us English.'

'Poor Henry.'

'In fact, I've got a problem on my hands. I'll tell you all about it over lunch.'

Which Henry did. Margaret could not complain that he was one of those husbands who keep from their wives everything that they themselves take seriously. And, immediately lunch was over, Henry had to dash off to a different conference with Larsson, and Falkenberg, and the other local ogres. Margaret did not have to consider further, as she had been considering now for more than twenty-four hours, how much she should tell Henry. It was unlikely that at any time she would have to tell him anything crucial about what had happened to her. 'You're still looking under the weather, old girl,' said Henry, as he tore off. 'Even the reception people and the waiter seemed to notice it. I saw them glancing at you. I don't know when I shall be back. I should go and get some sleep. Just trot upstairs and relax.'

He kissed her – really most affectionately.

Margaret did not feel at all like sleep; nor, for that matter, did she feel particularly out of sorts. None the less, she went to their room, took off her dress, and sprawled on the bed in her blue lambswool dressing-gown. It was quite reasonable, after last night's traffic, that she should be short of rest, and perhaps even show it. All the same, no sleep came; and Margaret faced again the problem that there was nothing more to do in Sovastad. Henry's solution to that would undoubtedly be a resumption of sociabilities with the Larssons and Falkenbergs and their kind; which, as he had already observed, would kill two birds with one stone, keep Margaret occupied while assisting business. One reason why Margaret felt unattracted was the time-limit on such associations: she could not, on the instant, become gay and intimate with strangers, and then, on the instant, cut it all off. And it was even worse when the time of cessation was so mobile and indefinite. Margaret could only give, or even take, when she had some consciousness of continuity. Probably, she thought gloomily, it was a serious limitation in the wife of a businessman.

In the end, she put on her dress once more, went out to buy three more postcards, and sent them off to her children. She continued to prevent her mind from dwelling upon all that had happened since the previous triptych of postcards to Dinah, Hazel, and Jeremy.

But it was not until well past midnight that she began to

feel alarmed: to be precise, when she heard the tinkling church clock strike three, as she had heard it strike one and two.

Even then, she thought, it might have been simply the fact that once more she was sleeping with Henry in the room. Heaven knew that Henry slept noisily enough to keep anyone awake, especially one who a second time had exerted herself so little during the day. Henry rolled and squirmed. He groaned and snored and panted. Sometimes he cried out. Margaret had to admit that Henry was not (to use his own idiom) good publicity for the institution of slumber. Not that many would sympathise with his wife's predicament: it was too utterly ridiculous, and probably too familiar also. A good wife would take it in her stride; restricted though the stride of a good wife might be.

The tinkling clock struck four and five and six, and Margaret never slept at all. It also struck a single, delicate note at the intermediate half-hours. At some time after half past six, with heavy rain, which had begun to fall about an hour earlier, beating drearily against the bedroom window, Henry sat up, trained auxiliary to the day's commands.

At breakfast, he said that she still looked odd, and she noticed that he was watching for the Swedes to be eyeing her. She still did not feel anything out of the ordinary. She had said nothing to Henry about not sleeping. She remarked to herself that to miss one night's sleep was nothing at all by the standard of people who slept badly. Or, at least, by the proclaimed standard. She had

441

been immensely exposed to the suggestion of insomnia; could hardly have been more exposed. Normality, her own possibly rather notable normality of somnolence, would probably be restored when she was returned to her own proper bed. On present evidence, that looked like being the day after tomorrow, but one never knew. The road ruled all.

'Hedvig Falkenberg was asking after you,' said Henry. 'Rather pointedly, I thought. Make some kind of contact, will you? I can't have a coolness with the Falkenbergs on my hands. On top of everything else. They can be damned sensitive, these foreigners.'

Margaret more or less promised, and meant to keep her word. She did not even have to tackle the terrifying Swedish telephone, as one would at home. She had merely to walk the half mile or so up to the Falkenbergs' house on its low ridge above the town. Visitors seemed at all times to be not merely welcome but awaited. The walk would do her good. Even the steady rain might wake her up or make her sleep: it was striking how a single force could lead to antithetical results. But Margaret let the hours pass and did nothing. And when Henry returned that night, she did not even have to make an excuse.

'Everything's settled, Molly,' he cried, almost exuberantly. 'Thank God, we can go home tomorrow.'

Possibly it was owing to the lifting of the weight on his mind that, on this second night after his return from Stockholm, Henry slept much more quietly; much better, as people say. Margaret heard him purring gently and evenly as a child: hour after hour after hour, while the church clock chimed and the rain pattered. As this second sleepless night slowly passed, Margaret ceased finding explanations, making excuses, pretending to herself.

If only she could walk about! A few minutes after the stroke of five, she got out of bed, and, in almost total silence, drew on her shirt, trousers, and anorak. She stood for a long time looking out at the infinitely slow and laboured dawn. She would have liked to escape, but in this place the door would be locked, and a night porter, even if there was one, would shrink away from her and be beyond communication. She must still, for a spell, be reasonable.

She hid away her clothes and crept back into bed. Henry was still purring away, but as she drew near to him, he seemed to give a single, curious sigh, as of a man dreaming about the past which is always so much sweeter than the present.

'Henry,' said Margaret after breakfast. 'You have said several times that I'm not looking very well. As a matter of fact, I haven't been sleeping. And quite by chance, I've found a place where people from all over the world go when they don't sleep. Would you mind very much if I stayed behind for a while? Just for a short time, of course?'

The argument took every bit as long as she had expected, but Margaret was developing new resources now, even though she had little idea of what they were.

'I'll let you know immediately I get out of the wood,' she promised. 'It's one of those things you have to live through until you emerge the other side.'

443

Growing up with Robert Aickman

by Leslie Gardner

It's a shameful thing to admit, but I had never been to the opera before I arrived in Europe. And as a new American expat, now probably-to-be permanent resident of London, I'd certainly never been to the Royal Opera House in Covent Garden. My friendship with Robert Aickman changed all that and much else too.

I had arrived via the University of Iowa's International Writers' Workshop and a few years spent in New York City's publishing world, and I was now eager to establish myself in the UK. After a stint at the BBC I joined the large British talent agency London Management, which had an entertainment division, actors' and directors' divisions, and a small literary division headed up by Herbert van Thal. 'Bertie', as he was known, represented writers and put together collections of ghost stories and horror stories – 'speculative fiction', except that science fiction was beyond his ken. My first job was to read for Bertie and to back up his efforts to find niches for these writers in the marketplace. And so I came across Aickman. I'd already heard about Robert in New York through my friendship with T. E. D. ('Ted') Klein, the brilliant American horror novelist and short-story writer who knew him well. Ted warned me that Robert could be 'precise'.

When I finally met him, I found Robert to be cultivated, humorous and a great companion for evenings as I made my way around London during those first years. When we spent time together he told me more about himself and I heard plenty about England's inland waterways – mostly gossip about his fellow conservationist campaigners. (He had his own ideas that sometimes clashed with theirs – he always sounded right to me.)

But our main common interest was his stories. At his flat in Gledhow Gardens, some evenings, he would read me whatever he was working on, then I would take carbon copies in to the London Management offices and also meet up with Clarence Paget, veteran publisher at Pan Books, who had made a successful career with Pan Horror and ghost-story collections. (Driving around town with Clarence was a death-defying experience in itself as he couldn't talk without looking at his passenger; but more of that another time.) This was, essentially, when I became Robert's agent, in cahoots at that point with Kirby McCauley in New York.

The rest of Robert's life was never brought up much in conversation. He would refer to the Swedenborg Society, which interested him: he would describe meetings he'd attended there and at other psychic societies, and tell me about successful presentations of material that he'd made, along with his personal responses to other members and to the head of the society at the time. But he never spoke much of his personal life. I was to learn more of that later, after his death. He was certainly expert at compartmentalisation. As I read more of his work, some of his anxieties and urges to keep things and people secret became more evident to me. (What was he holding back, or holding down?)

But I will always remember his stories of Elizabeth Jane Howard living with him across the street from Kingsley Amis, and the disgruntlement he felt at her choosing Amis over him. He and Howard published a volume of stories together in 1951 and he felt himself to be a kind of mentor to her. I think he even jumped out of a window once to hide from one of her then husbands. Or was this a flight of fantasy voiced aloud to entertain me? No way to know – and I just enjoyed the recounting.

When he would read parts of *The Attempted Rescue* and 'Laura' to me there was always a private grin on his face, and his eyes were lit up over the page. He would chuckle over the parts he used to lift the story out of its conventional byways. Now when I revisit his stories, and especially his novel *The Late Breakfasters*, I can still see him sitting there reading.

At the time I was involved also with an Irishman, a producer of radio drama at the BBC and he and I listened to classical music – my preference too – but not really to opera except on Radio 4. Wagner was his taste, and so I had a thorough grounding in Germanic psychological and mythical stories and romantic music. Robert approved of Wagner, but he thought a trip to the opera house was on the cards for me, and that the piece ought perhaps to be something not quite so heavy.

(It occurs to me now that he was also competing with my Irishman over opera aesthetics. Later on, when I took up with an Italian – whom I later married – Robert tried to defuse an overheated situation he had stoked up; he knew enough about himself to know how pugnacious he could be. He and 'that Italian' (as Robert called him) were together at a disastrous dinner party for four at my rather tumbledown Knightsbridge flat; it had been Marianne Faithfull's, and I still used her gigantic flat bed, which dominated a corner of the 'dining room'. 'The Italian' brought a friend, Jean Liedloff, a popular feminist writer on psychology, but Robert and she soon fought about misogyny. Later, he informed me that he'd disliked the woman whom he thought was the Italian's partner, but assured me that, though he normally didn't like Italians, he did like 'that one'. I did not disabuse him of his idea that they were an item: he would have been too prickly. But he did manage to smooth things out with Jean in the end, seeing my unhappiness, by listening attentively to her tales of travelling in Italy with the publisher and writer Longanesi.)

But back to the opera. Benjamin Britten's *The Turn of the Screw* was on at the opera house. Neither the Irishman nor the Italian would have recommended Britten's work to me, but here I was in England and Robert thought it important. (He also taught me about the distinctions between the Scottish, English and Welsh parts of Great Britain.) So, it was the great British composer I should hear. I knew the Henry James story but not Britten's angle on it, nor the music. To Robert's chagrin – always charming even when he chided me! – I had not prepared. But we met at the opera house, and went in to see and hear this terrifying ghost story with its soaring music. Robert was, of course, the perfect companion for this opera, and at the interval he told me about its nuance and provenance, as well as describing to me in words what it was I was hearing. These whispered and fluent explications truly enhanced the experience, and thereafter I would always probe his reactions to music that we listened to. Needless to say, the evening was memorable and a great success; I think Robert took pride in my enjoyment.

We met again at the opera house one late afternoon. I remember watching him before I made myself known: Robert, alone, staring out the window of the Chanticleer café in Bloomsbury, dreaming. He had obtained permission to show me around the back-stairs and corridors backstage and around the audience boxes in the house. I remember ducking through short doorways and clambering up thin staircases with him. He showed me where to peek out through the curtains, and where to spy on the theatre flats, scenery and costumes. It was memorable and splendid, an enchanting thing to do with him.

When we ate together *à deux* at his place he would have a meal ready, the table set and the wine decanted. (I had never experienced this before: my Midwestern mother and cocktail-drinking suburban dad never had wine with dinner.) Of course, someone would have arranged it all for him. It was slightly implied that he

449

done all the preparation, and I went along with it, but it was hard to believe. We ate what seemed to me entirely British-style food, simple and well served with all the right implements. I suspect I was easy to impress but he didn't hold that against me.

The last time I saw him was in his flat as he recovered from treatment for the cancer of which he died. He refused the rough chemical treatments then available and tried homeopathic cures. He got thinner and weaker, but he was well looked after by Felix Pearson, who became a friend of mine too. She was not the only one, of course: he had many devoted friends, though they didn't always meet (at least, not until we all saw each other at his memorial service). But on that late afternoon, despite his frailty, he still had his slightly wicked laugh, and I won't ever forget that.

LESLIE GARDNER *is director of the London-based literary agency Artellus Ltd.*